DNA BUST

RENE MAURICIO MENJIVAR

Published in the United States of America

Brilliant Books Literary
137 Forest Park Lane Thomasville
North Carolina 27360 USA

ISBN:
Paperback: 979-8-88945-337-6
Ebook: 979-8-88945-338-3
Hardback: 979-8-88945-339-0

The US Review of Books
Professional Reviews for the People

DNA BUST

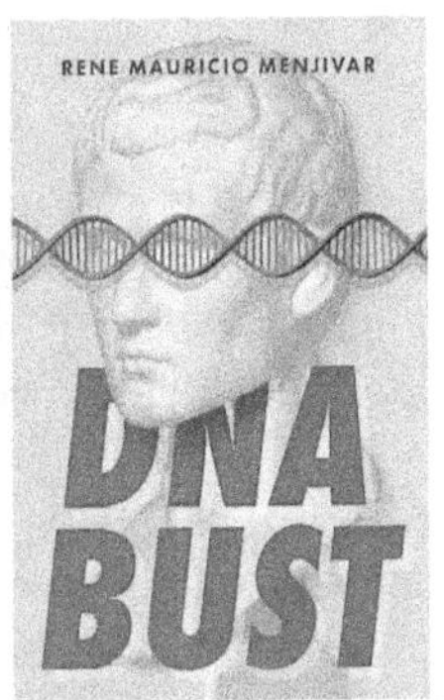

Author: Rene Mauricio Menjivar

Publisher: BookBaby

ASIN: B0C95DWL39

Genre: Crime Fiction

Book Reviewer: Mary Jacobo

Rating: ★ ★ ★ ★ ☆ (4 out of 5 stars)

Rene Mauricio Menjivar's book, DNA Bust, is a riveting tale of heist crime that unfolds through intricate storytelling. Set against the backdrop of meticulously planned and executed criminal activities, the narrative delves into the minds of individuals who set out on a dangerous path to secure assets and wealth. The author's writing style shines through as he skillfully weaves a story of audacious plans, unexpected camaraderie, and the intricate details that make up the world of crime.

The book's narrative voice is a standout feature, offering a glimpse into the characters' motivations, decisions, and inner thoughts without explicitly revealing their identities. Menjivar employs a unique approach, focusing on the crime scheme's logistics and the relationships between the characters while withholding their names. This strategy adds an air of mystery and intrigue, compelling readers to piece together the puzzle as they follow the events unfold.

Menjivar's attention to detail is evident as he vividly describes the settings, from jewelry stores to marinas, and even the cozy coffee shop where pivotal conversations take place. The author's ability to capture the essence of these locations immerses the reader, making them feel like active participants in the unfolding drama.

The US Review of Books
Professional Reviews for the People

The central theme of trust and partnership plays a crucial role in the story, with characters forming alliances that go beyond typical criminal partnerships. The bond between Ron and Brat is portrayed with complexity and depth, showcasing their distinct personalities that somehow complement each other perfectly. Their interplay highlights the contrasts in their decision-making processes, giving the reader a deeper understanding of their dynamics.

While the storytelling is compelling and the characters intriguing, the deliberate decision to avoid explicit character names or backgrounds might occasionally challenge readers who are accustomed to more traditional narrative styles. However, this experimental approach also contributes to the book's unique charm and adds an extra layer of engagement.

In DNA Bust, Rene Mauricio Menjivar has created a captivating crime story that showcases his prowess as a storyteller. The book's narrative innovation, attention to detail, and exploration of complex relationships make it a prime candidate for a gripping cinematic adaptation. If you're looking for a crime novel that stands out from the crowd, filled with calculated schemes and unexpected alliances, DNA Bust is an excellent choice.

He said: Some criminal events take place with the intention to secure assets, and wealth so, the individuals in this recount had started with the confidence that the plan behind the event will succeed to procure the expensive items. Let me tell you by the word succeed I mean secure the money, the valuables, the jewels or whatever is precious and scape the crime scene unharmed with the illusion to evade apprehension forever.

Some of these events are plain, effortless but aggressive, and rough, but others are more subtle and keen, yet most of them have a very sad ending. Worth noticing the cost is much more than what the profits yielded. These sad results are not just for those who are involve, they still implicate the lives of others that are not part of the illicit activities. As stated before, these are the accounts of a series of planned, rehearsed, and executed assaults that occurred in…let's say pleasant ways.

That was the initial account from Miller to Jack Wayne.

The master plan as Ron, the leader of the group called it, was thought out by himself. The details were added with the help of his confidant and second in command as Ron had appointed, his longtime friend Brat.

Brat and Ron had met when both worked at the jewelry center in a large mall. A commercial center with few small and medium size in square footage stores that sold primarily jewelry of what is consider of lower-grade quality.

Ron had the opportunity to travel as assistant manager to wholesale jewelry distributors to select lesser quality merchandise with a much cheaper price. He learned to identify small but legally acceptable differences in precious stones, in expensive gold and silver jewelry, and the subtle imperfections on some cuts in diamonds.

Brat was more knowledgeable on the natural pearls, and various types of rings, and pendants. He was more attracted to jewelry for men. Even though he did not care to wear large chains, or excessive jewelry.

Brat had a deep affection for his friend Ron, he saw him and treated like a family member. Ironically Brat had two brothers and one sister, but they did not get alone. Brat had more sympathy for his friend than for his siblings. Ron trusted his friend more than his own family. Ron and Brat had experienced few successes and had times of disappointment, and despair, which had brought them closer. They had different personalities that in a rare form complemented each other. When things did not work out Ron reacted with despair, but Brat took his time to analyze and try to see what could be learn and have some benefit out the situation, Ron had learned to listen to his friend, wait for Brat to express his point of view, then he could move on. Not always in agreement, but rather settled. Brat on the other hand on times of celebration did not want to linger in the same place or moment for too long, but to some degree move to the next project. Ron took his time and reviewed everything that had contributed to the success in order that their experience would guide them to increase the number of projects with the most profit and no trace for the police to catch them.

THE VERY FIRST PROJECT.

The very first robbery was carried out only by Ron and Brat themselves. It was a successful hit because the loot brought them an amount of profit quite good in proportion to the time, they spent planning and executing the job, apart from the amount of the stolen goods.

It was a small town along the bay with a small marina, which gave Ron the option to dock a small boat. Ron had monitored the place for over three months to learn everything about the routine and choose the best time to carry on the heist. Through his watch he learned the best day for the job was Tuesday, with the ideal time just before noon. The store had two full time employees and two part time assistants. Ron had learned on Tuesday mornings the store had only two employees. There were no security guards posted outside the small Ark Row Shopping Center complex. Ron walked in and asked one of the employees to show him a few stones, then he inquired some details about the gems, while the staff member was explaining, Brat walked in and ask the other employee to show him a few rings that were locked in a different case. While Brat waited for the employee to open the case and take out some of the diamond rings, Ron pulled a small gun and pointed to the employee ordering to give him the jewels. Brat played to be a casual client who had nothing to do with the robbery. He tried to leave and went to the front door, but Ron yelled: do not move or you are a dead man! Brat pretended to be very nervous.

Ron continued with a command in a strong voice-In fact you take the rest of the jewels and then tie down the employees. Brat obeyed and there was no resistant from the employees. Brat had dark sunglasses and a hat. Then Ron ordered Brat to clip wires, take the video recording camera, and put it with the stolen gems, soon after, Ron pointed with the small gun the door, indicating Brat to leave. Ron exited after Brat, both men walked out of the store named Excellent Jewelry with the loot and the recording video of surveillance system.

They were able to leave the crime scene without being follow or chased. Despite their choice of transportation for getting away. Ron and Brat used couple old basic bicycles to escape from the store to the boat docks. Once there, they walked the bikes and load them on the boat acting very calm. Then proceed to leave the docks area in Tiburon keeping the compose while observing if anyone was coming on the streets after them. There were no police vehicles, no sirens or other vehicles arriving at the marina looking for them. Brat and Ron bragged about how things worked out, they kept the story just between themselves. They told to each other, in a very arrogant way, the account of the event, they grew egotistical every-time they repeated details of the robbery.

That was their conclusion of the first project, after few weeks it was label a "success" because they never felt under police surveillance, and law enforcement officers never questioned either one. They had enough profit to pay off the charter boat.

'I have a question,' said Jack Wayne.

Miller said, 'yes, go ahead.'

Jack Wayne: 'where did they get the boat?'

Miller: 'Ah yes, the boat. Ok, let me continue.'

Two months before the heist the search for the boat was conducted by Ron and Brat. They looked on the internet for places within 10 miles where he could go to inquire about small boats. Brat also walked by the docks looking for small boats when he found a local bar near the marina. He and Ron talked about who should go and find any information, Ron wanted to go himself. They were as usual in Ron's garage. He had set up a sofa, a small table next to an old bar, a couple of wall mounted shelves with four bottles of different liquor drinks. He had an old tv monitor to watch occasionally some sport events.

Ron: 'look Brat I feel that I should go and find the boat, I know I can do it.'

Brat: 'bro, I know you can do it, but something tells me that it should not be the same person who looks and finds the boat, and then charters the vessel. Let me say it this way for safety reasons. Just to be cautious.'

Ron: 'I don't follow. What are you saying?'

Brat: 'never mind, just let me go one more time to look and let's see what I come up with, ok?'

Ron: looked down to the floor, contemplating the words from his friend, then walked to the window and look outside as if the confirmation for his friend was out there. He noticed a light breeze through the Gracilis bamboo hedges. Took a deep breath and then he said: 'go for.'

Two days later, Brat walked the small block, where he had seen the bar while he smokes his cigarette, he smiled when he saw the old sign with the fainted fish "Grumpy Fish Bar" Hanging on the side of the old wooden, one story building.

He went inside through the patio seating area with small wrought iron round white tables and white chairs with small blue umbrellas. The double French doors were open, the sound of a country western song was played on the small speakers one on each corner on the wall behind the bartender. Brat looked around and there were few people sitting at couple of tables, then he notices two guys at the bar near the left corner. It was obvious they were seamen. He sat next to the old guys. They were having beers along with cheerful laughs. Brat listened to their conversation, while he orders a tap beer. Jack was reminding his friend Ezra about the time that he (Ezra) was in that old boat with the broken bathroom and Ezra needed to use it kind of urgently, he had no choice, and found a large bucket to take care of business. Ezra laughed and reminded to his friend Jack that just when things appeared to be ok'd the boat took off and things got a bit messy. They both laughed even harder. Brat heard the whole account and could not help to laugh with them. They both stop and turned to Brat to ask: 'did it happen to you as well?' Brat felt a bit embarrassed and replied: 'not really, but could I ask who was driving the boat?' Ezra turned to Jack to point with his finger: 'that old bastard'. Jack replied: 'it was supposed to be a practical joke, nothing more.'

Ezra said,' we were a lot younger back then.'

After that a short silent pause gave Brat the time to ask for information about a charter boat, I'm looking for a small boat. It turned out that Jack had the phone number of a guy who used to charter his boat on certain days. Brat took the number just in case. He finished his beer and thanked the two old fellows for the good laugh and the number, then he left.

Brat gave to his friend the details and the phone number for the charter boat.

Ron called the number and the person who answer did not sound too friendly. Ron asked about a boat for charter. The other person said, 'who needs a boat?'

Ron did not want to give the wrong impression and just ask the owner to meet to see the boat. The boat that Ron found was almost ten years old but in great condition.

He had watched an episode of an old show about a boat chase in a river and how the fugitives managed to escape despite having a smaller and slower boat, they simple hide behind some plants and bushes to wait until the bad guys on a bigger boat had gone by far enough to allow the smaller boat to get back to the dock area, tied the boat get in their car and ran away unharmed.

Ron did not know much about boats and when he saw the name of the craft - "The Dream Chaser" he was dreaming. He liked the small motorboat.

Ron walked on the dock and observed the colors of the hull, the deep blue, the contrast with the red and the white as the main color. He thought the name was very appropriate for his project. He came aboard to examine the cockpit and the windshield. He took a quick look at the cab area under deck, opened the small door of the bath, he noticed a slight smell in the air, a residue of a chemical disinfectant. He opened the closet door, inside a small shoe box, forgotten from the previous charter trip. Ron shook the box without opening it, his phone buzzed with a text alert. He set the box right back on the same spot and close the door. Brat had texted Ron asking, "had you seen the boat?" Ron did not answer right away. He continued to check the rest of the boat. He liked the sleeping area. The canopy covers in the main area to provide shield from the sun was rolled up. Ron thought we should not use it; it would be less details in case anyone tries to recall what the boat looks like! A very small fold up ladder is installed in the stern. In the bow a small rail, on top there is an antenna, the bowsprit is painted white. Ron was very careful to not mention any other name or details of his plan to Mack, the boat owner. He asked for a test drive and both men went on a short ride.

Ron asked Mack: 'do I need some kind of license to charter and operate myself the vessel?' Mack with a stoical face kept looking straight ahead and said: 'you don't really know squat, do you?'

Ron felt stupid and replied: 'just answer my question.' He tried very hard to match Mack's unemotional demeanor.

Mack, then asked: 'what do you have in mind?'

Ron replied: 'I need the vessel for two days, taking a short ride within the bay, just my girlfriend and me. It's her birthday, I would like to give her something different, something especial a boat ride on the bay for her will be nice, you know spend a night on the water alone, go for breakfast hang out for the morning, and then return to the docks. I understand the weather forecast for the next few days is fair and calm, no chopping waters.

Mack said: 'You pay a deposit double of what I pay for my insurance. If you get in trouble, you are responsible for all the cost and my time. If nothing bad happens, I'll return your deposit, after two weeks. Ron asked: 'how come after two weeks? Mack replied: 'that's the usual time to check that everything is ok.' Ron took a short moment, and then replied, 'DEAL!'

Mack gave a brief explanation about the fuel and where the floating vests are kept, also a general description of the control lights, anchor buttons then he unlatched the canopy and rolled it out, so Ron could see how it works. They came back to the docks and berth. Mack told Ron pay close attention how I maneuver and bring the boat to berth. This is how is done! Ron was impressed with Mack's proficiency. He was told it will be easier for you to have your girlfriend on the dock helping with the lines. Ron had to pay a deposit separate from the contract that he signed, two days on a single week. No weekend days because Mack must be the pilot, and the rate increases.

Ron left the marina with great enthusiasm. He was very excited when he called Brat to tell him about the "The Dream Chaser" charter. He told Brat I even booked a session to go out with the owner and practice how to shove off from the docks, and then come back to berth using the dock lines.

Ron and Brat charter the boat for two days with the agreement to pay in equal parts from the profits they gain in their project.

On day of taking the boat, Ron showed up alone and told Mack his girlfriend was waiting for him at Clipper Yacht Harbor in Sausalito. Ron pick Brat a few docks away from Mack's place, from there they went on a test drive to see the location where the job was, as well as to gain experience handling the boat. While on the ride Brat went down under deck cabin and came back with the small shoe box. He opened and pulled a small stock of flash cards. Some had recipes, some had random notes and some silly jokes. Brat started to smoke a cigarette while reading a couple of cards to Ron.

Brat: 'hey Ron these are sailor jokes, listen to this one, why can't the sailors play cards?'

Ron: 'you tell me!'

Brat: 'because the sailors are standing on the deck.' Brat started to laugh.

Ron: 'don't be silly, that's corny.'

Brat: 'wait here's another What's the difference between sailors and gluttons?

One worries about pirates while the other worries about pie rates.'

Ron: 'put that away'

Jack Wayne started to laugh enjoying the jokes. Then said: 'that's funny, why Ron did not like them?'

Miller turned his head to look at his phone for any messages, then he said: 'let me finish there is more.'

Brat: 'here's one for nowadays tech, If Apple was a pirate ship, what would their sailors wear? An iPatch.'

Ron: 'I'm getting sick.'

Ron: 'Come on! This one is clean, why do sailors eat so many carrots? It helps them sea better.'

Ron: you better stop or I'll through you and your box of cards overboard.'

Brat: 'ok one last card What kind of oranges do sailors eat to fight off scurvy? Navel oranges.'

Ron just made a disgusted grim face.

Brat: 'Ok, ok I'll show myself out.'

ASSOCIATES OR COLLEAGUES SAME AS ACCOMPLICES

Ron knew a bigger store has more inventory but also more employees, and more security. He considered the possibility of increasing the band with someone with dedicated skills. Someone who is knowledgeable in electronics, that is in computerized security, and the like. He thought maybe one more or perhaps two more recruits to have a maximum of four members. Ron discussed with Brat the possibility of recruiting more members for their enterprise. (As Ron called it). Brat thought for a moment and remembered Pete. Not exactly an old-time friend but on the other hand not a stranger either. Brat asked himself if he could trust Pete? He told himself, 'Sometimes you got to take few risks in life in order to gain and move up. I need to evaluate few things before I take a chance with a candidate.'

He mentions to Ron that there was a person that he would talk to and have an idea if he was a candidate. Ron told him 'Do what you think you ought to do' and then he said, 'I would like to hear details. Don't rush anything, ok!' Brat nodded.

Brat had known Pete for a relative short time, less than five years. He remembered how he found Pete. Brat had trouble with the starter motor of his black car a 2003 Saab coupe. The vehicle needed other costly repairs. He had to jump start every other morning usually asking a neighbor to help him out. That Tuesday morning his Saab did not start, and his neighbor who has a truck was gone. That left Brat looking around for someone else. Pete left his apartment and open his garage door to start his old faithful

Kawasaki. Brat crossed the street to ask Pete for a quick jump start for his Saab. Pete had seen Brat a few times before but never had talked to him. Pete felt some sympathy for him and went to get his jump box. The car started right away. Pete disconnected the cables from the battery, and put the jumper box away, closed the garage door, waved to Brat and left in a rather hasty way. Brat did not have an opportunity to talk to Pete.

Few days later Brat got into his Saab and started right away, but before he had a chance to put into first gear and release the parking brake, Pete had walked to him and knock on the passenger window to greet Brat with 'How are you doing?', 'I see it started fine' Brat was late but he rolled the window down and decided to chat with Pete and thank him for his help with the jump start. Brat shook hands and introduced himself. 'I'm Brat, by the way, thanks for lending me the jumper cables and rescue my old Saab the other day' Pete and Brat exchange few words. Brat kept looking at his watch and Pete realize that he needed to leave. Pete told Brat that he had to go and offered his jumper box anytime. All he had to do was call him and he would bring it out. Then Pete left. Brat pulled away slowly thinking that Pete seemed to be a good guy. Brat had observed Pete working on his bike in the garage from time to time. Brat approached Pete on one occasion and offered a beer and pizza just to hang out, and chat for a bit. Pete liked the idea, and they got together one sunny afternoon while Pete was working on his Kawasaki in Pete's garage. Pete insisted that his apartment was a much better choice to associate rather than the garage, but Brat said that he will not be in nobody's way, I would like to keep company here as you change the oil. Pete asked about Brat's Saab, and Brat mention the car has other issues the steering wheel controls, no working horn, water pump failure. He mentioned all this while he lit a cigarette, I just had it with this old car. I am working to get me another set of wheels. I thought about this, I would like to upgrade my ride, you know. I will play my best and be smart, I must be careful, I don't need to rush things, you know. Pete just listened and nodded in agreement. They kept in touch from time to time, Brat realized that it had been almost four years since they spoke for the first time.

Two weeks later, Brat rang the doorbell waited a short moment, but there was no answer, then he called on his cell phone after few rings all he heard was the default greeting from the system to leave a message. Brat waited few minutes then call again, after the third time of the same response, he decided to knock on the door again, still no one answered. Brat walked around the front towards the garage just to see if Pete was in the garage. The garage door was closed with the visible pad lock. He lit a cigarette, passed his left hand through his hair, leaned against the old broken post for the gate, and smoke thinking what would be his next step to contact Pete.

Pete had left his apartment that morning, leaving the front room curtains halfway open. He was gone for the day. Pete did not take his bike, he had to run an errand, he had walked the three blocks to catch Muni bus and then Bart. He wrote himself a post note about the need to replace the padlock on the garage door, he left the note on the back door, but the wind blew the post note off the door and had landed just outside the back door. Brat noticed the note on the ground by the door, he picked it up after he read it shrug his shoulders then walked to the garage door and posted at the padlock.

Jack Wayne was puzzled by this short detail and asked: 'what is the purpose of the padlock and the note?'

Miller vaguely listened to Jack Wayne and responded: 'listen in every story there are points that they may never be connected for our full satisfaction or understanding, let's move on.'

He had not seen or spoken the last six or eight months to his longtime friend Rudy. Pete became self-conscious about thinking of Rudy for no reason, he thought, 'I wonder if Rudy is in some kind of dilemma?' Pete's attention shifted to talk to the person greeting him at the hardware store. He had walked in to look for the new padlock. For the next few weeks Pete did not think about Rudy.

Rudy was in a state of uncertainty, a life without a purpose, as if something had put it in suspension. He was just in survival mode. He was a very different Rudy from the one Pete had seen and talked last time they met. Rudy started to frequent a certain coffee shop couple blocks from his favorite park. The place was called Caffe e Dolce.

The "Garden Barista Park" is the official name of the recently renovated park, located South of a well-known Army Street. The name approved by the city council on recommendation of the Parks and Recreation Department. This was the result of the number of coffee shops nearby, and their contributions in adding many amenities, such as covered park benches with trellis and solar panels to illuminate at night. Many ornaments amongst them are the custom signpost with the four cardinal points. Rudy's favorite sign is the arrows pointing far away cities, Osaka in Japan, another arrow pointing to Singapore. There are other arrows pointing to places found in the heart referring to emotions. Rudy was looking for the right pathway to leave his state of isolation. When he saw the arrow 'compassion' He thought of having to move to another city to find compassion. Rudy was at home three days a week in the midafternoon.

His neighbor Susan lived in the back unit sharing the same driveway for the garages.

They had talked briefly on few occasions when the delivery package for Susan was by mistake left at Rudy's back door. Rudy had petted Susan's dog a few times and they both Rudy and the dog were acquainted. One week she happens to be home for a couple of days, she noticed that Rudy was home early. She asked Rudy if he was home often before six in the afternoon. Rudy said: 'yes, at least three days a week.' Susan asked him if he could take her dog Tuki for a walk as early in the afternoon as he could. Susan offers to pay Rudy for the inconvenience. She explained that there are people doing business by taking care of people's dogs. Taking the dogs for a schedule walk for a fee. 'Now,' she added: 'since we are neighbors, I thought, I ask you first.' Rudy was not sure what to say, he was surprised for the request. He asked: 'please remind me what's the dog's name?' If Rudy was mildly bewildered by the request of taking the dog out for a walk, then hearing the dog's name was even more puzzling.' Tuki. Rudy in a low voice asked Susan: 'What does it mean?'

Susan smiled and responded: 'it means Sweetness, an old Jewish word. Rudy shrugged his shoulders dismissing more questions that came to his mind, then called the dog by his name. Tuki was lying on the ground by the garage door, got up and walked to Rudy waging his tale in a friendly greeting. Susan exclaimed; 'see he knows you!' Rudy petted Tuki again and said: 'we'll go for a walk around the park, I guess I'll take the job. Besides I could use the extra money.' He thought.

Rudy took Tuki to the park and after a few walking times the dog became close to Rudy. He enjoyed the company and talk to the dog as he would talk to a friend. One afternoon in one of the walks Rudy stop by the custom signpost to read and said to Tuki: 'Compassion' you know Tuki not too long ago I read this arrow and I understood I needed to move to another city to find myself some kindness. Now the sign right under the word compassion, reads 'distance unknown' Rudy commented: 'I get it.'

They kept walking and Tuki stop to sniff the ground

Rudy said: 'the distance is measured in numbers, but not lineal miles, feet or yards is in the number of painful experiences. It's an individual own path on the 'road to growth. You know what I mean, buddy?'

Rudy smiled and kept walking along the cobble stone shape like an S. He stops one more time at the gazebo right in the middle of the S. 'Let's go home Tuki, I had a bit of enlightenment today thanks to you. You're a good listener.'

Brat tried calling Pete a couple of days later and he had the same result just the greeting with the polite request: 'leave a message.' Brat thought, maybe Pete is screening calls, and he doesn't recognize my number, I should leave a short message.

Brat was surprised that a minute later after he left a short message, his phone rang and when he answered it was Pete returning his message.

Brat: 'how is everything with you? Long time no see or hear from you.'

Pete: 'I'm well, how are you? Where have you been?'

Brat: 'things are good, let's get together and catch up.'

Pete: 'How about tomorrow late afternoon?'

Brat: 'Sure, do you have any particular spot?'

Pete: 'There is an old bar by the marina. It's call 'Grumpy Fish Bar.'

Brat: 'really? I'm not sure if we want to go to a bar, how about the caffe place by the park? They have sandwiches, coffee, wine, and beer. In case we want some to eat.'

Pete: 'What's the name of the place?'

Brat: 'Caffe e Dolce.'

Pete: 'sounds good.'

The two friends sat by the window in the only small table available for two. The place was crowded because it was Friday and there was a game on tv.

Brat explained to Pete about their 'enterprise' as Ron calls it. He told Pete they already had done couple of projects and things worked out very well. They plan everything with details and the risk is very low. He himself knows about the exclusive merchandise and Ron knows quality stones, because they both had worked for large companies in the jewelry industry. They learned to recognize the real deal. Pete got very excited and asked why he was call into this? Brat told him, because I know you. You have mechanical skills; they are very handy. I think I could trust you. Pete felt flatter.

Brat told Pete: 'We might just need one more guy to joint us. Then we should be set for larger projects. He thanked Brat and had a slight obligation to prove that he was worthy. He also though of Rudy to contribute to the group by mention his old-time friend. Pete mentioned to Brat about Rudy. Brat said: 'I need to know how well you know this, Rudy. Brat pulled a cigarette lit it and gave a deep puff, then said 'Why do you want him with us? What are his skills, and does he have close family?'

Pete asked why do you need to know about his close family? Brat answered in case we need to go far away for some time, kind of a 'cooling period' and no way to trace you through family or girlfriend. Pete smiled and replied 'I think he might be a good candidate. I need to talk to him.' Brat said: "be careful do not and I repeat do not give any specifics. No names no places not even disclose how many people are in the group.'

Pete said: 'you can trust me I know about his family; I will find out about close girlfriend.

I can tell you this he is quiet.

Pete calls his friend Rudy, leaves a message asking him to get together. There are projects that you and I could do in cooperation. The rewards are sizable. That was Pete's message for Rudy. The next day Rudy heard the message. Rudy thought about answering his friend's message, but he wanted to see and talk to Pete.

Rudy sensed the road to find compassion included the opportunity to mee this friend in person. Rudy went to Pete's apartment without calling or texting, he just took a chance he followed the nudge.

Pete was not home, but Rudy knew that his friend should be back sometime soon.

Rudy sat down to wait by the front door on the first of two short steps. The dim sunlight was on Rudy's face, it did not bother him, he raised his left hand to cover his eyes and looked up to the bird's racket in the small trees in front of him. There was a light breeze blowing some leaves, there was a quiet moment that his mind was distracted, and a few minutes went by. Then a roaring piercing noise of a bike approaching fast brought his attention back to where he was seating. Pete coming back home notice someone getting up from his front doorsteps. He slowed down and recognize Rudy. He pulled right in front of him and shut the bike off, pulled his helmet and talk to his visitor.

Rudy stared at his friend with his hands on his hip. Pete saw this and he understood that Rudy was ready for a challenge.

Pete: don't just stand there, come'er I'll give you a hug. Rudy took two steps and hug his longtime friend. Then he looked at him as to examine his wellbeing, and said: same blue eyes, same light eyebrows, same height about six feet and couple inches, and lankily! I say you are… what's your name? Pete and Rudy laughed for a moment and Pete looked at Rudy with serious scrutiny eyes. It was his turn to inspect.

Pete: 'let's see, same hazel eyes, same long nose, same Scandinavian straight loose thin hair, and about same height as me. Congratulations! You pass.'

They both laughed even harder and walked toward the garage. Pete put his bike away and they went inside the apartment to sit down and have a long warm conversation about the last few months of each other's lives.

Pete explained Rudy about the projects and the potential profit returns. He told him about the risks but also the possible chance to do something substantial. Rudy stared at the window without looking at the window and for a short moment kept silent. Pete sat and waited; he knew his friend is thinking.

Pete remembered what Brat told him. Don't rush it!

After a short moment Rudy told Pete that lately he was not doing anything, he felt like his life was on hold. He didn't have any place to go or motivation to do anything. He was just on survival. Pete told him this is probably what you could do and do it well. Do it for you, for yourself and for the group. Rudy nodded and whisper: 'ok I'm in.' Pete said: 'I need to know something.' Rudy raised his head and looked at Pete, waiting for the question.

Pete: 'I have a question. Do you have a close girl friend?' Rudy smiled with a sad face: 'no, I don't even have a dog.'

Pete: 'ok then I'll talk to the other guys, and we will meet later.' Rudy left Pete's place and went home. There were few things to consider. He sat and closed his eyes. He thought about the pleasant moments from the last couple of days, and warm memories of the park came to his mind. He could see himself strolling through the place. He could see the LED lights and the surveillance cameras connected to the local police to prevent crime. The restrooms in the middle of the park by the gazebo. He knew the baristas had contribute and added many things to the park. The tempered glass mirror for the women bath, two urinals and a sink low enough for children in the men bath. The crosswalk at each side North, South, East and West were paved with cobble stones. The two main Streets cross walk were raised to control traffic speed. The light posts inside the park were custom made. The cardinal points with the arrows pointing to the far cities, and the distance from the park. The post also indicated closest place with the most historic facts. The state border in the correct direction. There are other arrows pointing in different directions with some unusual destinations. Rudy read this many times and still could not figure it out what the signs said. One sign reads 'joy' the number representing distance is the scripture chapter from the Bible. There are other signs that reads 'peace', 'self-restrain', 'wisdom', 'maturity', 'love', 'patience' This post was paid by a pastor that was very popular among the youth. Rudy could not figure why a post with such signs was allow in the park. 'Those words are esoteric,' he told himself. What do they have to do with the actual city places and distances. Makes no sense, for him. He likes the small bulletin board by the gazebo. The board had from time-to-time flyers about community activities in the park, morning yoga, afternoon chess tournament, bocce ball games played on the grass area. There is a large lithograph copy of the grounds before the park was built. A computer-generated image from about hundred years in the past. Rudy smiled when he remembered the enlarged image showed a small creek that unfortunate no longer exists.

Rudy opened his eyes and felt relaxed and a bit excited. 'Now I'm ready to think about this offer, I need a cup of coffee.' He walked through the park and sat on the Northwest bench. The light wind blew some of the chimes hanging on the small trees. He enjoyed hearing the sweet sound of the chimes and looking at the small trees stager with the LED light posts along the cobble stone trail. The artificial creek runs next to the trail and ends at the small fountain. Someone just recent had added two clay ducks hand painted. Rudy wanted to think for a minute about the job his friend Pete had offered with the band. But he was getting distracted. Pete had explained the general details about going with two more guys to rob a jewelry store. Rudy got up and went to his recent favorite coffee shop Caffe e Dolce, he ordered a cappuccino.

Angela was setting observing people as they passed by, while sipping and enjoying her cappuccino. The young man appeared suddenly in front of her. He walked through the front door up the line to order, and he was unnoticed by Angela.

He did not notice her either, because his mind was preoccupied by the details of joining the enterprise.

Angela turned her head to her right and there he was standing waiting for his cup of coffee to be served. She looked at him and was attracted to his demeanor. He appeared to be sad, and lonely but at the same time had a strange look of staring to a place in his mind. His order was ready and did not respond to the second time when the barista motioned to his cup, Angela supposed that he was too distracted for whatever reason, and she proceeded to tell him that his cup was getting cold. She said: 'if you are not taking your coffee I might as well take it before it gets cold.' Rudy reacted like he came from another world. He utters a strange mumble sound. Angela gave to him a look as if she was trying to decipher a strange unknown language. Rudy realized what had happen and just busted laughing. Angela laughed also. Both started to converse. The time passed quickly, and they realize they were late for their next meeting. A rushed goodbye was exchanged along with phone numbers as they both departed. Two days went by, and Rudy was too busy to even call her, Angela did not want to initiate the first move, so she waited for Rudy to call her.

Jack Wayne was sitting down and slowly got up to come closer to his storyteller and said in a soft voice: 'that was the first time she talks to…' Miller interrupted to replied, 'please let me tell what happens next.' Jack Wayne noticed the emotional strain on Miller, then he sat down quietly listening to the rest of the account.

Few days had gone by since Ron and Brat talked about recruiting one or two more members. Ron called Brat to check how things were.

Ron: 'Mister B how are you?' From time-to-time Ron called Mister or just 'B' to Brat. When Ron used those words to address his friend it meant Ron is very serious and official, and depending on the tone of his voice, it means he wants to demonstrate his affection, as it was on this occasion.

Brat: 'hey Ron, I'm well. I got news from our new potential teammates.'

Ron: 'we better get together and discuss your findings.'

Brat: 'agreed, where do we meet?'

Ron: 'my place can you come tomorrow, afternoon?'

Brat: 'would you like to meet them?'

Ron: 'let's just meet the two of us and then we'll figure out what's next, ok'

Brat: 'I'll see you tomorrow.'

First Encounter with Bullets

Brat left his apartment around four in the afternoon on his way to meet Ron. The police patrol at full speed with lights and open blasting sirens passed him three blocks before he arrived to Ron's place. Brat had time to pull to his right and make room for the patrol car. He was perplexed and said to himself 'What the heck is going on' immediately two more police cars went by just as fast as the first one. Brat stayed in the same place for a short moment and another police vehicle block the interception at the end of the block. Brat could see the police closed the street. He said to himself 'man this is serious I've better get out of here' He made a u turn and decided to go around the block towards Ron's home. He could hear sirens in a distance approaching the streets where he was turning. The next corner where he needed to turn was closed by the police. He stopped to observe for a moment. Then he said to himself 'Are you kidding?'

More cars were behind him forming a line and no one could get through. Some vehicles turned and left for the same way they came. Before he could turn couple guys passed running on the sidewalk and several gun shots hit the cars parked on his right side. One bullet hit the windows on the vehicle just next to his and the glass shattered into many small pieces. Brat opened the door and threw himself on the ground. People were screaming and he could hear many running away from where he was laying down on the ground. Brat was talking to himself or better yet praying 'Oh please God don't let me die here!' A moment of silent gave him enough time to realize his engine was still running, slowly he crawled back into his car, reached for the keys in the ignition switch, and shut the engine off. He pulled the keys and suddenly more gunshots, but this time they were not hitting anything close to him. At a short distance he could hear people yelling and short after more shots of a heavier caliber, probably rifles. Brat's heart was about to explode in his chest, but he kept imploring for his life 'Oh God I'm done nothing wrong don't let them kill me' More police sirens on a distance approaching the area. Brat dragged himself out of the car and rolled under trying to hide and find shelter. He listened very carefully to any sound. More single shots and several heavy shots from automatic rifles. It was clearly an exchange of bullets between police and whoever had a smaller gun. He tried to think what he could do to get out of the place alive. He couldn't see anything or see anyone. He asked himself if it was safe to roll out the car and crawl towards the sidewalk risking being shot. Brat stayed there for a few moments and tried to encourage himself. There were sounds at a distance probably the police directing vehicular and foot traffic.

Brat's heart had calm down to the point that allow him to think what to do next. He decided to move in between the parked vehicles. More shots exchange and more voices from the police ordering or giving some kind of indications. The sun light starting to change, he knew the sunset will be soon along with the evening's dark sky. Brat peaked through the cars and all he could see was some police officers hiding behind cars with rifles and guns in their hands. He peaked to the opposite side no one was there. He reached in his pocket for the pack of cigarettes and realize that he had lost it probably when he threw himself out the car the first time.

Brat thought: 'if I wait till it gets dark maybe no one will see me, I have a chance to get out of here alive,' then he reaffirmed himself by thinking aloud 'that's it, I got this! Soon a small voice told him, 'On the other hand if police see me in the dark can't identify who I am and I may be shot by the police'. He heard a commotion of heavy trucks moving where the police were, he saw a heavy armor truck from the police squad parked right at the corner on to the sidewalk. Brat felt fear taking hold of him. He tried to call for help to the police. His voice had abandoned him. All he could master was a soft moan noise. He cleared his throat and tried again. He was too far for the police to be heard. He was still hiding behind the parked cars. They could not see him either. The day light was diminishing, Brat took a decision and got out his hiding place and walked next to the cars away from the police. His legs were heavy and felt sluggish. It was only forty yards to reach the corner, it took only about 8 minutes, but Brat worked hard stumbling from vehicle to vehicle and hide behind every other car. The time for him felt hours. When he reached the corner, he went around, and he was wet and soak in sweat. He bent over, hands on his knees with difficulty breathing from the stress. He squatted down, slowly sat on the sidewalk with his back against the wall, his wrists resting on his knees, and trembling hands. The sound of loudspeakers brought his attention. The police were giving orders of some kind to someone, he was too far to understand. He stood up, put his hand in his pocket looking for a cigarette and remembered they were lost, then he looked around, and proceeded to walk towards Ron's place. The streets were deserted, and dark. The last few yards about fifty before reaching Ron's front door Brat ran as fast as he could. Rang the doorbell and at the same time knock on the door desperately. Ron opened the door; he did not have time to say anything. Brat pushed the door and Ron out the way and got inside. Brat shut the door close. It was 7:30 pm.

Ron grabbed Brat by the shoulders and asked if he was ok. Brat just nodded and started to have mild nerves break down. Ron pulled him to the couch and said: 'hold on Mr. B' then he went to the kitchen, opened the refrigerator and grabbed a cold beer. He brought it to his friend and said: 'drink slowly take a breath, have another sip.' Then he said pointing with his index finger, 'wait, not yet! I also need a beer myself don't go anywhere.' He patted Brat's sweaty face. Ron and Brat had few sips of their beers before Brat felt settle and able to tell his friend what a long, horrible ordeal he had.

Ron told Brat: 'try to forget as best as you can. Everything is fine. We'll go back in the morning to check on your car.' The news on tv had the whole incident. The special squad division from the police force had a stand-off with one active shooter for about three hours and the suspect had surrender, no one was hurt or kill. Ron told Brat: 'you better spend the night here; I'll get you a blanket and comfy sweatpants. Tomorrow we can talk about business plans and candidates.'

Next day Brat explained to Ron about Pete's reaction to joint their enterprise offer. Pete also has a friend. His name is Rudy, they known each other for a long time. Ron wanted to meet Pete first and then Rudy. They met Pete in the park, Ron observed for a short time Pete while Brat was telling how they had met months ago. Ron shook hands with Pete and ask him how he felt about working with a team under his command. Pete answered: 'is about trusting each other, if you guys trust me, I can trust you as well, I would like to know what it is what we'll do.' Ron looked at Brat smiled then turned his head to Pete to say : 'it's about profits for jobs well done, details are discussed at the proper time and place.' Pete grimed to say: 'I'm in.' They had a moment of excitement, Brat fist bump with Pete, they turned to Ron, and all made the same move. Ron added let's move to the next step. Brat wanted to mention that Pete had a friend who could also join the group. He told Ron: 'what about Pete's friend? Ron nodded in agreement. 'When can we meet your friend?' Pete said: 'I thought we were all meeting today. Ron proposed before we meet your friend first, we will do a try out, Brat will fill you with the details tomorrow. Pete said: 'fine.'

Ron wanted to have a small simple task for Pete as a try out before they can meet his friend. Ron had Pete to find out from a store the amount of inventory and the most valuable items. Pete had the liberty to choose the store. He had two days to present his results. It was not a difficult task for Pete and Ron was content.

Two days later they met Rudy in a coffee shop on Great Highway near Golden Gate Park, the other side of the city.

Business Begins for The Band

Ron called everyone to a business meeting. They met at Ron's place in the living room with the curtains close. Ron spoke in general terms the illicit nature of what they were about to sign. The need for everyone's safety to keep extremely confidential. I will not kill anyone here but listen to me! One or all of us might die if anything is compromised. We must be in total agreement. In fact, what we must do is take an oath.

Our sworn statement should guarantee any information from our circle not to be revealed. Failure to our oath means death for all of us, is just simple, straight and harsh like that.' Ron added: 'Any questions?' While he looked at everyone very seriously. No one said anything.

Ron stablished the rules, including the oath for each member. They also promise to keep from becoming involved in any serious relationship with a lady. Ron submitted if anyone from us have a sweetheart, I mean, a serious sweetheart, I guarantee, that lady is a liability for our safety. Police can trace all of us through such lady. Anyone can have a lady but nothing serious or we're doomed. At that time everyone agreed and signed with the oath.

Ron proposed to figure a plan for a series of 'small projects' The idea, he explained is to try different methods to gain experience and confidence. We need to learn how to observe details that brings success or failure. No one objected. He asked from everyone to think how they would carry off the whole operation. Each one had one or two things to say but not a complete plan.

Ron asked Rudy to act as secretary and start to write what everyone is saying. At this point they all moved to the kitchen-dining area. Rudy sat at the small table in the kitchen with the small notebook and pen in front of him. Ron spoke: 'Let's have some order on this, let's see, you are the first one, go ahead,' and pointed to Rudy. They all noticed Rudy looked surprise and said: 'me?' No one said anything just looked at him waiting and listening. Rudy took the pen and without saying much he started to write few notes. Ron raised his hand indicating a pause, for everyone: Wait!

Brat got up from his seat and walked out saying: 'I'm right here just getting a smoke.' Pete looked at Ron and shrugged his shoulders and crossed his arms. Rudy put the pen down and looked at Pete and Ron. Brat noticed that Rudy was ready.

Rudy said: 'ok it's not a master plan just couple ideas of how we could start.'

1. 'select the location, this may require all of us,' he added
2. 'check their inventory, Ron and Brat are the experts.' He continued.
3. 'decide when to go in, and just do it.'

Everyone was silent and Pete said: 'Ok, that's a very general idea. We need to fill few other details.' Ron said: 'number one sounds good, select the location. That is a good place to start. We need more than that before we move to number two.' Brat said:' We need to check on their security system.' Ron interrupted and told Rudy: 'here is when you continue to write everything is said. Got it?'

Rudy took the pen to write what Brat suggested. They spent few hours taking notes and contemplating ideas. The day grew into late hours, Ron exchanged couple of glances with Brat, they nodded to each other in agreement, then Ron dismissed everyone for the day. He told them that they were all in the right path, he had a good feeling in how things were coming along. After three weeks they had a general plan and started to rob small stores in different cities. Cities at 20 to 50 miles from their hometown. Brat assigned Pete to drive one of the rental vans with the tools and the uniforms to use for the job. Rudy oversaw posting guard at the door while Ron and Pete were inside, and Brat was outside in case something unsuspected happened. If the police or someone else came he was to create a diversion to allow the rest of the group to escape. Pete disagreed with Brat, and he wanted to post guard on the door. The reason being the person at the door was the last one to leave the store no matter what. Pete wanted to protect his old-time friend Rudy. Brat and Pete got into a heated argument and they both called each other names. Ron had to calm them both and literally order Pete to stand down. He suggested to Brat to just switch the damn roll for Pete's sake! Right after he said it, he realized the expression of Pete's sake! Right after he said, he realized the expression "Pete's sake", he raised both hands and bowed as giving thanks to the small audience. Rudy was the only one who applauded Ron's performance. Brat went outside to smoke and calm his nerves. Pete came out and said sorry and both did fist pump. 'Things were back to business.

Angela was busy at work, and she saw a small note on a file 'Time flies when you are having fun' She opened the file that had old papers from a task that it was completed and dated. The date was the same when she met Rudy, now she did not relate it to the encounter. She thought about getting a cup of coffee at Caffe e Dolce, the coffee shop by the park. Once she walked to the park, she remembered Rudy, she realized that it had been two weeks since they met at the same coffee shop. She looked in her phone for contacts and Rudy's number was not there. She looked in notes, no number. Then she remembered they exchanged text messages and then confirmed that Rudy had not contact her since they met. She thought about texting him, but she decided to wait.

Rudy has been preoccupied with the details of his new job. He had helped Pete and Brat to go and find places where to rent vans, where to buy uniforms and even some tools for their different assignments. He thought a couple of times about calling Angela, but it was either too early in the morning or too late at night. He told himself 'Tomorrow, I'll text her around noon.' But before he could realize two weeks had gone by. Rudy woke up and saw the time 6:40 am. 'I need to get few things before I go to meet Pete.' Rudy left his apartment but before he started to walk, he texted Angela: 'good morning, Angie, it's been a while how is everything? This is Rudy.'

They selected their targets in small commercial centers, pawn shops, and stores where they could mingle disguised as service personal. They took on full working clothes such as Plumbers, electricians carrying a small tools belt, pest control including a handheld pesticide sprayer, cable technicians carrying a clip board with fake invoice forms, wearing a baseball hat with the local cable company in order to appear official. These ideas came from their meetings. In some jewelry stores, they went in at noon. In other stores they showed up late, a few minutes before the store closed for the day. They introduced themselves with the reason to check water lines shared with next door neighbors. The statement they used was: There is a small leak inside the adjacent wall we need to make sure there is nothing affecting your area. In other cases, they said we need to check the gas line and make sure of no leaks. In every case once they were inside the store one of them stood by the door and close it, while they carry out the merchandise. Because they experience success in every assault they committed, Ron called for a 'cooling period' and everyone went on to be on their own affairs for two weeks and not to communicate with one another. They had to work regular jobs.

Angela heard the phone buzz, she looked at her messages and with surprise she saw that Rudy had sent her a text. She was on her way to work but responded with a text telling him that he had been a stranger for two weeks. The only excuse for his silent could be he was abducted by aliens, and he just escape from the aliens and had returned home the last hour. After Angela pressed send, she read it and wished that she had not send it. She shook her head put her hand on her mouth and said: 'how silly.' She left for her office. Rudy read the text from Angela, and he smiled. He texted asking her to meet maybe that afternoon after work or the next day for a cup of cappuccino at the same coffee shop where they met. She answered, sorry no time for the next couple of days. Few extra things to do at her office. Her boss is taking a trip out of town, and she oversees getting the itinerary including booking hotels, and airline tickets. It takes time to have all that ready, she must stay at her office after work. She would have more time the following week after the boss leaves. Rudy and Angela were able to meet the last week of the cooling period for the band. Rudy enjoyed seeing Angela and he apologize for having schedule himself for work out of town the following week. I'm afraid I will be absent again, he explained.

After this 'cooling period' they expanded their 'projects' to the Southern part of the state, San Diego, Malibu, Santa Monica. They also learned how to disguise their own personal appearance. They also mimic some of their favorite movie characters gestures, Ron tried to imitate the voice of Steve Carell, Felonious Gru character in the movie Despicable Me. He could not do a good enough or acceptable impersonation that he opted for, to make his own version. Brat kept the sarcastic comments to Ron as a way of making fun of his friend. This is not that simple, Ron uttered: 'despite my best efforts invested in perfecting Gru impersonation.'

Brat seized his chance to give Ron a nick name. Ron: 'from now on you are our Feli short for Felonious Gru. I think we just call you 'Gru'

Everyone laughed and gave their approval. They also selected different accents. Pete tried Scottish accent. Rudy chose a French accent spoken by an American native speaking English. Rudy's nasal component for his French accent proved to be a lot more challenge that he could anticipated. They tried to be as natural as possible when talking to other people (in their own characters). Ron wanted for a big project take a cruise ship to go on a trip where the ship stops in several touristic places where souvenir shops, and jewelry stores offer deals, and the merchandise is available for the vacationers. Because of the idea of being on a ship he liked to call each other mates.

When the target for their next project was selected Brat and Pete had a disagreement in some of the factors that were not included. Brat insisted that those elements were not relevant for the result of the operation. The factors whether to eat the last meal one or two hours before the launch. Pete wanted Brat not to smoke any cigarette while on the job for not to leave traces of cigarettes butt. Brat told Pete no need to be concerned with those aspects. It was not the first time that Pete had disagreements with Brat. Ron had approval for Pete's concerns, but Brat and Pete had argued too long over the similar issues, and Ron consider he owe to his friend Brat and leaned on his favor. Pete respected Ron and submitted to his decisions. Ron felt responsible for his friend Brat. He needed to cover all the basics and Pete was right with the possibility to trace them through the cigarettes.

Rudy Smokeless Approach

Brat did not even suspect that Rudy ultimately will seek out a way for Brat to substitute the smoking habit for something healthier. Rudy disliked the smell of tobacco very much. He did not think about the word quit for Brat. Instead, he prefers to think on the idea of slowly reduce the amount of tobacco smoke in a day. Rudy first mentioned to Pete by asking 'how much longer is he gonna smoke?' Pete looked at him and said, 'who knows, why?' Rudy asked Pete 'doesn't bother you the nasty smell, and the smoke in your eyes?' Pete responded 'sometimes, with a face expression of being taken by surprise. He added: what do you have in mind?

Rudy answers: 'I don't need to start an argument with Brat, you've known him longer than me. Could you suggest to him to take it easy with the smoking when we are working together.' Pete said: 'no, I don't think so. We already banged heads more than once. This time is you and your subtle ways, buddy.'

Rudy smiled and said: 'well hear me out, I have a suggestion for him, don't think of quitting instead light the cigarette as usual, but don't finish the whole cigarette. Put it away before it reaches the end. Do that with few cigarettes, you could cut the end of your cigarettes before you light them.' Pete looks straight forward nodded and said, 'sounds good. Write it down and give it to me I'll see where it goes.' Rudy replied: 'I think there is more than that. I must work in more details. Thanks for hearing me out.'

The beauty of the bay besides the well-known aquarium, watching gray whales, Humpback whales, and White-Sided dolphins includes a small touristic town near the ocean. Carmel-by-the-Sea known for many galleries and museums, they found a small store with low security, hence an ideal target. It was considered an artist town because in the past many artists came to live for a short time. The artists found inspiration to write, to paint, and some worked doing small metal sculptures. The tourists often visit one of the city's jewelry stores, a small store with excellent valuable merchandise. The band thought it was the ideal store due to a simple security system. The store was on the second floor of a business's complex. The plan was to create a strong diversion away from the jewelry shop. The first floor has a storeroom with several cardboard boxes. The door has a basic door lock. 'It will be effortless to break in,' Pete assured.

Brat, Pete and Rudy had synchronized watches as part of their plan. Ron and Brat had 50 seconds of head start allowing them to enter the jewelry store before Pete gave the sign to Rudy. Once inside, Ron could look for a specific diamond. Brat did ask specific questions about the origin of the pearls. Both Ron and Brat acted as separate clients. Ron talked to the other employee. After the 50 seconds, Pete gave the sign to Rudy 'let's go.' They went to the storage room, broke into and started a small fire inside with the cardboard boxes. Then they alerted the security guards about the smoke coming out of the storage room. They created a commotion big enough that disrupted other stores and people started to run out of the complex. The security guards standing on the second floor went downstairs to see what the chaos on the first floor was. Ron broke few cases and grabbed everything he could. Brat ordered the two employees to lay down face to the ground and stay there or he will shoot them. Brat had a small homemade smoke grenade that set it right in front of the store preventing the employees to run after them. The group left the small town in two separate vehicles and gathered later at a cafeteria to have a sandwich. It was a successful operation.

The police interviewed the two employees and took a detail description of the suspects. No fingerprints were found. The security guards gave testimonies about the fire, but they never saw the suspects.

The use of DNA traces to recreate a face of an unknown person was a form of art. There was an artist who made busts for a gallery exhibit. It was not a tool in an investigation of a crime, not at the time of this crime.

DISGUISE IDENTITY

Brat kept an eye on the news for any report on the job that they had finish. There were reports of the robbery, but not a solid identification of any of the band members. He watched the news of a bank robber in a different city. The assault was recorded on video surveillance. Police had identified the suspect and made an announcement to solicit help from the public to call the sheriff department when anyone sees the suspect. The suspect was arrested two days later after the news showed his picture on TV.

Ron summoned a meeting to discuss a detailed plan in how to create a professional costume beyond uniforms. 'A costume to help us change our natural appearance.'

Pete said: 'you mean like in the movies?'

Ron: 'as much as we can make it look natural, we need to change our faces. We already have a good start with the fake accents. So far, I'm impress how the Brits accent is coming along for everybody.'

Brat: 'we could dye our hair and add wigs.'

Pete: 'I like the idea of wearing clear glasses, it changes your face.'

Brat: 'I need to go and get me some smokes; I'll be right back.'

Rudy suggested to investigate how the actors get theirs make up to alter their faces.'

Ron: 'ok, it's everyone's job to search for a specific detail from professionals. I will look about the extra 'fat' on the cheeks. Pete, you search anything about the eyes, contact lens with different colors and so for. Rudy you can help Mr. B to find everything for the hair including eyebrows, and mustaches.'

Rudy: 'great I get to work also on the smoke program.' He looked at Pete and raised his eyebrows. Pete just smiled and gave him a thumbs up. Everyone engaged very diligently on their own assignment. This was a task that everyone enjoyed. They considered by doing this project, set themselves apart from any other band. They thought of themselves sophisticated. Rudy and Brat got along doing their part. Everyone said at the same time: 'we got this Gru!'

In their first meeting after gathering all the information and respective kits for the costume disguise, Ron asked them to work for a while with the kits adding facial hair, the false eyebrows, and change hair color. They also had thick prescription glasses, and silicone gel to add around their cheeks to appear fatter and make the face to look rounder. Rudy mentioned to Brat, he could look like British and should speak with the proper accent. Brat worked on his British accent. Everyone encouraged him. Brat thought that he could add a cigar to appear like a gentleman with taste. Rudy shook his head and pointed that the smell of the cigar could be annoying or not pleasant for some people.'

Brat replied to Rudy: 'I assume you're right; I didn't think on the smell part. I suppose you can see that; thanks' Rudy was stunned! He could not believe what Brat had said. Pete turned his head in a similar disbelief and looked at Rudy pointing with his index finger and just lip movement 'what did you do?'

It took a short moment for Rudy to respond and ask Brat if he had considered reduce the number of cigarettes smoke in a day. The answer was just startled. Brat was not ready for any changes just yet. The smoking, he explained calm his tension, and helps him to take a short break to reconsider whatever is going on. Rudy understood Brat's point and agreed, he also offered a simple guide to reduce the amount of cigarettes smoke, whenever Brat was ready. Brat thanked him and said: 'maybe later.'

The meeting to discuss details and test their 'avatar characters' was done with a conference phone call where everyone was using a false name. They kept moving, changing their individual locations to pretend their conversations were being recorded by the police. Ron did not want to be trace to their places. Everyone was pleased with their efforts. The next step was to meet in person with their costumes to create a scenario and try the accents. What Ron called role play, the band auditions.

Ron's place was the best site in the garage.

'We will meet at my place, you've been there before few times in the living room and kitchen, but you didn't know that my apartment has a large garage, and the owner built an addition on the side into the back yard, he even ran some plumbing for a toilet and a sink, it is handy, not roomy but we have that extra space. I got a small table and couple chairs with a couch and a tv. That is going to be our headquarters/ recording studio.'

They came very early in the morning before six am ready for a long day of full costumes, complete make up with the extra facial hair, dye hair, and heavy clear glasses. Brat included a small fake scar above his left eyebrow. He walked pretending to have one stiff leg. They were ready to give their best.

Pete was chosen to film their show. The actors pretended he was a stranger not in the room. The objective was to have a film for the group to watch later and study what works, and what might need change or correction. The first three performances were not as good as professional actors, but they were acceptable. The whole band became excited, and Ron had to remind them that the idea was to use the best act to get the jewels, the pay would be better than an actor because it would leave no trace for the cops.

THE SMOKE SAGA

Rudy kept thinking every time Brat was smoking How to approach him without creating a situation for Brat to get defensive. 'I know he is open, and he said not yet maybe later. When is later? I must take initiative, can't wait forever.' Rudy asked Brat if he could hear something that Rudy read in an article about the dollars cost for the cigarettes. Brat: 'what is it? Are they increasing the tax again?' Rudy: 'it's not just about the tax.' Brat: 'what is it then?' Rudy: 'people pay $8.00 for one pack of cigarette. A-pack-a day runs $2,920.00 a year. That is one pack, if the person smokes two a day that is $5,840.00 a year! Later, the expense of medical care due to health issues related to the smoking habit. Consider some long-term effects, like the increase risk of stroke, and brain damage, eye cataracts, macular degeneration, loss of sense of smell and taste, yellow teeth and bad breath. Cancer of the nose, lip, tongue and mouth. Decrease skin temperature, decrease appetite, dizziness and headaches. Brat was in disbelief. Brat responded: you're shitting me!

Rudy shook his head and said: 'I am not.' Brat had never heard all that before, not all those terrible things together just for having a smoke. He told Rudy: 'that's pretty f...ing bad bro.' Rudy replied: 'I guess is pretty bad in the long run. It's not just the cost per pack, but it adds up through the year, doesn't it?'

Brat said: 'man! I need to think about this. What else is in there, I can see you are not done.'

Rudy: 'well you might as well hear this, no cigarette smoking, no waste, no ashes, no butts, no fire hazard. No inhaling smoke instead of air hence oxygen, no smell either. No short of breath, no cough. In short no health issues from the terrible nicotine addiction.'

Brat replied: 'this is too much to process all at once. I need time.'

Rudy: 'I understand, I'll tell you what, you take some time to think about it. I will write few suggestions to follow. The idea is to decrease the number of cigarettes in one day. This is not a completion. Take it as light or heavy as you can. If you give it a try for a few days, hopefully it will help to reduce the number of cigarettes per week. It will be up to you how far you want to go. I will have it ready sometime next week. That is if you want to read it and give it a try.'

Brat: 'you sound sincere. I will read it. I'm feeling mess up already. Not sure if I should thank you or give you a cigarette.'

Rudy: 'hey we are taking far more risks in our projects.'

Brat: 'Right! But we are gaining profit too.'

Rudy went home after their long day of performances. He was tired but did not wait for the next week or even for the next day to sit down to write what could make a difference for Brat in terms of quitting the smoking.

Rudy wrote the same suggestions that had mention to Pete. He also made it as a direct personal note to Brat.

Rudy wrote: 'Hey bro, I mean Brat you could start by cutting a tip to your cigarettes and throw the butt when you're done. The reason to do that is to start smoking less. You'll still go through your pack, but you'll be smoking less. You will probably cut the equivalent of four maybe four and a half cigarettes. I know what you're gonna say. It's my money! I agree it's your money and is your health, remember. Try to do that for a few days. Then you can cut a little bit more than just the tip, you could cut some of the cigarettes in half, take it easy you don't have to do it all at once. If you can survive cutting half to say 8 or 9 of your pack, guess what! You have reduced the number of cigarettes that you smoke. Keep up the good work! Your target is to cut in half at least 15 cigarettes of your pack. I'm not sure if you could get to this point by yourself.

No one can do all this alone, trust me. Cheer up! There is plenty of support available.

Next step, keep cutting in half the cigarettes. Put it in your mouth as usual, but don't light it right away. Hold on to for a moment, then go ahead and smoke the darn thing. Hold on now stay with me. The idea to have the cigarette in your mouth for a while is to indulge the habit of nicotine. It will take some time for you to master the impulse to light the cigarette right away. This is the beginning of reducing the quantity of cigarettes a day. You could skip smoking a cigarette by holding the lighting of it the same number of minutes that it takes for you to smoke one single cigarette.

You can count on something concrete here. You have control over the amount of tobacco that you are smoking. You are getting closer to take the radical step. Keep with the routine and little-by-little you can skip one or two cigarettes to stretch the interval in between cigarettes. The day will come when you skip a full day with no smoking. It is the reverse of starting to smoke. You did not smoke a full pack the first day of your smoking tobacco life.'

Rudy looked at the note, he read it twice and put it away in an envelope. He wrote on the front. To Brat for smokeless days. Or reduce number of cigarettes per day.

Rudy was excited about the long note that he ended up writing for Brat. He texted Angela asking her to get together after work. Angela was pleased to hear from Rudy.

She was busy that evening helping the senior center as a volunteer with the bingo game. Angela mentioned it to Rudy that she helps not just with money, but also with her most precious commodity. Her free time. They went out the following evening to their favorite coffee shop. They had an informal light dinner. The soup, salad, and sandwich that they shared was a better alternative that a pizza. Rudy couldn't wait to tell Angela about his long note for Brat in his effort to help Brat stop smoking. Angela read the note and made an expression with her face, her eyebrows slightly furrowed, her lips pursed, and her chin raised. She did not say a word, but it showed her disagreement. Rudy was puzzle and asked Angela.

Rudy: 'you don't agree that he should stop smoking?'

Angela: 'I agree, he should. Your note is long and kind of complex. I doubt if he could follow, that is if he wants to, in the first place.'

Rudy: 'but, but... it's all there! Well, is almost all. It has all he needs; it is a good start.'

Angela: 'maybe you could divide the instructions in two or three sections and offer the first, if he goes through the first, then give the second and so for.'

Rudy: 'Angie, you are so right. Actually, you are more than that. You are an angel, that is your name after all.'

Angela: 'Please! You are the hero behind his wellbeing.'

Rudy: 'you know what? The note states that no one can do it by oneself. It takes the help from others, and here you are helping him. Amazing!'

Angela: 'let me know how it goes after you give him YOUR instructions.'

Rudy: 'Wow! I wrote them, but I did not make all of them. I'm just the messenger. I will split them and hopefully it will make a difference for him.'

The lesson here is Rudy depression has practically vanished the moment he sat down and wrote the instructions for Brat about how to reduce the number of smokes. Rudy is focusing on helping Brat and in doing that he is receiving the uplift on his spirit, he already forgot the feeling of sadness or just surviving as he told his buddy Pete. He can't help to show his excitement when he tells Angie.

The Brits

Ron and Brat talked about the next project and how well things were going. Ron asked Brat what he thought about naming the group. Brat responded a name. what's the reason for?' Ron indicated that their enterprise was heading for a long term. The fact that among the different accents which are fake, phony, imitation or whatever you want to call them, the British is their best.

It starts to sound genuine. Brat admitted: 'is true! I myself like to think that perhaps some of my ancestors were British.' Ron interrupted, 'stop! Don't tell me that you are descendant of Sir Galahad Mr. knight.' Brat and Ron burst in laugh. Ron thought for a short moment and said to Brat: 'wait there's more' Brat said 'oh no"

Ron had that mischievous face when he called him: 'Tin Man' Brat had a frown on his face, a raised corner of his mouth and said, 'huh?' Ron laughed even more adding: 'the knight's armor, get it? Tin Man'

Brat responded: 'I see" Ron continued and declared: 'Tin Man is your new nick name instead of Mr. B. I like it.' Brat replied: 'ok Gru.'

They had few successes with small, quick projects. They had gained confidence to act natural and use the 'other' identity. Ron felt confident about the acting of each one with the fake accent. Their trips to Southern Cal had served them well. They had better timing, The experience in selecting their assignments was improved.

Ron and Brat were convinced, that it was wise to wait for some time after each project. They labeled: "Let the heat cool off." Let police report to us on the news about progress on investigating the robbery jobs. The small amount of the loot was considered less valuable than the time for planning. No amount of profit will be worthwhile if they neglected time to plan and prevent an error, a fatal error they underlined.

Their purpose of the projects was to obtain whatever number of jewels, at the same time avoid the attraction of police suspicion of the modus operandi. The police could alert other jewelry stores about the robberies and possible the size of the band.

Ron discussed carefully with his close friend Brat the need for everyone to continue with their actual jobs. It will be preferable full-time work. The reason, on which they both agreed was to have steady income while they waited on the news for police investigations, and reports, after their small projects. A further reason eliminates the need to cash out, too soon, and give a clue to jewelry insurance agents looking for the sale of stolen items.

Brat mentioned to Ron that Rudy was the only one with no steady work. Rudy works when the recording studio needs extra personal for the installation of mics, music stands and the like. Ron asked: 'what about the touring bands?'

Brat laughed and said: 'no touring, the shows of small bands are irregular in some night clubs. When a band needs help with the set up on the stage, they call Rudy for the assignment.'

That afternoon Miller meets Jack Wayne at the park where Rudy had met Angela. Jack Wayne makes the affirmation: "And so the Brits with Gru and Tin Man go to work?" Miller replied: 'yes, you can say that.'

GRU TIN MAN AND THE BRITS

The next project for the band with their costumes and rehearsed accents was selected by Brat after he searched extensively for a profitable place to rob. A city with a port, a destination for cruise ships with many tourists. The port offered few attractions to the short-term visitors, souvenirs, handmade items, local food vendors, and small jewelry stores. Brat made an emphasis about the relative low level of security in general. Brat observed for two seasons the number of tourists and their origin. He considered the hours when travelers disembark the ships. There was a group, tourist scheduled to come from Great Britain.

The plan was to mingle with the tourist while they were in town. Carry on the plan meaning rob the jewelry shop, then remove costumes with the hope that after the heist, police investigation would be much harder. The police would go to the cruise ship, request list of passengers and possible search the cruise ship. This is time consuming. Ron and Brat had the confidence they will have all the time needed to leave town with their true identities and not having to fear for the police running after them.

The police did not have a clue because the robbers were in town for a short time. They did not aboard the ship at any point. Not before the departing port and not on the disembarking port where they committed the crime.

The evening local news broadcast mentioned a robbery had taken place earlier on the day in a small jewelry store near the port. No one was hurt, only loss of merchandise. Police were conducting a throughout investigation including a possible implication of a cruise ship.

Pete made a short comment to the rest of the gang, after hearing the news: 'Police figure it out too late. We were never passengers on the ship, ha!'

The band arrived on two different vehicles. They came to town three hours before the arrival of the cruise ship. Ron was in one small commercial van. A plain white rented vehicle with no windows, by himself, no passengers. He had most of the cosmetic kits, two small folding chairs and one small portable table. This is used to set up the makeup sets. The other vehicle a full-size commercial van, no windows and a bicycle rack in the back. Brat as the driver Rudy front seat passenger, and Pete in the back. They all wore plain light color jackets, baseball hats, and sunglasses. The van stopped before entering town to drop Rudy with the bike. He rode the bike in town the last three miles. Pete received a text from Rudy about ten minutes after Rudy started to ride the bike. Brat and Pete were on their way to the supermarket, Pete checked the message. Rudy needed help. He has a flat tire and no way to fix it. He was too far from town to walk all the way to the supermarket. Pete texted Ron and explained the small change of plans, hence they would be slightly late to their rendezvous. Pete called Rudy and told him to find a clear safe spot and wait for them. We don't want anyone to see us together outside of town. Rudy agreed and walked back by 2 or 3 hundred feet to a spacious road shoulder. He found a spot with few bushes to hide behind. Perfect for Brat to pull the van and fix the flat tire. Pete helped Rudy. Brat got out and while they work on the tire, he smokes a cigarette. Rudy alluded to Brat, remember, no more smoking during the performance. Brat replied: 'yeah, yeah.' They went to town right after the tire was fixed according to their plan.

They all went and met at the supermarket to buy sandwiches and drinks. The meeting place was at the parking lot of the port. Rudy gave Brat the written suggestions in reducing the number of cigarettes smoke in a day. Rudy apologizes to Brat: 'here you go, sorry for getting in your nerve, I just would like that you find a way to start saving some of the profits that we are about to acquire.' Then he gave him a fist pump. Brat grabbed the list with a stern face and thanked him.

They parked amid vehicles inside the parking lot. They went to the small souvenir stores not in a group but each one as separate visitor. One by one went to check the location of the jewelry store. They each rehearsed their own route and learned any possible alternatives. They considered any alleyway or street. Ron knew the time when the cruise ship would dock and the time for passengers to disembark.

They wore their customs with makeup. They worked in couples to help each other with the customs and applying the makeup. Ron helped Pete, and Brat worked with Rudy. It was Ron's idea to keep Brat and Pete getting into any silly arguments. Ron told Pete 'You work with Tin Man.' Brat immediately interrupted Ron and told Rudy: 'you work with Gru.' They all laughed! Ron commented: 'this is good we all need to be relaxed, and in good humor. We just need… correction you guys', pointing to Pete, and Rudy: 'need your nick names.' Pete looked at Rudy and rolled his eyes. Rudy just drew his lower lip between his teeth.

When they entered the jewelry store, they spoke with the British accent. The clerks at the store thought they were from England, and they must be on the cruise ship. They pulled handguns and took a substantial amount of small diamond rings, some earrings, and neck laces. Then they tied down the employees and exited the store. Then they went to the large van. It was parked in the alleyway behind the stores. They removed the customs, cleaned the makeup, and went out of town driving at the speed limit.

THE BRITS AND THEIR HONEST JOBS

Brat had a temporary job as a clerk in a distribution center for electronic industrial parts and components. He worked only during high demand from the vendors. His boss call him only for three or four months in winter or spring. He liked the job. It was busy with long days. He worked shifts of 10 hours a day, for four days, then he had three days off weekend. What he enjoyed on the job, it required him to open and review some of the technical information, then match to the correct box of components. Different parts came from various manufacturers. Brat became very interested in electronic mostly in devices that control locking mechanisms, security surveillance rotating video cameras, among other controls.

Pete was a service mechanic for motorcycles. He worked for different mechanic shops, mostly to work on different bikes. It was challenging to learn about the electronic parts of the newer bikes, but he found enjoyment and it was interesting. He worked alone most of the time. He had a habit to listen to music with headphones and learned the difference in the quality of sound. He became attracted to the engineering behind such components.

Ron worked of a variety of places as a clerk. He worked from time to time in a jewelry store, in a bookstore, music instruments shops, and in rare occasions as assistant to vendors in conference auditoriums. He was an excellent salesman. He had a style and good attitude to convince people about many topics.

DNA BUST

Rudy worked in a recording studio, and through a few acquaintances that referred him for help as a stage crew, on local discotheques. The stage crew work was very tiring and demanding with long hours at night and the pay was next to nothing. When Rudy got paid, he called Angela to ask her out. He was looking for ways to spend time with her without spending too much money. He knew Angela preferred simple meals, inexpensive entertainment, besides she rather give her money to those who did not have much.

THE MORAL COMPASS

Rudy was sitting at the coffee shop Caffe e Dolce, the tv monitor at the upper corner by the table of condiments and extra napkins was on with the local news. The place was nearly empty in the early Saturday afternoon.

Rudy watched the weather report, the temperature was in the mid-seventies, a few clouds with light winds at 16 miles. He looked outside through the window to check on the clouds, then he turned his attention back to the TV. The newscast was about a series of burglaries to convenience stores. The crimes were done by the same suspect alone. The video surveillance had the clear image of the same individual wearing different jackets committing the criminal acts. No one had been hurt, but damage to property and the small amount in some cases had been taken. This was the least of the problems for the suspect. The individual should be caught any time. Rudy thought: 'this is an amateur, who has no idea how the surveillance cameras work.' Rudy whispered to himself: 'He is so stupid, changing his jackets does not fool anyone.' He thought about the suspect's inexperience, when Angela arrived.

Rudy did not think about the news anymore. Angela very perceptive had observed Rudy for a short time before approaching the table. She noticed Rudy staring the tv but clearly submerged in thoughts. She asked him if everything was all right. Rudy mentioned about the suspect committing stupid burglaries for a very small loot. 'This guy will be catch anytime and will have to pay way more than what he took.' Angela asked Rudy: 'do you think the amount of money robbed should be greater? I mean or equivalent to the risk of haven broken the law. Which in neither case does not justify the criminal act.' Rudy was blown away and he could only respond: 'that's not it! It's the fact this guy does not care about all the video cameras taping his face. He might as well surrender himself to the police instead of waiting or hiding somewhere. I'll bet he will be catch in no time.' Rudy had a stern tone in his voice, he even spoke a bit louder, to emphasize his statement. Angela replied: 'so you think he should have disguised himself in order to not be identify that easily?' Rudy answered: 'well, at least make an attempt, you know, he's not smart.' Angela said: 'you mean wise.' Rudy agreed and said: 'yeah! That's, it he is not wise.' Angela exhaled and pointed to Rudy: 'you see wisdom is not found on twisted criminal, and immoral minds. He is committing robberies that is criminal. It doesn't matter the amount of money. He will suffer the consequences.' Rudy said: 'Angie that sounds rough.' Angela replied: 'that is his choice. He could have an honest job, if he desires one.'

Rudy was attracted to Angela and was very impressed by the depth of her comments and observations. The sincere tone of her voice and her confidence pulled Rudy's mind to a place of serenity. He could not pinpoint a single trait of Angela that explained him why he felt calm in her company.

One time Angela in a sincere tone, she asked him what kind of books he was reading. Rudy felt embarrassed by not having an answer. He was not reading any books. She asked him why not? Rudy stumbled with his words and attempted to make too many excuses, none of which sounded valid or acceptable. Rudy realized he couldn't come up with a good lie. Angela smiled and suggested to him to read something that he would like. 'Pick the topic that is interesting to you. You could read an article in a magazine, perhaps it will be a thread for you to unwind in a fascinating road.' When Angela said this, she came closer, and opened wide her dark brown eyes looking directly at Rudy. Rudy almost felt off his chair. Completely enchanted.

Rudy asked Angela: 'how about you, what are you reading?' He frowned and tried to fold his arms close on his chest. He pulled away from the table.

Angela observed him dismissing all his moves with a smile. She went on to disclose that there were books that she would love to read, but currently she was focus on reading a bit of history, and some literature. 'I like to read the latest prize winners. I read in three different languages.' Rudy was inarticulate. She added, 'I also read about art and technology.' At her job she needs to keep current with certain aspects of art exhibits, and some general information about security systems. Her boss owns art, he is involved with some small galleries and private exhibits. He travels a lot to art auctions and some museums.

Rudy felt that Angela was in a different world. Rudy thoughts: 'no wonder she is highly knowledgeable. Rudy knew Angela is an intellectual, and more sophisticated that whatever his small world was. Despite all those differences, he started to call her Angie. Angela appreciated the tenderness and respect from Rudy.

Angela had talked to Rudy about moral principles and the truth about reaping what is sown. The respect that Rudy had for Angela kept him quiet when she talked about those concepts. Rudy sat, looked at her, and listened, many times fascinated, but sometimes in disagreement.

Rudy did not want to hear a lecture in moral principles. But Angela had a sincere way to present the ideas in a simple form. Every time Rudy had a conversation with Angela about truth, ethics, justice, decency, and virtuous behavior, he had sleepless nights. He spent time playing in his mind what she said. He could hear portions of the conversation again, and again. It seemed that he had undertaken a study on moral concepts. Rudy asked himself few times: 'where does she get this information? Why is she telling me all of this?'

'Actions have consequences' Rudy heard in his mind, remembering Angie's words. Angela does not know anything about his friends and their activities, and how they have been accumulating all those jewels. It is their own treasure. 'Sure, all that is illicit. Does it mean terrible consequences are coming?' Rudy felt under a raid of thoughts. 'What is going on here? It does not make sense! I can't explain it! This is exhausting!'

Angela did sense that Rudy had some type of preoccupation. He must have something heavy in his mind. Angela asked if everything was ok. Rudy had his reservations. He just pretended to dismiss the real answer and utter: 'sure all is well.' Rudy did not want to talk about his illicit actions. Angela through her conversations with Rudy, had learned that he had lost his family. It happened when he was a young teenager. A classmate who was close to him had help him. The family adopted Rudy and treated him as a relative. They all helped in high school, the last two years. Rudy considered his friend Pete as family, perhaps his close cousin. They shared many good and bad moments. It had been two years since they had separated, each at his own apartment. Every day communication had become a once a week.

When Pete talked to him about joining the band to work with Ron and Brat for a series of projects. Rudy asked what kind of projects. Pete mentioned, jobs in the jewelry business. Pete added, to be specific take possession of jewels from stores and then selling those items for profit. Pete winked his left eye at the same time. Rudy looked straight but his mind was not in the same room. Pete insisted and told Rudy that everything should be fine. No worries. You can use the money.

Rudy felt that he had to come along. It was his friend whose family had help him. He felt obligated, he decided to be there for Pete. Rudy perceived Pete's friends or associates did not inspire confidence.

THE ROAD TO VINDICATION?

Rudy had a crush on Angela. She inspired trust to him. Angela was educated, she spoke about interesting subjects, among them arts, and literature which made Rudy aware that his world view had changed. This reorder had happened gradually through the conversations with Angela, which both enjoyed. Rudy was conscious that he no longer needed or wanted everything for himself. Rudy wanted a fulfillment in his life. He was aware of subtle changes, the desire for satisfaction with his actions. 'It's not easy explain it to others' Rudy thought. This concept of having a moral compass. He understood compassion to others was a pretty good start for the consequences of his actions. 'One thing I know, for sure, the more I practice, the stronger is the darned affirmation!'

There is a sense of unexplainable peacefulness. The bits of Angie remarks hunted him as a whisper, 'you will have peace that surpasses human understanding.'

The Rudy that was in a survival mode as he had told Pete, was now on thriving mode. It had been few months since he felt depressed or alone. Thanks to Angie. Lately he was aware of a nagging voice.

Rudy tried to ignore the guilt feeling from his conscious. Every time he did something wrong. Not just with day-to-day actions, but slowly had sneaked to make him aware of his thoughts towards others. It was more than a feeling. It had taken a form of a force with life of its own. That conscious voice that spoke to him at times it was just a whisper, but at times it is shouting so loud that Rudy struggle to keep it quiet.

It was through repentance that the voice first got softer, then silent.

Then to Rudy's surprise, the same voice came back to support him. It saluted him with cheers.

He spoke with Angela about what had taken place. He told her: 'I must be crazy. I'm hearing voices, again, it's insane! This time the voices are encouraging my decisions to follow what is supposed to be virtuous.' Angela commended him. Rudy muttered: 'I'm no hero.' Rudy still could not grasp the idea of 'setting others before oneself' He reasoned, 'that just means yield your spot, or earnings, or your sweet moment to someone else for what reason? For Rudy it did not make any sense. It was contrary to his belief. 'In life one must hold on to own possessions including the place where we are because no one else will do it for you.' He explained to himself 'to yield own possessions is a ludicrous action.'

It did not dawn on him that Angela had been modeling such behavior for him.

'Angie's beauty is wholesome,' Rudy said to himself. 'She is beautiful outside and just as beautiful on the inside.' Rudy longed for Angela. The question 'how could I have her heart?' Run through his mind. 'I really need to show her that I am her guy.' Rudy thought that perhaps using some of the false personality rehearsed for the jewelry job could impress her and make himself more interesting to Angela.

Rudy saw a banner advertising a classical music concert. He knew Angela will appreciate such music. He bought tickets for an afternoon concert and invited Angela to attend the performance. He had never assisted to something comparable, but he hoped Angela understood classical music. Rudy hoped this could help him to establish a deeper connection between the two of them. Angela was surprised and pleased of Rudy's interest of classical performance. The concert was scheduled for Joseph Haydn, ensemble trio for violin, cello and clarinet in E-flat Major No 2. Angela looked at the program and asked Rudy: 'how come did you choose such concert? Rudy did not have knowledge of what to select from the concerts schedule. He just saw the best time he knew both could attend and bought the tickets.

Angela commented: 'it's a month away, we could talk about how this music works.' She explained, 'the pieces of this performance are enjoyable, but you need to be familiar with Haydn music.' She explained with specific details about instruments and how Haydn had written the music for each instrument to be played in an ensemble. Rudy paid close attention to Angela's description; he was delighted with the concert. He enjoyed the live music, the acoustics enticed Rudy to become a fan of Haydn. To Rudy having Angela's company was a truly priceless experience. Angela observed him with intriguing eyes. The performance, the seats that Rudy picked, the venue, and each other's company created a lasting memory. Rudy had selected an event with all the components that made an unforgettable afternoon for both.

Rudy could not perceive that what he had done in terms of the concert was a small result of his exposure to a cultivated mind as Angie, he himself started to acquire appreciation for art and gain a bit of wisdom.

Rudy talked to his friend Pete about having second thoughts on the jewelry jobs.

Pete was surprised by Rudy's comments. Pete questioned Rudy: 'what exactly is that you have doubts about the job.' Before Rudy answered, Pete blasted: 'is the actual value of the merchandise? Or is our capability of pulling in the deal.' Rudy realized that his friend did not even have a clue about the moral consequences. Pete disregarded much the criminal implications. He decided to leave the conversation as it was. Rudy gave a dismissive shrug with a low cast look and mumble: 'all-right, no problem.'

Rudy kept Angela from meeting any of his associates, The Brits. He never mentioned to the group anything about Angela either. Rudy saw Angela as a treasure of his own. The oath that everyone had taken was in the way.

The day for the band meeting, Rudy took a nap after work before their meeting. He overslept. He was late and called Pete for a ride to Ron's place.

Pete will pick Rudy on his way to Ron's place, he left his apartment when he turned the corner of Folsom and 6th Street a car in front of him changed lane without turning any signal or giving any warning sign to Pete, causing Pete to slam on the brakes avoiding a near collision this made him extremely angry. Pete accelerated towards the other vehicle cursing aloud and making the gesture with the middle finger up. The other vehicle oblivious of what had happened slow down to check the address on the building. She was looking for an address to do a delivery. Angela had volunteer to drop some food for a senior, a member of the senior center who had moved to an apartment with a granddaughter. Angela did not notice that Pete was on her tail very close. He was upset. Pete pulled next to her, lower his passenger window to give a very intense and clear derogatory message of how not to 'cut' someone in traffic. Pete realized right after he had yelled in rage that the other driver was an attractive young girl. She could not comprehend what was Pete doing. Pete calmed down, looked at her. He, in a very loud voice told her: 'watch where you're going, bitch!'

Angela asked: 'could you help…!' Pete did not wait for the girl to finish her question and dashed out the scene. He was even more furious cursing the whole moment. Pete said, 'a dumb chick' she is not very smart! Pete went home with a nasty taste in his mouth. He had a rather hard grip on the steering wheel and a strong tension on his shoulders. Pete pulled close to his apartment and realize that he started to go to Ron's place when the incident occurred, distracting him, and he for a moment forgot where he was going. He just went back home.

Jack Wayne with wide eyes open cover his mouth with his left hand and said, 'he called her dumb, but he is not acting very smart, who is the dumb?'

Miller laughed and added: 'life could be amusing. Let me tell you what's next.'

Rudy 's call came to Pete. 'I still need a ride where are you?' Rudy asked. Pete yelled on the phone: 'get your butt here if you want a damn ride!' Rudy answered: 'calm down, don't have a heart attack, for Pete's sake!' It was a customary for Rudy, and Ron to use the British equivalent of 'for crying out loud' with Pete as a punt intended.

Rudy arrived to find Pete seating in his car. After Rudy got inside Pete's car, they talked for a short time. Pete was much better. Rudy heard the reason of Pete's rage. Rudy did not say much in favor of anyone. Rudy thought: 'I wonder who the dumb chick is" They went to see Ron.

The First Cruise

The Brits discussed the points to consider selecting the destination for the cruise ship. Ron announced: 'listen everyone our gathering is officially open. We are discussing what we want for our next project.'

Brat said: 'let's go to another country for excitement's sake.'

Rudy: 'you mean for Pete's sake!'

Brat: 'No! For all of us sake!'

Pete: 'Whatever.'

Rudy: 'I vote for a short trip. No trip of six weeks or more, if it's possible.'

Pete: 'Alright! We have a potential winner. There are few cruises to consider. On the West Coast there are cruises from Los Angeles to Mexico, or to Canada and Alaska.

Ron: 'That's true, also on the East Coast there are trips from Miami to Mexico. There are some to the Caribbean Islands as well.'

They chose a 6-day cruise, from Miami to Cozumel, Mexico and return to Miami, Florida.

The itinerary includes two stops in popular ports for enjoyment of the passengers. Miami, Florida day 1, Key West on day 2, at sea cruising on day 3, Cozumel, Mexico on day 4, at sea cruising on day 5, Miami, Florida on day 6.

They had counterfeit money to buy jewelry in Cozumel. The paper money they used was supposed to be a Hight quality. They had hundred-dollar bills to facilitate the transactions. The amount they carried was over four thousand dollars. Ron planned and expected to use most of the fake money. He relied on his convincing method to acquire the jewels.

The Brits band used false, but high-quality personal identification documents to book their tickets. They utilized fictitious addresses to protect themselves from the police. That included their homes and workplaces. Everything was calculated to the meticulous detail. Evading all possibilities of being caught. Each member of the team used his own money to purchase the ticket along other expenses. Each one brought for the cruise trip a small vacationer luggage. They rehearsed a fake occupation for each one. It was an individual choice to select the occupation. Ron played to be a real estate agent. He as well as the rest of the band learned some basics about each occupation. They agreed to know some about the field in case anyone encounter a person who work in such profession. Ron added a brief background to his fictitious profession. He made a story about he is in the middle of a divorce, needed to be away from work, and did not want to talk property deals. He just wants to have time off from everything.

Brat was an accountant for a small personnel company that was indicted of fraud. He needed a break from the ordeal at work. The boss was under investigation, on his return from the cruise, the prosecutor wanted a detail review of the last few months of his work. Brat himself was not accuse of anything, but the stress was intense.

Pete was a technician of a startup computer and security systems company. He was on vacation. Rudy was simply enjoying a gift from his grandparents. Currently, working in a recording studio as a sound assistant, he was happy. Rudy perceived this made-up occupation a bit enticing. He developed a curiosity to know more about the sound engineering. At the time he did not know, it will be his pursuit.

They researched many aspects in detail related to the cruise. The allotted timetable for the different activities.

Time to disembark once the ship has arrived at a port, the time that is allowed to go around town. They studied all this to weave their planned moves for the robbery. They already had a good experience with the previous cruise ship. The time they needed to pretend they were British passengers when they entered the targeted shop.

Rudy learned that doing research was a time-consuming task, but it had a serendipity component. He found the worth of learning certain facts has many benefits. He also concluded the use of these facts to commit a crime, is clashing. That is his moral dilemma. The internal conflict started to grow. He knew that small voice was coming. The question lingered in his mind. "Why spend time to educate oneself in order to hurt others and possibly to hurt oneself. To learn is for the intellect and the intellect should guide away from danger. I have a fricken conflict.'

Ron asked Rudy to jot down many of their ideas to use for the plans. Ron read to all of them the final scrip.

Ron: 'listen up now, once we leave, we follow all aspects of our plan. We do not chat with one another for any reason. Maintain minimum dialogue with other passengers and crew members. We are traveling as separate individuals. We do not know each other. Remember this is not a vacation for us, we are on our serious important business trip. Our safety depends on all of us. We know what to do with our costumes in case of evacuation. Everyone pulls the regular "street clothing" In case the whole trip is cancelled, we all go back home, and wait for two full days before we initiate com-munication. We all agreed to select the peek time of the season. It is crowded, it should work in our advantage. It is expensive, so enjoy, but with awareness of surroundings. We hope the loot will pay for this and leave a substantial profit.' Ron added: 'any ques-tions?' Brat walked outside and mumbled: 'I'm getting a smoke.' Pete indicated: 'I'm going home all it's well. I'll see you guys tomor-row for our last rehearsal.'

Rudy clarified telling Pete: 'is not tomorrow, is in two days.' Ron replied: 'that's right.'

Two days before the departing day Ron had everyone together in the garage. The place had been converted into their den. They had a small bar, a tv, and a board for shooting darts. It was con-sidering a routine for the band to rehearse with their costume, and make up. There was a tension because it was the first cruise ship trip, and they were to be confine for few days. They wanted to have their accents as close as a natural speech. They recorded their last rehearse.

Ron: 'hey guys great work! Looks like we need some fine tuning, don't we?'

Pete: 'hey man your accent sounded ok, but your speech was kind of choppy.'

Brat: 'we all sound phony, and in need to be better actors.'

Pete: 'are we contenders for academy award? Say best support actor!'

'Ron: 'this is no joke, Pete.'

Brat: 'is no joke, but we can still have some fun while we are rehearsing here.'

Ron: 'let's review the notes. It's been long enough for now.'

After the performance, they sat and watched the video in order to fine tuning and make it more natural. After they viewed the video, and took final notes, the video was deleted.

They all went home to study their notes and work on the last details of their performance.

Cozumel, Mexico.

The day they arrived at the port it was sunny with few dark clouds and the temps at 88oF. The weather forecast called for a passing rain in the late afternoon. Aboard the ship the atmosphere of anticipation among passengers was contagious. The band could not help to catch some of the excitement for getting off board and enjoy the local resort. The first shops to be encounter by the visitors played Mexican music through a good quality sound system. Balloons of different colors, rows of small pennants from local beers, and banners flapping with the wind were greeting the animated crowd.

The band disembarked and walked as planned. Ron was several steps in front of Brat. They went to survey the streets, to figure alternative ways to get back to the ship. Rudy was behind Pete and did the same scanning for the other jewelry store.

Ron and the rest acted under the assumption their counterfeited money was discovered, soon after they had left the stores. The time to get back to the cruise ship was limited. Police would be looking for them. It did not happen as they expected. The number of jewelry stores in the resort was small. The idea was spent about a thousand per store. Rudy spent $400.00, at the Diamonds International on Rafael Melgar Plaza. Punta Langosta. Pete spent $600.00 in the same store. Brat and Ron did a similar purchase in Milano Diamond Gallery store, on #101 Avenida Rafael Melgar. Both stores on the same shopping center in Cozumel.

Ron and Brat walked together into Milano Diamond Gallery store. They pretended to be a gay couple. Brat did not say many words, only Ron spoke with his best British accent, Brat just pointed to the jewels, Ron asked the clerk to show them close to Brat, then he nodded, and Ron asked to be ring and pay for. Ron had a brilliant pink short sleeve shirt and a Cozumel cap. He asked to see items under one-thousand-dollar price. He bought a total of $2,500.00. Brat wore a brilliant yellow short sleeve shirt. He had light lens sunglasses, his left forearm wrapped with a white bandage, to simulate he had a fake injure. They walk out of the store holding hands. When they turned the corner, they removed the brilliant color shirts and they had light blue and white t-shirts under. Brat removed quickly his bandage.

They all got back to the ship with their items. Rudy had a small Mexican hat with light gray sunglasses, Pete wore dark sunglasses, and he had a local cap that he bought when he disembarked. They all removed their costumes. Everyone kept in their own rooms until the ship left the port.

In Miami at the return on day 6, the last day, the Brits put on a show with their full costumes and British accent. They went into an elegant jewelry store and did a stickup. Brat ordered the employees to lay down on the floor. Rudy and Pete tied the employees with duct tape, fold blind them before they left the store. They took many gems. Ron and Pete took a local bus to the train station. Brat and Rudy travel on Gray Hound bus to West Palm Beach airport. The loot was divided in four parts. Each one was packed and shipped to their own home. It was wrapped and label as electronic parts. Pete had printed labels before they left for the cruise. The labels were of a fictitious company.

The next day after they returned home went back to their legit jobs' routine. It was prudent to wait for two days before they had their first post operation meeting. Ron asked everyone to give own analysis of their actions. Then give a score. Brat gave a B+. Ron said: 'that's a grade, I'll take it.' Pete gave a score of 8.7. Ron also liked it. Rudy gave A-. Ron gestured thumbs up. Everyone looked at Ron waiting for his score. Ron told them 'Got to wait until merchandise is sold and cash is collected. I'll give a B+ for the whole operation. They were highly encouraging and started to talk for a possible next operation.

Brat had put the note Rudy gave him with his favorite lighter. The lighter was left in his dresser, he kept there to prevent getting lost.

Brat reached for his lighter and saw the note folded. He read it; at the same time, he smoked a cigarette. His first reaction was indifference. He looked up and saw his reflection in the mirror.

The last words he read were, you didn't start by smoking the same amount of what you smoke now. Brat thought on this, and he curve his mouth and gave a slight nod. He agreed with Rudy. His mind was working. He read the whole note again. He called Rudy. The first thing Brat told Rudy was: 'ain't no loser. Your note about quit smoking. Only losers quit.' Rudy had to think fast for an answer after a short moment, he responded: 'Brat you are not quitting. You are reducing the number of cigarettes smoked in a day.' Brat: 'is that what you are telling me in your stinky note?'

Rudy: 'look, I'll come over and we both go through the steps.' Brat and Rudy were near the bay, in a place away from everybody and Rudy explained the first thing. 'Your first step is cut a small section of your cigarette, then lighted and smoke. The amount will be less because you had cut out the tip. Follow the rest of the steps, give some time and you should oversee the darn habit. Brat was not sure if it will work, but he could start by chopping a bit of every cigarette. Rudy encouraged Brat by telling him 'You are un-re-starting.' Brat asked 'what the fu..k is un-...' Rudy intervened to finish the word, and said: 'relax is very simple, I just made-up that word. I added the 'un' to the re-start. You know some words have the 'un' in the beginning and it means the opposite. For example, un-happy, un-occupied, un-known, and so for.'

Brat pulled his top lip upward at the left side, turned his head slightly to the left, and reluctantly gave thumbs up. 'He said I'll keep with the rest. No promises.' He walked away lifting his hands in the air.

Angela was at work, Rudy sent her a text, few minutes before her quitting time. It was an unexpected message. 'Hi Angie, could we meet after work?' He asked her. Rudy had texted her about four days before stating he was busy with a timely operation. The project didn't allow time for his personal communications. 'Not to be alarm,' he added, 'it's just the nature of the installation in the basement room. The Wi-Fi, and regular phone signals aren't that great.' Angela left work and returned the message. She said: 'I did not expect you back in town! When did you get back?' Short after, her phone rang. She answered: 'Hi Rudy!'

Rudy: 'Hi Angie, how are you? Got back late last night. Can we meet?'

Angela: 'I'm well, aren't you tired from your trip? I'm busy today after work, it's my evening at the senior center. I have a date with a gentleman, it's his birthday. We are having a party.'

Rudy: 'what? You have a date! How old is this …person?' Rudy was jealous. Angela did sense a bit of hostility in his voice. 'Why? It doesn't matter his age. He is old enough to date on his birthday.' Rudy perceived a rebuke and changed his tone: 'I suppose! But Angie could we just get together for few minutes, then you could go to the old birthday boy.'

Angela: 'Are you jealous? What exactly are you insinuating? Shame on you!'

Rudy: 'Uh hmm, oh. I'm sorry, I just meant, you know.'

Angela: 'No Mister I don't know. But I'll tell you what, you can redeem yourself and do the following.' Rudy experienced grace, now he was willing to do anything and responded: 'surely, tell me!'

Miller noticed Jack Wayne had frowned his eyebrows, but the moment he heard that Rudy was willing to do anything, his expression turned to a satisfaction, he was pleased with Rudy. Then Miller said: 'if Brat had learned any of this, he would have called Rudy a "sucker!" Jack Wayne giggles.

Angela: 'Buy a small gift for a senior, don't need to spend more than $10.00. Then meet me at the coffee shop. How is that?'

Rudy: 'Angie for you anything. What do you want me to buy?'

Angela: 'that is for you to figure. Thanks, I'll see you in a little while. Bye'

Rudy: 'ok, bye. He hangs up and told himself: 'she is too Darn clever man!'

Angela reflected on what she had said. Felt remorse in the way she treated Rudy. Then she justified her action as a gentle form to tell Rudy have respect. The question came to her mind, 'Does Rudy feel entitled to have right over me?

Maybe! Hum…maybe is my fault, then we both need to talk about this. I must think about this a little deeper. I must admit he responded with respect and submission. Reminds me about the fruit of the Spirit. '

Rudy and Angela got together at their favorite coffee shop. Caffe e Dolce. Rudy: 'Hi Angie, great to see you.' Angela: 'Hi Rudy, how are you?' Rudy:' fine, here is the gift for the birthday boy. It is a gift certificate for a smart speaker. The sound quality is above average, he can listen to anything from the internet, he just needs wi-fi signal. Angela: 'Rudy I said no more than $10.00 this is way more than that. I can't give him this, you shouldn't have to spend all this money. Rudy: 't's in your name. It's fine. I don't have any idea how old he is but trust me music is always a great gift. You could help him explaining how this certificate works. Have him open and then show him the choices about the smart speakers with the $ amount. You can use your phone if he doesn't have access to the internet. It won't take long.'

Angela: 'Rudy, we need to talk about something serious. Rudy: 'you mean this is that serious?' Angela: 'not this gift certificate. But it has to do with our relationship.' Rudy was not sure what exactly Angela was referring to, therefore, he spoke sincerely: 'Angie in case you wonder I'm not marry, I'm not engage, I don't have a girl friend or living with a lady and hiding it from you.' Angela:' ok, well that all is…I mean it was not, is not what I meant.' Angela did not expect anything like what Rudy had disclosed. He was sincere, but Angela had for a moment no words. She instead just stared directly to Rudy's eyes and contemplated his unpretentious being. Rudy noticed Angela was at a loss for words too long, she even stumble on her words. He felt terrified by the thought, 'something is wrong. Maybe she is married'. Rudy finally asked her: Angie, are you ok? Angela took a deep breath and said: 'I'm fine. What I want to talk is if you are not marry or engage and you don't have a lady hiding somewhere, all that is good, thanks for telling me. They both smiled and felt relieved. There was a light tension in the air for a short moment. Rudy had to ask: 'Angie, are you marry?' And hold his breath!

Angela smiled and firmly said: 'not yet! But that is not what we need to talk. Then the thought came to her mind 'maybe'. Rudy felt the pressure on his chest being released.

Angela: 'Rudy in simple terms tell me what you expect from a girl?'

Rudy: 'I see, I'm not sure what do you mean.' He squinted, with slightly pursed lips.

Angela: 'Rudy is not that hard, ask me the same question.' Rudy felt at ease and asked her the same question. Then she responded setting her left hand over Rudy's right arm. Angela: 'I want a gentleman, a man who respects and knows how to treat a girl. These should be his qualities: self-restrain, patience, honesty, with himself and others. A simple person who loves sincerely and appreciates what life gives, even if is not luxury. Rudy said: 'that sounds kind of simple, but is a perfect man, some kind of hero.'

Angela replied, 'is supposed to be a life journey, a learning growth and application of oneself. Any way now that you have an idea tell me Rudy what do you expect from a girl?'

Rudy looked at her and with one finger on his bottom lip said: I have never thought about that. I probably follow along your lines and describe a perfect lady, but I can tell you that I'm extremely lucky. It just happened that I already know the perfect girl.'

Angela was intrigued and said: 'really? Are you sure? How do you know? I meant you must have spent lots of time with this girl of yours to get to know her this well. She must be in your dreams.' Rudy was confident when ha said: 'you're right she is in my dreams.' Angela's face became pale, she put her left hand over her forehead and cover her eyes. She looked Rudy through her fingers. She anticipated his answer. She had set herself up. Rudy was ready to pronounce, to proclaim an honest declaration.

He said: 'what I expect from a girl is all in you! Angie. I am very honest.'

Angela almost felt off her chair. She was very nervous, could not find a word. She looked at her watch and remembered the senior center. She just stood up and said: 'Oh gosht, I'm late for the senior center. Got to go, I'll see you.' Rudy didn't even have time to get up. Angela darted through the coffee shop. Rudy waved and whispered: 'don't forget to help the birthday boy with the certificate.'

Monaco

The band waited few days for the buyers to liquidate their jewels. Ron had contacts in Chicago and Los Angeles that bought hot items. He had sent messages to both cities and pictures of the stolen goods. Chicago's offer was a few more dollars than Los Angeles. It was less complicated to sell to Los Angeles. Pete insisted on sell everything to Los Angeles. 'Let's get rid of the whole thing and get our moneys.' Was his opinion. Brat always cautious recommended to Ron not to rush anything. Ron agreed and suggested: 'there is no need to force anything, let's not complicate the simple part.' Pete maintained that they should go to another venture overseas, but they needed the money to take care of the trip expenses. Few days went by, and the band agreed to finish details for the next trip. Rudy, Brat and Pete were very animated with the place they all selected. Ron had persuaded them to not to sell off the loot from Cozumel, and Miami until they had returned from the trip overseas.

The selected target was a store in Monte Carlo, Monaco. This time the logistics involved the entrant to the city which was by train, from Savona, Italy, and the same way to leave after they completed the job. Once the band arrived in Europe, they would flight from Barcelona, Spain to Genoa, Italy. The flight was over 7 hours. They checked in a hotel near the train station in Genoa. They rose very early in the morning. They applied the makeup and dressed in their costumes, then went to the train station.

The trip from Genoa to Savona is under two hours. This was the last time they all travel together and practice their roles. Pete suggested the unthinkable, learn the names of train stations between Savona and San Remo. As usual Brat objected and asked Why? Pete argued: just in case anyone must get off the train before we get to San Remo. It will be useful. Ron intervened and agreed in a grouchy mood. Brat learned the names practicing with his buddy Rudy.

Brat: 'again Rudy, say, the first darn station is..'

Rudy: 'Quillano Vado.'

Brat: 'the next one is, wait don't tell me I know Spotorno Stazione'

Rudy said: 'wow you sound like a local Italian, the next one is finite Liturgy Stazione.'

Brat busted a big laugh: 'not even close it is Finale Ligure stazione.' Rudy couldn't help laughing as well.

Brat: 'next is Pietra.' Ron explained: 'hey Tin Man, it means stone.'

Rudy: 'next is Borghetto Albenga stazione.'

Brat: 'the last one is Alassio.' Rudy: 'what do you mean last one? There are three more and then San Remo.'

Ron said: 'ok is Pete's turn.'

Pete: 'let's see Laigueglia stazione.' Ron: 'Impressive that's a mouth full.'

Pete: 'Is your turn.'

Ron: 'hum… Imperia.' Pete: 'not bad, Gru.'

Pete: the next one is Taggia-Arma, and then San Remo.' Ron was surprised that Pete could remember long Italian train station names. Brat asked: 'how you do that? You must be cheating. Pete tried to keep his straight face and just disclosed: 'I'm reading those freaking names from the train pamphlet itself. You don't really need to memorize the whole thing. Dah!'

Brat told him: 'I'm gonna kill ya!' Ron and Rudy were rolling on the seats.

The next train was from Savona to Monaco it was 4 hours and 40 minutes. On this train they were in individual seats apart from each other.

It was ten minutes after twelve mid-days, when they arrived in Monte Carlo. They meandered into some of the stores and mingled with other visitors. One unplanned visit to a wine tasting spot from Brat took place. He had a peculiar habit of savoring dark chocolate in combination with red wine. Ma Cave Prive'e a wine shop in the way to the jewelry store with the wine tasting sign posted outside. Brat went to see at the window the menu it read "vin (wine) petite Sarah, au chocolate noir (with dark chocolate) Brat utter:' Ahh!' His temptation was stronger that all the plans and agreements with his mates. He needed to take just one quick sample. He gulps down three different wines and tasted three different samplers of chocolate. He had hazelnut, and cashew.

He used three different glasses, with three small serving forks. He did his best performance of his British Anglo accent. The clerk at the wine store had no doubt that he was from England. Brat was in a haste; he was worried for the schedule. Brat knew, he was late for the jewelry store. Brat's part was to wait for Ron's signal indicating the place was safe for the job. Brat arrived a minute late. Ron couldn't do anything but wait until Brat showed up. Then he signaled Rudy and Pete.

Pete and Rudy waited until Brat went inside the store, then they started the small fire, as a diversion. The security guards rushed to find out the cause of the commotion that Rudy had started. People around the store moved also away from the store in curiosity. Their plan was executed close to perfection, the confusion about the fire was so great, even the store manager left the store for a moment to check the disturbance out in the hallway. Ron motioned to Brat to proceed to brake glass cases and take many pieces. Ron kept an eye on the clerk and manager. When the manager came back inside the store Ron sprayed a heavy dose of anesthesia right on his face. That provoked him to fall semiconscious. The clerk came behind, and Ron asked the clerk to help the manager. Ron sprayed an equal dose to the clerk. Both men were on the ground too drugged to do, or even see anything. Ron and Brat left the store with a large loot. They walked away in a casual way. Everybody gathered just behind the train station to remove the makeup and change quickly the shirts and jackets. It took some time for the manager and the clerk at the store to recover from the effect of the gas. The manager sobered for few minutes before he called the police. Ron and his associates had enough time to return to the train station. They caught the first train departing to Mento Garavan. From there they boarded another train to Genoa. Everyone settled in the train to Genoa. Ron Talked to Brat, he asked what had happen. Why was he late at the jewelry store. Brat said in his way to the store a lady from the train station asked him few questions. He answered them in a polite manner, and it took couple minutes longer, he did not want her to be suspicious. The real reason was the wine tasting stop that he did. Ron noticed a small hesitation but did not say anything. They knew with every mile they traveled they increased their chances of escaping. The Brits succeeded. They caught a flight from Genoa, Italy to Barcelona, Spain.

POLICE AT WORK

The police received two calls at the same time from the same place. A commercial plaza where tourists were high in number. Locals mixed with visiting shoppers. Some were tourist from the cruise ships that stop by for few hours and let their passengers disembark at Port Hercule. The one-mile distance from the port to town has few shops, and a couple souvenirs stores. There are small groups of visitors that enjoy strolling the hills. Lieutenant Depardieu was called to visit the place to open an investigation for robbery and a small fire. The small fire was put out by the time lieutenant arrived. The fire marshal stated no injuries were reported due to the fire. Then he proceeded to the jewelry store Le Diamand Fou. The place where the stealing had occurred. He interviews the manager and, the clerk of the jewelry store.

Lieutenant Depardieu introduced himself to the store clerk monsieur Belmondo, after greetings, the manager monsieur Jean-Paul Garrel came to meet the lieutenant and his company. There was a detail description of the events prior to the commotion of the fire. Both jewelry clerk and manager gave their own version in a separate room. Their statements of the robbery as each one could recall after being overcome by the gas.

Lieutenant Depardieu: please tell me about the gas.

Monsieur Belmondo: 'one individual talked to me, I showed few diamond rings, then he wanted to see pendants. All the sudden a commotion was going on outside. The robbers went outside followed by the manager monsieur Garrel, 'I went out also to see what the disturbance was.' It's a fire said the manager monsieur Jean-Paul.' He went back inside the store, 'I followed him he was falling on the floor. The guy with the French hat said to me help him, I bent over to hold the manager, and got a heavy dose of spray in my face. I lost my consciousness for a moment. I could hear noise but couldn't do anything. When I came back to me the assailants were gone.' Lieutenant Depardieu interviewed the manager in the back room. Deputy Rene Clouseau stayed in the front room with the clerk. The testimony from the manager was very similar to the clerk. The sprayed gas had neutralized both employees long enough to allow the robbers take many items, and leave. The manager and the clerk could not disrupt the burglary or delay the escape. The police closed the store for three hours to conduct a complete inspection. No fingerprints were found. The video from the security cameras showed partial image of their faces. One man was wearing a French hat with a small feather covering part of his face. He had dark glasses hiding his eyes.

The other man had a goat tee and thick clear glasses with a rather large frame, The police figure this was part of a costume to hide their true appearance. The manager and the clerk agreed that both men were from England because of their accent.

Lieutenant Depardieu had his assistant Rene Clouseau to make a detailed list of British tourists, that had checked in the hotels. Make the list for the last three-four days and a list of those who have left the city, after the heist. He asked his assistant to include a sketch of the suspects. Make the best profile possible using the descriptions from monsieur Garrel and monsieur Belmondo. 'Then' he said, 'let's compare with the security video, we may find something helpful.'

The search needed to include the lists of cruise ships that were in town during the robbery. This was more complicated because the ships were considered international jurisdiction. Local police needed authorization as well as help from other countries. The paperwork was different for each country; hence it will require some time to be processed.

The ships were on different schedules for different destinations. Lieutenant Depardieu had a suspicion that the perpetrators, if they were in one of the ships, they had plenty of time to change their appearance. They must had left the ship and disappear. The first two days of the initial investigation provided no results. Lieutenant Depardieu had neglected to visit and interview the other small stores, that tourists had visited when the ships arrived. He and assistant Rene Clouseau visited twelve of the sixty stores and coffee shops without any results. Ma Cave Prive'e, the wine shop, was closed to the general public. Lieutenant Depardieu commented to his assistant Rene Clouseau about the possibility of an employee from the wine shop had seen any of the burglar suspects. 'We need to come back and talk to the wine shop staff, when they are open.' The wine shop was nearby the jewelry store Le Diamand Fou. The day of the heist the wine shop closed early. The wine shop was hired to provide beverages to a small wedding, a private reception, for a wealthy family. The wine shop needed to prepare sets of champagne, wine, and cocktail glasses for the reception.

When Lieutenant Depardieu interviewed Hugo, the clerk at the wine shop, he did not learn anything, because it was a different employee the day of the robbery. Andre, the employee that worked the day of the incident was on vacation. Hugo pointed out a note with a box of glasses, Andre left the dated note, explaining the glasses were used for tasting the day of the robbery. Assistant Rene raised a brow, and inquired: 'what about the box?' Hugo went on to explain the glasses were set in the box uncleaned due to a chaos of a fire. The glasses were used for the last customer a few minutes prior to the fire alarm. The three uncleaned glasses were supposed to be washed on the next day but, Andre was on vacation. The following day of the heist was the reception, and no one had a chance to clean the sample glasses. Assistant Rene took notes of this detail that Hugo had provided to him. He mentioned to Lieutenant Depardieu.

'Let's examine those glasses,' he said to Monsieur Garrel. Lieutenant Depardieu and assistant Rene had a rational expectation.

DNA BUST

The police department had a plethora of cases that demanded the attention of Lieutenant Depardieu for the following three weeks. The burglary on Le Diamand Fou jewelry store, was set on the side as less priority.

The jewelry store insurance adjuster requested a report on the investigation from the police department. The insurance adjuster wanted to review any progress on the identification of the robbers, and the possibility for retrieving some or all the stolen merchandise. The insurance company objective was to avoid paying the high claim. The deductible was high, but the total amount of the value was in the range of $90,000.00. The robbers knew what to take in the short time. The police did not have any leads that satisfied the insurance company. Time was against the insurance company; it had been a week since the act. It just seemed the longer the police took to have any real facts to identify and capture the perpetrators, the least change it would be to recover any of the merchandise. Monsieur Laurent from the insurance company remembered detective Liam from another city that had help him in a different case.

Monsieur Laurent hesitated to call detective Liam because he did not have any trust on detective Liam. There was a rumor, that detective Liam was accused of taking bribes from different sources in order to obtain extra cash. The reason allegedly, he was addicted to gambling and needed extra money to cover his bets. These were all falsely created notes made by Martini Pavard. The false facts were mentioned only on social media. Detective Liam did not care for social media. The facts about detective Liam were all twisted because his reputation within the police department was impeccable. This generated an envious rival for a promotion. Detective Liam was not aware Martini had become his rival. It was the case; Martini had received assistance resolving complex cases from detective Liam. When Martini Pavard was transfer to another division the whole affair ended.

The incident was short lived, Monsieur Laurent was relief to confirm what he suspected. Detective Liam was acquitted, not by any jury, but in Monsieur Laurent's own mind.

Monsieur Laurent called detective Liam and explained the whole situation about the jewelry robbery. His frustration was at the little progress the local police had made in the case. Detective Liam agreed to review the report from Lieutenant Depardieu and see what else could be done. Detective Liam requested authorization from his office to be transfer for a short time to help with the update Le Diamand Fou heist case. He was not in charge of the investigation. Detective Liam proceeded to reexamine the video from the jewelry store.

Detective Liam noticed one of the suspects from the video, did wear a rather unusual hat. He made a note, it could help the witnesses to remember something else about this person. Detective Liam on his early forties, had gained experience in analyzing crimes, he considered small details, and consulted with his peers. He did not act with urgent haste.

He came to the shops nearby of the jewelry store to interview the employees. He showed a picture from the surveillance video of the suspect with the hat. In two of the stores, they remembered the suspect with the hat. One was Andre from the wine store.

He recalled that the man from England was in a rather rush to leave. The client took three different samples of wine, which he enjoyed with the dark chocolate. Detective Liam asked to view the surveillance video from the wine store, together with Andre. He hoped for the image to be clear enough, to identify the man with the hat. The video showed clearly the man had drunk three different glasses of wine and used three different small forks for the dark chocolate. Detective Liam only hope that some traces of the fingerprints were left on any of the glasses or the small forks.

Andre from Ma Cave Privée, reminded Detective Liam, the box containing the glasses were still in the closet. Lieutenant Deperdieu had labeled as evidence. No one had taken the box to the police station. Detective Liam took the box himself; he gave Andre a receipt for it. He indicated: 'when our lab is done with it, I will return your glasses myself. Merci monsieur'

Detective Liam proceeded to the police lab with the box of circumstantial evidence. He requested to run fingerprints from wine glasses with British criminal data base. 'Let me know if there are any matches,' he instructed the lab technician. No positive results were shown from that search. Detective Liam solicited to just run the fingerprints with international criminal data base even if it was not British, no matching results.

While the technician was working with data bases, detective Liam visited some nearby hotels. He showed the picture from the wine store surveillance camera. That was the best, and clearest image of the suspect. No hotel had any guest with that description. The only source left to investigate was the cruise ships that were at the port the same day. Detective Liam realized the challenge on this attempt. He wrote out the factors to be cover. The list was an outline as part of his proven strategy to map out a plan. A way to check points covered, and then complete and close the loop to uncover the mystery or resolve the puzzle. He wrote number one the distance from the port to the stores, number two: the time for the suspects to escape and the possible routes,

Number three: 'we need the list of passengers. Assuming they were on any ship, then is an international affair. We need assistant from other agencies.'

Detective Liam checked the date of the robbery, it had been a week. He had an impossible task, interviewing the staff and crews of the cruise ship that had docked the day of the crime.

The DNA Factor

Doctor Judy Chan had read an article about the unique creative work done by New York artist Heather Dewey. She had some success reconstructing parts of a human faces with certain features from DNA samples. The results were incomplete consequently, she had to randomly select age for the faces. DNA science and knowledge stablished features such as the color of the eyes, the color for the hair, the gender, and complexion, and ancestral attributes. Doctor Chan knew from Heather results that DNA samples from cigarette butts, chewing gum, and hair samples can be used to create a face that resembles somewhat a face of the actual person. It is not an identical copy of the face but, nevertheless does provide an entertaining possibility to look like the genuine face.

Why was Doctor Chan interested in working on the DNA busts? In her application for college her aptitude questionnaire her second choice on the list of occupation was sculptor or an artist that can create images of people. This is far from being an artist although, it gives her an ample chance to form a solid image. She enjoys using her scientific knowledge with a bit of creativity. She adds details such as the particulars contour of the nose, the lips, the chin bone and the length of the neck.

Doctor Chan had read an article of a cold case. Police did not have any witnesses, still not resolved. A trace of DNA was collected on the crime scene.

The DNA sample did not match any of the files from the police data base. Doctor Chan hoped with the use of DNA could help to recreate a face of a suspect and provide a lead towards the actual criminal. The trace of DNA was an incomplete source to attempt to recreate a face. She needed to consult the latest developments in genomic technology.

Detective Liam was busy working on the images that he had, from the video surveillance. A copy of the report of his investigations, was sent to monsieur Laurent from the insurance company. A side note from the report stated there is a remote possibility of using DNA traces. 'You can read in my report the circumstantial evidence of wine glasses used by a confirmed suspect. We had collected DNA traces from these wine glasses. However, our search so far on the data base of local police and from Great Britain did not yield any favorable results. We continue with the investigation.'

Little that Detective Liam suspected what he will encounter during his investigation. His stoic behavior will transform into a more affectionate and tender Liam.

WORDS OF WISDOM FOR RUDY

The day after the Brits returned from the Barcelona trip, the Monaco project as it was label. Rudy had to go back to work at his job at the recording studio, he called Angela right after work.

Rudy: 'hi Angie, how are you?'

Angela: 'hello, who is this? Must be a wrong number.'

Rudy: 'Angie! Is me! Rudy.'

Angela: 'what a nerve! I don't recall you saying goodbye or anything.'

Rudy: 'I had to go for a business trip but I'm back, and that's why I'm calling to hear from you.'

Angela: 'oh yea! Well, I'm busy and I got to go. Call another day.'

Rudy resented not having told her before his trip that he was going out of town for few days. Now he had to be patient and wait another day to call her to apologize.

Angela had some time to think on the last time she and Rudy talk. She knew that Rudy was sincere when he told her all he wanted in a girl, a perfect girl was in her. She heard the whole conversation in her mind a few times. She discovered her feelings for him were perhaps reciprocal. Why did I get so nervous, she asked herself. It was my own fault insisting on asking who his perfect girl was. Angela concluded out of the abundance of the heart the mouth will speak it.

Angela wanted to call Rudy after couple of days after the birth certificate incident. She resisted the temptation the best she could.

After more than a week of Rudy's silence, Angela was very upset, angry, frustrated, but all those feelings later became just worrisome. She had call him, but no answer. She did not leave a message. Now she was missing him. Then Rudy called out the blue.

'No wonder I almost hang up on him,' Angela She was at ease knowing Rudy was back.

Angela received a bouquet of flowers and a note with an invitation for dinner.

She sent him an email almost immediately in fact she knew it was a rushed response, but it was too late try to delay her reply. Angela had thanked Rudy for the invitation. I'll see you tonight. She replied. Angela checked her calendar after pressing send, on her phone screen. Then she had a premonition about her commitments, and needed to be sure she was clear for the evening. To her dismay she was supposed to help at the senior center for one hour, from 6:00 pm to 7:00 pm. Dinner with Rudy was schedule at 6:15. Rudy received an additional email from Angela explaining her dilemma. She apologized and asked for a rain check. Rudy wanted to see her, it was easy to change the time for dinner, he knew that was a gentleman's way to treat a lady. He texted Angie about the change of dinner time and promised to be in a place rather simple but elegant. Rudy wanted to treat Angela to an exceptional place. His intention was to make up for having neglected to communicate his plans of leaving town without telling her. Angela agreed to meet right after her collaboration at the senior center.

Rudy took in consideration what Angela thinks in the way one spends resources and utilizes time. Rudy was glad that he reflected before making reservations for dinner. He decided to invite Angela to a well organize, clean and moderate restaurant. They did not even need reservations. Rudy hopes the place would have an open table for the two of them at the time of their arrival. 'I got to be careful and not over do this,' he told himself.

For the benefit of Rudy and Angela the cozy restaurant, Fatto In Casa, own and run by Italian family had a small table near the window with handmade curtains, for privacy. Angela looked around while the table was set for them, she raised her eyebrows with a smile. Angela approved and liked the restaurant.

Tom, the owner walked them to their table. He greeted and addressed them as a family. Tom said: 'good evening signore and signora, I hope I'm correct madam welcome to our place. My name is Tom I have the pleasure to wait you and your husband tonight. Any drinks?'

Rudy wanted to correct Tom, but Angela raised her hand and very polite responded.

Angela: 'well, I thank you, we are close friends, not married. Rudy interjected quickly, 'yes, we are not married, although you my friend might as well be a prophet speaking into our future.' Angela couldn't help to grab and squeeze Rudy's hand, while she looked at him with scolding eyes. Tom apologized for the assumption he had, and to redeem himself offered appetitive on the house while they decide for their meal and drinks. Rudy turned to Angela who still had her hand over his, and said, 'I already like your choice Angie, bringing me to this place, how did you find it?' Angela squeezed even harder and told him 'You are incorrigible'. Looking at his eyes intently.

Tom excused himself and went to prepare appetizers. After a few minutes, they were settled. Rudy told Angela that he was working with a friend on a kind of boring project, and he should spare her the boredom with details. Angela perceived some hesitation in the words of Rudy, but she kept quiet.

Angela told Rudy; 'I'm not going to insist that you tell me more about your trip out of town.' Then she said: 'Rudy, tell me how you are doing with those voices. Do you still hear them?'

Rudy: 'well, I'm not sure if we want to talk about me and 'voices.

Angela: 'Oh sure we do Rudy. Are you practicing generosity?'

Rudy: 'what do you mean? Remember I contributed with a generous gift to a gentleman's birthday. By the way whose birthday was this time?'

Angela: 'my visits are not only for birthdays. And yes, you sure did give, I thank you for your great present. But that was after

I prompted you. I am referring to generous actions prod from your own initiative. '

Rudy's demeanor changed gradually from a quizzical to shameful. Then he spoke: 'ah yes, I've been so busy, haven't got time to think about that.'

Angela: 'keep it simple, you don't really have to think about you being Rudy, you are you, Rudy.' Angela gave a sweet smile, and lightly tapped Rudy's cheek. He was blown and hesitated to respond right away. He took a deep breath and cleared his throat.

Rudy: 'I must admit Angie, you're all that I want in a girl. Please don't get me wrong, I say this with all respect, and admiration.'

Angela: 'come on! We've been here before. Seriously how are you doing with the voices.'

Rudy: 'they're still around. Let me ask you what this thing about generosity is?'

Angela: 'A generous person will prosper; whoever refreshes others will be refreshed.

I'm quoting proverbs, the book of wisdom. I just leave it like that.'

Rudy: 'ok, I heard you.'

Jack Wayne asked: 'she always had a word of wisdom you said before.'

Miller: 'yeah, later on I'll tell you why she even conveyed few words in my head, actually those were implanted in my brain, I could not break out from them.'

Jack Wayne: 'It happened more than one time ha! Now please tell me what happens next with Angie?'

Miller: 'don't you wanna know how the band picks the next project?'

Jack Wayne: 'Oh sure. Tell me.'

Back To the Band

Ron gathers Brat, Rudy, and Pete to celebrate their return home with no incidents and with a very good loot. They waited for four months to hear anything on the news about their latest project. Each member stored his own share of the loot and waited.

After those four months of no calls or inquiries from the police, it was time to enjoy the financial gain. Ron decided to sell part of their jewels to cash out the profits. They connected the contact in Chicago. Ron hope, the Chicago client will buy their jewels at a very good price. They sold about 40 percent of what they took from the store, and it came to be around 40 thousand dollars.

Ron and the rest of the mates as he calls them were very delighted and thrilled, so much that a new project was planned. Perpetrate another visit the following year with a similar agenda of two different cities, comparable to the trip to Cozumel and Miami.

They were confident and almost arrogant about their successes.

The logistics included a different approach for each store.

Let's use the Canadian accent for the first store, then for the next robbery we should use our well-rehearsed Australian-English accent. They all agreed to continue with the magic touch of the make-up. The results so far have been very encouraging. There was no need to be concerned with the video security cameras. Their identities were hidden. They rehearsed their acts through the months before the trip.

In the meantime, they kept working at their regular jobs.

'Let's all keep a low profile' was Ron recommendation. 'We need to be very careful in everything, including our meetings' They implemented a system to check if anyone is following their footsteps.

Rudy and Brat couldn't figure if anyone was asking anything about their affairs. They asked their neighbors, coworkers and stores they frequented if anyone had asked about them. They explained a family member out of town has a friend who may be looking for Pete or Rudy. Brat took the same action. Ron decided to wait and check every time he left home if anything was out of the ordinary. They all reported things are quiet.

Ron kept telling them: We should not assume that everything is clear.

Brat was working with Rudy selecting the cruise trip, as well as the ports the cruise ship stops. Brat kept smoking behind Rudy. Trying to keep his habit from Rudy's sight. One late afternoon Rudy came across with an article about behavioral side effects of the nicotine habit. He cut it and posted on the cabinet where they kept snacks and drinking glasses. Rudy asked permission to Ron. Ron read it and gave his approval saying: 'I sure hope he gets it. The smell is getting out of hand'. The cabinet is in Ron's garage, where they meet.

The article title is: Reflections On My Nicotine Addiction." It read: as a result of my smoking habit my monetary squander in tobacco and lighters goes beyond dollars and cents. When I run out of smokes, I usually go out and get some more. But occasionally I must go out my way to satisfy the craving. This addiction has no shame. Or better said we smokers don't have shame. We are willing to run the risk to be denied by asking a total stranger for a cigarette. Including in extreme occasions beg or try to make someone to have pity on myself. There is also the other side of the coin, a stranger will ask me for one of my smokes, most of the time I yield, but there is an occasional bad moment that irritates me, for whatever reason is bothersome and I tend to lie by claiming is my last one. Most of the time I tell the truth. I feel bad knowing the terrible sample I show to children. They don't understand how serious the health hazard is. They playfully pretend they are smoking imitating the motion of puffing, holding the smoke then slowly let it out. I have seen them. Rudy added at the bottom. They are oblivious of the terrible damage by oxygen deprivation at the cellular level.

Brat noticed the paper posted on the cabinet. He quickly read the title and pretended to dismiss it. He read it later alone. He cursed Rudy and all his nosy innuendos about cigarettes.

That same evening Brat was on his way to the store to buy a pack of cigarettes two young girls asked him for a cigarette. Brat was distracted when the girls asked, they asked him again with an attitude he was annoyed, and reacted very angry telling the young girls they were too young to be smoking. They should not smoke if they can't afford it. The girls cursed him and told him it was not any of his business. They walked away very fast before Brat had a chance to say anything else. Brat remembered the article. He went home pull the note about reducing the number of cigarettes smoke in a day. Rudy gave the note some weeks ago. Brat read it twice, he was bother by an internal conflict he hated the way people acted towards the smoking. Brat realized 'is against smoking not against me,' he despised the whole situation. The next day when he saw Rudy, Brat asked for help. Brat told Rudy the whole incident with the two young girls. Rudy reaffirmed Brat: 'you're right, people don't have anything against your person! What everyone points out is the nasty smell that is surrounding the person who smokes along with the other bad things from the cigarettes. Brat this is between you and my little help. Let's start, I will hang as long as it takes.' Brat felt like a true brother had come to his rescue.

PROBING CAREER

Ron and Pete worked searching online the websites of jewelry stores that disclosed its selection of precious stones. Pete was fascinated with the alarm systems. He worked hard learning how to hack and disconnect those systems.

The plan was ambitious in the number of stores with the possibility of a large loot.

Pete was interested in alarm systems, precisely in the science behind the computer network, he wanted to know the nuts and bolts. Pete took it as a form of hobby to read as much as he could. He registered and completed an online course for a diploma as a certified technician in security systems. The course provided him with proficiency in how to install and troubleshoot alarm systems for businesses. Establishments that require a relatively small area of surveillance. Brat encouraged and supported Pete. Ron called Brat to ask him how things were coming along.

Brat: 'Hey Ron I got to tell you this, Pete is really doing some progress in the alarm system.'

Ron: 'really how is that?'

Brat: 'well he has completed a course online about installing alarm systems. I asked him to install one in your garage as a tryout for him. He is very encouraged.'

Ron: 'oh yea! What's next I will need a pass code every time I want to go to my garage? The rats will trigger the sirens so the cops will run to check on it?'

Brat: 'Aw come on! The idea is to have Pete practice to be good and proficient so he can hack into the system. Later he could disarm systems that we encounter in our projects.'

Ron: 'now you're talking! Let's do it! And by the way from now on his title is the science techie, or for short 'TECHIE'

Brat: 'he will be honor, it would give him a chance to show off his prowess, he has worked very hard to earn it.'

This made Pete feel special. Pete installed a small, sophisticated alarm system in Ron's garage. The system installation was a headache for Pete for the first attempts, but he persisted, Rudy kept him animated, after a few times of frustration the system worked. Brat asked Pete try to hack into his own system, meaning: 'don't type the password, but try different codes and see if you can figure a back door.' It was a real challenge for Pete, but he came around and succeeded. This experience gave Pete the inside of making changes to the system's outside manufacture specs but made the system even more complex to hack into. After all that work, Pete could change the original password and install his own! Ron was so puzzled that asked Pete "what do you mean install your own password?"'

Pete said: 'let me explain it to you this way. I change the door lock and install my own door lock and I'm the only one with the key, get it?'

Brat: 'ok Techie, I get it. I'm proud of you.'

Rudy was so greatly influenced with Pete's success on the alarm installation to the point that he felt very encourage to read more about sound engineering. He commented to Angela his enthusiasm for the electronics. Angela inquired; 'what area specific in electronics?' Rudy explained his friend took a course online and now his friend can work with computer systems. Rudy did not want to give too many details to protect the nature of these friends and why his friend was working so devoted. Angela noticed Rudy's genuine interest; she insisted asking on the specifics. Rudy asked Angela: how come are you so persistent to know any specifics?

Angela: 'I can't help to notice your authentic interest' Then she suggested: 'you could take a course, just like your friend did, and learn more deeply the specifics that you like.' Rudy thought for a moment. He put his index finger over his upper lip, his eyes staring straight, but not looking at Angela. Then he replied, 'I need to find out what do I need to do' Angela asked: 'would you like my help?'

Putting her hand over Rudy's arm. Rudy felt all her warmth, he came close to melt. Rudy saw in his mind a flash account of Angela's virtues plus her skills. He can see the benefits of Angela's help. She reads in three languages, her savvy in other fields, science, arts, history among others.'

Rudy surrendered to such sincere proposition. He wanted to hug and kiss Angela. He just couldn't risk being misinterpreted and offend his lovely Angie. Rudy thought she is exceptional to me. Instead, he made the motion to give her a friendly hug and said: 'thank you! I accept your help.' Angela smiled and gave him a tender hug. Rudy said: 'I am interested in the field of sound engineering.' Angela searched for the best course online. While they were sitting down at Caffe e Dolce enjoying a cappuccino with some biscotti.

They found the school Conservatory of Recording Arts and Sciences.

The curriculum focuses on the basics to begin a long career in music, video sound, broadcast audio, live sound, and audio for film and tv. Rudy was delighted with the wealth of information in terms of all the sound engineer covers. He was captivated when he read to Angela the range of job opportunities.

Angela observed how Rudy responded to just the beginning or the entrance of a new career. Rudy went on to read the many places where he could find work. Among them are recording engineer, game audio designer, live sound engineer, audio visual technician, corporate media technician, tv/video scoring engineer, broadcast engineer, foley engineer and few more. His excitement was contagious. Angela knew he was into a better future, somehow, she was part of it, not officially but, it was evident.

After understanding what was needed to register, Rudy sorted out which classes to take and with the help of Angela he determined the schedule and started his classes.

The very first level for him was a certificate as a sound technician. Followed by a master recording program of 36 weeks class and 12 weeks internship.

Jack Wayne tells Miller: 'wow! Sounds like that was an excitement time.'

Miller responded: 'it was for both, now let's go back to the Brits.'

THE BRITS SIENE RIVER VENTURE

The enthusiasm was high among Gru, Tin Man, and Techie. They wanted to start planning for another operation. Their eyes gleamed with anticipation for the next trip. Ron and Brat ordered Chinese food for everybody; Pete brought enough beer for all of them. Pete noticed Rudy's demeanor was the opposite of the rest. Pete called Rudy on the side and asked: 'Rudy, what's the matter?'

Rudy: 'What do you mean?

Pete: 'Who do you think you are kidding?'

Rudy with a gloomy face responded: 'I don't think I'm kidding. I'm ok.'

Pete: 'either you are afflicted with some terrible disease, or you are so sad because someone has passed away.'

Rudy: 'no not at all! I just feel tire from work and classes, but that's all.'

Pete: 'I know you! Come on, we need to talk, now how bad is it?'

Rudy: 'I don't think I…I mean, I shouldn't continue with the band.'

Pete: 'why? You're not content with what we have profit so far?'

Rudy: 'actually is more of the opposite. I am concert with the consequences of what we have done.'

Pete could not believe what Rudy had said, he could not connect their business association with Rudy's sadness. It was outside of his judgement. Then he asked: 'Rudy what the heck are you talking about? You are mumbling consequences! I'll tell you what the consequences are, to start we had accumulated a small fortune. All these was done through our hard labor. Don't you remember all those hours rehearsing our accents. The time working on the f' cken make-up!' Ron and Brat were talking while they were eating, sitting at the small table. Brat got up to bring two beers to the table, Ron noticed Pete and Rudy standing close to the window having some kind of arguing. It looked like Pete was reprimanding Rudy. Brat got back to the small wooden table and looked toward Pete and Rudy. Both Ron and Brat called Pete: 'hey guys, is everything ok?' Brat added: 'the food is getting cold.'

Rudy had a very heavy guilty feeling and did not want to argue with Pete or anybody else. He looked around and told Pete: 'I guess you're right we do have a small fortune.' Pete responded: 'there you go! That's the Rudy that I know. Now let's go and eat, those guys are not gonna leave anything for us.' Pete walked towards the table pulling his pants up and rubbing his hands together. They set out the scheme for the next journey. The cruise was on the Seine River one of the popular routes from Paris toward Normandy.

After few weeks of Rudy's online classes, the time for Seine River the band's next project came up. Rudy resolved to stop the classes for the sound technician certificate. It was a hard choice, but it will be the last time he robs anything. Rudy got together with Angela at their favorite place Caffe e Dolce.

He told Angela: 'I'm leaving town for few days. I'll return to class as soon as I can.' Angela could not understand why? They both knew interrupting three consecutive classes was equivalent to drop the semester. Angela first pleaded not to leave town. She asked: 'what could be more important, the school or a one-time job helping his friend?' Rudy tried to affirm Angela on his determination to finish school, when he's back. At that point Angela demanded an explanation. Rudy could not disclose his stupid oath, the real reason of his absence. He, with clasped hands promised Angela, 'I will finish this course, no matter what it takes, but this project was planned before I thought or planned on any class. It will be the last time I..I, get involved.' Angela could not hold a small tear coming out her eyes. She stood up to dry her eyes. The hanging lamp was right above her head, Rudy could not see her face, then she turned around to leave, and said with a tender voice: 'I'll see you when you're back.'

Jack Wayne asked Miller: 'Why did the band agree on this particular trip?'

Miller replied: 'there were few components that looked beneficial.

They hope few factors will work on their favor. Choosing the busy season when many tourists are causing in some degree a congestion which could help in terms of blending with the crowds and making more difficult to law enforcement and security to identify, trace and even capture any suspects.'

Ron thought about creating a diversion using the general public by trigging a scare sound of shots, or small explosion and causing panic if the need to escape ensue. The cruise on the river offers many alternatives to move away from the jewelry shops, one the most obvious by boat, then there is the public transportation bus, train and ultimately by automobile. They were determined to obtain a considerable loot, enjoy the scenery, taste some of the gourmet foods and enhance their expertise in the robbery endeavor.

THE SECOND CRUISE

Following such rationale, they selected an 8-day cruise on the Seine River with itinerary of few ports and excursions. The voyage starts in Paris with the first day welcome everybody aboard the ship.

Day one passengers settle into their rooms. Ron and the band had time to work on their fine details of make-up costumes. Tin Man assembled the two cigarette lighters' fuses to use them as small bombs.

During the trip, in a collective agreement the band will call each other using only their nick names. The reason for such change is to protect each other real names. 'If we are very diligent with our rehearsing and costumes, but neglect one obvious detail such as our real names, then we reveal part of our identities.' Ron told the band. Therefore, from the time we all depart for the job: Ron to be called Gru. Brat to be called Tin Man. Pete to be called Techie. Rudy was the only one with no official nick name. There were suggestions as Ru for short, but it didn't sound right. Gru proposed to be a simple nick name, let's call him: 'mate' since we are working in a boat.

Brat was not happy with the nick name, Pete frowned his eyebrows, Rudy himself shrugged his shoulders. Gru wanted to have a nick name for him, and he said: 'Oh for Pete's sake.' At the same moment that Ron started to say Oh for…the rest of them in unison said: 'Pete's sake.'

On the first day, they found two stores with similar security systems. Pete figured the systems were relatively easy to hack the store's surveillance network. Pete, the Techie, did his magic from the ship he broke into Lydia Courteille jewelry store. He disrupted the system 15 minutes before Gru and Tin Man walked into the store.

Pete created a false alarm call, that trigged the loud alarm in the store. The manager turned the system off, then checked the cause, it was just a false alarm. Techie turned on the alarm again to create a second false alarm, again the manager turned the system off. Techie did a third time false alarm, and now the manager a bit frustrated called the alarm company. Pete Intercepted the call, Gru impersonated a representative of the alarm company. After listening to the manager's frustrated complains, Gru informed the manager that their monitor system did not register any false alarm. Gru instructed the manager that a technician was dispatched to check the system in few minutes.

Gru provided the store manager with the name Pat as the technician representing the company. Pete was playing the technician with the name Pat as the trouble shooter, he was sent to check the false alarms. Gru even provided the estimated arrival time. He also mentioned: 'our technician is a new member in town, but with extensive experience. He happens to be from England.' Tin Man had a false identification badge as a technician. Pete showed up at the store introduced himself and displayed his badge with his tools. He requested to see the panel of the alarm system. The store manager himself showed the cabinet with the controls. He proceeded to open the panel to pull couple of the connections. The small closet for the alarm system control panel was tight for one person. The store employee observing Pat the technician initial work left Pete do his job by himself. Tin Man pulled a small tablet to hook the wires and run a test. He informed the manager the store doors require to be close for a few minutes and the locks must be set, 'I need to run a test to try the system as if the store was closed. We need to do this to check sensors,' he said. In the store at the time there were four other people besides the employees. Pete said, 'there is no need to ask clients to leave or to evacuate the store.' Pete added, 'just announce to everyone what we are doing, ask them to stay close to the middle of the main room and don't move. Anyone could trigger a sensor provoking a false alarm. It is a matter of a few minutes to run a test of the system.' Techie disabled the sensors and Ron took some items without any alarm turned on. Techie set a one-minute delay to turn another false alarm. He went to the electric panel to switch the main set of lights off. Mate had gone to a caffe on the same block that Lydia Courteille jewelry shop was. The coffee shop situated at the corner with some tables outside on the sidewalk. Rudy waited 15 minutes for Techie to work with the alarm system in the store. Then he called the police to report a suspicious bag at the corner caffe. Rudy had set under one of the tables placed outside the coffee shop a backpack filled with some newspapers and a couple aluminum cans. He bought three large sodas in aluminum cans, with a knife that he took from the cruise ship, he scratched the cans to make them look more suspicious.

The jewelry shop doors have an automatic locking mechanism. Tin Man locked the doors when he turned off the lights and set the siren to sound intermittent for 4 seconds three different cycles. This created a small chaos, and confusion. No one could open the doors and leave. Gru took more items. Techie pretended to be confused and turn the whole system off. Then he told the manager one of the sensors is shot, it needs to be replaced. He left the store claiming to have his service van in the parking lot. 'I have a replacement set; I can go to my van to check for the right sensor.' Gru and Tin Man took more gems before they left the store together. Techie set the locking mechanism to bolt the doors right after they left, trapping the rest inside. Meanwhile the police had arrived at the coffee shop, they had spotted the suspicious backpack, and evacuated the place. The band hope this will allow them to move far enough from the store before the police could be alerted.

Techie was chewing gum while working in the store, he used the chewing gum as a temporary filler for the sensor. Techie needed some substitute to bridge the connection within the circuit. His chewing gum with a paper clip seemed to be ideal.

Police investigating the suspicious bag at the coffee shop needed more than 20 minutes to clear the small area where the table had the questionable object. Once the bag was confirmed to be inoffensive, it was removed the coffee shop was clear the business was reopened. The call from the burglary came few minutes after the employees were able to call and inform the police dispatcher what had happened in their store. The lieutenant in charge of the coffee shop investigation was notified of the jewelry store robbery. He was the closest police officer to the crime scene, that could go and take the preliminary notes. The lieutenant in charge needs to leave a deputy in custody of the coffee shop before he could walk to the robbed place to start with the investigation. One hour had passed since the Brits had left the store with the loot. The Lieutenant inspected the electric panel and the alarm system after the declarations of the employees. He found the chewing gum holding the metal paper clip causing the short circuit with the front doors locking mechanism. He took it as evidence and sent it to the lab.

The band went back to the ship.

That evening each one stayed at his room for dinner, in case the police were looking at passengers scanning for the robbery suspects. The ship dinner provided a gourmet meal that overindulged their sweetest fantasies.

The schedule for day two had a guided tour in the most touristic locations near the port. Ron and Brat went to survey the planned sites for the "potential gems clearance." Ron made these observations, 'look Tin Man, these shops are in a wide-open plaza. There aren't many spots to hide in case the cops are chasing.' Brat replied: 'I agree, the time for passengers to disembark and return to the ship is too short, the port is too far away.'

Ron concluded: 'too much risk. We better skip this spot.' Brat said: 'we still don't know how hot the search from yesterday operation is.' They both went back to the ship to tell Rudy(mate) and Techie about their findings. All together deemed the port not worthy of any risk. They enjoyed the day off from the bijoux and diamants business.

Rudy bought some eggs, a small carton of milk, and took to his room some vinegar from the dining tables. He prepared two stinky bombs.

Day three La Roche Guyun, there is a jewelry store called Equestrian Shop inside a commercial square. Techie and Tin Man had an idea to provoke a mayhem inside the jewelry store. Make a homemade stinky bomb from the food items that Rudy had bought the day before. He mixed in two empty coffee cups the eggs, the milk and vinegar. Rudy had sealed the coffee cups with a small piece of plastic. Tin Man had two large lighters; he modified the tips to insert a small fuse. They intended to use the lighter with the fuse to ignite a small fire. The small explosion should startle everyone without causing any alert outside the store.

Gru when inside the store and asked to see some exclusive design sets of pendants and earrings. Dimitri, the assistant manager, brought Gru to the inner back part of the store. Gru had one of the cups of coffee with one of the homemade stinky bombs. Tin Man was in the front with Ralph another employee. Pete, the Techie walked with the other homemade stinky bomb. Marcelo an assistant employee invited Tin Man to have a seat in the section for watches. Rudy(mate) came in few seconds after Tin Man was sitting observing the watches. Marcelo excused himself and went to greet Rudy(mate). At the same moment Pete opened the stinky bomb and tossed it off behind a display case. The rotten smell starting to spread. Ralph noticed the fetid smell and went to see what is going on. Tin Man lit the small fuse for the lighter bomb, he set it by the front case. When the lighter exploded, Dimitri the employee with Gru returned to the front. Gru opened his stinky bomb and spilled it right in the middle of the back hallway. In a few minutes the whole place was a horrific scene. Gru broke a case and started to take jewels in the back. The employees were overwhelmed at the front by the bad smell and the small cloud of smoke from the little explosion. Tin Man set the other small fuse for the small bomb. At the second small explosion Techie and Rudy pushed very hard the employees to the ground and tied them. Tin Man grabbed many small rings, earrings, and some precious stones, then he left the store followed by mate (Rudy) and Techie.

The whole operation lasted ten minutes, no one had tried to come into the store while the commotion took place. Ron and Pete waited for Rudy and Brat to leave in a very calm mode with their large bags full of precious items. Ron and Pete had to cover their faces to avoid getting sick from the stinky bombs. Once they left the store each one went back to the ship on different streets.

Ralph, he had worked in the store for 15 years. He was a trusted, knowledgeable, and appreciated employee. He commented, 'in all these years I never had any bad experience of being in a robbery. Granted we did not see any guns, but the small explosions got our hearts sank it is still a crime. We were victims of stinky fumes to immobilize us down. Thanks God it was temporary. But I'll tell you, it still is just as traumatic as if a weapon is pointed to you. Once the terrible smell effect passed, the adrenaline rush took over and the nervousness was uncontrollable, to say the least.'

Marcelo the one employee who remembers the horrible experience of being at work in a jewelry shop when it was robbed, few years in the past. He had a more frighten experience because gun shots were exchange between assailants and security guards. He was not hurt but he saw the dead bodies of the assailants. It took few days for him to recover and not think and see the same scene of dead bodies in his mind. Five years had gone by since the incident. Now, this time, during the robbery, he had his emotions in under control mode. In the aftermath, he was composed, and kept telling the other two colleges to remain calm everything was fine. The robbers had gone, no guns were fired, and the explosions did not hurt anyone, nor did it cause any damage to the store.

He was hoping that due to the ordeal he could go home earlier to call his new girlfriend. He wanted to tell her what just had happened. He hoped to impress her with his courageous behavior facing incredible danger. He had a story for her, now after the whole thing was over.

Dimitri the more mature among the three of them, could not help to make a comment. He was a jester. The moment Dimitri started to speak Ralph put his hand lightly over Marcello's chest, indicating hold on, let him speak. Ralph knew something hilarious could come from Dimitri. Marcello lowered his chin slightly and looked intently to Dimitri.

"It not only happens among fisherman when they tell their stories, let me correct that the hyperbolized stories of how big was the fish that escaped, and how much bigger was the second catch that also escaped. It also strangely occurs among robbed victims to dramatize how long was the ordeal, the recount how the robbers were intimidated by the brave employee! By all accounts the number of assailants armed to the teeth was enough to ransacked two or three stores at the same time.' Ralph laughed accusing Marcello 'I hope that is not you.' Marcello just smiled and said: 'nah, I'm cool, I'm glad we are fine.'

Lieutenant Pierre Bauer was called to investigate the robbery and small explosions inside the jewelry store Equestrian Shop. He interviewed the staff, and concluded the suspected robbers were from Great Britain. According to their English accent. After he had reviewed the surveillance video, the suspects seemed calm, and knew how to control the staff. Lieutenant Pierre Bauer had distributed few pictures of still images from the video. He proceeded to follow the guidelines for the investigation. The results did not provide any leads. The cruise ships received a request from the police to provide a list of passengers from Great Britain. Two days had passed since the Lieutenant sent the request to the cruise ship. The voyage was in day 6 of their trip. The staff members on the cruise ship in charge of greetings passengers were asked to review the pictures sent by Lieutenant Pierre Bauer. The results stated the list of passengers from Great Britain did not resemble any of the suspects from the photographs.

Lieutenant Pierre Bauer sent an alert to jewelry stores near the other port cities about the robberies in the cities of Paris on the Western side of Seine River, and the city of La Roche Guyun.

The insurance adjuster monsieur Laurent received the email report of the robbery with the police long file attached. He opened and after he read it, email detective Liam. Dear Monsieur Liam hello, my friend I have another case of jewels' heist. Please respond, I need your help. kind regards from Laurent. Detective Liam was in his office when he read it. It took a moment for him to remember the name and to related with a previous investigation on jewels. He responded the next hour.

On day 4 the harbor scheduled to visit was port Rouen, Ron and Brat decided to let the heat from the recent jobs cool off. They knew police will be extremely alert and vigilant in the shops around the port. Ron announced to Tin Man, Techie, and Mate: 'we are officially on vacation, stay out of trouble, keep your eyes open. Go to town with the rest of passengers but come back couple minutes before everybody.

Pete and Rudy were in the same room. Tin Man heard that Mate was not going out with the rest of the passengers, he tried his best to motivate Mate in going out to check the famous places in Rouen. Brat noticed that Rudy was downcast, so he felt compelled to cheer him up. Brat appreciated Rudy's interest in helping him to reduce somehow the number of cigarettes smoke or at least manage the consumption of tobacco smoke. Rudy told Brat: 'you go ahead I'm just going to take it easy and stay in the ship.' Tin Man resolved to give Mate some time alone, then he told him: 'as you wish buddy take it easy.' Mate's mind was back at home always thinking of Angela. Brat was sharing the same room with Ron. They kept adjusting the plans and decided to split the group after the next port. Pete came back few minutes before the rest of the passengers. He found Rudy trying to check on his classes online. Pete felt admiration for Rudy's dedication, then he told many facts about the Famous cathedral of Notre Dame, the church of Arc de Sainte Jeanne, although Pete could not remember how the French say it. He also told Rudy the day was simple beautiful, sunny and in the low eighties. Then Pete became preoccupied with a disturbing thought, he asked Rudy: 'did anyone inquire for our group? You know the Brits' Rudy shook his head.

Day 5 at Normandy, Ron expected police looking for them. Brat and Pete suggested stay on the ship. Ron opposed to the idea. 'It will raise suspicions if we don't visit the city. Let's all be prudent, go out and keep an eye on any police with uniform and undercover, we can recognize them, they are all the same everywhere. The moment you see something suspicious you know what to do.' They went off the ship to see the historic places. They went to see about police observing the passengers. That would have been an indication of a large search. Each one went on a separate route. They never talk to each other in public. They kept a prudent distance most of the time away from passengers while on the streets.

Pete went to see works of Claude Monet; he bought a small book of the famous painter. When he stood in line to pay at the register a lady from the ship recognizes him. She happens to be from Westminster district in London. She asked him where he was from. Pete stumbled and the only thing it came out of his mouth was Westminster. She extended her hand and said: 'please to meet you, I'm Florence Woodward. We live on Margaret Street near Regent Street you know. It is not too distant from Cavendish Square Gardens.' Pete face became pale, sweat started on his forehead, he knew he was in big trouble. He hesitated to say anything for a second, but he asked her: 'is there a museum nearby?' To his surprise she replied: 'Yes! The Cartoon Museum is very close.' She continued telling details of the neighborhood. Florence told the stories of her family before her parents marry.

She extended the conversation for a while making Pete uncomfortable, he thought she would be asking him at any moment something from his own family, he thought he was about to faint. Florence kept talking not allowing Pete to say much. It was Pete's turn to pay at the register. He paid and grabbed his book. Then turned and shook Florence's hand again saying: 'nice to meet you I have to go now.' She replied: 'likewise, and goodbye.' Pete exited the book/souvenirs section and started to run to get away from the crazy lady.

Rudy laughed for a short moment to Pete's report of his encounter with Florence. Rudy asked: 'What name you gave to this friend of yours?' Pete said: 'What friend?'

He explained the lady never stop chatting: 'I did not have time to say much except for really? And an occasionally right! To agree with whatever, she kept yakking.' Rudy asked Pete: 'did you tell Ron?' Pete answered: 'haven't had a chance yet. I don't want to go out the room and encounter her again.' Rudy agreed and said: 'I will explain to Ron and Brat.'

It was at Les Andelys on day 6 Ron and Brat decided to have a different approach and scout the streets adjacent to the jewelry store. Techie had search on the internet the stores close by their position and had found Perle d'Or a jewelry store. Pete had hack into the website of the store and decipher a way to alter the alarm system for a short time. He explained to Gru: 'the system has a backup, and my short circuit causes the back up to reboot itself and reconnects the system. We may have only a few minutes before the system goes back online by itself.' Ron asked: 'how long do we have?'

Techie answered: 'maybe five minutes, maybe less.'

Gru replied: 'ok, here is our plan.'

Techie short circuit the alarm system one minute right after the store opens. Ron and Brat enter the store seconds after Pete has hack the security system.

'We know there are only two employees at this time.' Gru and Tin Man use the same technique of igniting a small fuse of two cigarette lighters to mimic small bombs. The employees are subduing to Gru's commands to lay on the ground. Brat announces the threat of a powerful bomb was set to explode and will destroy the whole building if they moved. Brat bags few gems with the help of Mate.

Rudy tied a small nylon wire to a metal empty box of chocolates inside of a paper bag. He points to the employees: 'here is the bomb, the wire line is attached to a sensitive detonator. You move and the bomb goes off.' The Brits take five bags filled with many precious stones and leave the store. Ron and Pete go back to the port through different streets, Brat and Rudy use a shorted straight way to the ship.

The Brits worked the plan to a near perfection. The operation at Perle d'Or was consider successful in the first stage or the 80%. The transportation of the loot back home and the selling of the gems was the second stage or the other 20% to complete the project. But they had acquired few pieces of gems in a matter of a couple of hours and got back to the ship without any incidents. Pete had lingering bad feelings about the encounter with Florence. He was really concert about the possibility of being identify as a passenger if the police requested travelers to see pictures from the surveillance video from the jewelry store.

Ron had to adjust the plan quickly after hearing Pete's encounter with Florence.

Rudy and Pete left the ship just before passengers got back on board for the evening. This was done with the idea to avoid any potential encounter between Pete and Florence, because she could engage in a longer conversation and introduce Pete to any other friend or family member of hers. Ron also wanted to reduce the stress on Pete. The common agreement was the moment they leave the ship they also leave the false identity. Each one takes back the true American English accent. They took three pieces of luggage. Pete had placed the stolen gems inside the luggage. Pete concern was Florence, she knew he was on the ship, she can recognize him now. If the police came to the ship with photos from the video surveillance, she could identify Pete. Ron decided along with Brat, the best move was sending Pete and Rudy to Paris with the loot. Ron said: 'we need to prevent any possible way that authorities can trace any one of us.' Techie and Mate took the bus.

Pete's tension was reduced to a serene mind. He was able to concentrate, and found an auberge St. Christopher's Inn, a hostel. Rudy asked at the bus depot for a taxi to 159 Rue de Crime'e. The back wall of the building was right at the water. The rooms were very clean, with basic furniture two twin beds, and area rug with a small wooden table. The view of the water canal through one mid-size window. Their room number was 24 on the second floor. Pete asked Rudy: 'why is 24? There are only four bedrooms on each floor and there are three stories in the building.' Rudy said: 'we are on the second floor, our room is number four, comprendre?' Pete responded: oui monsieur. They both laughed.

Rudy walked in setting two pieces of the luggage in the middle of the room. Pete followed him with the rest of their luggage.

He said: 'the bed next to the closet is yours, I'll take the one next to the small table.' The men's bathrooms where at one end of the hallway with four shower stalls, and four individual enclosed toilets two sets of lavatories with common mirrors. No TV, no refrigerator, no microwave not even a coffee maker was provided in each room. The lobby has a small area set with tables and basic kitchen utensils for the guess. Pete told Rudy, with an air of appreciation: 'can't complain about this spot for the price that we are paying and the location. This is fine, is very low profile, we'll do. We wait for Ron and Tin Man to find the hostel, which means the next three, possible, four days stay out of trouble and enjoy the neighborhood. I think I can be at ease and relax.'

The hostel was right at the canal in Paris. Rudy was busy he set in three different boxes equal parts of the loot. Then he shipped them from Paris to Ron's home. Techie had printed labels for the boxes, indicating the content electronic parts. Pete boxed the rest of the gems and shipped them in the same way to Rudy's home.

Day 7 Paris Mantesla-Julie the day the ship docked it was a warm sunny morning. Most passengers were eager to visit the historic places right after breakfast. Groups of 6 to 8 people have become friends and going together for the excursions. Ron and Brat avoided all the groups for the sake of keeping their identity. Brat mentioned to Ron how tough was for him to resist the temptation of joining other smokers even just for couple puffs. Ron asked him: 'how are you doing with your plan to reduce the number of cigarettes? Brat initially reacted with resentment, but then he calmed down, and replied: 'I'm working on it. I think is making a freaking difference. I am following the stupid technique of cutting the tip off a cigarette before I light the darn thing. I know I have cut the number of cigarettes that I smoke now, still long way to go. You know what I mean!' Ron gave him a thumb up and said: 'keep it up. I know you will find a way to succeed, let me know if I can help.' Ron gave a short pause and then added:'...I have a fire extinguisher in case I see you smoking.' Then he laughed giving Brat a pat on his right shoulder. Brat just smiled looking down and muttered "thank you man you and your help are a real pain in the neck" Ron just added: 'Don't take it too hard on yourself.'

Through the day Ron reflected on what had happened the past four days. Things had worked well for us. He called Brat they sat down and studied what could be the next step for the police. 'Tomorrow is the last day of this cruise' said, Ron. Brat posed the question: 'what would be expected from the band?' Then he answered himself 'Flee the place. Right?' Ron thought for a moment then said: 'what will be the unexpected? We will try to do the opposite, instead of leaving will stay, in fact let's book another cruise this time a little longer.'

Brat in a sarcastic way said: 'elementary dear Watson!'

The main plan was to go from Nice to Lisbon. Brat showed Ron the route for the train from Paris to Nice. In the map Gru saw the city of Lyon, then he smiled and turned his head to Brat: 'Here is our stop before Nice. We may have some precious business with our mates.' Brat started to check train timetables from Paris to Lyon and from Lyon to Nice.

On the eighth day, the ship docked back at the port for the destination. Passengers were dismissed and some transported to the airport.

Brat did not have enough time to finish buying tickets and complete the ideal itinerary. But he had all the information to complete the traveling plan. They walked away from the ship looking for any suspicious police observing the passengers disembark. They felt relief when they got into the taxi in their way to the hostel.

'We will stay two more weeks.' Said Ron to the group at the hostel. 'If the cops are looking at the airports, they can keep looking for ghosts in the next two weeks.' Brat spend the whole afternoon working on the new plan. He aspired to find the optimal schedule.

He had a tentative timetable for the following two weeks. He found on the web site two cruise ships departing from Nice, one on Thursday at 5:15pm, and another on Saturday at 5:15 pm, as well. Their plan for the next cruise trip had many details including a preliminary timetable for the travel time from Lyon to Nice. Brat felt proud of his initial plan. He checked the options for the two ships departing from Port de la Sante, Nice. The two ships had the same route schedule from Nice to Barcelona, Spain. Oddly enough, tickets were still available.

The 8-day cruise takes the passengers for three beautiful small port cities to enjoy some of the unique cuisine such as Cassis, the fisherman competitors in Se'te, and the gorgeous sites in Collioure to finally end at Barcelona.

'It could not be better for us,' said Ron. 'We can survey gem businesses that have minimum security, hence, constitute low risk for us in Nice.'

From St Christopher's Inn, they go to the train station on time for the ride to Lyon. Everybody was pleased by the way the hostel worked out. The price was right for a clean private, room. The amenities were basic, and convenient. They consented to stay in a hostel at Lyon.

Lyon

Pete found a hostel in Lyon, Away Hostel and Coffee Shop. The name indicates possible American own or manage. Brat commented: 'who cares who owns it, the price is even better than the one in Paris.' Ron added: 'this is not Paris; the price should be a little less.' They arrived to the hostel in two separate groups. First Ron and Brat registered, ten minutes later Pete and Rudy. The same early evening they went to check the jewelry stores. They selected Bijouterie Joaillarie Salam on 19 Rue Paul Bert on the West side of the Saone River in the old or Vieux Lyon. The East side of the same river, Pete found a control box for the alarm system for Teller Jewelry Lyon, on 3 Rue Simon Maupin. They formed two groups in pairs to figure out the alternative streets back to the hostel. Ron insisted on learning the streets names around the dormitory with easily distinguishable landmarks. He suggested: 'look for a tall building with unique features, or a bridge tower. The idea is in case of running from a chase you can quickly reorient yourself back to the hostel.' Each one draws a personal map with few key words for street names and obvious tall buildings.

The next day, early morning Pete and Brat went to Perrache railway station, on 14 Cours de Verdun Gensoul. The train station was a walking distance from the guest house. They came back on time for breakfast. They bought tickets from Lyon to Nice. They could only purchase tickets the day of departure.

The schedule was perfect. Departure time was 12:45pm for the train for Nice. The Bijouterie Joaillarie store opened at 11:15am. It only took 25 minutes for them to walk into the store and subdued the staff.

They snatched a considerable number of gems before the Brits absconded. They crossed the river from old Lyon. Once they came back to the East side of Saone River, they went into Teller Jewelry Lyon store. Talked to the staff to distract them while Pete set the alarm from the outside box.

After the employee had turned off the system, Ron threatened the staff with a fake bomb in a bag. Ron and Brat ordered employees to unlock a couple of the display cases for Rudy who took plenty of gems into a backpack. He left the store and watched for any sign of potential trouble. Ron kept an eye over the employees while Brat seized few more items into another backpack. When they left Ron ignited two small bombs made with the cigarette lighters and set them in front of the door. The whole deed took less than eight minutes. Each assailant walked away in different directions. Everyone carried a backpack with their tools and equipment. They also had a designated post to go to change their appearances. The plan included change the shirt used in the jewelry stores. The video surveillance in the shops will have recoded the images, chances those videos are in color. 'We'll give them something very distinct. We had to alter our appearances' said Ron, 'before returning to the hostel.'

Brat went to Guillotie're the bridge on the Rho'ne River. Brat wore a dark blue shirt with a matching hat. It was 11:50 am when Brat arrived at the bridge entrance, at that moment a guided group of tourists gathered next to him. The tourist guide is an American residing in France for over ten years. He had on, a dark blue shirt, same as Brat, a twist of Fate. The American tourist guide explained few facts about the bridge Guilloti'ere the oldest bridge in Lyon. The bridge was destroyed completely during War World II.

Two ladies in their sixties with the tourist group observed Brat's blue shirt same as their guide. One winked her left eye to her friend pointing to Brat, then they both walked very close to him. They greeted Brat saying:' hello there,' with a mischievous smile. Brat saw the two ladies as troublemakers, he answered: 'hello.' Immediately one asked him: 'are you the assistant of the tour guide?'

Brat responded: 'Oh no, I'm not sorry.' The same lady replied: 'you are wearing same color as your friend, and you are handsome.'

Brat said: 'our shirts are the same color? it's just a coincidence, he is not my friend.'

Then the lady dropped a bomb to Brat by asking: 'are you marry?' Extending her arm with her hand touching her friend. Her gesture was to tell her friend do not interrupt, let him answer. The two ladies could not see Brat eyes because his dark sunglasses. Brat had just closed his eyes trying to comprehend what did she say. He could only say: 'pardon me?' At this the other lady, said: 'Liz my friend is just trying to be friendly, you know.' Brat knew the two ladies wanted to play with someone. He gave his best British accent and smiled telling them: 'that is a secret.' Liz insisted, and asked him: 'are you going to take the two of us to your apartment for drinks? Perhaps we can figure out your secret.' Her friend let go a loud squeak laugh. Brat murmured: 'what the heck!' Then smiled, and said: 'I must go, have fun, bye.'

They asked him one more question: 'where is Fourvie're Hill?' Liz blew a kiss, and the other waved goodbye with her fingers as he left. Then he moved quickly behind a large delivery van, where he changed his dark blue shirt, and his blue matching hat. He put them into a plastic bag and dumped it in a small garbage collector stand, next to the bridge entrance. Brat noticed a large hill in a short distance from the bridge. The sign next to him with an arrow pointing Fourvie're Hill. There is a basilica on top of the hill. The view is wonderful.

Pete went to Pont Gallieni on the Rho'ne River. He saw the esplanade under the bridge, there he sat for a moment on one of the benches and contemplated the few ducks swimming. He changed his dark red long sleeve shirt for a white collarless cotton shirt. He unzipped the removable legs off his khaki cargo pants. He also put on a 2-inch brimmed light khaki hat, and dark gray sunglasses. Then he walked across the street from the tall four towers on the elongated building, he had an affiche (small flyer) of the basilica, he admired the front columns and a terrace with balustrade one tower roof has a small peak a golden statue the other 3 towers have a deck with a large mast and a cross. The front has a set of tall narrow windows with a cupola with a medium size statue on the roof. There were couple of pictures illustrating the different aspects of the building.

Ron went to Pont Wilson on Rho'ne River. He put on a blueish-gray chambray shirt that morning. He changed to an Ivory polo shirt, and a hooligan light steel gray hat.

Rudy in his way to Kitchener-Marchand bridge on Sao' River. He walked by a small group of four people who were setting their musical instruments. Rudy noticed one girl cleaning a long metal instrument. Rudy was curious how the sound of the clarinet will be on the outdoors. He heard a tall girl oversaw the musicians, but Rudy needed to alter his looks and put on a different shirt. He could not stay and wait until the tall, short hair, brunet young girl started to play. Rudy walked behind a small brick fence used for hide garbage cans, then he discarded his dark magenta shirt, to put on a light-yellow linen shirt with a black bucket hat. The sun was reflected brightly on the ground by large windows from across the river, the Eastern side. Rudy stood and stared to a modern skyscraper building with large windows. He looked around making sure he was not observed by police, then he headed to the guest house. Walked by the Street with a grassy area, where three musicians were playing under a chestnut tree. One local young man an art student played the violin, the other young man played a cello, and one girl played the flute, who works evenings at the restaurant. One other blonde girl helped to set the portable music stands, and the folding chairs. The girl playing the flute sat in the middle, the cello to her left and the violin to her right.

Rudy stopped at a distance behind the small audience sitting on the grass in front of the three musicians. Few others perhaps four or five standing forming a semi-circle. Most of the audience were friends of the musicians. Rudy can hear the music to his surprise he recognized what they were playing. It was beyond a doubt the same piece he and Angela had gone to see live. Rudy remembered well, it is Haydn, the No 2 in Flat Major. The music brought emotional memories of that unforgettable afternoon. Rudy was overwhelmed. He thought about Angela, he missed home and wanted to cry. Rudy realized how precious this time was to be alive. It was a short moment to enjoy the beauty of the city, the simple ensemble played with such grace that evoked a melancholic mood.

A warm sun was cheering the day. Everyone around Rudy were enjoying the music. He started to walk away with a heavy laden of guilt. Rudy could not stop thinking on Angela, his thoughts took him to a horrible question What kind of man did he pretend to be for Angela? How shameful, one needs to be, he regretted his deeds. 'Could I talk to Pete? Maybe Ron? Who can understand this predicament? This must be a ruse of someone. But what does it matter? When I am guilty of every charge!'

Ron stopped at La Boîte a' Cafe' the coffee shop at the corner from the hostel.

The fresh smell of roasted beans was too strong to resist. He walked in and closed his eyes to take a deep breath of the fresh brew. He ordered a cappuccino. Found a seat next to the window, the perfect view to the street in the direction of their dormitory. It was difficult to keep his mind on what just transpired while sipping his cappuccino. For a moment he observed two motorcycle police officers blocked the street at the intersection. Ron's heart started to race. The motorcycle cops held traffic two patrol vehicles closed the incoming traffic. He did not have a clear view of what police were doing. He got up from his seat alarmed. The light traffic became a congested busy line that reached more than half the street. Panic seizes his whole being, he whispered: 'Oh sh…We're busted' Pedestrians gathered to catch sight of the action. Two other police cars with their top lights flashing were escorting a black limousine, followed by two motorcycle police. It must be a cabinet minister. Ron sat down again, to say it to himself: 'false alarm!' but keep an eye on any suspicious movement, then he exhaled in relief.

Everyone made back to the boarding house. The time was 12:40pm. They paid for an extra night because the time to check out was at 11:00am. They knew their operations will pass that hour. Ron justified the extra £130.00 disbursement as an insurance. It was better to have a place to pack and remove make-up before they headed to Perrache train station. The trip to Nice lasted less than 6 hours.

Lieutenant Pierre Bauer had sent alerts to the 20 districts known as arrondissement in Paris. The report from the burglary committed on Perle d'Or in the city of Les Andelys came to lieutenant Pierre Bauer attention in the middle of an investigation of a violent homicide. The priority was to find the murder suspect or suspects. The burglary was important but considered less violent. Lieutenant Pierre sent the pictures he had from the video surveillance to hotels, airport and security agents at the train stations. No suspects were reported. The details of robberies committed in the city of Lyon were presented to lieutenant Pierre, one day after the incidents.

The accounts were from two different jewelry stores. They were done the same day one in Bijouterie Joaillarie Salam and the second on Teller Jewelry, in the city of Lyon. Lieutenant Pierre suspected the same criminals were acting again. This time he sent the alert to Lyon's police department with a copy of his files from the previous burglaries. The file contained the fingerprint results from the lab. Lyon police alerted most of the jewelry stores to reinforce the security and look out for four individuals who were using different tactics to overcome the staff, these criminals were to believe from Great Britain. At the same time notifications for hotels requesting guest lists from Great Britain that had registered the week of the robberies. The police chief added a note of urgency with the hope some information will return from the hotels and provide a lead to the suspects. 12 hotels provided a total list of 25 guests from Great Britain with the names. The police clerk called those hotels to request specific information about the guest's description. In the response from the hotels only two persons fit the general description in terms of high and age. Unfortunately, those guests had check out the day of the robberies.

Lieutenant Pierre Bauer called Lyon's chief of municipal police to suggest posting undercover agents with a copy of the suspects pictures at the airport and train stations. 'Look for four individuals traveling alone with possible light luggage.' Lieutenant Pierre could not predict which direction the Brits were moving next. Is it Geneva? or Turin, maybe they stay in France Marseille, Nice or Monaco.

It seemed once again that Gru and Tin Man had successfully selected an ideal route and region to evade law enforcement agents.

That evening at the hostel, the loot was divided into four parts, they had 12 rings of different sizes with diamonds, 6 pairs of gold earrings with pearls, and diamonds. There were few pendants with small emeralds six bracelets with very high-quality pearls. Ten women gold watches and four men gold watches with diamonds. The mood was a mix of uncertainty and victory. They had the loot and so far, no one had approached them to request an interview or question their activities in France.

Ron gave them a word of caution: 'let's not think we are not being pursue.' Pete perceived Rudy melancholic aspect. He nevertheless remained focus on the task, he did not say a word. There was too much to do and not enough time to deal with whatever was his issue.

They place carefully each group of jewels making sets for rings, earrings, pendants, and watches. They bag the wrapped portions in soiled shirts to disguise the valuables. Ron and Brat left the guest house five minutes apart. They assumed police were following any group of four individuals that fit the profile. Pete and Rudy left three minutes apart and took off in different directions towards the train station. Ron had a feeling of confidence of being successful if they all boarded the cruise ship.

He told the group: 'let's abstain from a deadly sin avarice, gluttony in other words we have enough for this trip.' Brat asked: 'why are you talking about gluttony? We haven't had any excess of food.' Pete said: 'I think you Ron are talking about greed, not necessary food, right?' Ron nodded: 'yea! Between the shipment from Paris and these collections there is enough to pay for these two weeks and then some more. Now if and only if at some point during the cruise we encounter a shop vulnerable with low security then maybe we attempt to do business with them.'

At the train station Brat walked around the station to check for any police monitoring. He found in the small office a picture of them from the video surveillance in Les Andelys jewelry store. Fortunately, the makeup they wore helped to disguise their appearance. The suspects in the picture were different men from the real delinquents. Brat alerted the rest, and everyone made sure to cover their heads with their hats and wear the sunglasses. They kept the distances from each other as if they were complete strangers.

City of Nice

The first train was schedule to depart Nice station at 6:25 am, but due to a glitch in the main computer that controls the safety light on parts of the railroad track, caused a delay of 52 minutes. A maintenance crew was sent to replace three LED light components on two tower lights of the change rails. The engineer in charge at the time of the glitch determined the malfunction displayed on the computer main screen was not a software issue, but a mechanical and authorized replace the LED bulbs. No trains can run in any direction while crews are on the tracks.

After the bulbs replacement were completed and tests conducted the system was back online, then, announcements on the affected train stations were made inviting passengers to aboard trains for the first run of the morning.

UNSCHEDULED DELAY

The train the Brits took left Lyon at 8:25 am it was the first train of the day after the LED lights incident. The four individuals boarded the train by different doors. They waited for the train to stop on 2 train stations, then they sat together and were able to discuss the plans for Nice. The train had traveled about one hour, and they arrived in Valence the train station to connect with the train for Nice. Then, passengers with destination to Villefrenche-sur-mer trasnfered train, including the Brits. After 20 minutes of travel the train came to a full stop in the middle of two train stations. The announcement in English was shorter than in French.

The reason for the stop at no train station was not an emergency, but a safety directive from the command control center. The first ten minutes passed and not action outside the train, and no comments from the train operator. Some passengers mostly locals were conversing in French, the Brits could not understand what the matter with the train was. Another fifteen minutes went by, and the train moved very slowly only 20 feet, and came to another full stop, after three minutes the new announcement in English, the train coming in the opposite direction had suffer a mechanical failure and the repair crew is working on the issue. The tracks need to be clear, and all trains are halt for safety reasons. Time estimated to repair the mechanical issue 40 minutes, time estimated to open tracks for trains 50 to 60 minutes. After the announcement in English, a long, and more detail was followed in French. Many passengers got up and retrieve their luggage and started to walk towards the exits. Brat, and Pete asked a couple travelers to please explain what is happening. One person disclosed the train in the opposite direction had derailed and it will take anywhere from two to three hours to move some of the cars out of the way. In the next 25 minutes a bus should come to the near train station about 750 meters corresponding to 7 city blocks and pick passengers to continue the trip to Nice. Anyone who wanted to continue the trip to Nice by bus needs to leave the train at once and walk to the train station where the bus provided by the railroad transportation agency is coming. As soon as he said that he excused himself and walked to the exit door.

Ron, Brat and Pete felt as if they had suffered the derailment and were stuck with no hope.

Rudy was thinking: 'here is our reward, our debt is catching up with us.'

Ron could not even contemplate the idea of dragging their luggage from the train to the train station and getting into the bus on time. On the other hand, what was the alternative? Wait in the train until the tracks open and possibly miss the cruise ship.

The next 5 minutes passed very fast most of the passengers walking for the bus had left, only few ladies and couple other travelers who did not have an urgency to reach Nice remained in the train. The next announcement in English indicated the fact the opposite train had derailed and everyone who stayed in the train is safe. The estimated time to clear the tracks was about 5 hours maybe more. Passengers are encouraged to remain in the train, but they are free to get off the cars for a short walk and exercise extreme caution always looking ahead on the tracks both ways. The announcement in French was twice as long.

Rudy made a comment after the French bulletin: 'It looks like we are staying on the train until the tracks are clear and we probably will need to get on the cruise ship next Saturday. Not bad, let's hope the cops are searching everywhere except this train.'

Ron had no idea of the damage on the tracks, didn't know either if people were hurt wounded, broken bones or even dead. Brat started to have a concern about how long we need to stay in the train, he felt vulnerable and with nowhere to go. Pete observed Rudy after his comments, but he also felt anxious about having the evidence that now he was not sure if he wanted to hold on the jewels or get rid of them before anyone sees them. The band was under enormous stress for the unexpected delay. Each one sharing similar thoughts but kept silence.

THE FRENCH CONFUSION

One person walked into the car from another section and greeted Rudy in English, he had a heavy French accent. He asked Rudy if the seat next to him was open. The whole car was empty except for the two seats they were on. Rudy looked around and answered with his good British accent: 'no, I think whoever was sitting there is gone.' The guy on his thirties sat next to Rudy and started to talk about what he heard on the other section of the train, he said: 'I heard it was an accident.'

Ron asked: 'do you mean to say the accident caused only minor damage to the other train, and people are okay?' Then he answered: 'yes, by the way my name is Pierre are you guys together?'

It was obvious they were together. They were sitting close and talking to each other when Pierre slid the car door open and saw the four of them were the only passengers in the whole car. Ron cleared his throat, then responded in his well-rehearsed British accent: 'for the moment yes, we are here together including you now.'

Ron, Brat, Pete, and Rudy did never prepare for a complete unpredicted situation like the one they were caught in. No one had an alternative name to use in a moment of let's just say, emergency.

It was truly a French shock; the train halted due to the derailment and now Pierre, the French traveler, asking too many questions.

Pete ventured to say: 'I'm Harry and this is George.' Pointing with his index right finger to Rudy. His voice sounded apprehensive, and he paused waiting for either Ron or Brat to take over. Pierre said: 'hello,' and turned to see Ron who was next to Pete.

Ron mumbled: 'oh yeah! I'm … er Ian and I think he said his name is William' looking at Brat. Each one of the groups was clearly stun! Brat was looking down with his right hand over his head. Ron called him: 'William Are you ok? Mister William.' Brat looked up and said: 'I'm stress out because this bloody mess.'

Pierre admitted the situation is demanding, 'were all of you going to Nice as well?'

Everyone turned to see each other and nodded.

Pierre added: 'if that is your destination for the night you will need a room in a hotel. Hotels are book around this time due to the cruise ships season.' Ron replied: 'how about you?'

Pierre said: 'Ian, right? I do not need a room in a hotel because I lived there.'

Brat said: 'Pierre may I ask a question?' Before the French answered Brat added with a tone of anger in his voice, 'where do you think I could find a bloody room in Nice at whatever the time might be when we finally get there.'

Ron immediately interjected: 'Mister William for Pete's sake! Calm down.'

Pierre answered: 'It's alright Ian, I understand how frustrated you all must be. I hope the estimated time to have the railroad tracks open should be in 5 hours, since there are no injuries. The time to arrive at Nice is another 3 to 4 hours, in short, we all should be in town between 7:00-7:30 pm. I'm not sure if you could rent a room for the evening. Maybe one of you should look the web for hotels in Nice and try to phone inquiring for rooms available later tonight.'

Pete grabbed his phone and looked at hotels in the area of Villefrenche-sur-mer and hotels in Nice. He found couple hotels near the train station, but he needed reservations 24 hours in advance for all rooms. The hotels further inland had rooms available, each one of the occupants for each room needed to call and make his own reservation.

Pierre smiled and said: 'I'm glad you all can make reservations and have a room. Even if is a bit far from the train station.' Ron asked Pete: 'excuse me Harry, could I have the phone number of the hotel closer to the train station? I should better make the reservation before we get to Nice. Harry replied: 'of course Ian, I'll finish booking for myself.' Then Mr. William said: 'Harry could I also have the same number for my own reservation?' Then George suggested: 'why don't we all inquire for a discount if we make a reservation as a group?'

Harry said: 'that is a brilliant idea, let me ask to the clerk.' After a few minutes Pete hang up. Everyone was looking at him waiting for his explanation.

The hotel provides group discounts 24 hours in advance. They only have private large suits available at this moment with no reservation. Harry added: 'I'll give you the phone number of two other hotels to try, perhaps you will have a better luck.'

Pierre said: 'I hope you can find a room. It looks like finding a place for tonight is a challenge. I live about 20 minutes walking distance from Villefranche-sur-mer train station. My place is not huge, but If you do not find a room for tonight, you are welcome to spend the evening sharing the living room in my apartment.'

Ian spoke first and said: 'let me try this number and see what the hotel has.'

Mr. William called another number; he spoke with the clerk with no results.

Harry found a place about 10 miles from the train station.

Pierre reaffirmed his offer to share the living room for the night.

Rudy answered: 'If I do not find a room when we get to the train station, I'll take your kind offer, merci beaucoup monsieur!'

Pete also responded: 'I don't know about the other fellows,' pointing to Ron and Brat, 'but I also appreciate your hospitality. I promise, I'll be going early in the morning. I don't snore, well not too loud I've been told. Everyone laughed.'

Ron said: 'I will consider such generous offer as a backup. I'll try one more hotel.

Brat, for everyone's unbelief, hesitated and said: 'Hum, I don't want to impose any inconvenience.' He paused for a short moment, and then in a way to make it sound as reluctance he added, 'but since all are for one and one for all…'

Pierre laughed at the truly British way that they were behaving, even though, he did not suspect the band was performing one of the best acts. It just came very naturally; the Brit's anxiety had subsided considerable.

Pete commented: 'since we are settled for the rest of the trip, I'm taking a short walk outside, I need a little bit of fresh air.' Brat added: 'good idea, I need a smoke' and looked at Rudy with a slight shrug of his shoulders. Ron excused himself for the bathroom. Pierre told everyone: 'I need to go to the refreshment car and get me a drink, I'll see you all later. Nice to meet all of you.'

Rudy got up with everyone and the moment Pierre left the car, he sat down again closing his eyes with his mind on Angie.

Once outside of the train Pete and Brat walked on the other side of the tracks away from the train. They wanted to keep distance from the train to talk about the whole incident with Pierre.

Brat tells Pete: 'so, Harry ha!

Pete says: 'that's right Mr. William.'

Brat: 'what about Rudy?'

Pete: 'he is George.'

Brat: 'right! And Ron is Ian'

Brat: 'what the hell is going on? The whole thing has gone under, we don't really have a chance!' When he said this, he lit a cigarette.

Pete tried to remain calm and replied: 'not everything is lost, so far, we still don't see cops on us, I hope they don't even suspect where we are. We at least had made a connection with this dude Pierre and hopefully we can stay at his place for the night in Nice. Brat continued with his cigarette and ask Pete: 'why don't you go back inside and tell Ron to come and meet me here. We need to talk away from that Pierre. I don't trust him.'

Pete replied: 'I'll go back to see if Ron is not too suspicious, and he can come out. Wait for about 3 minutes in case Pierre is around.'

Brat agreed. Pete added, 'in the meantime I'll get acquainted with the surveillance systems available in Villefrenche-sur-mer, and in Nice, one good thing is we still have access to WIFI in the train.'

Ron came out of the train to look for Brat where Pete told him they had talk freely.

Pete saw Ron approaching the small bend on the tracks with a few small bushes that covered the view from the train cars. Pete called: 'hey Gru or should I say Ian?'

Ron gave a slight grin and replied: 'Oh Yeah! This is Ian from here to Nice, Mr. William.'

Ron observed Brat lighting another cigarette, then he said: 'aren't you supposed to do something to the darn thing before you light it?'

Brat heard it, and knew it was about the plan to reduce smoking, but dismiss the whole hint, he just replied: 'I'm too stress out this ordeal is too much. What do you say about this guy, I mean Pierre. I don't trust him. Do you?'

Ron said: 'calm down! One thing at the time. Let's start with cut the cigarette or just put it out before you get to the end. We need to remain calm.'

Let's talk about what's going on with the train, we know the tracks will be clear in few hours and we will proceed to Nice. This fellow Pierre, I don't trust him either, our problem now is, he has seen all of us, and we don't really have an alternative but stay in the train until we all get at nice. We will figure out what to do once we get in town. One thing we could do is, two of us spend the night at his apartment and since Pete found a place the other two spend the night there. Pierre could be intrusive and ask too many questions. We need to reduce the chances for him to discover more than he needs to know. Remember we all met here in the train stuck, due to the accident with the train in the opposite railroad tracks.'

Ron and Brat returned inside the car, to talk to Rudy and Pete. They agreed to the idea of all have met while traveling in the train. Ron and Rudy will spend the night at Pierre's apartment if they do not find a place for their own.

Brat and Pete will go to the hotel that Pete found.

Ron instructed Rudy not to mention anything that could give a clue to the French host. 'We don't even know what he does for a living, he might even be a cop. '

The Brits confronted with such bizarre circumstances had devised a feasible plan.

Three hours passed and each member of the band had taken a separate seat away from each other.

TIME TO PONDER

Each one had absorbed himself in his own thoughts. Pete had inconspicuously opened his bag and observed the gems that he had. He was dreaming of what he could do and obtain once he cashed out his part of the loot. The powerful attraction for the money was strong enough that he had forgotten the precarious situation that they are in.

Ron anxiety had subsided enough that he was playing scenarios for the next few hours. What should they do as soon as they arrive in Nice, how they will gather before boarding the next ship. If the police were waiting for them what should be the next step, 'should we dump the gems and have no evidence? Or should we give them to Pierre, and accuse him to be an accomplice? The police will have a lot more work to do.'

Brat Had become tired of thinking the worst from Pierre, the worst from the estimated time for the train repairs, he was a bit hungry but decided to take a nap and had fallen asleep.

Rudy's contrite started as a soft voice asking the obvious in terms of his current affairs, Rudy tried to answer himself, but the soft voice became louder with more pressing questions. 'What have you done to deserve honor?' He tried to block the questions and thought of Angela. The voice kept a shameful tone, 'do you expect rewards for your illicit accomplishments?' Rudy was enduring the nightmare taking place while he was wide awake. He just could not stop hearing the voice pointing all the wrong actions and consequences. 'Your admiration for your techniques is obvious and disgusting.'

Rudy tried to justify to himself or to the voice the results of their fine techniques. Rudy said: 'look we hacked the security system of the stores that prevented anyone of getting hurt or police running after us.' The voice kept hammering the actions pointing the prideful attitude: 'Your boasts are as empty as your empty deeds. All your high esteem for your loot a stolen treasure is call worship, guess what you are worshiping, a lifeless idol, it can't do anything for you, what is worst you become what you worship. It is worthless.'

Rudy again arguing with himself thought: 'we are building a pretty good treasure.'

Angela had given a heavy dose of moral values, so the voice added: 'that treasure of yours is in fact subjected to be stolen from you, loose its value or be destroy.'

Rudy came back and said: 'there are stupid thieves and there is our enterprise highly professionals in every aspect of the operations.' All that to hear the voice in an angrier tone: 'you despise in others what you despise the most in yourself. You learn to lie to you first, then to others, it shows in that brazen look of yours.'

Rudy was engrossed on his thoughts he looked through the window the small hill in the far background, then his gaze fix on the closer bushes to the window, his silhouette reflected on the window glass made him change his focus. He became self-conscious and notice the train made sounds of starting to move. The voice from the car speakers announced: 'we are happy to announce the railroad tracks are open and we are clear to proceed to Nice, please return to your seats.'

The train after two minutes continue with the few passengers that remained through the delay. The scheduled stops were made but only taken one or two minutes because many passengers had taken the buses provide while the train was halted.

After few minutes of the train continuing the trip to Nice, Pierre came to the car with the intentions to confirm the four strangers recently acquainted with each other, were still traveling in the train. After all, he may be hosting two strangers that so far behave fine. 'I wonder if I can trust these brits to spend the night in my apartment once we arrive in Nice.' Pierre asked himself.

Ron saw the sliding door open, Pierre walked in the car. Brat was the one sitting closer to the door which Pierre came in, but he kept walking, then nodded to Rudy who was three seats away from Brat. Rudy saw Pierre's nodding, and just raise his hand saying hello. Ron was four seats after Rudy, Pierre stops to talk to him and sat next to him. They exchange few words mostly about the estimated time to arrive at Nice. Ron dared to ask Pierre: 'what his occupation was in Nice.' 'I work in a small store, I do many things, I am responsible to open, have everything ready for customers, once a month I do inventory, and then place an order for more merchandise.' Ron asked: 'what kind of store?' 'We have what is consider souvenirs, including local wines.'

Pierre asked Ron, 'what about you, what do you do?'

Ron had thought about this question and what to say. He will stick to his original alternative occupation about an estate agent, as it is called in the UK a real estate agent. Ron supposedly works in commercial properties. The next question from Pierre was 'where are you staying in Villefrenche-sur-mer or in Nice, or you are just passing by.' Ron said: 'I'm not sure where to go from Nice, I'm in the middle of a messy divorce and just need some time off from everything. I may go to Montecarlo for a couple of days and then go back home.' Ron then asks Pierre: 'were you on vacation in Lyon?' Pierre stated the reason for his trip to Lyon was to visit family over the weekend. After few more minutes Ron excused himself and said he needs to use the water closet.

Pierre got up from the seat and told Ron: 'I'll go to buy some food and coffee, it has been a long trip already, we should be in town in less than two hours, I'll see you then.' Ron waited for Pierre to leave the car to the front of the train, then told the rest of the Brits: 'if you guys are hungry better go right now to the food section get as many snacks as possible and drinks then leave that car get away go to the rear cars, the idea is to keep distance from the French guy.'

Ron and Rudy stayed in the same car where they met Pierre. Brat and Pete went to the last car in the rear of the train hoping that Pierre would not come looking for them.

When the train made it to Ville franche-sur-mer station the time was 7:35 pm. Pierre came to the car where Ron and Rudy where sitting expecting to see him. Pierre saw only the two of them and asked about the other two Harry and Mr. William. Ron said: 'I have not seen either one since we continue after the railway tracks were announced clear.' Pierre replied: 'maybe we'll see them again after we get off the train, before we leave the station.' Rudy mentioned: 'they have a place for the night.' Pierre asked Rudy: 'did you talk to either one?' Rudy said: 'only while we were all together and they made the reservations, after that they must have gone to another car, I have not seen them.'

They left the train along with the rest of the passengers and waited to see Brat and Pete. After fifteen minutes they can see only few passengers walking in the train station. Brat and Pete were not among them. Ron asked Pierre 'how far is your place? Should we get going? It looks like the other two fellows have gone to their own rooms for tonight.'

Pierre realized it was late, therefore, it was time to leave, and since the other two were not around it was better head home and rest, next morning he needed to be at the store and open as part of his duties. He told Ron and Rudy 'let's go home it has been a long day already.'

Brat and Pete had taken a taxicab for the hotel La Regence-Chez Betty, where they made the reservations.

Brat told Pete: 'let's get to our rooms, Ron knows where we are. We should get together again in the morning.'

Pierre was tired due to the long delay that had stretched the traveling day over 12 hours. During the walk with Ron and Rudy, from the train station to his apartment, the talk was short and only basic questions, mostly from Ron.

'Do you have a dog?'

Pierre: 'no, I don't have a dog because I don't have time to care for one.'

Ron: 'I see, same here, no time for dog. I will be going very early in the morning.'

Pierre: 'No worries, I myself need to be at the store before 7:00 am. We probably all be going no later than 6:15 am. But Ian and George, let me ask you two, since both of you are from London, something that I must know.' Ron and Rudy held their breath, not sure what is coming to them and have the potential to ruin everything.

Pierre continued in a casual mode: 'you must follow one or perhaps two teams which one is your favorite or according to your knowledge which team is the most popular in London?'

Ron answered: 'I beg your pardon, what teams are you talking about?'

Pierre laughed! Then said: 'you must need to be very ceremoniously before you answer a simple question-I'm talking football from the Champions League.' Rudy dared to say: 'Well mister that depends on who do you ask.'

Pierre gave a big hint by mentioning two names. 'Let me guess is between Chelsea FC and Arsenal right.'

Ron grabbed the hint and very firmly stated: you're right! It is fifty-fifty! I consider myself all Arsenal, but I can guess, George here is Chelsea.' He winked his left eye to Rudy. Then Rudy put his right index finger on Ron's chest and said: 'that is correct mister Arsenal.' Grouching and showing teeth.

Pierre looked at them afraid they would start a fist fight right there in his living room. He said: 'Ok, ok. I see. Don't need to illustrate the passion any stronger. You both are in the land of Olympic Gymnasie Club Nice. But that's enough about football, wouldn't you say? We all better get some sleep, if you need something let me know. Good night.'

Early the next morning Ron, and Rudy got up and were ready to leave, when Pierre came from his bedroom to offer coffee. Ron thanked him and said: 'I really need to get going. Rudy added: 'I would not want to be much more trouble.' Then Ron very formal said: 'I'll be happy to compensate you for helping me with your kind hospitality.'

Pierre understood the two Brits were anxious for leaving to plan their next step for the day or days ahead. He did not insist with the coffee and refuse to get compensated for providing lodge. Ron and Rudy left without much more to say.

Ron and Rudy went back to the train station the same way they had come to Pierre's apartment the night before. They had exchanged text messages with Brat and Pete they all agree to meet back at the train station.

Ron and Rudy arrived at the train station quarter after seven. They bought a cup of coffee at the cafeteria along with a delicious pastry, while waited for Brat and Pete.

They went to inquire with the station agent about transportation to the harbor for the cruise ships. They learned public transportation was on a 5-hour strike. The bus to go from the train station to the harbor was supposed to be back on service at noon, that means the Brits would be on time for the cruise schedule.

The cruise ship was scheduled to board at 3:15pm, departure time 5:15pm. There was a gap of 7 hours before the time to board the cruise ship. Ron reflected whether to walk to town dragging their luggage and backpacks, due to the strike or just walk to the beach spend few hours looking around until midday find a restaurant and have a pleasant long lunch. The Brits left the luggage in the paid lockers at the train station. They proceeded to check the bay of VilleFrenche-sur-mer.

Ron and Brat learned the bay has three different beaches, they decided to go see the western part of the bay. Ron saw the small sign that read Plage de la Darse. Next to the Port Royal of la Darce. They both stood observing from the Westside to the Eastern part of the beach. Andre a local taxicab driver noticed them and approached to greet them: 'bonjour messieurs.' Ron and Brat turned to the man with the amiable voice had greeted them. Ron couldn't help to be suspicious and did not response, instead he looked around to see if there were any other men with Andre. Brat saw a sincere smile in the man on his fifties. He replied bonjour. The taxicab driver introduced himself and offered his cab in case they needed to go anywhere. He knew about the strike. Ron more relaxed, asked any update of the strike, he was informed the short suspension of public transportation service was a relative brief, mostly a way to protest for the high tax on fuel, and full service should restart at noon.

Ron kept looking to the water, then he mentioned, in the marina area, there are many small docks. Andre explained: some docks are for medium vessels 25+ feet size other docks are to berth small boats less than 20 feet, however, there is no parking for vehicles. Many people ride their bikes to the beach from Nice, and Villefrenche-sur-mer. Then he added: this beach is one of the cleanest beaches in the bay, many people visit for a little while due to the roughness of the surrounding terrain, is composed mainly of pointed rocks.

Andre also mentioned to Ron and Brat: 'before you gentlemen head to the beach area, is recommended to wear heavy rubber shoes.' Andre paused for a short moment to change his advice: 'wearing rubber shoes is essential to protect oneself on the rugged landscape. Ron looked to Brat both agreed to Andre's warning. Brat venture to ask: 'What else is good to know about this area, Monsieur Andre?' The cabdriver with a courteous gesture answered: 'The beach has a public shower to rinse oneself from the sand and salty ocean water, but there are no other facilities like snack bar or posted signs of no lifeguards on duty. You swim at your own risk.' Pete and Rudy went the opposite side of the bay. They hiked to Plage of Marinieres. From the beach they see many boats on the bay.

They kept strolling all the way to the far end of the beach, they passed the parking lot to discover another beach. Plage de l'ange gardien a smaller serene place. They saw a portion of the cove that is use for pet owners walking their dogs. Pete was aware of the surroundings in case police were waiting. Rudy was the opposite, oblivious of any person that could be a police officer or anyone following them.

In a common agreement the four individuals came back one by one discreetly to the train station just before noon. They hope the strike will be over or at the very least service would be restored allowing them time to plan the next move before going to the harbor.

Nothing was out of the ordinary or very suspicious for Ron, Brat and Pete. They decided to look for a restaurant to have lunch.

Plage VilleFrenche-sur-mer beach was a nearby public beach, they walked and found a great restaurant with splendid view. Ron ventured to order a salad that he could not even guess how to pronounce it.

An American couple in their sixties sitting next to their table heard their conversation and the horrible stumble in voicing the French menu. The lady in a subtle voice explained what the menu offered. She asked them what they would like to order. Pete gracefully thanked her and told her: 'we appreciate your kindness but shouldn't interrupt your lunch.' The husband gave a booming laugh and said: 'We're from Texas, you all can drop civility. No one is interrupting anything. Now go on take you shot at the French grub, it ain't bad.' Brat laughed and asked the couple if they had time to joint them for a drink.' The wife in a ladylike manner explained: 'thank you but we just finished lunch and our driver is waiting to take us to our boat.' Ron immediately asked: 'Are you on a cruise ship?' The husband clarified: 'not exactly, we have our own yacht. We like this restaurant; you picked a good one.' The lady explained the entree's, the main course and the poissons/fish food items. Rudy wrote in English, quickly as much as he could while she translated details.

Ron and Pete following her suggestions they shared a salad the sahimi tuna tartare with wakame and sour vinaigrette dressing (tartare de thon sashimi et ses petale de noir de St Jacques). The main course, they both also order each grilled squid virgen sauce with basmati rice and fresh vegetables (calamari A' la plancha, persille's et a L'hulle d'olive) Brat and Rudy, shared an entree' sea scallops carpaccio with summer truffle (Carpaccio de noix de Saint Jacques A l'hulle de truffe de d'ete') They also ordered a main course plate for two sea bass, mixed vegetables and grenailles potatoes (Loup legumes et de pommel de terre grenailles)

During the fabulous meal the comments was focused on what they had enjoyed so far. Brat said: 'the landscape is amazing,' Pete added: 'how about the unique azure color of the sea,' they all nodded in agreement. Ron gave an expecting look to Rudy and waited few seconds hoping for a comment. Rudy dismissed the whole innuendo he kept eating. Ron said: 'the mountains behind us suggest something mysterious. At this Brat asked: 'what do you mean?' Ron replied: 'It looks like the mountains are hiding a secret. I heard the old town is a labyrinth of alleyways on cobble stone.' They lamented not having enough time to go into town. The early sunny afternoon brought the ocean breeze, a welcome relief for the intense heat. This was not the first time they enjoyed gourmet food. The previous cruise ship in Seine River their meals were very tasty and rich. The difference was they ate separate from one another. They haven't had a meal together with leisure to truly enjoy it.

Ron asked: 'how are we doing time wise?'

Brat checked the time and said: 'we still got a couple of hours to kill.'

Pete said: 'we can't stay here too much longer.'

Ron: 'we could have some coffee and stretch it for another 40 minutes, the place is not crowded, anyway, but we should get going.'

Pete agreed and suggested: 'let's all go, not together though, just in case. Let's find out what is the status of the strike.' Brat asked the waiter about the public transportation strike. It turned out buses were back on the regular running schedule. Each one being cautious, apart from each other returned to the train station to pick up their luggage. Then, they all caught the bus for Nice. The band reached the port and one by one boarded the cruise ship without any incidents.

FROM NICE TO BARCELONA

Day one, Nice

The ship's crew welcoming passengers and their families created a good atmosphere, calling each traveler by name and title according to the personal information provided by each traveler at the time of ticket purchase.

Great enthusiasm and excitement were among the passengers as they carry the luggage. The air temperature was perfect at 76oF, and clear skies. Dinner was offered with formal attire in the main dining room, for those who wanted a more casual setting there is a section with tables that did not require tie and coat for the men. Ron ate his dinner at the bar with a drink three seats apart from Pete and Brat. They kept an eye on those who were around them. The evening was uneventful for them. Rudy sat at one of the small tables next to a window looking to the city lights. He wanted to take a moment to write a note for Angela.

Dear Angie, today as I walked by a small, picturesque bridge in a pretty city I came across of a trio what is called an ensemble. I was gladly surprised to hear they played one of the Haydn compositions I think is something call Flat, and something else, I don't really know, but I'm sure is Haydn No 2. I remembered the wonderful afternoon that we had when we went to the concert. After I listened to the small group play for few moments, I had to walk away from them, it made me so sad I really missed you. I am home sick, badly, I am Angie sick!

Day 2 At Sea

The calm seas with light winds offered spectacular views. Few high clouds due West, but otherwise great weather forecast for the next week was the captain's announcement first thing in the morning. Rudy kept writing what it has become more than a note. He fell to the temptation in writing out some of his secrets. Even though, he resisted with all his might, he still exposed some of his inner fears, Rudy did not have anyone to go for encouragement or comfort, even though, he was in a cruise ship full of passengers and crew members, the rest of the Brits were there, Gru, Tin Man, and techie, yet he felt all alone.

Ron suggested to everyone to just enjoy the day at sea. 'Let's all keep a very low profile, minimum interactions with anyone, with any of the crew members and with any other passengers.'

The ship maintains a distance from the land as it navigates Southbound in the Mediterranean, but passengers who are outdoors standing on the decks can still see the hills on land from the different towns. There are other vessels coming Northbound, other small fisherman boats steer clear from the cruise ship. The sunny, clear day allows some private sail boats to come within the safety distance and wave to passengers on deck. The ship captain announces the two small islands near by the town of D'Hyere. They can barely see the islands, lies d'hyere, and lie du Levant. When they approached land, the town le Seyne Sur mer was at a distance, suddenly, the ship had to maneuvered towards La Ciotat in order to avoid a collision. A private sailboat that had a mysterious missing crew had drifted on the water with no pilot or crew, it came dangerously close to the ship. There was no one on board to steer clear from the cruise ship. There was a great commotion, many passengers rushed to the decks and windows to see the sailboat, even some of the crew members turned their attention and held their breath in an anxious moment, but no one was hurt on the near collision thanks to the alertness of the captain and crew members to alert and alter the ship course from Cassis to La Ciotat. The captain immediate announced and assured the entire ship was in no danger. He invited everyone to continue to enjoy the views and relax. He went on to explain the change of direction was short on the distance but being a large vessel the time to slow down the ship and then return safely to the proper route will take few more minutes. Maritime authorities were notified, and the empty boat was taken to the port for proper identification and investigations.

Ron and the rest of the Brits shared the collective concern, along with the mild anxious feeling of everyone on board. The captain and the rest of the crew reassured the safety of the vessel and passengers, therefore there was no cause for alarm. The incident was over, and the captain focused on the enjoyment aboard the ship. He changed the musical show for the evening to start one hour earlier with the purpose to divert attention from the tense incident to a more relaxed atmosphere.

Day 3 Cassis

The evening had passed with no complains or inquiries from the passengers in regard of the early afternoon close call collision with the empty sailboat. The captain invited all passengers to enjoy the time allotted to disembark. The morning activities after breakfast included an excursion to Cassis town.

The announcement included the opportunity to try the fine white wines from the local vineyards.

Rudy observed the many hills around town. He read in a small article included in the cruise ship brochure, that Cassis has few wild caves. He was intrigued about who may live inside the caves. Rudy could not find information about exact details for trail or road leading to the area and venture to visit one or more of these caves.

Ron and Brat inquired about the jewelry stores. There were few in the shopping area. Pete walked up to one of the shops, he noticed an alleyway where the deliveries and service entrance is. He found the electric box panels and circuits, after he inspected, he knew the alarm system can be hacked, then, sent Rudy to tell Ron what they had found.

It was a simple alarm system for the Bijouterie ciotat Or. Pete looked up the name of the store and found that it means 'gold jewelry' Rudy commented on the name: 'it is a simple name, just like their security system.'

Ron and Brat went into the store, held a fake plastic gun to the two employees, bound them up, then Pete emptied two display cases of gold rings, and small jewelry. They left the store with the loot before anyone had come into the store. It took five minutes to do the job. They made it to the ship just before the ship call to board at the end of the day.

Brat learned about the humidor room with the fine selection of hand rolled cigars, as well as the lavish selection of cognacs. He was not aficionado of cigars, it was a bit too fancy for his taste, but he admitted to himself, smoke a cigar! It has an enticement of its own. To drink cognac was out of his class, he thought, too ostentatious, for him a good beer was satisfactory, on an especial occasion he might consider a drink of whiskey.

Brat had worked on the plan that Rudy had provided to reduce the number of cigarettes consumed per day, however, the plan did not consider a very critical point, any time Brat was under stress the plan did not have any alternative suggestion to overcome the urge of lighting a cigarette. Everyone in the band was affected by the disturbing events of the previous day. It had left an unsettled feeling. The trip had already been extended beyond the original plan, no one in the band had spent long time away from home. The fatigue was increasing due to the pressure of maintain a fake attitude of vacationists who are enjoying themselves. They had a common apprehension about the law enforcement agents were right on their heels.

Brat needed a quick way to calm his nerves, smoking a cigarette had an immediate sedative effect, that lasted only for a few minutes, hence, he needs to smoke another cigarette within the next hour or resist the temptation for about two hours. The cruise ship designated area that allows smoking is the fancy humidor room. It was the best scheme for Brat to have a short moment of calmness, and keep the smoking out of sight from everyone, including Rudy.

Brat had visited the humidor room three different times at the same hour. There were other passengers sharing the same room at the same hour that Brat had visit. One of the passengers had noticed Brat visiting for a third time.

He greeted Brat, to engage in a short conversation. Ryan wanted to know more about his mate for the smoking hour. Ryan not only like to smoke but also drink a little too heavy. Brat did not want to offend Ryan by treating him rude and dismiss his company. Ryan noticed Brat's British accent and inquired where he was from. Brat remembered Pete's incident with the British lady Florence, when they were on the Seine River cruise. Brat blabbed: Westminster district.

Ryan disclosed he was from Boston and had visited London twice. Ryan did not know much about this part of London and with a polite tone asked specific facts from the district. Brat had taken the time to read few facts about that area of London. He looked straight ahead and with confidence and shrewdness in a casual manner mention what he had read.

Brat said: 'well you know some of the famous sights are the Buckingham Palace home for the queen, Westminster Abbey church used for coronations.' Ryan looked at Brat and asked him: 'how many times have you gone inside to see the ceremony?' Brat with a grimace responded: 'not one! I only see them on tv, do not ask why.' Ryan nodded in silent. After a short awkward moment Ryan requested: 'what else is there?'

Brat kept quiet as thinking, then he added, 'ah yes! The tower Big Ben clock, and the neighborhood gardens, most of them are small but locals love to frequent every day. To mention a few the White Hall Gardens, Christ church gardens, Millbank Gardens, Riverside Walk Gardens one of my favorites. Oh yeah there is a small museum, the recent open Cartoon Museum. I do not want to sound like a tour guide, but that is what the district must see has.' Ryan replied: 'wow! Next time I get to go to London I have to check your hometown district.' Then he excused himself to go and order another drink. Brat remained on his chair with a bad feeling. The more he thought about his conversation with Ryan the more his apprehension grew.

I can tell you this: he was disgusted with himself, because he knew he had talk to Ryan unnecessarily too long. Ryan could identify him later. Brat needed to leave the humidor room quickly before Ryan return with another drink, and more stupid questions.

Day 4-5, Sete, Languedoc bad sardines.

Passengers were informed with their options and recommendations for the two days in port of Sete. One major attraction is the abundance of sea food. Ron and Brat felt they could pair up to watch for authorities observing the passengers. They needed to be defensive and observe who was watching passengers all the time.

After couple hours in town there was obvious police watch, but it was a general security, and no one was distinctly followed. Ron and Brat felt they could relax a bit and enjoy the rest of the day.

Pete asked Rudy: 'hey bro how about a short visit to the museum?'

Rudy replied: 'what time do they open?'

Pete: 'I think around 9:30 maybe 10:00'

Rudy: 'Ok, I'll meet you at the entrance.'

Pete: 'Are you going to a particular spot?'

Rudy: 'Not really, by-the-way don't wait for me go in once the doors are open.'

Pete: 'Oh no, last time I went into a museum I met Florence, from Westminster district in London. The goofy lady who told me everything about everyone in the neighborhood. I had enough of that.'

Rudy started to laugh and added: 'who knows maybe she is waiting for you again. I don't want to interfere with your date.'

Pete laughed and said: 'cut it off, it ain't funny!'

Rudy: 'Ok, I'll meet you at the door, no worries.' Rudy adventured to visit a small shop for women cloths, he found a perfect blouse for Angie. He needed to keep it in secret for the rest of the band. If not a series of inquires will follow from each member. Questions to confirm what they would suspect. Who is the special gift for? You are guilty of having a serious sweetheart. He will be considering a traitor by the whole band. Little that anyone could suspected that Angela is the ideal girl to provoke a paradigm shift in Rudy's thinking, that ultimately would contribute to what is inescapable, the gang's wreck of activities.

The gang is incapable to even see Rudy's reasons for attempting to be honest, truly a dismay. Their fears are based in part on how law enforcement investigations are conducted, however, that is only one component of the consequences.

After the visit to the Musée d'Art et Traditions Populaires de Cassis, Rudy told Pete: 'let's take a look at the market.' They wandered through one of the fish markets, they saw among the specialty's oysters, mussels, clams and fried squids. Many tempting fresh sea food items were on the menus. Pete did not want to spend too much money on meals since the cruise included good selection of gourmet food.

Rudy indicated: 'I know the ship lunch time starts at 11:00am and runs until 2:00 or 3:00pm, but I would like to try some fresh sea food.'

Pete looked at some of the food, the sweet aroma, and the freshness snared him. They wondered to a cozy shop and had the grill oysters (huintres grillees), and clam soup (soupe de palourdes) They ate the soup and the oysters around 1:30pm Brat also tried some sardines with a cocktail. He gave some of the sardines to Rudy and told him: 'wash them down with this drink. '

Ron and Brat while inside a store, heard a couple next to Brat asked the employee information about the famous 'Joutes de Sete' The clerk gave a big smiled and said: 'I'm member of 'blue team' this year we have a strong squad (e'quipe forte)' The couple asked: 'where is this tournament?' Ron heard the details and had a strong curiosity to witness this confrontation, which takes place during the Fete de Saint Louis.

Back at the ship during dinner Ron and Brat talked with Pete and Rudy. It was obvious the interest from Ron about the fishermen competition. Pete proposed: 'let's all go tomorrow to check out this battle of boating knights.'

Rudy kept writing from time to time his long notes for Angela, they resembled a report. He found on these writings a certain comfort for his mental anguish. Rudy along with Pete, and brat went to see the Joutes de Sete. It was an exciting event; they joint the crowd in the cheering as the justing took place. The event reanimated Rudy and gave him plenty of material to share with Angela. Once they went back to the ship Rudy took out his writing pad to tell her about his day.

He started his exposition: dear Angie, today we attended a competition which I learned is a tradition in the Languedoc region that dates to the 17th century. They called it the Joules de Sete It is a jousting tournament on boats rather than horseback. The teams have 10 strong fishermen, these are married men with the red shield, and the opposite team 10 equally strong bachelor fisherman with blue shields. I find this arrangement or formation interesting considering the occurrence that married men usually are older than bachelor men. What's more, married men are committed to succeed, and to bring honor to their families, on the other hand bachelors typically behave with an adventurous spirit.

They propel the boats with oars. Each boat has and oboist and a drummer sitting in front of their boat playing a traditional tune. The jousters dress in white. The competition is to throw the opponent into the water by pushing him of the 'tintaine' a small platform on each boat, where the jousters stand.

They use a lance, a long wooden spear. They hit the pavois o wooden shield. The lance has an iron tip, which can hit the pavois quite hard. The man who falls into the water is then followed by another jouster from that boat, who continues the battle. The winner can battle again until he too falls in the water. The winner of the Saint Louis joutes gets eternal fame, his name is engraved on a jousting shield in the Paul Valery museum. I can tell you this Angie, you are my winner because your name is engraved around my heart. I know what you will say my heart is not a museum. But in there is where I keep my treasure.

After all the writing Rudy did not feel good. He started to experience a light headache, and his stomach felt uneasy. After much plead from Ron and Brat, they all sat at the same table for dinner. Few hours later they were very sick.

The cruise personnel followed all protocols of sterilization and sanitation for food and beverages to ensure the safety of all passengers and crew. Sadly, occasionally contamination occurs during food transportation. A malfunction of the cruise kitchen and storage fridges is not common but takes place. The clam shader soup that was served was not suitable for eating, because the temperature had fluctuated, and bacteria had grown contaminating the soup.

Rudy, Ron and Brat ate some of the spoil clam shatter soup. Pete was the only one from the group that did not eat soup. Forty-five percent of the passengers became sick with food poison. Some passengers had mild symptoms with headaches, and nausea lasting two days for some of them. There was a small group with headaches that lingered a third day. Other passengers with preexisting conditions developed more severe symptoms lasting five days, they needed medical attention.

Day 6 Colliuore Time for Illness

The health condition of many passengers persuaded the captain to alter the schedule and remain at Colliuore, Catalonia for the entire 6th day. The captain consulted with the doctor on board, and he was advised to keep the ship stable at the pier while the passengers health condition improve. Few passengers due to dehydration were transported to the Centre Hospitalier, a relative nearby hospital. They had to administrate some IV solutions. Ron had a mild case of food poison, he did not suffer severe dehydration, he did not even need IV solution. He recovered in shorter time than Brat and Rudy.

Brat and Rudy on the other hand, were afflicted in a serious state, but not critical. They spent few hours of the 6th day of the cruise, at the hospital feeling very sick.

Brat kept encouraging Rudy by telling him that their precious cargo referring to the loot was all worth the misery in which they found themselves. Rudy had a completely different reasoning. It was difficult for Rudy to appreciate what Brat was trying to point. He thought: 'how can he justify this hardship for the stolen gems? We are reaping in part the consequences of our actions.'

Brat and Rudy were discharged from the hospital in the early afternoon, there was a small van rented by the ship as a shuttle to transport passengers back to the port from the hospital. Brat and Rudy asked the driver to drop them off three blocks from the port. The shuttle driver was not in complete agreement, 'I am supposed to bring everyone direct to port for the cruise ship,' he told them. Brat pleaded: 'monsieur s'il vous plait!' They wanted to walk for a short distance and discuss their points of view.

The driver took a deep breath and with two blocks from the port, replied: 'ok, c'est bien, but go to your ship.' He pulled over and let them get off the shuttle.

Brat had portrayed for Rudy, the many benefits of the wealth on account of the gems. They were immersed in their conversation and Brat was oblivious that Ryan had spotted him from across the street and was approaching them.

Brat heard Ryan's voice greeting him. He was bewildered. Brat had not seen Ryan since they chat in the humidor room, about three days ago.

Ryan asked the usual question: 'How are you Brat?'

Brat turned his head with a vague look in which apprehension slip through.

Rudy kept walking hoping to be unnoticed by Ryan. He knew Brat was already familiar that was not a good idea. 'If Ryan could recognize two of us that is really bad.'

Brat still a bit surprise to see Ryan mumble something like I'm ok. Ryan inquired: 'are you ok, you look tired!'

Brat shook his head lightly and answered, 'I just got back from the hospital, I was dehydrated and I'm tire, I'm heading back to my cabin for some rest. If you could excuse me Mr. Ryan.' Ryan waved his hand indicating not a problem. Then he added: 'so sorry buddy. I'll talk to you later.' He just stood on the street waving goodbye to Brat.

Day 7. Barcelona, Spain

The final day, a sad ending for the cruise and its passengers, they were dismissed with a voucher to use with a huge discount as an apology for the food fiasco.

Doctor Chan was with medical personal attending sick passengers on the cruise ship. She provided medical attention to critical sick passengers among them Brat and Rudy. Brat and Rudy had to stay in the hospital for few hours with some iv intravenous fluids to recover from a mild case of dehydration. They had removed their costume make up but retained their fake names. Doctor Chan did not need to check photo identification, because they were sick passengers on the ship due to the spoiled food. Doctor Chan had seen and attended about 800 sick passengers. Brat and Rudy did not have any peculiar sign or symptom from the rest of the passengers.

Ron and Pete check in a modest motel, they could not leave Barcelona until Rudy and Brat health condition improved. One day later the four of them took a direct flight back home. They landed in the early afternoon, after 13 hours flight. Ron told everyone at the airport while waited for the luggage: 'go home and rest for a day. We all need to get back to our jobs if we still have them. I'll check on you guys' tomorrow late afternoon. This was a good business trip, too bad that illness got us at the end. We will have our profits in a few days. Rudy and Brat, if you guys need anything let me know, you are not on your own.'

Brat replied: 'thanks bro.' Rudy said: 'I appreciate the offer.'

Rudy walked in home and set his luggage on the floor, after closing front door immediately texted Angela, it was just after four in the afternoon. He sent a simple salute.

Rudy: 'Hi Angie, I'm just got back home from a long trip, I confess I'm very tire. I also need to recover from a bad case of food poisoning. I'll be ok, I wanted to check with you. I miss you a lot.'

Angela heard the phone notification, but she was busy with many emails to read and replied from her job. Ten minutes came to be twenty and then it was time to go home. She logged out her computer and closed her desk, then she read the text notifications. Rudy was back, it was a bittersweet text. She re-read the last affirmation, 'I miss you a lot' She uttered her response: 'I miss you too.' The wish to see Rudy and talk to him was almost overwhelming. Angela texted back asking how serious his health condition was. Rudy was embarrassed about his health condition; he was not completely recovered. He told Angela: 'I need to rest; I'm recovering for the time being.'

Angela resolved to called and asked: 'what exactly is your condition? Have you seen a doctor?'

Angela's questioning conveyed her concerns for Rudy's well-being. She also presented evidence of a deep sentiment, a feeling that she can't declare untrue. Rudy heard a melody in her insistence about his condition. It was Angela's tone of voice. Rudy had texted a magical declaration in a sincere mode. Rudy did not know what he had done. Rudy said: 'hi Angie, is a long story but I saw a doctor and stayed in a hospital for few hours with an IV to treat my dehydration. I'm much better now, as I said I need to rest, and I'll be ok.' Angela said: 'Ok, I can stop by your place to bring you some soup, you need to eat along the resting.' It was impossible to say no for Rudy, the longing to see her was greater than his humiliation, he accepted her kind offer.

TRUTH SHALL ENDURE

ngela came to visit Rudy at his apartment after work and brought him the soup.

Angela wore a smile that was accentuated by a light lip stick. She had the pair of earrings with an Indian touch, one small light-yellow feather on each white gold earring that Rudy bought for her on an occasion. Rudy had forgotten about the earrings. Angela's blouse was the right red Burgundy to contrast the light yellow of the feather earrings. She came to the front door and rang the doorbell. Rudy had unlocked the door and posted a small note for Angela. Angie, please come in. She walked in 'saying hello, anyone home?' Rudy was seating in the living room and greeted Angela.

Rudy said with an apprehensive voice: 'hi Angie, how are you?'

Angela felt nervous for a reason she did not want to acknowledge, she just said: 'hi how are you?' Rudy with a wide smile responded: 'I'm ok, but how are You?'

Rudy: 'I'm better but still feeling weak, I guess due to my dehydration. Oh my! You look charming! Nice set of earrings!' Their eyes locked in a moment and Angela confirmed what she suspected. She had to focus and answered.

Angela: 'thanks. You bought me the earrings somewhere in Barcelona. But let's talk about you. Your weakness could be also due to the infection, do you still have some antibiotics?'

Rudy: 'yeah, I should finish them tomorrow. I also have a doctor's appointment. Thanks for the soup it is delicious, I feel my stomach kind of tender and can't eat a lot yet.'

Angela: 'Don't rush it, is better to take it easy. Keep drinking fluids through the day.' Angela went to the kitchen to get a glass of water, and brought it to Rudy asking him: 'Now tell me what happen?'

Rudy could not ignore how attentive she was by bringing a glass of water, he said: 'oh, is no big deal, I feel stupid, you know.'

Angela sat next to him and placed her right hand over his shoulder when she said: 'please don't say that. We all can get sick from time to time even if we are careful. But really tell me what happen, I would like to know how your trip was besides you getting sick.'

Rudy could not believe the girl of his dreams was so close to him and insisting to know the truth. Rudy had enough strength to handle only one affair, the story behind him getting sick, but not the real job they went to do, he said: 'well, the "job" went well I suppose, my friend Brat also got sick. We think it was some kind of contamination of the food in the kitchen where the food was prepared. We know it was not intentional but an accident. Good thing it happened in our way back home after we had finish with the job.'

Angela: 'Oh good thing! You said, what kind of job was this?'

His heart rate was getting faster, and he was sitting down not moving at all, but he can feel the anxiety was getting too high. His hands started to feel sweaty, and he could not fully answer to the simple question. Rudy's mind went through most of the moments of the robbery with a lighting speed. He was not prepared to answer such question in a convincing manner. All he could utter was uhm, well, …

Angela observed how his demeanor changed from feeble of being sick to a nervous and uncomfortable person. She noticed that he started to sweat a little on his forehead. He gave a quick glimpse to her and try to simulate a smile. Rudy kept looking to the floor, then pass his hand on his forehead, to dry his sweat in a casual way. He knew Angela was observing with all her attention and focus on every detail on his torment. Rudy was doomed.

Then he looked at the ceiling, at this point in a moment of recovery he thought about Pete's task, hacking the alarm system.

He said: 'my friend had a job to check a system that the owner of a commercial place needed to modify, I was his assistant, even though I'm not much of a techie.'

Angela fixed her eyes focus laser on Rudy as she said: 'so you're not qualified as a techie, but this friend of yours, takes you away, and gets you sick. What was more valuable? Go away for a job even though you are not qualifying or continue with your classes and obtain your certificate.'

Rudy wished he could disappear at that instant, he was sorry, but he mumble: 'well, you know,..we, I mean, he is a good friend, and how was I supposed to know that the food was contaminated?'

Angela was frustrated, but she felt compassion when she saw Rudy genuine sorry, she added: 'Rudy, I'm sorry that you are sick. All I want is that you realize that when you decide to do something valuable, and you abandon it not for an emergency there are consequences good and not so good. Besides when you signed up for a class you are giving your word to stay committed and do your best for you, for your future and for your teacher. I understand that Pete is a good friend, but it was not an emergency, he could respect your decision about pursuing your desire to obtain a certificate.'

Rudy could melt with such grace, Angela's voice had all the wisdom and love he needed, Rudy said: 'Angie, thanks, I suppose you are right.' He thought without saying a loud word, 'but you don't understand even if I tell you what the real job was.'

After this moment Rudy became silent and did not say much. Angela just looked at him and realized that Rudy was embarrassed and probably needed to be alone.

Angela: 'I got to go now. Call me if you need something. I hope you get better soon. I miss you too. Take care.'

Rudy looked at her, gave her a smile and said: 'what! Oh yeah, I miss hearing your voice. I'll make it up to you, thanks.'

Rudy had a heavy dose of Angela's love. It was more than he could handle. He knew she care for him. He needed to correct his actions. The thoughts about Angela's care were slowly replace for his actual condition. Rudy was alone in his apartment and did not have any sense of time, but he started to regret his involvement with the band to rob the jewelry stores. He felt so tired and drained, he could not even think on how much money he may get from the loot. He came to contemplate his resignation from the band and just walk away from everything, but he knew it was not that simple. There was also that stupid oath. He was involved deep enough, he knew too much, they probably will not let him go without a valid explanation. What could he do tell everything to Angela then ask her for help? Now that was even more ludicrous. Rudy asked himself: 'how the heck did I get into this? I'm trap.'

Jack Wayne felt sympathy for the affliction of Rudy and exclaimed: 'was there any way to escape or just leave the band?'

Miller answered: 'there was an incorrect allegiance for the faulty reason. Let's see what law enforcement was up to at this point on the story.'

Detective Liam Collection of Details

The police of Lyon went to check the crime scene on 19 Rue Paul Bert, the store Bijouterie Joaillarie Salam, and on 3 Rue Simon Maupin, the store called Teller Jewelry. The crimes were committed on the same day few minutes apart. The report stated the description for the assailants was the same on both stores. The employees' testimony on both stores, indicated the attackers were either from England or Australia due to their accent. No fingerprints were found on either store. There was a piece of chewing gum on the alarm control panel, and a couple of cigarette butts on the floor outside the second store. The police lab report provided samples of DNA but no matches through the criminal records from local data base. Substantial lost was reported from the store Bijoutere Joaillarie.

The insurance company called monsieur Laurent due to his expertise in claims from robbery. Monsieur Laurent came to visit the store he learned that the description and accent of the men who robbed the store was like the robbery still unresolved in Monaco at Le Diamand Fou, from about a year, which is an ongoing investigation.

Immediately, he called detective Liam and informed him about this situation. He remembered how detective Liam had traced the evidence to establish few similarities. Suspect's description and accent was a common thread in both cases. Perhaps the same men were back on business. Detective Liam following a comparable process did not find any leads but there was a common factor, cruise ships come, and their passengers come to town for a short time.

Detective Liam sent a notification to cities that have port for cruise ships about the robberies targeting specifically jewelry stores. He included few details about the suspects British accent and maybe four or more in the same group or possible more than one group. The suspects are to believe travel as passengers in the cruise ships. He also asked to notify his office of any robberies in the future.

He checked the ships that were in town the day of the incident and he called the ship office to inquire about any unusual event when the ship was in town.

The report from the ship indicated only an incident that was label a matter of safety hygiene. Further details were not available at this time due to ongoing settlement between the cruise ship insurance and passengers. Detective Liam had to use all his police influence and obtain an order to have the ship office disclose further details of such incident. The full report including medical details was presented to detective Liam. Perhaps this was an unexpected lead to something more concrete. Detective Liam reviewed the other stops for the ship and called the other police department cities to check if there were any robberies while the ship was in their towns providing the dates. One other report came with a robbery on Bijouterie Ciotat Or, a jewelry store in Cassis town. A city known for its fish specialties and port destination of cruise ships.

Gaspard and Basile worked the day of the armed robbery. Their testimonies were taken at the store when police responded to the call denouncing the theft. Basile insisted the accent was Australian, although one of the suspects said few words in bad French pronunciation. Gaspard had the opinion the accent was closer to English from Great Britain. Marius the third employee, had called in sick and missed the trauma of a dreadful episode. 'Why was this mentioned in the testimony?' asked detective Liam. Gaspard pointed to the fact Marius was trained with the special arm forces unit and if he had been at the store that day, it would have made more difficult for the robbers to overcome three instead of two employees. This gave detective Liam a pattern for the robberies. He believed to be true, the assailants of Le Diamant Fou store in his own city, Monaco, Equestrian Shop in La Roche Guyun City, near Paris, and now Bijoutere Joaillarie, and Teller Jewelry in Lyon were the same individuals. These men also traveled on the cruise ships as regular passengers. Now he needed to find images from the cruise ships that match the images from the stores video surveillance. Then he could interview crew members of the ships, check the list of British passengers, or with British background. He also can review the tickets purchase records; he hoped this will provide a better lead towards the criminals.

It took several days for detective Liam to put together the information and book the appointments with the ship offices. Then, he set up interviews with members of the crews that had plenty of interaction with passengers. Detective Liam met manager signor Gino and together discussed the best way to hold a meeting with the crew. Explain to them the situation to request details that they remember from the suspects. Detective Liam showed the surveillance video from the jewelry stores to the cruise ship crews. Most of the crew remembered the passenger with the marked British accent. Detective Liam asked signor Gino about the safety hygiene incident and through him the name of the doctor who treated the passengers that became ill was disclosed.

Destiny Set in Motion

Detective Liam paid a visit to Doctor Chan.

When detective Liam walked into her office, Doctor Chan was surprised to have a visit without previous notice. Doctor Chan had taken the medical doctor position on a cruise ship to travel overseas, practice her profession, receive compensation, and visit cities that she only read and watched some videos posted by travelers. She enjoyed the idea of visiting few places, but planning the trips includes air fare, lodging, packing luggage and a detailed itinerary which was too much work for her. The position for a medical doctor in a cruise ship provided lodge without checking into a series of hotels. The job fitted her remarkable, for a season. This was her last cruise, and she had much paperwork to finalize, before she headed back home.

Detective Liam greeted her, then introduced himself as the police officer in charge of the investigation of a series of robberies. He begun to explain the situation. Doctor Chan intervened to ask: 'what does it have to do with me? You are unannounced, I'm busy. This police business is taking too much time.' Detective Liam asked her to let him finish. He said: 'you will understand in a minute, right after I show you the video and you can tell me about any of your patients.' Doctor Chan told him: 'now you are expecting information that I don't even have.' She asked him: 'if you are police how come you are not wearing your uniform?' He answered: 'I'm a detective, they don't provide a uniform for my job. Here is my badge.'

The interruption to Doctor Chan from the police came at the worst moment.

Detective Liam showed for a short moment his badge, then put it back in his pocket, the other hand with his index finger on his lips thinking. Then he added: 'Doctor Chan I apologize for being rude. I'm very sorry, I need to make an appointment at your convenience, you could grant me the minutes when it suits your schedule, then I'll explain the facts, and leave you alone. You are very busy.'

When Doctor Chan heard this, she also had a moment of silent, she thought: 'he is showing courtesy, perhaps he will not waste my time after all.' She resolved to accept the apology and hear what he had to say. She was forming the idea of a police officer being rude and without manners. But detective Liam had changed his approach. She added: 'you are right you needed an appointment, but instead you used a poor judgment by walking into my office asking questions. I accept your apology; you have ten minutes.' She watched the seconds hand moving from number ten to eleven, at her clock hanging over her desk. Detective Liam looked at the clock as well and thanked her. He proceeded with the explanation in the jewelry stores robbers modus operandi. 'In consequence they must be in the cruise at the time of the food poisoning incident. You probably treated some of them. The video from the jewelry store will help to identify any of the suspects. I am asking if you could recognize one or more, please tell me. You are not in danger.'

Doctor Chan watched detective face for a short moment, she felt reassurance, and responded: 'let's see the video again, please.' The tension in the room dropped. They both sense relief. Doctor Chan was hesitant to trust completely detective Liam, although he had shown indications of good manners. She was at ease to say the least.

The video unveiled different men from the sick passengers. The faces were not fully visible, but showed enough for Doctor Chan to determine they were not the same individuals. Doctor Chan explained she treated only two men with British accent. The video displayed three. She added: 'one was severe enough that needed IV to help with dehydration.'

Detective Liam considered the possibility of more members as part of the band. 'There are four different suspects in the other robberies. They must travel together. Perhaps only two became sick.'

Detective Liam started to suspect that the culprit could had some kind of costume and makeup that he had removed when he became ill. Detective Liam before leaving Doctor's Chan office, asked for any possible DNA trace from the time of the treatment. She answered: 'there are files with personal information from the patients, but now no DNA samples. I will pull the files and have them ready for you.' Detective Liam looked at the clock and the ten minutes granted had pass, in fact it was close to forty minutes. He decided to come back to check the files. He asked Doctor Chan: 'could I come back in couple hours to see the files?' She had turned back towards her desk and only replied: 'sure, I'll have them ready.' Doctor Chan's personality and professionalism matched detective's Liam. Task oriented very professional no nonsense but there was something that she could not figure-out about the detective, his personality had an attractive component. She dismissed the lingering sound of his voice as he said: 'I'll be back in couple hours to check the files.' She did not have time to find the files, there was no assistant to delegate such chore. However, something prompted to stop what she needed to do and, pull the files to look which was the right patient according to her memory. There were many sick males, but only three had severe case of dehydration and needed IV. She remembered that, but only she could recall the charge. It took close to thirty minutes for her to find the right file.

Doctor Chan had not stop for her lunch because she had worked through her mealtime finding the right files for detective Liam. When he walked in, she handled him the files, to her surprise detective Liam asked her if she care to eat something. She asked: 'what do you mean?' Detective Liam: 'you need to take your lunch, I appreciate your help, but please don't skip your lunch over this.' Doctor Chan could not help that she found him thoughtful. Doctor Chan mind set, task oriented and at the same time her vocation to care for others. She recognized the attentiveness from others. What made this time more relevant! It was from a police detective. They are supposed to be rustic and austere. A smile appeared on her face as she nodded. 'Do you care to eat something while we review the records,' she asked? Detective Liam was not prepared for such replied, and stumble on words. 'I did not mean to impose on you any of police business, the least that I can offer is company. Yes, it is my pleasure to joint you for a bite.'

She presented the medical files that she had from the passengers considered "persons of interest." That included a medical record indicating bios, blood pressure, temperature, height and weight.

There were two patients who presented symptoms of nausea, vomiting related to Norwalk virus. Three days later same patients suffered diarrhea, abdominal pain, headache, and low-grade fever related to campylobacter jejune. Doctor Chan suspected the two men who she remembered clear, were infected by two different meals. The two men had eaten food while they were in town, the same day they had eaten food at the ship. The files had the personal data name, address, and city of origin stated from the passenger list filled handwritten by each patient.

Detective Liam made a copy for his investigations. He noticed there were four passengers' males from the same city. Doctor Chan disclosed the coincidence share between the four passengers from the list and her own personal place of residence. She said: 'I live in San Francisco. I should see at least one of these patients for a follow-up once I return home, If he comes to see me.'

Detective Liam had a strong lead on the passengers who were sick, he needed to contact San Francisco authorities to send all the information. He needed them to check suspects home addresses confirm the dates of the cruise ship to match the days these passengers were out of town. He considered that personal data could be false.

Doctor Chan had scheduled a visit for further observation with the two passengers with severe cases since they reside in the same city.

The brits had no idea about the police investigation on the cruise ship, for this reason, Brat and Rudy did not have any reason to be suspicious to go and see a doctor the next day of their return. The follow-up for the food poisoning was schedule before they left the ship. The ship company had paid for these visits. The arrangement to cover all expenses was done as a gesture to correct the inconvenience to their guests. The day for the doctor's appointment Brat did not feel good, but it was not related to the food poisoning, he was exhausted felling the full effects of jet lag. He decided not to go out at all. His recovery from the intestines was 80 per cent. Rudy was feeble from jet lag, and residual effects from the food poisoning. He did not have any desire to go and see the doctor, but he knew Angela would kill him if he neglected the follow-up with the doctor. Rudy called Brat to check how he was doing. Brat did not answer nor replied to his text messages, this indicated to Rudy that Brat was not doing anything including talking to anybody. Rudy had the intention to call Angela to tell her he was not going to see the doctor because he was very tired from the trip. He was much better from the food poisoning, but there was no point attempting to trick anyone specially Angela about his poor health. Rudy, then mastered all his strength and went to the doctor's office.

SFPD did check the addresses provided by detective Liam, results: Street name exist, house number nonexistent, police rendered as false information. The police also investigated the credit cards that were used to purchase the tickets, it turned out the payment was done using a combination of gift certificates, cash, and money order. There was no way to trace the passengers, the police did not have a clear picture of the passengers, they only had the obscure photo from the surveillance video at the jewelry stores. Detective Liam did not provide detail information about Doctor Chan follow-up with two suspects from the cruise ship. Doctor Chan did not know that personal information from the passengers' cruise ship who live in San Francisco was false. When Rudy visited her office for the follow-up, he was never requested to confirm or rewrite his home address from the cruise company's office.

One week later after SFPD sent the results of the investigation to detective Liam, he decided to take a more direct involvement in the case. He collected all the information in a chronological order from the first robbery to the last robbery. In every burglary included testimonies from employees who stated the distinct British accent from the suspects. The still images from the store surveillance videos. The strong lead he had indicated San Francisco as the possible town where the suspects live. He presented the long file to his superior with the request to travel. It was very convincing. He had to answer one question. 'Who do you know in San Francisco?' His answer Doctor Chan the medical doctor who had a follow-up with two of the passengers from a cruise ship that was in the same city of the last burglary. The evidence turned compelling; he was granted to travel with the full support of SFPD.

Detective Liam had requested an appointment with Doctor Chan before he left Monaco. He stated the nature of the meeting police business. He received a confirmation for his police business meeting with an added note from Doctor Chan requesting more information about the length of his trip to San Francisco.

Detective Liam did answer her inquire with a short: 'thank you Doctor Chan, I will provide further details as soon as I have an update. I have seven days to examine the personal information of the suspects. The day of my departure is October 10 in the afternoon, I should arrive in San Francisco on October 11, I have a layover in New York for 6 hours.'

The day for the flight from Monaco the pilot became ill there was an unusual delay for the airline to replace the whole flight crew. Detective Liam arrived in San Francisco on October 11 late afternoon. He sent an email to Doctor Chan before he departed from Monaco about his delay. Doctor Chan read the email and felt a bit apprehensive. It was until October 12 detective Liam could talk to her. He was pleased to see her again. She was glad to see him also, she asked: 'how was the flight?' Detective Liam gave a brief recount for the cause of the last-minute delay. Strangely enough Doctor Chan found in him a familiar friendly face, they had developed a work relationship that detective Liam kept very professional.

Detective Liam was tired from the jet lag, but he had anticipation to hear what Doctor Chan could tell him about the suspects. She remembered clearly Rudy as the young patient, although the British accent was absent. The young patient had recovered nearly 100 percent, he did not need more medication. Doctor Chan had taken the temperature along with the rest of the vitals. Against rules she kept the tip off the thermometer with a sample of saliva in a sealed container. She provided physical description, height, weight along with DNA sample. Detective Liam had the police to check for criminal background. No criminal records matched the DNA sample. The conversation between detective Liam and Doctor Chan started with the subject of the suspects, and all the information gather, yet there was no single individual arrested, or called for an interview. Then they talked about the remaining time detective Liam had before returning home. They developed a professional relationship that gave detective Liam a pleasant environment, Doctor Chan changed her perception about the police image. She found detective Liam very discipline at the same time engaging. His edifying remarks about providing DNA sample from the suspect encourage her inclination to create a 3-D image from the DNA sample. A personal aspiration for a long time that Doctor Chan had waited to have the required elements to venture in the combination of sciences and art to create something more like an image, something tangible close to a human replica from DNA. She did not disclose her intention to detective Liam. She was aware the time available in the city for detective Liam was running out.

Doctor Chan was curious to see if she could use the lab for the recreation of the face using the DNA sample, unfortunately the face that she could recreate was incomplete, although she could remember enough to fill the missing details from her memory. Doctor Chan worked nonstop for the next 20 hours. She came up with a three-dimension image that she converted into a three-dimensional face that resembled the young patient. It was close enough to identify the real person. Doctor Chan was proud of her artistic hobby. She hoped the bust will impress, detective Liam, and help to apprehend the suspect.

Detective Liam received a call from Doctor Chan indicating that she had something very important that might help him to identify one of the persons of interest. Detective Liam looked at his watch to verify the time. It seemed odd to him this late into the evening, have an invitation to meet at the lab where she had done some work. Doctor Chan wanted to talk about this mysterious piece of information, and she did not provide specifics over the phone. He agreed to come and meet even if it was pass ten in the evening. The peculiar detail about this call was Doctor Chan identify herself with her first name Judy, and she sounded a bit excited. Detective Liam was very surprise and impressed to see an image of the face of this man who could be one of the robbers. Now detective Liam had something factual and very recent. He emails his superior officer back in Monaco with the latest piece of identifiable information provide by his friend Doctor Chan. His stay in San Francisco for the investigation was extended for another 6 days.

TIME TO HUDDLE

When Ron left work for home, that afternoon the sun set earlier, in the past three days, the temperature had noticeable cool down. It had change from hot towards pleasant. It was like any other late summer day; the wind was gusting strongly. The season started to change. It was the first week of autumn.

Ron had been busy and did not realize how many weeks had gone since their last voyage, 'has it been four weeks? Or maybe more.' He asked himself, 'don't matter they had gone by quickly. We had three successful cruise ship operations, it is time to go back to our jewels,' he texted Brat. He had not talk to Brat or check on him.

He himself had recovered from the food poisoning acquired at the ship towards the end of Lyon-Barcelona cruise ship trip. He learned from Pete that Rudy was doing much better. They had a mutual agreement: do not interact among each other the days following the heist. It was a preventive measure in case police were following any of the members. Ron sent a second message to Brat asking to have a meeting with everyone. 'We need to go over details, also want to know of any changes from any of you.' When they met their conversation took place on Brat's apartment.

Ron: 'Hi Brat, how are you doing?'

Brat: 'Hi Ron, doing ok, it's good to see you.'

Ron: 'How is everything?'

Brat: 'Everything seems to be good, I mean, nothing unusual as far as I can tell. How are you?'

Ron: 'I'm well, I noticed the season is changing, the sun in setting earlier, and we should consider what is next for our coffers.

We have a good profitable enterprise. You know that it has been few weeks since our French trip, I guess we all had been busy, I haven't check on things, I mean is time to review and rather than wait to see if anything happens, we should be looking if there is anything that indicate to us, that they are after our enterprise.'

Brat: 'you're right! What do you suggest?'

Ron: 'For starters tell me how Pete, and Rudy are. Do you know any changes on their part?'

Brat: 'Pete, I have not heard anything from him for about two weeks, which means no need to be alarm. Rudy has finally recovered from the FP; you know food poison. I need to call him and check on him.

Ron: 'Good please do that. Later, today and the rest of this week let's look in the news for anything about our trip. I will send a message to New York and see if they ready for another purchase of our product. They should know if police are looking for some of our jewels. By this weekend we all should get together and discuss our next trip.

Brat: 'I will look in the news for anything, I will send notifications to Pete, and Rudy.

Pete had done three jobs of installing alarm systems for three small warehouses as an independent contractor. He still doesn't have a contractor's license.'

Ron: 'That sounds great. How did he get the jobs?'

Brat: 'The first one was a referral from a friend. The other two jobs were a result of his first job installation because he had custom some of the features and created an additional code to increase security the owner was impressed and very pleased with his work and ethics. The owners of the other two warehouses had asked Pete's friend for information about his custom alarm system. Pete was recommended on high esteem.' Ron asked Brat 'how is Pete responding to all this?' 'He seems to be content and excited.' Brat responded. Ron said: 'I'm glad.'

RUDY RENOUNCES OR AT LEAST HE TRIES

Couple of days after Rudy had the visit from Angela and he had gone to see the doctor for the last time, he decided to call Pete to see how he was. He needed to talk to his friend. Rudy wanted to work all details about leaving the band. Pete was the one who recruited him. Rudy had joined the group only because his friend Pete had asked. Pete should be the first to know he was leaving the band. Rudy did not know the band had more projects for everyone. Pete answered his phone looking at the caller's name. Pete: 'Well how are you doing mate?'

Rudy: 'Hi Tin Man, how is everything?'

Pete: 'All is good, hey listen wanna get together for beer or coffee?'

Rudy: 'Sounds great. Where at the Caffe e Dolce?'

Pete: 'You know it, see you there in twenty minutes.'

Rudy had time to get ready and felt very animated to have a chance to talk to Pete.

Pete sensed in Rudy's voice his health was much better. He felt pleased.

They both met at their favorite coffee shop.

Rudy genuine wanted to tell Pete about leaving the band. He did not want Pete to misunderstand his motives. His number one reason to leave the band is moral conviction, sounds very odd, strange, peculiar or whatever adjective needs to be but they all are the same. Rudy did not know how to start the conversation; all he knew was 'I got to tell him somehow.'

Pete and Rudy engaged in a conversation concerning consequences of what is illicit. Pete argued most big businesses operate in such way and no one does anything to change the procedure, granted, Pete added, 'it is unwritten, and it seems there are no consequences.' Rudy paused briefly then said: 'it seems there are no immediate repercussions, which encourage to continue the immoral character of those involve, I can tell you this in reality it prolongs the decadence of the whole enterprise.'

Pete was a bit perplexed.

Rudy sustained: 'we are not big business.'

Rudy proposed: 'in life and in everything what we do there is a moral component. In other words, we say or just think out loud "what's in it for me?' Then they discuss the moral part of the business, the gain for them which is not related to drugs, or murder. Pete gets on the defensive side protecting what they had done, reminding Rudy, 'everyone is dishonest from lawyers, to cops, to supervisors cheating anybody all the time. For instance, car salespeople they always lie, insurance companies try to charge for everything and then when the client has a claim, they pay a lot less or avoid altogether paying. Cable companies don't disclose hidden fees but charge everything. You even hear from the Bible those famous tax collectors from Rome, always charge more than the actual tax.'

Rudy said: 'that is all true but does not mean we have to do the same if we have an alternative, besides stealing is for fools, the lawyers, cops, or companies may think they are smart and they get the counsel of attorneys, they label it wisdom but why fools should have money in hand to buy counsel or wisdom when they can't understand it. Get it, I know you do we are not fools.'

Then Rudy points to the positive, 'look at you, you are a good installer, you can make enough money by working in your own business, what's more you really enjoy your profession.'

Pete conceded and in one last attempt to defend his position added: 'whatever you steal you don't lose any part on taxes.'

Pete's phone rang. The caller was Tin Man, as Pete had it on his contacts. Brat called to communicate a meeting for the group. 'We need to reconnect and plan the next business trip.' Brat said and asked to tell mate. Pete answered for both without Rudy's opinion. Pete told Brat, in a serious business tone of voice: 'for sure Tin Man, we can make it. What time? Eighteen hours. Where? Gru's place. We'll be there. I'll bring some snacks.' Rudy saw Pete's demeanor, and knew it was a business meeting. Pete looked at Rudy to say: 'Friday at 6:00 pm at Gru's place. Don't be late, I got to work until 5:00 in a system for an office. I'll come as soon as I finish.' Rudy did not say anything just lowered his head and thought for a moment. It was an awkward silent moment for Pete, he decided to end the conversation to tell Rudy: 'Listen mate I got to go now. You're, ok?' Rudy looked at him and Said: 'oh yea! I'll see you Techie.'

Ron waited for the group then greeted each one with genuine gladness, they responded with equal enthusiasm. The whole group was happy to get together to catch up with the lates personal activities since their trip. Ron asked everyone for any unusual event. 'We just need to continue to practice caution in case the police were investigating. No one had any unusual report.'

Ron proceeded to announce some of their loot had been sold, and short after each one received a substantial amount of money which was just part of the total profit so far. He reminded everyone that this money was consider "hot" and they could not spend it freely because that will surely be the last time, they will have freedom.

'We just don't know how much the authorities know about each of us. We assume they are watching us. Maybe the FBI is waiting for our next move. A spending spree, or a lavish purchase will call attention. Police will be so suspicious and may ask too many questions and someone will end in police custody until everyone is caught.' Ron advised to keep the money, if possible, in an account in a foreign bank. 'Wait for few months then test the field and spend some. Take a vacation, use some of your profit.' Brat was not in complete agreement. He wanted to spend some money in the coming weeks. Use up some of it, maybe not a whole lot, but he wanted to take a short trip, enjoy fancy meals, and drinks. Live a little maybe get some fine clothing.

Pete wanted to use some of the money to open his own shop for the alarm system installation, but he needed few elements, an office with furniture and equipment, some tools and a small inventory of parts. These commodities cost money but will provide the image of a sanctioned business.

Rudy was not sure if he even wanted any of that money. He was having regrets about the whole operation. The last conversation, he had with Angela, made him feel embarrassed about what he was part of, and what he had done. For Rudy the only good deed he had done was taking his classes towards the sound technician certificate. He needed to focus on his biggest goal a degree in sound engineering.

Ron listened to everyone's comments then suggested to remain calm. He handed the money and reminded that everyone was responsible for the whole group. He said: 'consider the consequences of your actions. You don't need to go out to blow a whole lot of money.' He turned to Brat: 'go ahead Tin Man take your vacation is yours, but be careful, don't attract attention and get in trouble, actually get us all in trouble.'

Brat nodded in agreement with Ron. He looked around the room to the rest of the group, everyone had an expression of expectation. He kept silence for few seconds that felt more like minutes. No one had an idea of what Brat was thinking, not even Ron. Brat took the moment to observe his friends' faces. He drew a smirk and apologized to the group. He said: 'friends forgive me. I realize my excitement got the best of me. Ron is right should I or any of us start spending too crazy someone will notice. We have an enterprise that is very profitable, and this could be for long time. I will plan this trip and expenses with Ron's help, I got to be prudent.'

Brat's apology, and comments evoked Pete to realized that he also needed to rethink his plan, it was better for him to get a small loan for his startup company and then pay off the loan in a monthly installment with the money from the loot. In the long run that would be a better move to appear legal and not raise any suspicion.

Ron agreed and encouraged this plan.

Ron was pleased to know that Pete was working on security systems. No one thought the possibility of police linking Pete's ability and skills with hacking alarm systems. For all of them hacking the alarm systems was not only genius from Pete but also a clean job. No way to trace him, no witness, and no need to worry.

Rudy made everyone known, he did not have any plans for lavish spending or exotic trips. It sounded perfect for Ron. 'Mister Mate, just keep a low profile and let the months goby before spending some money. That is if you don't really need to get something. You don't have to suppress your needs either.'

Rudy mentioned that as soon as he completed his classes for the sound technician certificate, he was going out of town for a short time perhaps four days and spend a little bit of his reward. Everyone demanded from him to reveal who is the lucky lady. Do we know her? What's her name? Come on! We all want to know.

He dismissed the whole thing as a joke. Rudy answered by saying: 'I'm not about to give my share of the profits away.'

Ron told everyone in three or five weeks they will be back together planning their next project for the following summer. Brat said: 'we are done with our meeting. We can leave one by one with caution.' Pete was ready to leave when at a distance an emergency vehicle with the sirens approaching rather quickly, caused him to stop and listened for a short moment. Ron commented: 'there is no need to be panicky, sirens at a distance does not mean cops are coming looking for us.' The group gave a smirk dismissing the shared unsettle feeling of concern. Short after they could hear another vehicle with the sirens. Ron got up from his chair and said: 'no need to be concerned, although, something is going on.' Pete was close to the window and peeked, he could not see anything unusual.

The loud sound of a blast from a strong explosion prompted everyone to lay down on the ground, a qick response to protect themselves. The sound of the sirens was much closer. Ron yelled: 'everybody out!' Pete was closer to the door, he opened and ran out followed by Rudy, Brat and Ron. They could see a big cloud of dark smoke coming down from behind the homes.

The sounds of metal crunching, wood crumbling with the intense flames from the rapid growing fire, could be clearly heard on the street. The strong smoke smell was filling the immediate area, Ron told everyone: 'let's walk to the corner where the smoke and fumes are less intense.

The building behind Ron's neighbor was on fire. The explosion came from the garage. The sound of glass being broken and people running from their homes gave a sinister atmosphere. Emergency vehicles passed by with the sirens open. Ron's house and his immediate neighbors were not in danger. The wind was blowing in the opposite direction of his block. The fire grew quickly toward the adjacent buildings away from Ron's Street. Police closed the surrounded streets to all traffic. Pete, Brat and Rudy can't leave on their vehicles. Evacuation took place on the three blocks next to the fire. Ron and the rest of the band stood mesmerized watching the heavy big clouds of smoke blowing away from where they were. People ran toward the actual site of the growing fire. 'Not a good idea,' said Ron. 'Let's stay here for now, looks like the wind is taking the danger away from us.' Brat pulled a cigarette and started to smoke. Rudy looked at him and his cigarette without any word, but his silence said a lot. Brat shrugged his shoulders and said: 'it calms my nerves.'

Bystanders and neighbors commented no one was injure, despite the strong explosion. The sky was dark. The uncertainty of the fire, the dark night and the nature of their meeting had a unsetting atmosphere with the group. After forty minutes Brat said: 'looks like the firefighters have some control over. It is late, I think I'm walking home. The cops are not going to open the streets any time soon.' Pete asked Rudy: 'hey mate wanna come along? We are not taking our vehicles tonight.' Rudy said: 'what a mess, wonder what cause the fire. Let's go home Techie.' Ron stood behind looking as everyone walked away until they turned the corner.

The night grew darker and the intensity of the flames from the fire were reduced by the firefighters; the smoke was not visible, but its presence felt very strong. The damage left some people with no shelter, few homes were destroyed and few more were condemned. The material lost was high for the community. Most neighbors were traumatized, some could not fall asleep for the rest of the night. The news crews conducted some interviews from those affected by lost due to the fire. The lost was beyond what most insurance will cover. One or two witnesses who did not suffer physical property lost did answer questions from the media. From preliminary inspection the cause of the fire was a heavy piece of equipment run with the wrong electrical extension cord that over-heated and provoked the fire. The electrical cord was plug in the garage that had flammables containers such as two propane gas containers, many old buckets of oil base paint, a container of ace-tone and two plastic containers of gasoline without the proper cap. One of the frightened neighbors mention he though a person was fleeing the place at the time of the explosion, in other words a sus-picion of criminal acts.

A SAD IMAGE.

The alarming fire episode is an analogy to the Brits projects. They were criminal acts, which had cause damage and property lost to the shop owners. The incidents had traumatized employees, no one had been seriously hurt, but they had suffered emotionally. The intensity of their robberies (flames) had left a trace of heavy smoke of a different kind. Part of the inner self of the band members was scorched, but they choose to numb that pain. Ron, Brat and Pete were standing in the mist of the flames, but perhaps intoxicated by the fumes of greed. Rudy was feeling the heat, besides he had Angela to talk to him into some sense, but his confused loyalty was his biggest smoke screen yet to overcome.

An Attempt to Confess

Rudy called Angela to ask her if she had any events planned over the weekend. It was Thursday, Angela volunteering schedule for the senior center was on Wednesday's evening and sometimes on Fridays. Rudy hoped this Thursday they could get together after work for a moment, he wanted to go with Angela on a short trip over the weekend. Rudy did not want Angie to feel being imposed or force to do anything, he rather wish for both to do something relaxing, something consider as loose from any rigid agenda.

The weather was changing for shorter days and the temperature was cooler after sunset. Angela was a bit tire but agreed to meet for a short time and have a snack rather than formal dinner. She chose the place, a small caffe. Let's meet with one condition, she said: 'I want to be home before it gets dark, let's meet at three in the afternoon.' Rudy couldn't be happier to hear Angela's voice in agreement. He needed to talk to Angela, having to be concise for time's sake was the best circumstance for him. Rudy told Angela: 'I surrender to your condition.'

Rudy had few thoughts among them celebrate his accomplishment at the end of the semester. Rudy had some homework to do, but he wanted to ask her about going out of town for a shot trip at the end of his classes.

Angela arrived couple of minutes early and she sat in a corner table next to a window. She could see the Street and look for Rudy, if Rudy came in by the other side of the store he would walk in the hallway before the corner table, and she would still see him before he can notice her. She was wearing her leather jacket, her favorite jeans, with the short boots and matching leather purse. She did dress very elegant unintentionally. After all they were having just a cup of coffee. It was until Rudy walked in through the hallway and she got up to greet him that she noticed herself on the glass door in front of their table. Rudy was speechless when she got up to say hello. Her radiant beauty caused Rudy to take a step aside and gesture with his hand from head to toe how elegant and pretty she was. Angela felt very pretty, and at the same time embarrass.

Rudy: 'Don't you look pretty!' His heart was about to leave his chest.

Angela: 'hi Rudy! Come on! This is informal.'

Rudy: 'Thank you Angie for coming and coming ever so pretty.'

Angela: 'oh Stop it! Tell me how you are?'

Rudy: 'I'm starving! Would you like something, I'm warning you I have some money and we can have anything.'

Angela: 'you're funny, I just having some coffee and maybe a small piece of pie.'

Rudy: 'I'll go and order right now, be back in a minute.' Rudy got back to the table with the coffee, a cold drink for him, and three pieces of pumping pie.

Angela: 'thanks Rudy, you are hungry, aren't you? I'm only eating a piece of the pie. The other two are yours. Now tell me how are doing from your food poison? '

Rudy: 'I'm recovered now. He looks down as he answers.'

Angela: 'but… what's wrong now?'

Rudy: 'I must decide about working with my friends and I'm not sure how they are going to react. It has to do with some projects that I helped them. They expect me to continue, but I would like to do my own and… '

Angela: 'and was wrong with that? They will understand, right?'

Rudy: 'probably not, is not that simple.'

Angela: 'why not? Just tell them find another person and that is!'

Rudy: 'oh no, you have no idea. This project took a long time to prepare, we spent lots of time working on many details, it was a high risk for all of us, but we learned our parts and the whole thing worked well, so far.'

Angela: 'sounds a big involvement How come you are not interested anymore?'

Rudy: 'I'm not sure if you should know this. I just rather not to be involved anymore.'

Angela: 'now that's intriguing mister! What's going on here? Is this illicit?' She lowers her voice as she says the word.

Rudy looks both ways before he says.

Rudy: 'I'm just telling you, not to inquire anymore, or mention because is better to just leave it on the surface. Please.'

Angela: 'Oh Rudy I just want to help you, I don't need to know any specifics, no names, no places, I just wish you to be well. Let me tell you this "two are stronger than one," we both can think better than just one, and perhaps we both can think in a solution or at the very least an alternative for you.'

Rudy: 'Angie you are so special (looking at her eyes) I did not want to meet you today to talk about my dilemma. Let me tell you why I ask you here. You know my classes end the first week of December; would you like to go for a short trip out of town just to celebrate with me that I have completed the first part of my certificate units?'

Angela: 'on a trip Out of town? Where? How long? Just the two of us? We are not married you know!

Rudy: 'oh please Angie don't get me wrong we can get separate rooms, I'm not trying to take advantage, Where? How does Carmel or Monterrey sound? How long? For three days if you can. Don't tell me right now think and if you can then we can plan it.'

Angela: 'hmm, I'm not sure if it's a good idea going on a trip with you even if it is for a day!'

Rudy: 'I was hoping that by now we trust each other.'

Angela: 'let me think about it for a couple of days, can't promise anything.'

Rudy: 'that's fine. Now Angie I hate to rush but I better get going because I have some homework to finish.' He got up and waited for Angela to stand up and motioned a hug for her. Angela stood up and gave him a hug.

Angela: 'call me next week. I'm glad that you are physically better. Take care.'

Rudy: 'Angie you look marvelous! I love it.'

Rudy left the coffee shop giving himself a review of how well he had handled the initial steps to plan his withdrawal from the band. He thought: 'I did tell Angie my intensions to leave the group, I kept from disclosing the horrible things, it was not easy, but I did. Now I have to think out how I'm stating my reasons to leave the Brits, I need to be judicious telling everyone and not depart as enemies.'

Jack Wayne raised his hand to ask a question. Miller paused, looked at him and raised his eyebrows.

Jack Wayne: 'was any penalty for leaving the group?'

Miller: 'No. But I wished for the band had a written rule stating a reason to expel a member and maybe impose a heavy fine in terms of charging some percentage from the profits. The short answer is no, no penalty it was simple no one can leave.'

UNCOVERING SOME HINTS

Detective Liam had a very difficult task ahead of him. He did not have much information to go on this complicated inquiry, other than the image recreated with the DNA sample that Doctor Chan had provided.

-There was no file with the local police or international criminal background.

-The only positive lead was the person who was treated for food poison on the ship. Doctor Chan had identified the patient with the British accent as the same with the severe case, but the follow-up patient did not look the same as the one on the ship and he spoke with hardly any British accent. Detective Liam suspected that the robbers had use make-up, and costumes to disguise their identity. He also supposed they spoke intentionally with British accent, during the burglaries, and when they were on the cruise. Beyond that not too many leads to go on. He reviewed the police reports of the robberies. Some of the details mentioned the malfunctioning of the alarm system turned off by somebody, in one of the jewelry stores. The three false alarms incidents before the robbery. Not a coincidence detective Liam thought, instead he wonders: 'could this faulty function be caused by the robbers themselves? Then I need to check how the alarm system had some sort of short circuit. Maybe induced by the robbers.'

He contacted SFPD to request assistance in a case that he did not have jurisdiction in the first place. He was not sure if the city could press charges to the suspects because no crime was committed within the city and county limits.

SFPD designated Lorraine Clarice Dufour as assistant to detective Liam. A young energetic student of criminal law who wishes one day in her future to be employ for the federal bureau of investigation. Lorraine Clarice Dufour was an intern for the police department. Detective Liam explained her the kind of information needed to gather and the importance to keep it confidential due to the international nature. Lorraine's enthusiasm to prove herself with the SFPD and with an international investigator gave her enough courage to do her best. She saw this work as an advantageous occasion to learn and gain experience. Her main task was to collect information of proficient technicians capable to hack alarm systems like those surveillance in the jewelry stores robbed.

Detective Liam provided all the data in regards of the systems hacked at the jewelry stores. She spent few hours learning about companies that operate and service the area. Companies that supply parts, but their focus is on sales of systems for professional installers. Companies that install and service security systems and monitor the surveillance are numerous and vary on size of their employees. There are many small independent contractors that do not even appear on review sites but have many jobs from referral customers. Assistant Lorraine called a few companies talked to some technicians about the likelihood of their systems to be hack. She collected the data she deduced many systems can be broken into and there are many techies capable of doing such tasks. This information was valuable but did not provide specifics for any suspects. Assistant Lorraine presented the preliminary results to detective Liam.

He agreed with his assistant then he said: 'we can't find a suspect to lead us to the band with this data. Clearly this is the wrong approach.' Lorraine needed to have a different way to embark on the case. Detective Liam gave assistant Lorraine couple of days to examine one more time the data. He did mention: 'we know the suspects were on a cruise.' It was enough input for assistant Lorraine to consider a different approach to her inquiry.

She started with the dates of the cruise ships on the Mediterranean from Nice, France to Barcelona, Spain. The police report listed the cities where the robberies had occurred, along the cruise ship itinerary. She looked for passengers arriving from San Francisco. Passengers who left from San Francisco the day or days before the departing date for the ship and had returned home in San Francisco at the end of the cruise.

Assistant Lorraine obtained a list from two cruise ships. One list from a cruise ship with only European passengers, no American vacationers. The second list from a ship that had shorted the initial timetable due to a medical situation. The list from this ship included the names of two patients who reside in San Francisco. Her list of names included gender, city of origin, addresses, first time taking a cruise, traveling with family or alone, and more data irrelevant to her investigation. It was optional for the passenger include title or profession. Some people listed their professional titles, medical doctors, attorneys, finances. Assistant Lorraine assumed the reason to include this sort of information was to promote themselves, and hope to generate some potential client or business. Not one had any job or listed as professional technician. The information from the passengers was correct, later confirmed by the SFPD, the exception four passengers' full information was false. Detective Liam was not surprised to learn the four travelers were from San Francisco. This was the only correct piece of information.

There was one person who visited Doctor Chan for a follow-up examination, because it was consider a severe case. When the patient filled the paperwork to update his medical record, the question of his occupation/profession was optional even though, he did not disclose his occupation, the suspicion for Lorraine was strong. She believed this was a good lead and notify detective Liam about her interesting findings. She presented her report on a Wednesday afternoon. At this point it was unknown if he was a computer technician

Detective Liam was very satisfied of Lorraine's hard work and congratulated her for an excellent job. Then he added, 'this analytical thinking will certainly make a difference as you examen all the facts and weave the events with the details. Many times, these details are there with the facts, but they are hidden. You will expand your vision.'

LOOKING FOR CONCRETE
PROOF UNFOLDS
INTO AN IDYLL

Detective Liam needed another image using the DNA from the second passenger who was treated, but his personal data was false. He called Doctor Chan the next day Thursday morning, asked her to meet with him to discuss something not related to her work. Doctor Chan agreed to meet with detective Liam, after work, although she kept wondering: 'what the reason could be to talk, there was no other reason, she thought!'

The meeting was in a small restaurant that she had suggested. Because detective Liam was a visitor in town, and he had complemented the city variety of restaurants, but did not know enough for an acceptable French food, he had pleaded Doctor Chan for her choice. Doctor Chan thought about the perfect place, a cozy French restaurant in a quiet Street of Glen Park neighborhood, Le Pettit Laurent.

She could not help to make herself more presentable for a date rather than a meeting related to work. The reservation was for six thirty in the afternoon. She left work at three to give herself plenty of time to go home to conduct a small trial applying herself some make-up. The thought of acting frivolous crossed her mind as she lightly applied the lipstick once, she looks herself on the mirror, then applied a second pass feeling brave, and uttering the words 'Judy you only live once."

She needed an elegant dress, but she looked at her plain blend dress robe. She was a bit frustrated. She came to almost cancelling the meeting which somehow it was converted into a date. She could not remember how the meeting stayed on her mind since she left for work early on that morning. Time was getting close, but she came to terms to wear her new year's gown and do herself the best hairdo possible giving the circumstances.

Doctor Chan was feeling silly and vaguely nervous when she arrived at the restaurant few minutes early without giving much thinking, she orders a bottle of wine. She does not drink but it was after she had ordered she realized that she was acting out of control. What is happening! She asked herself, unfortunately before she tried to answer her date arrives. Detective Liam was dressed very much like any workday. He noticed that Doctor Chan was different very different and almost did not recognize her. He did not think too much about that and proceed to thank her for coming and meet with him after work.

Detective Liam: 'hello doctor Chan, thank you for your kindness to give me some of your time after work. How are you?'

Doctor Chan: 'hi! You're welcome, I'm fine. Please just call me Judy. She felt her heart racing when he shook her hand and she held to his hand for a bit too long and even squeezed him a bit.'

Detective Liam: 'may I offered something to drink? Judy'

Doctor Chan: 'I… well yes! But I took the liberty to order something already if that's ok?'

Detective Liam smiled and said: 'yes.'

The waiter brought the bottle opened to serve two glasses, and asked if they were to order appetizers.

Detective Liam: 'asked for a recommendation about appetizers and agreed to what the waiter suggested.'

Detective Liam: 'proposed a toast: 'to Doctor Chan as acknowledgement for her contribution to resolve this rather complicated investigation.' He also added: 'by the way Doctor Chan, I mean Judy you look "pretty" tonight, are you going out with friends after wards? I promise not to hold you too long.'

Doctor Chan: 'oh thanks, I don't have any plans other than stay and help you in what you need me, I mean in what I can do for you.'

Detective Liam: 'I apologize for my plain appearance. Let me explain the reason that I ask you to come.'

Doctor Chan holding her chin between her folded hands and elbows resting on the table, just stared and said: 'please no need to apologize you are just fine, and just tell me what it is?'

Detective Liam explained the work that assistant Lorraine had done and what it meant to have an image of the other passenger who was treated by her after they returned from the cruise. He explained that the information of four passengers was false. It was the best lead that he had since the video's images, which they probably were not their true identities.

Doctor Chan kept listening but just stared at him all time, and at one point she sighted. She helped herself to another glass of wine. She was already intoxicated but not from the wine, but from the feelings that she was riding. They had a conversation about their respective backgrounds in terms of their native cities. What they did before working on their respective fields, how each other found their current jobs. They both share the similar reason of staying single and not currently dating anyone. They both were busy with their jobs. Doctor Chan enjoys a hobby experimenting the recreation of images from DNA samples, but her interest came after she read the article of DNA phenotype, although she was not doing it for criminal investigation. Detective Liam had a different hobby. He likes to play chess. He claims that thinking about the game helps him to analyze criminal cases and helps him to figure out certain details crucial to the answers. Doctor Chan did not ask what the reason was to ask her for the meeting, she was enjoying the evening. It dawned on her it has been a long time since she had a male company outside work. Detective Liam lost tract of time because her company was charming, besides the conversation was not related to work or the investigation rather about personal interests. A pleasant conversation since he had come to the states. At the end of dinner, detective Liam ask Doctor Chan to make a second image of the other patient that had a follow-up after the cruise.

Doctor Chan: 'I'll be delighted to provide you with another image. But the second patient did not show for his schedule visit. There is a way to retrieve his DNA. The medical cabinet aboard the ship has the blood sample. I need to call the captain to request the vial with the blood sample. How soon do you need it?'

Detective Liam: 'I don't want to impose, but at your earliest convenience.'

Doctor Chan: 'I can start this weekend, could you come to the lab and help me?'

Detective Liam: 'err, I'm not sure if I could be of any assistant to an artist, but sure I can come to help.'

Doctor Chan: 'could I ask you something, rather personal?'

Detective Liam: 'sure, I hope I can answer to your satisfaction.

Doctor Chan: 'what is your name? I mean your first name?'

Detective Liam: 'Nolan. He felt a bit awkward.'

Detective Liam: 'Judy this was a great place, the food is delicious, I must get going I have much work to do. If I'm helping you at the lab tomorrow, I mean Saturday, tomorrow is Friday, is it not? I better get going.'

Doctor Chan: 'oh my what time it is? I need to get home and get some preparations for the lab. Prior to the blood sample arrival. I thank you for the lovely evening, Nolan.'

The cruise ship sent the vial in a box to Doctor's Chan lab on an especial delivery.

They met at the lab to work over the weekend on creating the other image.

Now they have two images in 3D of passengers from the cruise ship that had the medical predicament. The information stated on the cruise when they booked the trip was false, but nevertheless the images were closer to their true resemblance.

At this time, it was unknown to detective Nolan that one of these individuals from the cruise ship his occupation was alarm system technician.

Lorraine took pictures of the images from the DNA and showed them to the clerk where the tickets were purchased, she mentioned the dates when the tickets were sold for the cruise. The clerk did not remember the person or any details, she told assistant Lorraine: you see there are so many clients going through our office, but there is a video camera in the ticket office. Lorraine saw the video, the recording from the day the tickets were sold showed a glimpse of a person that resembles Brat.

Next, she requested an appointment for detective Liam to see the video. Detective Liam compares one still image from the video to the 3D image there is a strong resemblance. It was not an identical picture, but it was close enough for detective Liam to have a first clear image of one of the suspects. He also knew there were three more, whose images were not in the video. Detective Liam deduced this since only four passengers' information from the cruise data base was false.

The Brits Persist

Ron called Brat and the rest of the guys to get together to discuss details of their next project. He wanted to have a collective agreement to decide what type of costumes and make up they were going to use.

They all agree that their British accent was good, but it had worn out, somewhat. Perhaps it was time for a change.

They concurred they have it close to perfect and it comes naturally, the question was what could they tweak without embarking into something too big for the group to master in a relative short time? Maybe, they needed to switch characters. Ron was to wear Pete's costume, Brat was to wear Rudy's costume, and no funnier hat. Make the appearance a bit more formal. The ideas started to flow, someone suggested adding a limp on the walk with a cane. Brat was to rehearse adding a pipe, even if he did not smoke a pipe. 'I'll just add to have it when going to the jewelry store.' The three of them had a spur talking about how good they can perform. Rudy did not share the same feeling.

They did not form a detail plan including the stores or a specified destination. They relied on their previous trip to purchase one way airline tickets, later find the best target stores for the jobs.

They went to Barcelona, Spain, because Ron presumed the police will trace their initial destination to start a search. 'Let's pick a city for our arrival, then we move to a different city and country for our business.' Brat and Pete discussed the fact they had been in France, and they have left their mark, 'it will be clever to stay away from the same area.' Ron said: 'let's go to Milan, Italy.' Brat with the help of Pete can figure what city can be consider low profile and find rides on the coast. They all agreed approving the plan, this made them comfortable.

Brat looked at the train schedule from Milan to Genoa, he found all the details and they bought one-way tickets. Cost 23 euros, travel time 1 hour and 40 minutes.

While in Milan they found couple stores that had low surveillance and locations that had proximity to the several escape routes. They wanted to continue the adventure of stealing at the jewelry stores, they saw themselves as daring experts, growing confident to the point of consider each other self-reliant, but the reality was they were brazened, and cocky, taken greater risks. The intoxication from the greed and amassing more loot was driving them to the end.

The store target was found. It fits the profile they wished for.

Pete tried to hack the system, but he needed more detail information about this model, he asked Ron to create a distraction so he could get to the control panel and see the model and configuration. Ron told Pete: 'I can do better than that, I have an idea of different approach, wait for me.'

Ron went inside the store to present himself to the store manager as a proprietor of a small store of antique furniture and wanted to upgrade his security system he asked the manager for the type that they have in their store. Signor Baustelle the manager of the jewel store looked at Ron with a mix of skepticism but at the same time a degree of fascination. He was intrigue. Perplexed, he felt the need to ask one question to Ron.

Signor Baustelle said: 'tell me how long you had owned this store?' Ron was puzzled for a short moment. He did not anticipate such question. The manager did not believe someone this young, inexperience, naive probably immature, someone who have not earn the rights could own an antique furniture store. Unless it was handed to him.

Ron looked at the manager, then responded with a smile, 'it has been in our family for two generations, my grandfather worked for an antique store in his youth he had an opportunity to start his own store, then my father grew into the business, and then here I am to continue with now a tradition of our family.

Signor Baustelle demeanor changed from being suspicious to communicative, he saw Ron as a friend visiting from out of town. He wanted to show his system with a degree of content. He ushered Ron to the back room to show himself the security system, he explained what to watch for also how to handle most issues, he showed how to troubleshoot in case of a false alarm or a power outage. Ron discovered two things about the target place, a combination of technical detail, obtained through a shrewd approach. Techie was suited for the science behind the alarm system by now he knows how to hack it. The clever aspect what he called serendipity he discovered that pretending to be a store owner and presenting himself to other small jewelry stores he could gain some kind of trust and allow him to see more of the secure system.

Pete was elated with all the technical information that Ron brought him. Pete started to work on figuring how to hack the system as part of their plan. When Pete was ready to cancel the video monitor along with the security siren alert for the store then he gave the signal to Brat and Rudy, they waited for Ron to go back inside the store to talk to the manager. Then Rudy and Brat went inside with dark glasses, fake facial hair to demand the store employees to surrender the jewels from the cases, they were armed with back packs supposedly carrying explosives. 'If you don't comply, we will detonate the explosives, everybody dies.' Ron was supposed to be a casual victim caught in the robbery. He was ordered to carry a bag given by the assailants full of the gems. The employees did not want to take a chance to risk their lives, everyone obeyed then they were tied up with strong duct tape that Brat had in the backpack. Ron was ordered to tie everyone. Then they all exit the store, leaving behind the untraceable mark on the crime scene with the immobilized employees.

Brat and Ron gave each other high fives as a gesture of celebration for the newly discovered way to probe to gain trust from the store owners.

Rudy shared for a little while the optimistic moment, then when he was alone with his thoughts, he felt convicted of what they were doing.

He could almost hear Angela telling him that he was heading only for trouble. He resented those thoughts even though there was some truth about it.

Miller, the storyteller, makes a personal comment to Jack Wayne: 'now you see Rudy also known as the mate was not ready to retire from the business of crime, the elation from the burglaries was too strong. He will soon come to a crash point.

They took the train from Milan to Genoa.

They flee from Genoa to Savona by regular train. The short ride is about 23 miles, estimated time 55 minutes, the ticket for one way cost 5 euros. The reason to go to Savona was to catch the cruise ship at the port in Naples.

They felt watched, they felt uneasy, there was a certain apprehension, not paranoia. A muted sense of guilt of self-reproach, nevertheless Ron shared a common need to be mindful of their moves and interactions with each other. Ron instructed for each band member to keep minimum contact with other passengers do not contact at all among yourselves.

Their plan was to go to via Pietro Paleocapa to visit the stores there. They walked around the streets to figure their way to escape avoid getting lost from the port. They found a small market few blocks away from the jewelry store they agreed to run to the market and mingle there if it was necessary, before going back to the port.

Ron, and Brat went to the small jewelry store in separate ways. They pretended not to know each other.

They waited until no one else was in the store before they entered. Brat pretended to have a hidden gun in a shopping bag, He pointed to the clerks asking for the jewelry. Ron acted as he did not know anything he stood close to the clerk with his hands raised up, in surrender.

Brat pointed Ron demanded to take the bag to put the jewelry that the employee was giving. Ron pleaded not to be harm he was not part of the store staff: 'I am just a customer' Brat yelled at him to shut up and obey. Brat told the employee to turn off the alarm if he intended something his coworker along with the customer will be shot immediately. Ron whispered a bit loud: 'don't kill us we are innocent.' The alarm was turned off the employees gave as much jewelry as Ron could carry in two bags. Brat asked Ron to tie down the employees, he gave him a roll of duct tape. After this he asked for the front door keys he also asked if it was a back door, they locked the front door to exit through the back door. They had no incidents going back to the port. They boarded the ship an hour later the ship was on its way to port Naples.

The following morning the cruise ship docked at port Naples.

Ron had googled the city map he found a couple of the jewels stores with the address on via Gaetano Filangieri, and another on via Calabritto, both stores in the vicinity of the port. Pete had the brand name of the alarm system. He had inquired which kind of systems were commonly installed, use and service in Naples.

He considered the method of try and error as his first approach. This could help him to determine if he could break into store that Ron had from the maps. Pete dedicated himself trying to figure out the alarm system while they rode from Savona to Naples.

He had succeeded by disarming the system, but there is a protection feature the internal circuit has a backup that reactivates itself in less than 12 minutes. Ron hopes ten minutes are enough to collect enough gems and leave the place before the system arms itself to alert police. When the ship allows the passengers to visit the city, the brits had the plan set in motion.

This job was for team Brat-Rudy, team Ron-Pete were posted outside to secure things preventing any faulty situation. Ron also wanted to secure team Brat-Rudy escape.

If there was a need to create a distraction, Pete was ready to cause either a fire, or stage an accident by jumping in front of a vehicle with a scooter. The idea was to create a commotion forcing people to gather as witnesses maybe call for emergency response. Their plan was simple. Peter hacks the system with the objective to disarm it, as he already understood how to do it.

Team Brat-Rudy go inside the store, ask for the manager to show some of the rings and bracelets. Then Brat threat the staff by telling them of a powerful charge of explosives will detonate unless they comply with the demands to put quickly, in a bag the items that are at hand.

The large number of explosives are set by the front door.

Brat told the manager: 'your alarm system is disarmed.' He proved this when he asked the manager to check his alarm system demonstrated that it was already disable.

The manager believed everything they were saying and obeyed. Then locked the employees inside the bathroom then they left with the loot with much suspicion. The whole operation took 11 minutes. Their plan worked to the perfection without any complication. They all made it back to the ship.

The cruise schedule was a short stay at Naples during the sunset the ship left the port moved slowly to a short distance from the shore for the passengers to enjoy the scenery of Naples and its hills with the nocturnal lights. The next day they arrived at Palermo port.

The police in Savona had taken testimonies from the employees they went to the regular routine of the preliminary investigation by checking, hotels, for any British tourist. The port had three different cruise ships on the same day of the store heist. It had been two days since the Savona robbery when the police reviewed the ships passenger lists the only British tourist on board were couple families with young children that were heading back to Spain.

The other ships did not have any register British passengers. Naples police received an email from Savona police notifying about the jewelry store robbery. It was a day later of the Naples jewels store robbery. Naples police sent a warning to Palermo police to be on high alert with jewelry stores the department provided details of Savona and Naples robberies.

The police in Naples came across the notification sent some time ago about alerting cities with port for cruise ship with the link report from detective Liam about jewelry stores. The note also requested sharing any robberies taken place in their own city. The preliminary report from the police department of Naples was sent to detective Liam's office.

The police department in Palermo requested detailed information about the suspects to Naples police department. This request from Palermo police department was sent to detective Liam's office. Naples police did not have sufficient information of the suspects.

Detective Liam received the request from Palermo police department, then he tried his best to explain to captain Gino Cattarela the details about the jewelry stores robberies, but it was too long to include the fact that the suspects wear make-up, their British accent is not true, and they may operate in a different way. All this was taken too long to explain it over the phone, besides detective Liam did not speak fluent Italian and captain Gino did not speak good English.

Palermo police was just warned about a potential attempt to rob jewelry store or stores, suspects may come in one of the cruise ships, primary one coming from Naples. Detective Liam knew that it was a lot to ask for to search and locate suspects. He could not provide at this point a clear current photo of the individuals. He did not have any evidence for the police in Palermo in case there was any person of interest for an interview. They did not have witnesses to positive identify the suspects.

It was frustrating for detective Liam, he felt one step behind from the delinquents.

He was with Lorraine after his conversation with captain Gino Cattarela

Lorraine observed detective Liam concerned face, then asked him how long he had chased these individuals. The answer was: 'Not long enough! But I'm getting closer.'

Lorraine smiled with a word of encouragement. 'Detective they are ready to be caught, and they will have the honor to be apprehended by your relentless investigative work.'

Detective Liam appreciated the uplifted comment.

When Ron when to check a jewelry store on via Roma, Palermo he noticed undercover police standing near by the store. He did not even walk into the store. He asked one of the guards close by how the market was, but he used his most American English giving a bit of southern accent. The Italian guard asked: 'what are you looking for? The market has many things,' Ron responded some bracelet for his wife, but he wanted to surprise her. The guard smiled and suggested couple of the jewelry stores. Ron thanked him walked away.

That was a strong warning for Ron, as a result, he canceled all plans for Palermo. He gathered the other members to say with an emphatic tone: 'we are aborting all plans immediately! The police are waiting for us to arrest all of us or anyone who they can seize.' They did not panic after Ron told them what he had seen and how he interacted with one of the law agents posted at the corner of one jewelry store. They found ferry transportation from Palermo to Salerno without needing reservations. They bought tickets went to Salerno on the Amalfi coast. The train from Salerno to Naples took about one hour.

The trip from Naples to Milan and then to Turin was in the same day, a long day.

They left Sicily in the South to head north with the destination in mind of France, then Barcelona.

Once in Barcelona they divided the loot into four equal parts each one bought an inexpensive different small set of vases packed some of the jewelry inside the set of vases and ship it to a PO box, Rudy bought a medium size porcelain jars the most inexpensive with some local decor to pack some of the jewelry inside.

He also found a leather jacket with a matching small purse for Angela, he packed the rest of the jewelry with the garments to be shipped to his own home. Brat bought an espresso coffee maker, a well-known brand Illy, he wanted to have cappuccinos at home. There was nothing unusual about the machine other than it was an Italian brand. He opened the metal part to insert the best he could many small diamonds, along with some other small jewelry. The machine had a stainless-steel cup he inserted some other items from the loot. He repacked the coffee maker shipped it to his home. Pete bought a pair of shoes, pants, and a leather jacket. He included all the jewelry inside of his shoes with new clothes and shipped to his own home as well. All the merchandise they bought to pack the jewels was very inexpensive. The idea behind was not to attract any attention because what was hidden inside. They inquired about the time the shipments will arrive back home to be sure they will have returned home before each of their boxes with the jewels. When they received their boxes, everything was in perfect order. Ron had everyone to report their news even if there were not good news as soon as they had them.

Rudy waited until his box came with the gifts for Angela, before mentioning anything to her. The boxes came six weeks after they had come back. Ron had everyone together requested for everyone brought their loots to recount it all, and to celebrate their finest voyage even though they had to alter their plans in Palermo because police were waiting for them. They reasoned we were just 'lucky' to escape being capture.

Brat had an argument with Ron, he felt strong to disagree about been nearly capture.

Brat: 'you know Ron we did not see any cops looking for us.'

Ron: 'you're wrong Brat, the cops were there waiting for us. I told you the cop was posted at that corner by the jewelry shop waiting for us.'

Brat: 'how do you know that they even know who we are?'

Ron: 'I'm telling you; I had a gut feeling telling me they were there for us!'

Brat: 'nonsense! You are over reacting pal!'

Ron: 'look Brat, I know in the pass I had made mistakes, my foolish arrogance got in the way, but I had learned with your help to understand that there are times to see what is very difficultly to perceive but is there right in front for everyone, well everyone who has sight, the right sight.'

Brat: 'Alright RON, I suppose this time you're right and you did see the imminent danger.'

Pete: 'hey guys so what are we going to do, since the cops knew, and they were there waiting for us?'

Ron: 'we do absolutely nothing! We don't make any moves, no selling, no spending. We don't give away our identities, nor our place of residence.'

Rudy: 'what are we saying. Are we done? Are retiring from our trips and live a normal life?'

Ron: 'not so fast Rudy! All we are doing for some time is keeping a very low profile. We don't know how long we need to be quiet, but we have a very precise and profitable enterprise. Not even close to retire or close operations for good. We are just doing what is the smart thing to do, read the signs avoid any mistakes.'

Pete: 'it sounds as if we were legit! In the meantime, I will continue with my plans to open a shop to work on security and surveillance custom system. It is a good field, it pays well, and I really like it.'

Brat: 'hey do what you need to do bro. I will work on my job and wait out the storm, I know when is safe again we can go back and continue to build on my pretty fat retirement fund. Oh Yeah baby!'

Ron: 'we will get together once a month to check on things, alright.'

Rudy: 'I may take a short trip to celebrate the end of my semester relax for a while.'

Ron: 'okay guys just remember this not a word of our trips, or our enterprise our about our nest, silence is more precious than our jewels, okay! It's that clear?'

Brat, Pete and Rudy: 'CLEAR!'

The Presents

Rudy was with mixed feelings about the whole ordeal. He felt as if he had escaped from some kind of nightmare, he wanted to review the events, also he wanted to give the presents to Angela. He knew the longer he waited the less likely he would want to give them to Angela. Rudy could not see clearly if there was a curse that he had put on the gifts due to his illicit activities and he would have a resentment against his friends; one thing was clear the activities spoke louder to him, it was a matter of time for the curse to become real. When Rudy called her, she explained: 'I need to finish few tasks then I have to do some errands between today and tomorrow, how is next week?'

Angela was busy but also considerate in her answer. Two days later he called her to asked her let's get together for a short talk. Rudy hoped for some time to enjoy each other's company. Perhaps he could find with Angela's recommendations a way to figure out a resolution to his issues. Angela agreed to meet at their favorite place, she sensed in Rudy's voice some kind of stress, although when she answered she was glad to hear from him again.

Jack Wayne interrupted and said: 'let me guess, Caffe e Dolce.'

Miller smiled nodding his head in agreement: 'Ah but there is more to the story a Hiccup.'

The day before of their meeting Angela's office along with the entire building was evacuated caused by a gas leak. The fire department escorted everyone out of the building in the mid-morning. The gas leak occurred in the second floor but the main valve gas meter in the first floor were defective. It took the rest of the day until the next morning for the repairs. No one was allowed in the building for safety reasons.

Angela was behind with her daily work scheduled activities she needed to stay late to catch up with few things up to date. She called Rudy to reschedule.

Rudy was disheartened.

Angela: 'Rudy I hear what you are saying, let's meet the day after tomorrow is that good? '

Rudy: 'I suppose is fine.'

Angela: 'I'm sensing something is not fine with you. How are you doing?'

Rudy: 'I'm good, listen I'm sorry this gas leak happened in your building, it's not your fault, I was just expecting to get together for a little while. I haven't see you for a few days.'

Angela: 'yes I know, but I need to catch up with few things at work.'

Rudy: 'I'm glad that you are in no danger and the building gas leak is fixed. Now tell me when you would be available.'

Angela: 'I will be free the day after tomorrow in the afternoon after work around 5:30.'

Rudy: 'great! We still meet at your favorite spot Caffe e Dolce?

Angela: 'Right, I see you there.'

The next day Angela was running few minutes late she did text Rudy about her delay, which Rudy replied, 'no worries, see you when you get here.'

Rudy had brought the gifts from Spain in the original box with one of the stores bags. He rehearsed what to say and planned to probe Angela's mood for the long talk about his involvement with the band. Angela arrived with all kinds of excuses and apologies. Rudy: 'Angie! I'm so glad you made it. Please have a seat relax.'

Angela: 'I'll give a hug then I'll sit Let me put down my bags.'

Rudy: 'how about something to eat.'

Angela: 'sounds great! I'm hungry I think I'll grab a salad and a sandwich.'

Rudy: 'I'll get it, please sit down, where are you going? I see, to the bathroom, ok.'

Angela: 'could you get me some tea? I'll give you money later.'

Rudy: 'this is on me, allow me.'

Angela gets back from the ladies' room they have their food during a conversation. Towards the end Rudy pulls his backpack tells Angela that he has something for her.

Angela: 'what do you mean something for me?'

Rudy: 'here I got it while we were in Barcelona in our last business trip. Angie, I hope you like them.'

Angela: 'oh Rudy you probably spent your earnings on this.'

Rudy: 'no, not really, please open them.'

She sees the large plastic bag and wonders what's inside. Opened and pulls the beautiful leather jacket in small size. Perfect size for her. She gets chills to see the beautiful fine leather garment. The color a soft sage green with charcoal trim on the two front pockets gave an accent of fine finish and elegant design.

Angela: 'Ohh my goodness! This is beautiful Rudy, what a nice fine quality. It must cost a fortune!'

Rudy: 'try it on, I really hope that fits you.'

Angela: 'it feels so soft. I love it. It's my size! Thank you.

Rudy: 'you look so good! Here open this box now.'

Angela: 'one more? What is it? Oh, these are shoes, aren't they?'

Rudy: 'put them on as well.'

Angela: 'they're perfect. How did you figure this? The color they match with the jacket! You are amazing! I don't have a matching jacket with shoes on this color! I like it. Thank you.'

Rudy: 'Oh no Angie, the amazing thing is that I found these items in two different stores but with the matching color. The leather on the jacket is different of the leather of the shoes, but I guess they use same dye or color.'

Angela: 'Tell me what this special occasion is?'

Rudy: 'you are the special reason. Besides I don't know if I will have another change to visit Spain. I'm really considering not to go with them on another job.'

Angela: 'you mean you will concentrate on your classes to finish school?'

Rudy: 'yeah, something along those lines.

Angela: 'you are not telling me everything.

Rudy: 'Angie, is getting late. What about taking a short trip even if is just for a day.

Angela: 'you are bribing me. Rudy, no need for that we can go for a day to Monterrey Bay if that is where you would like to go.'

Rudy: 'Angie, I don't mean to sound as if I'm buying your decision to go for a day, but Monterrey Bay will be great for a day.'

Angela: 'You're right getting late. In two weeks, is Hallowing, we could go on Saturday the week before or the week after.

Rudy: 'how is the week before the craziness?'

Angela: 'that's next Saturday.'

Rudy: 'you said it. I'll text you details, time to leave, where to meet, etc.'

Angela: 'where to meet? What do you mean?'

Rudy: 'oh yea, I'll pick you up.'

Angela: 'ok, thanks again these are terrific.' She referred to her jacket and lifted the purse. Then she said: 'I like the color I love them both Rudy.'

Rudy: 'It is my pleasure, Angie. I'll send you the text and see you Saturday.'

Angela: 'bye bye.'

THE PLIGHT

Rudy got home with mixed feelings on one hand he was very proud of the gifts for Angela they were going on a trip, but on the other hand he could not find the time to tell her about the jewelry robberies. The week went by fast, Rudy rented a jeep hard top, made reservations for Saturday lunch in Carmel early afternoon.

Saturday morning at 7:45 Rudy with Angela were on their way to Monterrey Bay. Angela was with the expectation to see what Rudy was planning she wants to see how different he would behave. This was an opportunity for Angela to observe Rudy's personality and character. She wanted to see his best not just with her but with total strangers. It was a big test for Rudy, except he did not know it. Rudy had been thinking all week about how to tell Angela about his involvement with the band. He knew Angie was going to be disappointed, but he was already planning to quit the band.

Angela asked him what the first thing was that they will do once they arrive in Monterrey. Rudy turned his head to replied, 'whatever you feel like, we can be very busy going everywhere seeing everything or just find a small caffe place, sit down have some coffee and do absolutely nothing but contemplate the morning and talk.'

Angela before answering, thought about Rudy's response. This is interesting: 'I need to be cautious in what I say.' She remained silent for a long minute. Rudy asked Angela what she would like to do. Angela said: 'surprise me by disclosing what is your plan, after all, this trip is your idea.' Rudy said in low voice as if he did not want to be heard. 'Oh boy!'

All he can do to buy time was negotiate a compromise 'how about do the middle of the road.' Angela asked: 'what do you mean?' Rudy said: 'I mean find a coffee shop have some to drink, talk a little bit, then go for sightseeing or to the aquarium.' Angela agreed, 'we can talk about what have you been doing on your last trip in Spain. I want to know with details, including names, streets, what do you think is the most interesting thing in the morning, what was the most boring thing in the afternoon. Tell me what about the meals. Everything, we have time, correction you my friend have time.' Rudy started to sweat, feeling very anxious. The only thing he could think was: 'how am I going to start?' They arrived in the city Rudy drove few streets to find a small caffe with a view to the bay.

Angela: 'this is nice Rudy, I'm hungry I think I'll have pan cakes and coffee.'

Rudy: 'I'm not that hungry, I'll just have some coffee.'

Angela: 'Are you ok? You look distraught.'

Rudy: 'really? I'm ok'

Angela: 'Rudy! You do not know how to lie! You are obviously anxious about something. Please tell me perhaps I can help you.'

Rudy: 'Angie, first let's have some food then we can talk, I have time remember.'

Angela: 'ok, but keep in mind you can't lie.'

The young waitress came to take the order. The girl in a cheerful tone greets them.

'Hi guys, how's going?'

Angie responds with a radiant face: 'good, do you have waffles?'

Waitress: 'sure we do, they are serve with bananas, whipped cream and some fruit. Would you like some coffee?'

Angie gestures consenting, then she looks at Rudy extends her left-hand open indicating is your turn.

Rudy in a low voice says: 'morning, I'll have coffee please.'

Angie puts her right hand on Rudy's hands that are on the table tells him: 'you are eating an order of Florentine eggs with a wheat toast.' Then she looks at the waitress to winks her left eye.

The waitress writes the order, then says: 'I'll bring the coffee.' Turns and thanks them.

Rudy turns his head and stares at Angie, then just smiles salutes her with his right hand adding: 'yes madam.'

Their food was served. Rudy gave a general account of what the job was. Angela was very patient she did not interrupt with questions of details. After an hour Angela suggested to go to another place, they have been too long at this coffee shop. They walked out decided to sit by the water on the rocks beyond the aquarium. Right there Rudy confessed his participation, he felt ashamed and shaded few tears. He apologized to Angela but assured her that none of the money that he helped to steal was used for any of her gifts, or the trip spendings. Angela wanted to slap him to give a lecture. Instead, she felt compassion sat beside him holding hands in silent. Rudy wanted to run away full of shame. Angela after a few moments told Rudy that he made a mistake, a despicable one, he needed to tell the police what had happened. He should not keep silent any longer. In the future someone could get hurt or killed and then the matter would be deplorable, to say the least.

'Can't do that, not just yet.' Rudy uttered. 'They are my friends, and I'm no traitor. I'm not even a snitch.'

Angela raising her hands in a gesture of disappointment said: 'they are no friends. They don't care about you, they don't even care about themselves. They are going to meet with disaster. It took a long time for Rudy to say anything else Angela let him be. After Rudy felt settle suggested to go for a short walk apologized to Angela for dragging her into his mess. Angela said to him the reason he told her everything was his conscience needing to confess is the beginning of his healing and restoration. His actions have consequences he nevertheless needed to resolve. One way to resolve is tell the police, before the police come looking for him. Rudy answered: 'maybe but I'm not ready for any of that.' Angela told him you may not be ready but I'm sure the police is catching up somehow. Rudy asked her to just go for their lunch since they had reservations. Rudy said the trip was already ruined by his past actions. Angela agreed to go for lunch. They ended the trip right after lunch. Angela asked Rudy to make plans and arrangements for his confession to the police. 'Confront the consequences even if that meant time in jail.' She asked him to promise to do it. He could count with her. She told him that he will receive some reading materials for his conform, he could read at his own leisure. Rudy asked: 'what kind of materials?'

Angela said: 'here is one. One whose heart is perverse does not prosper.' Rudy asked Angela: 'what does it have to do with me confessing to the cops about our jewelry business?' Angela told him: 'What are your planning to do with the money you stole? Were you planning to buy something?' Rudy responded: 'well yeah. That is the whole purpose of getting money in an easy way. You can buy stuff!' Angela pressed deeper to said: 'Buy stuff like what? Material possessions that someone else could steal from you. That is not too smart going through all that inconvenience, and hassle for something that it could go just as easy!' Rudy thought about it then said: 'well maybe not to buy stuff but buying some knowledge.' He thought that was a clever answer. Angela replied: 'here is another reason to consider. Why should fools have money in hand to buy wisdom when they are not able to understand it?' Rudy was baffle.

He felt frustrated and embarrassed. He did not have a word to comment wanted to get away from Angela. He needed a time alone to process what she had told him.

Angela observed his long silent then added: 'everyone arrives to a moment of reasoning and welcomes the prompts from the conscience to discern right from wrong.' Rudy thanked her and said I don't deserve your wonderful caring. Angela spoke softly to said: 'there is a wonderful and joyful surprise for the soul when the mind submits to what is moral right and just, don't miss your chance.' Rudy felt disgusted dropped her off at her home, he promised to do something, but he could not tell how soon. Rudy left with heavy thoughts: 'Angela is right! She just knows, and if I have any smarts, I've better do what is right, I already blundered bad enough. Besides I rather experience the 'wonderful joy' as she says even though I'm risking everything mostly the harsh reality that is nothing more than another version of so-called moral principal. I must do something to settle this dilemma of knowing that there is something wrong with the illicitness of our actions and the application of our efforts with our talents. One thing for sure is not easy!'

He knew he will betray the whole operation when he tells the police maybe as anonymous voice or send a message a day before the operation without giving exact details of the time

Rudy started to have repeating thoughts about how wrong the stealing was, he tried to dismiss them. Then even at night the repeating thoughts invaded his moments. The loudness of the small voice got deafening over other thoughts. He woke up few nights due to the nightmare of his now constant struggle of what to do with the band. He recognized that his moral compass was broken. He needed to take a radical decision. He had come to the point of no more resistant, no more fight with his own self. Rudy was ready to give up.

The weeks passed by, the final classes, and the homework came to conclusion the time to review all material before Rudy's last exam on a Thursday early afternoon. He had given his best effort to do well with the exam. That evening he called Angie to tell her about his confidence-expectations to do well with the last exam. He wanted to celebrate together, she needed to be in the celebration since she had helped from the beginning. Angie was also excited with one question for him: 'what you have in mind Mr.?'

Rudy said: 'could we go away for a day or so please, let me try again, I promise not to ruin it this time.' Angie felt her heart touched to hear Rudy's sincere plead, with joyful surrender she agreed.

THE LOVE OF LOVERS

To say that Rudy was thrilled is not accurate he was in jubilation indeed in high spirits. The girl of his dreams had agreed to give him a second change going out of town in a short trip. Rudy could not help to think in a modest but delightful place to spend the day. His immediate thought was Monterrey for the second time, but something tells him to look at the small towns around the area he finds Capitola and Aptos. On Friday, Rudy called 3 places to make reservations for two separate rooms, but he is requesting for the weekend. There is nothing available because he needs to call a week before his requesting dates. There is one lodge a Bed & Breakfast Inn that gives him an option, write your name on a waiting list if there is a cancellation then you get the rooms. The reason there is waiting list is one single room is reserved from a couple coming out of the country and there is a possibility they may be delayed for one complete day. Rudy takes a chance writes his name on the waiting list, even though, is only one room. Rudy has a starting point plan not complete nor guaranteed but nevertheless a plan: 'I will confess to Angie I have included my name on a waiting list for one room. I will sleep in the vehicle. Then I'll show her the pictures of the gardens surrounding the property.'

On Saturday morning at 9:10 Rudy picks Angie and they drive on Highway 1 towards Monterrey. Angie has packed a small gym bag with a spare walking shoe, socks, a light sweater with pants. The weather calls for rain in the late afternoon and some showers through the night. She notices Rudy very enthusiastic in good spirit. She asked him: 'is this a surprise destination?'

Rudy turns his head to see her eyes starts to tell her: 'Angie, I love you,' then he continues: 'thank you for coming today to spend the day together. I can't lie to you. I called few places to make a reservation for the weekend you know spend one night then come back home tomorrow. I looked for two separate rooms, but I searched yesterday Friday. Nothing is available because is too close to my requesting days. Now I found one place that I am betting the people who has reservations for this weekend cancel and I get the room, I'm on a waiting list. They will call me after 1:00 pm, today.' He went on to explain the rest of the details, telling Angie she can have the room for herself, he'll be okay in the car through the night.

It happened that Rudy received the phone call; the reservation was granted to him. Angie was pleased to learn the bed and breakfast Sea-cliff Inn Aptos Tapestry is ready for them. They spent a couple of hours that evening having a delicious dinner in Monterrey Bay. Angie waited to be settled for the dinner, before asking Rudy: 'now please tell me how you are doing with your statement for the police?'

Rudy took a deep breath before started to tell her: 'I have planned this I'll call the police station to say I have information about a thief, I'll give the name, the address where he lives, with some other key details. I will let them arrest him first then I will put my things in order before going in and surrender myself.' Angie did not want to continue with the sensitive part of Rudy's plan. She added: 'let's finish with dinner first, then go to Aptos, I would like to see the place.' Rudy was excited he showed her the pictures of the Inn telling Angie: 'wait until you see it, the place deserves your presence.' Angie gave him look that meant "Stop It" After diner they went to the inn under a steady light rain that lasted through the night.

The house is nested in a flat area of the hills surrounding the town. The driveway is at the end of a short private dirt road with large pine trees on both sides. The house has a car port for the guests on the room above the car port, which is Rudy's room. A small garden patch to the left of the car port with two benches under a trellis with a large, beautiful wisteria.

They walked into the house, Rudy carried the light luggage, Angie carried the small paper bag with a couple of bottles of tea, water, a small bag of seedless grapes, a box of white crackers, a small container of cream cheese, and few cookies. They were prepared with some snacks to enjoy sitting by the fireplace. They opened the door for the room that was lit with the wall sconces decorated with fabric matching the curtain at the window. The table lamp has three settings, the light was on the second medium light. The bed set next to the left side of the room against the wall with a large drawing done in aquarelle, the painting depicted the front of the house showing the car port and the window of their room. The window in front of the bed the small fireplace to the right, a medium size walnut armoire with red stain mahogany trim. Angie stood at the door, she was dazzle, then looked around the room admiring the décor. She set the bag on the floor in silent, pointed with her index finger the wall sconces, then she saw the walnut armoire and brought her hands to cover her mouth in a gesture of admiration. Rudy kept an eye on her expressions then asked her: 'do you like the room?' Angie felt very special and pleased, she nodded gave Rudy a hug with a long loving kiss. The fireplace was off, Rudy proceeds to light the logs that were already in place. Angie fixed a small plate with some of the snacks and poured in two glasses the cold tea for both.

They sat on the area rug with heavy cushions in front of the cozy warm small fireplace. They cuddle to rest for a while. The silent of the night was accompany with the steady sound of the light rain falling on the laminated roof of the car port, just outside their room. They had a romantic intimate loving evening doing what lovers do in ecstasy. Rudy was supposed to spend the night in the vehicle, Angie asked him to stay, they spent the night together in the room with the fire going on for few hours. Neither one of them Rudy nor Angela had fireplace in their apartments, they enjoyed the simple but special feature of the fireplace.

DNA BUST

About a day or so after Ron, Brat, Pete and Rudy left Barcelona detective Liam came to Naples. He interviewed the jewelry store employees about the robbers' appearances, about their facial features, clothing any detail that they could remember. After their testimonies, he showed the pictures from the previous robberies, the employees identified the same men who perpetrate on both occasions the stores with a distinct British accent. This confirmation from the latest stealing about their appearances and British accent gave detective Liam a firmer conviction that the accent was fake and only a component of their act as to disguise themselves to avoid being identified and apprehended. Before he leaves for Monte Carlo his hometown in Monaco, he writes an extensive detail report of all the information about the case. He includes a chronological sequence of events, names of agents that helped so far with their agencies, photos from the surveillance videos, the testimonies of the employees that were present when the loot was taken. He asked to the different city police departments to include this report he also asked to keep his department updated with any new information and to alert the jewelry store managers in the areas about a potential attempt from the robbers Detective Liam suggested jewelry shops where the cruise ships visit.

He went home to study case by case he noticed a lapse of time from the first robberies to the second time. Was this a coincidence or was the modus operandi from the criminals? The robberies were done only in summer during the busy season. There was no action during fall, winter or spring, only during the long daylight of summer. The robbery in Naples was in September, the police in Palermo did not see any action, now it was October. If his calculations were right, there should be no action until June or so next year. Detective Liam spread everything on his desk, but it was too small to see it in front of him. He cleared an area of his living room at home and laid out everything on the floor. According to assistant intern Lorraine Clarice from San Francisco the last positive lead was in her city. 'A beautiful city!' He thought.

Then he remembered Doctor Chan his mind was absorbed on the pleasant moments that he had with her. 'Oh, yea she wants me to call her Judy. Come to think about it she is very attractive, also I remember in our last interactions she was acting a bit charming, which I don't mind. But she behaves like she is not herself. I wonder if she is seeing someone,' he thought. Detective Liam did not remember that they had this conversation already.

He will regret at some point not paying attention, especially after she initiated a very personal point by telling him, 'You know I'm always busy and no time for social life, but I'm sure on your case you go out with your friends very often you probably have a special someone back home, how lucky or fortunate she must be!'

At that time detective Liam did not see the innuendo he dismissed the whole point by saying: 'I don't go out for entertainment. And my last dog had to go because did not have enough time to look after him.'

'When was the last time we spoke? Last year? I should call her, or at least send her an email to say hello. I guess I like her! I need to think on what I'm doing here and not be daydreaming.' Detective Liam looked at his calendar, he thought: 'I could go to San Francisco to conduct a more in-depth investigation on these men.'

Detective Liam received the authorization from his boss to go to San Francisco spend a maximum of six days to perform his case study. This was towards the end of winter. He knew it was not enough time to conduct a thorough investigation He checked his vacation time, requested two of his weeks of vacation right after the six days. He could arrange this trip around March. He wondered: 'How is the weather in San Francisco in early spring?'

A GROOMS PLOT

Detective Liam sent an email to Doctor Chan informing her that his boss had authorized a visit to San Francisco to conduct an in-depth investigation of the jewelry stores loot. According to his research the suspects were in San Francisco. He briefly mentioned the only other person of the local police, who knew more about the case was Lorraine Clarice. The intern that has assisted him so effectively! Detective Liam concern is Lorraine is not a deputy or a police officer, she is not authorized to go out on the field for an investigation. She is not qualified. Her life could be in jeopardy. The email also included a petition that detective Liam apologize for, if he were to be demanding. His request was help him to find a good place in the vicinity of Golden Gate Park, hence he could walk a short distance to the beach. He also mentioned that he was planning to include a day or two from his vacation time.

Doctor Chan read the email in disbelieve of such a pleasant surprise. He had contacted her for further assistant on his police work. How thoughtful! He may not be demanding on his request, she thought. Besides, he is not just for business, there is a little time for pleasure, and relaxation. She wanted to answer him that he could stay at her place, but that is so improper from her. 'What is he going to think? What is my intention to ask a man to stay with me while he is visiting the city regardless of the reason for his visit. The idea is so unsuitable and could ruin everything. He could think many wrong things about my character,' she thought. The correct move was to respond to ask him: 'do you prefer the North side or the South side of the park?' Detective Liam responded: 'it makes no difference if the price is the same. My plan is to stay for a short time maybe a week or so.' He did not disclose the whole plan.

Doctor Chan initialed a full hunt for places on both sides of the Golden Gate Park. She looked a room with private bathroom. Her search produced few places within ten blocks from the beach, she narrowed down to a maximum distance from the beach of three to four blocks. She personally went to inspect one of the rooms and even paid a deposit with the provision of reimbursement if her "cousin" visiting from Europe did not stay. The agreement for the room was based on the arriving date that she obtained from detective Liam. Reluctantly detective Liam gave a different date of his actual arrival. Doctor Chan found one room that hope detective Liam would like.

The bedroom was on the second floor in the back corner of the house. She met the owners, Dave Lu and his wife Su Quan Lu. A retired Asian couple, who rented their son's formerly bedroom. He is married lives in Seattle with his wife, no grandchildren yet. Doctor Chan wanted to see the room personally. She walked up to the bedroom door, which was opened, stood at the doorway. She observed the whole room. The ceiling is white and matches the doors, the windows, the trim is done in a glossy finish. The walls are in a yellow that contrasts the red in the bed headboard, next to the bed there is a window with red wooden blinds. The window faces the South with a view to the back yard. The red wooden blinds are mahogany stain and varnish finish. Doctor Chan looked the bed is queen size, a new bed, there is a small desk with a chair, a dresser with a Tiffany lamp. Next to the lamp an old fashion alarm clock, a radio. The wall behind the bed headboard has a medium size lithograph copy of the Golden Gate Bridge Doctor Chan observed the bridge she tried to guess the time when the pictures was taken, she thought: 'either late morning or in the early afternoon. The day light is even on the bridge, it must be close to noon time.' Her sight continued, then she saw the window with the curtains facing west to the ocean. There is a quiet side street. The wall in front on the bed has a poster of El Capitan granite stone at Yosemite Park.

Looking at the poster she thought: 'when was the last time I was at Yosemite? I think maybe eight years ago. I need to plan a short trip to the park. Hmm maybe in winter to contemplate the beauty of the snow.' Doctor Chan's kept staring the poster, suddenly a thought came: 'stay in Yosemite for honeymoon must be lovely" The realization of such thought provoked her to come back to the room. She was self-conscious as if someone else was in the room and able to hear or read her mind. She walked to the window with the blinds, with two fingers push two louvers open saw the back yard. The small patio furniture set on the gray slate surrounded by fern and rose bushes, two wrought iron chairs with large cushions, the small round table an exterior propane self-stand gas heater behind the chairs. She turned around, to see the room from where she stood, she saw the closet door with a large mirror a mahogany frame. 'The room is fine,' she told herself, 'But there is something that I could add, what could it be? Ah I know, got i!'.

Doctor Chan sent an email to detective Liam informing him that his room was found. The arrangements were made it will be ready by the time he arrives in town. Doctor Chan requested a picture taken with his own cell phone camera, one of the streets from his hometown, actually his favorite street. Noting: 'no details is preferable your favorite street. Nolan,' she repeated in her email, 'please don't make much of it, just send me the picture. When you come to San Francisco I'll explain it to you, trust me. Thank you.'

The room has hard wood floor with an area rug with deep tone colors blue, green and red. The rug was bought just before renting the room. No TV is included in the room, guests could watch TV in the living room, if they follow the house rules. All lights out at or short after 10:30 pm in the common areas, hallway, kitchen, entry way and living room during weekdays. Saturday lights out at 11:30 pm.

Doctor Chan liked the house location, the room the home-owners. She was pleased and proud of what she found for Nolan, 'it will suit him,' she thought. 'I just hope he sends me the picture of his favorite street.' After that she went home.

Detective Liam was careful thought about his luggage with the possibility of Doctor Chan figuring out his actual staying. She had offered to pick him up at the airport. Detective Liam thought about how to go around Doctor Chan kindness not let her see too much. He planned to arrive at the airport take a cab check on a motel for the first night. The next day meet his friend Doctor Chan at the airport pretending he just cleared customs with only the luggage he will let her see, then go to his room. Later on, come back to his motel check out bring the rest of his cases to his room.

Detective Liam followed his instincts and thought about looking into doctor's Chan own personal life. He asked through an email to assistant Lorraine to find out doctor's Chan birthday, he added do not let Doctor Chan know you are helping me, it is a surprise from my office as a measure of gratitude for her hard work in assisting with the DNA images. Detective Liam asked: 'please respond that you understand this type of research.' He wanted to sound very official. Assistant Lorraine was exited to receive one more assignment from overseas, she did respond with the pledge: 'all investigations are confidential no one else will have knowledge.' Detective Liam knew he had an excellent accomplice. Lorraine sent a request to the cruise ship office for Doctor Chan's personal data information such as home address and date of birth. The reason she stated, the chief from the police department wanted to show their appreciation for Doctor's assistance he wanted to send some flowers with a gift certificate on her birthday, hence the request for such information. Lorraine added that the chief considers this information confidential as police business, no access to the public. She included her name, email, and phone number as a contact person. Lorraine used the police official email given to her for police business. The cruise ship manager office responded soon with all the requested data no questions asked. Detective Liam received the email from Lorraine the same afternoon local time, he was impressed with Lorraine's efficiency once again.

Doctor's Chan birthday was a week earlier than the date of his starting investigation in San Francisco. Detective Liam was pleased to know that. It could be a blessing in disguise because he could really set a great surprise for a delayed happy birthday celebration. He should have enough time to arrive, settle before getting everything ready for Judy, as he should call her now. He thought about buying something for her to wear, but how in the world can he figure the size? Maybe a purse and some matching shoes? No that is too complicated, better get some jewelry like earrings, and a pendant. He asked the attendant at the jewelry store what could be appropriate for a birthday gift? The lady suggested "there are stones for each month" many people like to wear them as part of their collection given through the years. He agreed bought a set of earrings, and a pendant aquamarine. He was told March birthstone aquamarine is the symbol for youth, hope and health.

In a birthday card he wrote: 'Dear Judy your radiant youth brightens those around you. May your birthday be full of health. I hope this humble gift makes for a belayed happy birthday.' He signed Sincerely Nolan.

After all this was done, he reflected to realize that never had spent so much time in preparing for someone's birthday before, 'she is a special lady,' he told himself.

The Band New Costumes

The time came for the band to get together and check on each other how things were going. All of them reported noting unusual perhaps it was time to consider the next trip. Brat was not sure if planning a next trip was too soon, after all it had been just three months since their last voyage as they call it. It was a close call in Palermo. Ron clarified: 'this is just a plan, and no one was stating a hard date, no one was booking a cruise or making reservations overseas. It was good to make plans and later depending on how things are they could consider a date, and further specific details.' Brat the second in command called Pete and Rudy to come together exercising caution in case they were being observed. Pete came dressed as a service technician with a blue coverall, a logo on his front pocket. Tradesman's glove sticking out of his right back pocket, with a small toolbox with hand tools. He had a baseball hat matching blue color to his coverall. Ron opened the door saw this person standing facing the wall inspecting the wires coming into the house. He did not recognize who he was. Pete turned to face Ron greeted in a very polite way.

Pete: 'good morning, sir, I'm da techie in our enterprise I had a service call from your second in command.'

Ron: 'what da...! You scared the heck out of me man! Don't just stand there, come on in.' He Gave a hug to Pete and smile showing a great affection.

Pete laughing asked: 'how was my cover up with my coveralls? Punt intended by the way.'

Ron: 'Genius! How did you figure this? It suits you very well. I did not recognize you at all, when you introduced yourself is all fitting. Great job Pete! I mean Techie.'

Pete: 'where is everybody?'

Ron: 'Brat should be here any minute, he is picking some snacks. You know him. Rudy is coming few minutes late. He has something going on with his girlfriend.'

Brat and Rudy came almost at the same time.

Ron: 'hey everybody I got to tell you what happened earlier when da techie got here.'

Pete started to laugh: 'that was cool!'

Brat: 'what!'

Rudy: 'what did you do?'

Ron explained the whole scene, everyone busted laughing, and congratulated Pete for his innovation if anyone watched him coming in, he has the perfect alibi.'

Pete: 'well is not just an alibi, seriously these are my work clothes when I have a call to install or service a system. There are times that I need to crawl in dirty spots like the underneath of houses, the attic, etc.'

Ron: 'so is not just an alibi ha you are amazing techie!'

Brat: 'I think we all need to follow suit in such a great idea.'

Rudy: 'what do you mean?'

Brat: 'we all need to have a personal appearance or a way to present ourselves using an alternative occupation. For instance, you Rudy how is your sound technician deal coming along?'

Rudy: 'I shall say. I'm done in a way there are couple of things I still have to complete, because last year I had to cancel some classes due to our trip.'

Ron: 'well there you are Rudy; you could start going around as a sound guru with headphones or whatever the sound guys do.'

Their conversations lasted more than they had anticipated they agreed to get together another day the following week to talk more about the next trip.

One week later they were back together with the purpose of working on the details for the next voyage. It was close to Christmas.

Brat had called everyone to remind them to come with their alternative occupation attire. No Santa Claus dress please. Ron wore a long sleeve shirt, a tie with slacks, and dress shoes. It was nothing expensive, but rather simple. He is a realtor. Brat a white button up shirt, khaki pants, casual black shoes. He is an accountant. Pete had the same outfit. He still is the techie. Rudy had no different appearance. He claimed that he was working on his sound engineering degree.

A Trip for A bride

Detective Liam was busy through the short month of February, it seemed that March came fast, one week away from his trip, he checked for a good price with the airlines, but it was too close to his departure date for a discount, he paid the full price bought the tickets. His department reimbursed the expenses, but he felt bad for not planning in anticipation time to take advantage of discounts.

Detective Liam had all the paperwork with files in his work folder, he reviewed them twice before putting everything inside his old leather attaché. He finished packing his luggage. The carryon piece of luggage was exclusively dedicated for Doctor Chan's birthday card, the earrings and the pendant gifts, his laptop, his charger, a small old set of metal chess pieces with a worn-out fold up board. He had place tape to hold the board together, it was falling apart but he did not mind., for him it meant character. He could get a new board but in his mind that could not be fair for the old metal pieces. He was used to play by himself as many chess players do, for the lack of other persons willing to play. Two days before of his departure he had done all his preparations of the arrangements for the work to be coordinated with the office in San Francisco assistant Lorraine was expecting him to share the limited space on her small desk that was assigned for her internship. Detective Liam was very appreciative of assistant's Lorraine willingness to accommodate him in her desk. Detective Liam bought a souvenir the small replica of the Opera di Monte Carlo building as modest way to show his gratitude.

He boarded the airplane a direct flight from Paris To San Francisco International Airport SFO. The duration of the flight was thirteen hours. During the first five hours detective Liam found plenty of file shuffling to do in his laptop, watched a movie, ate some and even took a nap. After five and a half hours he started to think on what exactly his relationship was with Doctor Chan, he noticed every time he thought about her on his mind, he calls her Judy.

He discerned that for a first time he had planned a vacation in a distant place besides he planned to spend it with a lady. He could not remember when the last time was, he had dated let alone spend vacation with a woman. He also opened the gift for Judy contemplated the jewelry. He saw they were beautiful. His thought about the stone was 'Aquamarine, ha. How this happened?' He smiled reaffirmed 'Yeah! She'll be pleased.' He closed his eyes tried to sleep for a little while. The voices next to him woke him up. He felt rested checked the flying time, two hours to go. Detective Liam ordered a glass of Sauvignon Blanc white wine and kept thinking on his strategy to implement in the hunt for the suspects. He knew that with the help of assistant Lorraine they could trace to locate the places where either they live or work. He felt confidence about this case. He was determined to make this long trip worth. He needed to study the band's past moves to anticipate on their probable next move. Then he took a glance to the gift box for Judy, he thought: 'what is going on here? She is stealthy. I don't think I can deal with a wife.' Then he smiled: "Even though she is kind, no that is not the right word. She is loving. Am I in pursue for a lady. We don't even live in the same country. I'm definitely not moving to San Francisco. I don't expect she is moving with me to Monaco! Whoa, whoa, is that what she's planning?'

It was their destiny because Doctor Chan has become accustomed to write his first name in all correspondence. She felt good about him, detective Liam was no longer what she used to think of him.

THE SHORT TRIP IN SPRINGTIME

The plan was simple, book the airline tickets around Valentine's Day to leave late April with a domestic destination, New York. The idea was to hide the oversea trip. This trip did not include a cruise ship for transportation from point of business to the place of flee. The agenda was different for everyone to travel in different airlines. Ron and Brat went from San Francisco to New York. Ron used Delta Brat United Airlines. Pete left after Brat in American Airlines, Rudy on British America. They all left the same day. From New York Ron and Brat left the same day at different times. The next day Pete and Rudy followed a similar timetable of Ron and Brat. They all bought tickets from different airlines to conceal their travel plan. The common destination was London. The Brits rested for one night the day of their arrival, then they regrouped at the Mad Bishop and Bear pub near the Paddington station.

Rudy walked into the pub looked around for his friends. He was the first to arrive, he sat on the left side of the bar near a small table. Attracted by some of the wall decoration including an old newspaper article about events in the borough. He noticed a young patron playing chess alone.

Rudy met Ian they talked about their common interest they had. Incidentally Ian was a sound engineer, recently graduate from Ravensbourne University London. A mere coincidence? Ian thought that it was not. He told Rudy that as far as he could tell nothing in life was a coincidence Everyone was designed for a specific purpose, but the mystery of life is figuring out what is the purpose and discovering what the talents were giving for the job of life fulfilling. It is harder to keep on the specific job life fulfillment than doing something consider grand, or spectacular to be popular, famous and rich, but feel no success have no real legacy for those who are close and being influenced by the actions. Rudy felt this type of conversation is too deep and reminded him of Angie. His mind wondered about how he had struggled with his own conscious about the job he had done with the band.

For sure, this job is not fulfilling for him. Rudy asked Ian if he was some kind of counselor or mind doc. 'What do you mean?' Ian asked. 'You had two items that are relevant with my life, if is not one heck of coincident then you must be sent by some… someone, er... that I know.' 'What are those items?' Ian inquired. 'You are a sound engineer, then you speak about life purpose just like my friend. In fact, you sound just like her, are you two related?' Said Rudy and at the same time gave a light punch to Ian shoulder as an amiable gesture Ian was about to respond when Ron and Brat walked in the pub, they saw Rudy. They walked towards him sat down next to him. Rudy greeted them and introduced Ian to both. Ron in a polite way told Ian that they needed a moment alone to discuss their business. Ian got up shoot hands with all of them then proceed to go. Rudy apologized to Ian: 'we will be talking again." Ian nodded in agreement then left.

Ron had everyone reviewed his own part of the plan recited to the group in a fast pace just to refresh everything. They ordered fish and chips with bangers and mash with the local beer.

The next morning, they bought the train tickets to go to the Netherlands. The group departed from London St Pancras Intl station to Amsterdam Centraal station in Netherlands. The train ride lasted under 5 hours; it has one change at Brussels lasting 50 minutes.

Once they arrived in Amsterdam Ron and Pete registered at Monet Garden Hotel.

Brat and Rudy registered on the Inntel Hotels Amsterdam Centre.

DNA BUST

The street Pieter Cornelisz Hoofstraat has many stores, the Brits selected a prestigious jewelry Lassan Boutique in the vicinity of central station as their target place.

They spent some time of the evening surveying the store. The next morning on the third day of May, they waited until passengers from a cruise ship docked behind central station disembarked and came to town. They walked to mingled with the tourist then went to the store before the passengers returned to the ship. They used their new approach; ask the manager the source of the precious stones if the response was information not available for customers, then Ron with his best fake British accent informed the manager they were not customers, but rather inspectors they were confiscating as many items as possible taken those items in small bags. The threat of a bomb in a backpack placed by the front door was the alternative of not complying with the inspector's request. Ron pulled a small remote control that looked like a fob with a small flashing red light and pointed to the backpack. He made a gesture of an explosion. Ron asked the manager to show Brat the alarm control panel. The manager pointed upstairs. Ron asked the manger to go with Brat take the customer standing next to him. He told the manager to comply with Brat's indications to disarm the security system, if he did anything else the customer will be killed, 'it will be your fault.' The customer protested but Ron demanded immediately to be quiet the manager was responsible for his life. The customer grabbed the manager to beg for his life. Before the manager or the customer did anything Ron demanded to be silent, 'go and obey. Time is running, you only have a minute,' he said, then he looked at the time and said: 'the bomb is ticking, the person outside the building needs to hear from me to deactivate the bomb. GO!' The customer pulled the manager jacket and pleaded: 'please help me.' The manager held the customer as he walked towards the stairs, he nodded this head to reaffirm the customer that he was safe. The customer was Pete. Ron remained downstairs with the other two clerks waited for the manager's return.

Once upstairs the manager opened a small closet door at the end of the stairs showed the control panel to Brat. Pete stood next to the manager observed the control whispered: 'I hope this is what they need for heaven's sake,' looked at the manager which meant this is not our control. Brat told the manager: 'is your fault that your customer dies here for not complying. This is not the control for the alarm as I asked you.' The customer heard this and grabbed hard to the manager's arm to beg 'please help me,' then he felt on his knees and started to sob holding to the manager's arm. At this point the manager was scared asked Brat to forgive him, but the alarm was monitor from outside the building by a private company he could not do anything to disconnect. Brat told the manager to call the alarm company tell them 'You are ok Let's go downstairs give to your dead customer a canvas bag to fill with all these items from the display cases here, hurry up now!'

Then Brat ordered the customer to tie down the employees including the manager inside the bathroom. They left the store. Ron and Pete went in the same direction to the central station. Brat and Rudy went to the hotel changed costumes for street clothes. They had no incidents left Amsterdam the next day early morning.

DISTRESSFUL RIDE

They went to Amsterdam Centraal train station to board the train with destination to K"oln Hbf station in Cologne, Germany. Brat had map out the strategies for travel from London, UK to Cologne, Germany. Ron had looked the map, and gave his approval, but also asked: 'where do we go from Cologne?' Brat looked at the map and spotted Bonn airport.

'There is one transfer at Arnhem Centraal station.' Brat explained, 'it is situated in a distance of 60-61 miles, as I read it from the details on their web page.' Then he added, 'the train ride takes about 1 hour and 10 minutes. The distance from Arnhem to Cologne is 102 miles, these are fast locomotor engines, hence the train ride takes 2 hrs. The trains ridership depends on the day of the week and the time of the day.' Pete told Brat: 'you started to sound like an "infomercial".

The train with the Brits was at 1/3 capacity, it was the right number of passengers to provide a comfortable ambience in the cars. There were enough seats for travelers to have a one full seat per person. They settled down on their seats to enjoy the scenery. Everything so far was proper, or it seem to be.

The ride from Amsterdam to Arnhem takes about 1 hour and 9 or 10 minutes. There was an incident on the last kilometer prior to enter the train station that caused a delay of about 1 hour. Passengers shared different feelings some were calm and patient, they waited for any announcements from the train operator, some were anxious being so close to train station but for safety regulations no one can get off the trains since there are no platforms high to reach the cars at the boarding doors.

The train operator gave a standard message through the sound system from the train cars. No details or specifics about the cause of the hold-up. Ron and the Brits along with the rest of the passengers could see through the windows no trains coming in the opposite direction, which meant the station was either closed for whatever reason or the railroad track in the route they were was obstructed near the train station. Brat, Ron with Pete speculated about what caused the trains to stop in the middle of the road. Brat mentioned about having headaches and trouble falling asleep. Ron advised to take couple of aspirins for the headaches, also while they were waiting for the train to resume its rout 'take a seat try to sleep. We are under stress; it takes a toll in our bodies.' Ron also admitted he himself felt tense with low energy and having an upset stomach. Pete came at this moment to join their conversation. Ron asked him: 'how are you doing in terms of handling stress.' Pete said: 'I'm having hard time falling asleep and my stomach feels like having a storm.' Brat and Ron looked each other nodded confirming all of them are suffering the effects of the darn stress.

Brat added: 'yea! Our business is not for wimps.' Pete uttered: 'we must have tenacity, determination some endurance or we must be suffering stupidity beyond any hope.' Then he caught himself and said: 'Hey! Don't tell Rudy what I just said!'

They all laughed for a moment. It gave them a slight relief.

They were concerned for the police may be tracing their last robberies in Amsterdam following behind in another train car or worst waiting for them at the next station.

The speed of the train was reduced in a similar way as when the train approaches the station, then stop completely, but after a short moment it continue very slow for about 3 minutes then ceased all movement, no announces were made for a long 10 minutes. Passengers called the operator through the intercom to inquire any details, the answer was: 'we are waiting for instruction from central station.' After 30 minutes of standstill the operator announces a vague message: 'there is an incident at the station, no details were provided at this time, we apologize for the inconvenience, as still waiting for further instructions.' The notification was the same in three different languages, English, Dutch and French.

Pete sat next to Rudy and commented: 'it could be something minor, maybe an electrical overload on some panel, or a light bulb is out. They just have to change, and we go to the station.' Rudy replied: 'I hope is not a major issue with the actual tracks, or a train car derailment.' They all remembered the similar situation on their way to Nice, although no one wanted to talk about that experience.

One hour had passed the train started to move back to a regular speed, no announcements were made. The speed was reduced as the train approached the station; Brat could see few railway police standing observing the trains coming to the station. He could not help to be apprehensive. He thought the police was looking for them, possible searched the previous trains in a combined effort to apprehend the four suspects of jewelry burglars. He expected the worst. In a short moment of 3-5 minutes his mind created the sad end of their enterprise. He drops his head as a gesture to capitulate. Ron came sat next to him to ask him: 'what could be the reason for the railway police presence.' Ron saw Brat's pale face in anguish, a face of a person being defeated. Ron noticed Pete came close to them he said: 'what the heck is going on here?' Ron in an effort to keep them calm uttered few words: 'We don't assume anything, we continue with our plan, transfer to the train for Bonn. No need to show worry faces. We do not have any reason to be anxious, so remember we have great endurance. In fact, we are not even frustrated for the delay. Let's go!' Interesting enough as Ron gave them an uplifting talk, he also felt encouraged.

The train came to stop at the proper place for the doors to open, those passengers arriving at their station disembarked. The Brits walked towards the platform to catch the train with destination to Cologne. No one asked anything to any passenger on the station, the police patrolled around the station in a calm demeanor. Brat walked behind Pete to board the next train for cologne. He sat, the doors closed, the train started to move leaving the station, but his tension was about the same for some time. Ron gave thumbs up to Brat as he walked by him. Brat made gave a slight smile in response. The train continued to move away from the station protected by the railway police without any events.

The train ride to Cologne was uneventful, they change trains from Cologne to Bonn's airport, Germany. No one said anything, no words, they were exhausted from all the tension and the extended delay. The group separated in pairs Ron and Pete took British Airways, and Brat with Rudy took Lufthansa they all went to London. At the London airport Brat was so drained that he thought he would not survive one more hour. The moment he sat on the airplane destined for San Francisco he closed his eyes and felt asleep for the next three hours. Ron kept an eye on him for the first two hours then himself took a long nap of two hours. There was no need to keep vigilant the flight last 13 hours hopefully no heavy turbulence, it was time to relax and rest for a little bit. They had a direct flight nonstop from London to San Francisco.

At their arrival to SFO San Francisco it was late afternoon with a mix of few clouds light fog temperatures in the upper fifties.

Everyone on the band was afflicted by the stress of the trip and the moments of uncertainty, the long-lasting travel time added physical and mental fatigue to their overall difficult situation.

Rudy was progressively tormented with the thought of telling the police his story without giving precise details about the main suspects.

He felt his physical condition had worsen, the awful feeling of anguish stayed with him. It was a nightmare tormenting him with horrible thoughts. He tried to substitute those bad moments by remembering Angie and what he had told her that time they went to Aptos bed and breakfast. It brought him some comfort, however soon after, he can see words from Angie's lips turning into boiling balls of fire chasing him as a result of his wicked deeds. He knew he had made corrupted decisions. He needs to make the changes that he had talked about, is just a matter of: 'when Am I gonna be ready?'

The police reviewed the surveillance tapes from the Lassem boutique.

The robbers were identified as British due to their English accent. After searching at the local hotels for British guests who had registered two days before the robbery, and guests that had checked out the day of the stealing there was no match with the images from the surveillance video.

The search on the cruise ships that were docked on the port the day of the robbery did not provide any leads; it was day number three from the robbery. Local police requested England police department assistant with the identification of criminal records with the video images. The alert that detective Liam had set popped in Amsterdam police department then notified the rest of the local police about the heist in their city. There were no specific details about which city could be next target. The notice had a general warning stating potential robberies targeting jewelry stores located near port cities where cruise ships can dock, and passengers disembark.

Detective Liam received a notification about Amsterdam hit. Three days later a notification from Cologne, Germany about a jewelry store robbery. He quickly calculated that the robbers may be on a cruise ship on the Rhine River because the geographical locations of the stores. He requested from the cruise companies the list of British passengers and travelers from San Francisco. The results were negative. The robbers were not on any ship this time.

The Brits' new decision to proceed with a different transportation approach was working just as they had hope for. Ron discussed with Brat about how the police knew their manner of transportation from city to city. On the cruise ships, this time he said: 'we are not on any ship, we are rolling on trains. They can't figure out our logistics.'

The Knight Is in Town

He arrived to SFO five minutes ahead of schedule. After he cleared customs located his luggage, took a taxicab and went to a Bed & breakfast on Church Street near Dolores Park. Detective Liam had reservation for the day of his arrival. The first night was a bit hard due to the jet lag. He used the alarm clock to remind him the hour to leave for the airport pretending his arrival to meet Doctor Chan. He forgot one important detail, the monitor that shows the arriving flights did not show any coming from Paris. Doctor Chan looked for in every arriving flight of Air France as he had indicated. She had come at SFO thirty minutes before the supposed arrival time that detective Liam had mentioned. Detective Liam walked casually by the waiting lobby saw Doctor Chan standing in front of one of the monitor sets looking at the arrival flights. There he realized about his faulty part of the plan. She knows he did not tell the truth. He stopped for a long moment to think. 'What could I tell her.' While staring at her, he noticed her figure and contemplated long enough to appreciate her height. She must be around 5'8" or more. Her straight hair hangs up to her shoulders. Suddenly he was compelled to tell her the truth about his earlier arrival, he dismissed the feeling proceeded to approach her to greeted her.

Detective Liam: 'hello Doctor Chan'

She turned fast and looked at him with puzzle and said: 'hello Nolan, when did you arrive?'

Detective Liam: 'what do you mean?'

Doctor Chan: 'I've been here for the last twenty minutes looking for the arrival of your flight and it never showed.'

Detective Liam knew he was in trouble. He looked to his right and to his left in a casual way, then just said: 'We arrived few minutes earlier I went to customs, I have my luggage and I'm ready. We can go now.'

Doctor Chan stared at him for a short moment with a dubious mind; but looking at his blue eyes and his smile she was glad to see him. She dismissed her suspicion gave him a quick hug. She tells him: "welcome, let's go you must be tire, I'll take you to your place, you will like it.'

Detective Liam was not ready for a hug barely responded with his hands still holding the two pieces of luggage. He thanked, and added: 'I'll be ok, just need to rest for a while.' During the drive from the airport to the house in the Sunset district they talked about his plans for the next day agreed to get together for dinner in a place by Embarcadero.

Doctor Chan pulled on to the side street next to the house where detective Liam room is. A corner house with the lawn continuous from the front door all away to the back yard into the neighbor's driveway. A medium size Palm tree right at the corner of the property line with some other plants. The front door has three steps with a wrought iron handrail. The porch has a small roof with tiles that gives a Mediterranean style. The windows on the side where she parked has flat bricks around three sides of the window casings. Mister Lu, the homeowner opened the front door and greeted them. Doctor Chan said: 'hello good to see you again Mr. Lu, this is Nolan Liam my cousin, Nolan this is Mr. Lu.' Detective Liam did not know anything about he was a cousin or relative to Doctor Chan. He did not have a chance to ask her any questions, because she just pushed his back as she introduced him. Mr. Lu shook hands and welcomed him inside. Doctor Chan told Mr. Lu to go ahead and explain house rules for guests.

Jack Wayne had a comment: 'let me see if I understood dad, I mean detective Liam did not disclose he was arriving one day earlier, and on the other hand mom, I mean Doctor Chan did not tell him about he is her cousin for the rental room. Right?'

Miller nodded saying: 'yeah, they are even wouldn't you say?'

Jack Wayne and Miller laughed.

She excused herself went back to her car explaining her phone is in her car she needed to check any messages. Mr. Lu gestured to go ahead and extended his hand to detective Liam to go ahead into the hallway for upstairs.

Doctor Chan had asked Mr. Lu ahead of time permission to set a framed photograph on the small desk in the bedroom. She explained that her cousin would suffer home sick the picture of one of his favorite streets from his hometown would help him to have something familiar and not feel home sick. Mr. Lu agreed. Detective Liam stood at the doorway of his room looked around quickly. He nodded in agreement, he was pleased. He noticed the picture but did not recognize it right away. The 8x10 picture that he had sent to Doctor Chan now framed next to a small old fashion radio, it all looked as part of the room decor. Detective Liam walked inside the room to set the luggage next to the small closet. Doctor Chan called from the hallway she asked if everything was okay. Mr. Lu excused himself and gave the house keys to detective Liam.

Doctor Chan entered the room with an expectative look, and a big simper.

Then she Inquired: 'how is it?' Detective Liam responded with an equal smile: 'the room is fine I appreciate your thoughtfulness adding the framed picture of my favorite street.' He walked towards her and gave her a hug as expression of his gratitude. Doctor Chan whispered: 'oh Nolan you cheer my soul.' Detective Liam heard this and caused him to tremble. He was not sure if it was fear or joy. Doctor Chan realized that it was not the right place to start a romantic moment she felt awkward. She excused herself asked detective Liam to rest the next day as they had made plans get together for dinner. Then she left.

Dave Lu and wife Su Quan Lu came back to detective Liam's bedroom to tell him: 'here is a copy of the house rules if you need parking for your vehicle, you are welcome to use the side space next to the driveway. If you need something let us know, we are going to be downstairs in the kitchen.' Then they excused themselves.

The Wedding's Dream

Doctor Chan arrived at her home inspired by what had happened the last moment with detective Liam. Her thoughts were repeating on her mind over and over. For her every time the charming grew a little bit stronger. Her enthusiasm grew to a point of daydreaming. After a short moment she yawned, she looked at the clock, and told herself: 'I need to rest.' She went to bed she has a vision.

While she was asleep in the REM stage, Judy saw herself walking on a park. She knew this park. She had been here before. She recognized the oval center with the distinct gazebo. It was the Garden Barista Park. She sat on a bench on a cool calm early afternoon, the sun on her face. It's a clear day, blue sky with the temperature at fifty degrees. A calm breeze made her to rearrange her scarf, extended her legs and reclined slightly. She put on her sunglasses, then slipped her hands in her coat pockets. 'This is a safe place to rest for a little bit' she thought. She took a deep breath, closed her eyes and thought 'I'll stay here for just a moment.' She felt the warm sun on her face so good, the chirping of the birds became pleasant, in a moment the place turned quiet. She took one more deep breath and her mind drifted from one thought to another.

First, she is fixed on 'I need to be sure to answer those messages from the patients' Then the next thought that enter her mind was 'did I do laundry? 'I need to buy more detergent and other supplies'.

Then an interesting thought came 'was Nolan trying to…' but then she saw the shadows of the Brazilian Pepper tree. Judy sees what a person who is walking on a small brick pathway, she can see the shadows of few branches that are moving slowly by the wind. She sees a small park bench next to the brick pathway, there are two engraved initials on the back of the bench N & J in a heart. Judy could not see who the person is. The shadow of this person is right in front on the pathway. Two small steps made of stone are at the end of the pathway, preceding a set of old oak double doors. The doors are open. The pathway is in the middle of a perfect manicure lawn. She can smell the fragrance of white roses, there are some plants with Arum-lily flowers, and bushes with white Hydrangea flowers along the grass. Inside, past the doors there is music that she can barely hear. She climbed the two steps and walked inside. There are people greeting, everyone is dress up as attending a very especial event, they are standing on both sides indicating for her to continue walking. The middle is an aisle, she can see that it is a church. She hears the music. It is the weeding music, because it is a wedding! But why is she walking the aisle while the music is playing? People on both sides of the aisle are looking at her smiling with radiant happy faces, some ladies have their heads slightly tilted as a gesture of satisfaction and congratulations while taking pictures of her with their phones. The loud sound of emergency vehicles on the street woke her up. Judy realized that she had a dream. She had more than a dream, there was a vision within the dream. She looked at the clock it was three fifteen in the morning. Very early for her to start the day. She smiled and knew that her future was to be marry. She went back to sleep. She never saw the face of the groom, but in her mind, she knew who this person is. She told herself the fact that the sound of the siren woke her up is a good indication of the relation to police vehicles, and to Liam's occupation. She did not argue with herself about this connection even though it was a long shot, but she was satisfied she could not be wrong. Her mind drifted again felt asleep. After two and half hours she got up, felt rested, she did her routine to be ready for work, interesting enough for her, she had a spring in her step. Then she left the house in a cheerful mood and went to work.

Jack Wayne raised his hand to ask a question.

Miller paused and said: 'do you have a comment?'

Jack Wayne said: 'I have a question.'

Miller motioned yes.

Jack Wayne: 'how do you know all this?'

Miller hesitates then elaborates: 'that is part of my research for the story, let me continue with what happens with the assistant.'

Jack Wayne with enthusiasm says: 'ok.'

TIME IS THE ESSENCE

The data that assistant Lorraine provided included the receipts from the pharmacy where Brat and Rudy bought the medicine. The antibiotics Doctor Chan prescribed.

They used credit cards to purchase the antibiotics. The medicine was purchased with two different credit cards one issue to Rudy Miller and the other to Brat Walker. These two names were not on the list of passengers of the cruise ship. The prescription from Doctor Chan had the names of Richard Miller and Ian Walker. Detective Liam deduced the names used as passengers were fictitious. The police department requested to the credit card administration office the address of both card holders. The credit company administration office sent the information directly to detective Liam.

When detective Liam knocks on the front door of Rudy's apartment, no one responds, he (Rudy) had gone on a short trip for a couple of days.

Detective Liam looks for someone on the units next door to Rudy's searching for information about Rudy. He doesn't find anyone to answer his inquires.

This happened on the last day of his approved trip from his hometown office.

At this point, he does not have anyone under arrest, nor he has an interview because he could not find any of the suspects. He knows that is hard to justify the approval of more time to continue with this work. He wants to sort few things then decide. It seems to him this has become a race against time.

He went to his apartment, sat at the small desk in his room, stared the photograph that she requested from him, he needs to move from work time to his vacation time, then he can stay a bit longer, ten days. Detective Liam looks around the room and realizes how much of all this is her care. The photo from his hometown reminds him the city and somehow gives comfort. He would never have thought such way to transform a strange room far from home make it feel more like he is with family or longtime friends. 'She is clever,' he thought. 'I like this, the room, the house is just the right distance from the beach. I have what I need. Do I need her?'

Doctor Chan has been busy she had gone out of town the last three days for work. He has nothing planned for his first day of vacation other than wait for Doctor Chan return home. Her trip was a last-minute arrangement to attend a conference in Los Angeles, CA. The determined factor for her to decide to go for the conference was detective Liam was busy with his investigation did not have much time for socializing. He was looking forward to spending some time with Doctor Chan, now a more intimate relationship since they call each other by their first name. She had demonstrated her feelings for him. She was sincere and loving. It was hard to resist her affections. He even had a surprise revelation during his flight. He uttered the word wife, he told himself 'A romantic long-term relationship can't work because we don't even live in the same city.' Can he afford to have a wife? Now he finds himself in her city, oddly enough, every time they talk, he finds the idea more appealing. He told himself: 'don't need to rush anything.

Tomorrow when she is back, I will have time to assess and decide, once I ask her. I hope to have enough courage instead of having this preposterous nervous feeling. Am I afraid? I will find out.'

Judy got back home with many things to do. She needed to catch up with her patients' files, the information from the conference sparked few ideas for her desire to write a book about her profession, but some research needed to be done. The last thought in her mind was about detective Liam. She forgot for a short moment that he was in town.

DNA BUST

Detective Liam was anxious about talking to Doctor Chan but wanted to give her a day or so to get herself up to speed with all her affairs. Doctor Chan returned on Sunday afternoon, detective Liam call her on Tuesday mid-day and after greetings he asked her out for diner either Tuesday or Wednesday. Doctor Chan was delighted but she could not go out Tuesday she had to accommodate patients who missed their appointments when she was out of town. Wednesday she was feeling very sick she did not want to pass it on to detective Liam. The agony to wait until Friday or maybe Saturday was terrible for detective Liam, his vacation time was coming to an end, but he could not do much about the circumstances. He found the waiting days useful for his investigations.

INSPIRED BY LOVE
RESOLVED A CASE

Lorraine Clarice received a call from detective Liam asking her to help him with some details about the suspects information in the jewelry heist case. Lorraine is about to finish her internship and continue with her studies which meant no more office at the San Francisco police department. Detective Liam just needed to confirm dates and addresses from two of the patients treated by Doctor Chan. After all the information was corroborated detective Liam observed Lorraine's hands then asked her if she could do something very special for him. Lorraine hesitated to answer because she noticed that detective Liam had been looking at her hands. Detective Liam apologized: "excuse me, let me explain what exactly it is. I wonder if you could try a ring that I would buy for our friend Doctor Chan, I think that your hands are about the same size of Doctor Chan. I can always exchange the ring for the right size. But...' Before he finishes Lorraine interrupted to say: "No problem I would be glad to try a ring to help you figure out her right size, are you proposing? Congratulations!'

Detective Liam was dumbstruck for few seconds, he started to blush. He just realized what Lorraine had decipher. He had no idea how that came to be. He desperate wanted to go back in time and never had asked Lorraine for her help with the ring size. He never planned anything about a ring. It just came out of his mouth without any warning. It was too late; he might as well continue take advantage of Lorraine assistance to find the best engagement ring. Lorraine understood how embarrassed he was, she felt awkward and tried to minimize the uncomfortable feeling that both had, she said: 'when would you like to go to select the ring?' Detective Liam started to sweat on his forehead, he mumbles something: 'to-to-morrow... if is ok with you'. Lorraine answered 'in the afternoon? That will work.' Detective Liam just nodded with his head staring at the notes. Lorraine smiled trying to reaffirm him. She said: 'Detective Liam is ok to be nervous is a big thing what you are doing it means a lot! She will be enchanted with the ring, I'm sure.'

Detective Liam looked at assistant Lorraine with an expression of insecurity beyond his control. 'I did not plan this, I just acted without thinking. It is not me, I meant is not what I usually do.' He spoke.

Lorraine responded: 'love does not think, just points the way, you love her, I'm sure she has a lot to do with your feelings for her. She probably is waiting for you.'

Detective Liam apologized for involving her in his personal affairs and shook his head as switching back to the reason of their meeting.

He felt energized and encouraged then he told to his assistant, Lorraine: 'I appreciate all your assistance on this case, now there is enough information for the police department for an interview with two of the suspects. The local police could go back to find the two suspects that we have names and addresses. Once they are brought for interviews more information will be available to arrest and charge them with the robbery of jewels from one or more stores. The facts should provide a complete picture to confirm the suspects are the same individuals committing the stealings. Let's connect the dots: first the dates of the cruise ship docked, second the robberies, and third the food poison of passengers. What is the common thread? The dates and the place of these events are the same.'

'The figures made based on the DNA samples of Doctor Chan and images of the surveillance video are considerable close. We could present these pictures from the video and the DNA images as evidence, It is a long shot and much work needs to be done.' There was much work for the police to do in terms of collecting the evidence caught mostly on the surveillance cameras on the different jewelry shops that had record of the robberies. It was a considerable effort done by detective Liam, he spent many hours reviewing the tapes, mapping the stores' locations, he also made a chart with the dates and times of the robberies. A copy of the large file was sent to the SF police. Later he updated the file with Doctor Chan's 3D image of the suspect who was treated for food poison at the cruise ship. From this image detective Liam was able to identify one of the suspects in the recorded video from the jewelry shop. The names and addresses from the pharmacy receipt provided a strong lead to look for Brat and Rudy.

THE DOOM IS NEAR

The police looked at all the evidence that detective Liam had gathered. The police chief Craig Nelson provides full support with the investigation, then detective Joshua Ferrigno and detective Eduard (Eddy) Ness were assigned to the case. The information included images of the individuals that became ill with food poisoning while on the cruise ship that happened about one day or so after the date of the robbery. The heist was committed on the cruise ship route.

The detectives needed to find the two individuals for an interview, also to corroborate the image from the DNA provided by Doctor Chan.

The first door that detectives Ferrigno and Ness went back to knock on was Rudy's. He was not home for the second time the police came. The second door was Brat's, he was not home either. Detective Liam was present on both occasions with the police officers. The police inquired with neighbors. This time Brat's neighbors provided more information about his coming and going. An officer was posted 24 hours to wait for Brat to show up.

When Brat came home, he was prudent, before he walked to his front door he drove by his entrance and parked at the corner. He surveyed for any unusual individual or vehicle near his apartment. He spotted a parked vehicle with a male that it seemed to him a cop. He was right. He went into his apartment by the rear service door. He did not turn any lights, did not make any noise to alert the neighbors. He spent the night in his room risking being discovered, the next morning he checked for the vehicle it was gone. He rushed to take a quick shower, change, packed few things and left by the rear door. He just had come to his vehicle when the same car that was parked the day before turned by the corner. The driver did not see Brat getting into his vehicle. Brat started to sweat but tried to remain calm waited few minutes to observe the undercover police detective. Brat saw the cop getting off his vehicle walking to the front door of his apartment rang the doorbell. He felt sick on the tip of his stomach, his heart rate accelerated, his hands got sweaty. He thought he was dead. He had never been arrested. He waited few moments around five minutes then saw the cop gone back to his car. Brat started his vehicle drove few blocks away, he parked to call Ron.

Jack Wayne asked: 'did the police follow Brat at a distance to see if he goes to his friends. '

Miller: 'no, the undercover police never saw Brat, so he couldn't follow, but that is a good strategy. You learned that from your dad, didn't you?'

Jack Wayne says: 'not really. You see it all the time on the movies.'

Brat and Ron talked for about twenty minutes finally agreed to meet at the coffee shop to go over everything. Ron called Pete and Rudy asked them to come at the coffee shop after work but told them what had happened to Brat. 'Be very careful of your surroundings, you guys need to be discrete of who is behind you. Don't panic!' He told them. They agreed to spend the night out of their homes, and check into a motel, just to be sure that nothing goes sour. At the coffee shop they talked about how close they were to be arrested, what was the future for all of them. Ron after thinking couple of scenarios of what if, he convinced Brat into proceed with their plan.

He emphasized: 'you better leave the city soon, go to a different town where you could stay for at least a week to wait if the police had more information about them. At this point we need to be one step ahead of any move from the cops.'

Rudy and Pete were not sure if that was the best way to respond to what they called the inevitable fall. Pete had a cousin in Santa

Rosa near Russian River where he could go for a week and could bring Rudy. Brat and Ron both had places outside the city where they could go for few days. Rudy ended up accepting Pete's offer.

After a week on a Thursday early afternoon, Rudy came back to the city, but before going home he bought pizza borrowed a friend's deliver car with the delivery hat and pretended to be a pizza deliver. Then he went to his apartment to deliver a pizza. He checked the street did not see anything unusual. He went inside to pack few things, including all his costumes with the makeup and the receipts for the previous trips.

On the same day at later time everyone else came back to check their places. Nothing was different no police was posted anywhere waiting for them. That weekend things were for the most part normal, and for this reason the brits went back to their regular schedule days. They had a premonition of a changing situation, Ron told Brat: 'it is like if we try to read a hidden message in the dark.' Brat agreed gave his point of view saying, 'Yeah, I can't tell what the silhouettes are pointing in the thick fog.'

They all together decided that everyone had to move away from the city to another town not in the bay area but further away, maybe Sacramento or San Diego. Pete suggested: 'how about to another state.'

Rudy had to do something drastic, he was running out of time.

Rudy pulled out some jewels he still had from the last trip along with $15,000.00 money from the loot sold few weeks before, now he had a grand total of $95,000.00 he remembered what Angela had told him about generosity. He decided to be generous. That Saturday midafternoon, he went to the center that Angie frequently volunteer. He donated $12,000.00 attempting to feel better; this should also show Angie that he could be very generous right on the spot. The good feeling was short live.

Soon he was tormented by the fear of being arrested by the police, he had an awful feeling the law was about to find out who they were. He needed desperate to talk to Angela.

Miller noticed that Jack Wayne was thinking in what he had told about the donation, thus, he asked Jack Wayne. 'Do you understand what I said?'

Jack looks at him and said: '$12,000.00 That's a lot of money!'

Miller smiles and continues with the story.

On Sunday, he reached out to Angela asking her to spend some time to talk over the advice she had provided few times. Angela smiled and told Rudy: 'I remember what you said in Monterrey Bay while we enjoyed dinner,' then with much kindness replied: 'we had been here before you need to go to the police to give your own statement. I am happy to help you in any way I can if you are ready to take a definite step.'

One last time Rudy pleaded with Angie about the notion of come true with the police and at the same time clear his conscious, Angie answered: 'I understand your dilemma, please consider this. The corrupted (wicked) are brought down by their own criminal doings.'

Rudy under Angie's pressure and fighting his own conviction, betrayed his friends.

Monday late afternoon, he placed a call to the local police. The sergeant asked him what the nature of his call was, he said: 'non an emergency, I have information about a burglary.' The sergeant Police asked: 'what's your name?'

Rudy: 'I rather be anonymous.'

Sergeant: 'ok but this is deemed serious business, if you are trying to place a prank call you are in trouble.'

Rudy was very nervous, he started to sweat, with a trembling voice he answered.

Rudy: 'I'm serious and don't have much time.'

Sergeant: 'go ahead what is it that you have to say?'

Rudy: 'his name is Ron, (he paused) …he, he stole few jewelry items from a shop in Amsterdam.'

At this point Rudy shock up and could not say loud enough any word. He started to weep struggling to hold tears.

Sergeant: 'Ok I understand, take a deep breath and tell me more.'

Rudy: 'sorry, I just want to correct things. His address is 4515 Folsom Street, green front door. He might be home.'

Sergeant: 'is he alone is he arm and dangerous?'

Rudy could not hold the heavy terrible guilt he broke down and sobbed. He just hangs up the phone.

Epic Bust!

The sergeant made the best of the brief call gathering the information to make sense before reporting to the officer in turn.

The caller yields enough information of a certain individual having some jewelry items from a heist perpetrated overseas. He provided where the house is situated. The police had to move fast to confirm if the caller was saying the truth. They did not know who or how many persons could be at the address.

The chief police Craig Nelson was notified of the anonymous call, the unusual detail of the call was about jewels stole in Amsterdam, that caused him to link the call to a case under investigation with a detective visiting the city from Monaco. The large file for the case provided by detective Liam included names and address for two suspects. He realized the call might be connected to the same case, he immediately dispatched three units with five officers in search of Ron. 'Be very careful!' He said, 'don't play hero we don't know how dangerous this guy could be and how many more individuals may be with him.'

The time was 6:45 pm on Monday, two of the three patrol cars stop at the front door, the third one stop blocking the long wide driveway to the double car garage. The driveway continues to the back yard. They all got off the vehicles three officers approached the front door with drawn out weapons on hand, the other two walked near the rear door by the garage.

The duplex layout of one-story apartments shared one common wall; the tenants had view to the back yard through the back windows looking the fence which is covered by the Wintergreen boxwood shrub trimmed up to the high of the fence boards 6 feet.

The open side runs from the back fence to the front of the property line which is hedge with Gracillin bamboo that covers the whole fence. It adds a beautiful sight of a woody area giving much more privacy from the neighbors. Ron has cut some branches between the bamboo and the back of the garage at the roof line. He installed three brackets and a small wooden box to hide few of the jewels that he has from the projects. He anticipates someone could search his place to find the loot. The box is well hidden amongst the bamboo branches behind the garage.

The sidewalk at the front has two threes 6' tall Princeton American Elm they provide an aesthetic shaded area.

The house has a hallway with one doorway to the left for the front room extending from the front door that ends at the bedroom with the bathroom to the left. A doorway in between the bathroom and the bedroom that leads to another small room that does not have a closet. Ron calls it his office. The front room or living room is connected to the kitchen with a small eating area for a table next to a window that oversees the driveway. The living room has two bookshelves one by the wall next to the front door, the other is on the wall in the hallway. The office has a small desk with Ron's laptop, a base cabinet and some shelves above containing few books with some magazines. There is a door to the back yard. The bedroom has a small closet with two sliding wooden doors. The room has two windows one on the wall to the back yard and the other window faces the end on the driveway at the garage. The garage has a small addition into the back yard. The room has a water closet with a small sink. The garage is for two cars long enough to accommodate a sofa and a bookshelf. There are two long windows on the garage wall facing the back yard, the windows provide plenty of light during the day even with the garage door close.

One police officer knocked on the front door and step aside expecting some shooting. Ron was seating at the kitchen table oblivious of what was taking place outside. He did not have the slightest idea. He got up walked to the front door when the officer outside knock again, Ron in a loud voice said coming! He opened the door and the three officers pointed their guns to his face and ordered: 'hands up! Turn around and kneel!'

Ron obeyed without saying anything in a total state of confusion.

He was pushed to the floor face down, hands brought to his back and handcuffed. One officer asked in a rather low voice, 'who else is in the house?'

Ron answered: 'no one! Is just me, I live alone.' The other two policemen went into the house, one behind the other, they checked the living room, then the kitchen. They came back to the hallway with hand signals pointed to the back rooms, both walked in a stealthy manner. The bedroom door was slightly open, the bathroom door was closed, they could see the small office but could not see the whole room. One officer pointed to the bedroom first, but the other shook his head and pointed to the small office first because no door. They both went to check the office. One went to open the back door allowing the other officer to come in to help with the other two rooms. They opened the bathroom door first then they opened carefully the bedroom door. One officer pointed to the sliding closet doors. Two stood on each side of the doors and one in front with their guns ready to use in case there was someone hiding inside. They confirmed no one else was in the house.

The lieutenant in charge of the operation explained to Ron what was going on. We are looking for stolen jewels. Then asked: 'where are the jewels that you stole?' Ron looked at the officer and responded emphatically: 'I don't have any jewels, I don't steal, you are out of your mind!' Then the officer said: 'Okay I will ask again where you have the jewels that you allegedly stole?' Ron responded: 'you are in the wrong place with the wrong person.' The officer gestured to the others to take him away. Ron was taken to the patrol car parked in the driveway. The sergeant took the suspect into custody to the police station. The time was 7:55 pm, nearly one hour after they arrived at Ron's place. The other two remained at the apartment searching for the stolen jewels, with any evidence that could incriminate the suspect. The police searched in the garage and found on the shelf a small box with makeup kit with two different sets of fake eyebrows a plastic container of silicone gel. The officer who found the makeup box did not know about the surveillance videos from the jewelry stores that showed the four suspects with distinct facial features, only detective Liam could connect the makeup box with the possible costumes of the thieves. The makeup kit was left on the shelf.

Ron was brought up for questioning his name, and address, to corroborate the information given to the police station by the anonymous caller. Ron was searched to see if he had a weapon conceal with his clothes. He had his wallet in his pants rear pocket. Ron kept his cell phone on the kitchen table but this time he had set it on silent mode and left it inside the pocket in his jacket that he hanged in the closet. He forgot to pull the phone after he put the jacket away.

The commander posted one police officer outside the house until detective Joshua Ferrigno or Eddy Ness showed up to wait for anyone who might come looking for Ron.

They did not find any jewels, but they took Ron's bank files with his laptop.

He was arrested and brought to the police station for questioning. He was charged with a theft crime, although with a limited time for the detection since the police did not have any evidence. The police needed to establish few facts and find hard evidence otherwise Ron goes free.

They needed to confirm the crime committed at the jewelry store.

The evidence needed to be found to place it under police custody.

They needed to prove he was at the crime scene the day of the burglary.

The police needed to find proof of him performing the crime or a witness to identify him. It was crucial to find the anonymous caller for an interview.

The police at the time of taking Ron for interview had not review the entire file that detective Liam had provided with. The information connecting Ron and the rest of the Brits was included.

One crucial piece of information was not included on detective Liam's file, the names of Ron and Pete.

The chief police Craig Nelson called detective Ness once Ron was apprehended and under custody at his place of residence, which was provided by the anonymous caller.

Chief: 'detective Ness this is chief Nelson.'

Detective Ness: 'yes sir, how can I help you?'

Chief: 'hey Eddy this is Craig, we just apprehended one individual who you may want to interview, is related to the jewelry case that you and your compadre Josh have been assigned.'

Detective Eddy: 'I'm on my way sir, does Josh know about this as well?'

Chief: 'who Am I? Call center? I'll let the two of you talk to each other, just keep me in the loop. I'm going home for the night, see you in the morning.'

Detective Josh was still at the police station when detective Eddy called him about the suspect being transported from the place where he was apprehended. He was informed about the anonymous caller and the jewels stolen from Amsterdam. Detective Josh read the file from detective Liam to search the data about the Amsterdam steal. He texted Eddy the facts about the robbery, the date, the name of the store, and the number of suspects. Ron showed some confusion when detective Eddy asked details of his affairs on the date of the Amsterdam jewels robbery. He was asked: 'were you in Amsterdam on May 4, to be precise on the Lassan Boutique?' Ron thought for a short moment and answered: 'never being in Amsterdam.' Then detective Eddy asked Ron: 'you and your friends took few jewels from that boutique, where are the jewels?' Ron responded: 'I told your buddy at my apartment that I don't have any jewels and you guys are out of your minds, I don't steal.'

Detective Josh came in to tell Ron: 'I want you to see this video from a robbery on the commune La Roche-Guyon on the banks of Seine River', then showed the picture of Brat and Rudy. 'Do you know these individuals? What are their names?' The video is from the Equestrian shop jewelry. Ron responded: 'you have the wrong person; I don't have anything to do with that.' Josh kept asking: 'tell me your location the week of 20, 21, 22, 23, 24, 25 and 26 in August.'

Ron opted for a default answer, he could not remember. Detective Eddy told Ron: 'you know the same dates the cruise ship stopped in the city of Sete, most passengers became ill. Were you in that cruise ship as well, did you suffer any symptoms?' Ron becomes nervous, he keeps silent thinking 'I got to be very careful how I answer.' Detective Josh taking turns asking many questions to Ron. He inquiries about his vacation trips. Ron is getting confused. At this point the robbery that took place at the store Bijouterie ciotat Or in the city of Casiss, France was not mentioned, however, Ron makes a fatal mistake when he absolves himself claiming he has nothing to do with the heist.

Detective Eddy confronts Ron asking: 'what robbery are you talking about?' Detective Josh says: 'did you committed a robbery? He asked you if you suffer any symptoms, now you are telling us you have nothing to do with the robbery.'

Ron was sweating and said, the police had asked him about the robbery of some jewels, when he was handcuffed at his home. Detective Eddy read the reason for his arrest. 'You committed a burglary of some jewels in Amsterdam, but now you are talking about a job in Cassis, France.'

Ron responded: 'all I said is I have not committed a robbery; I did not mention a city.' Detective Eddy takes couple of steps around Ron's chair leans over him from his back and speaks in a low voice very slow, 'our conversation is being recorded, you better have a good explanation of your statements. Go ahead, you tell us who these guys are, their names, where do they live,' but Ron looked down and uttered: 'I don't know who they are.' Detective Eddy asked again: 'where do they live? They are your friends, where are they now?' Ron repeated: 'I don't know them.' Then detective Josh said: 'Ron you have their phone numbers text them. Ron kept silent. Detective Eddy did not realize Ron had left his cell phone in his jacket hang in the closet.

Detective Joshua had read the file that detective Liam had sent, then he texted detective Eddy the details of the band trips in France, and Italy supported by the surveillance videos. The images on the videos identify two of the four suspects treated in the follow-up for food poison infection. The identification of the same individual was provided by Doctor Chan. Detective Eddy asked Ron for details of his last two trips overseas. He told Ron that the police from Savona and Naples had video recordings of the suspects of jewelry store robberies, and one of the suspects matched his appearance with the same height and complexion. Ron denied any thing with the heist, at this point the police told Ron more arrests had already done in connection with this evidence. One of the suspects had already given names of the other participants, he was offered a deal if he could provide the names of the other suspects and surrender the jewels. Detective Eddy told Ron that if all the jewels were returned the charges would be different.

Ron was in turmoil; he could not speak a word. Detective Eddy continued to request information he told Ron in an austere tone: 'look let's start by writing the names of your friends, the addresses, where do they work.'

Ron's head was in a complete chaos, his face was pale, his eyes glazed over. He was in shock. The police looked at him understanding what the matter with him was. Detective Eddy said: 'let's take a short break give him few minutes, let him recover then we'll ask him again in a stronger tone. He'll get it.' Detective Josh told Eddy: 'look it is already pass 9 pm, it's getting late, let's get some sleep go home and come back tomorrow.' Detective Eddy agreed they locked Ron in a cell for the night, then they went home for the night.

After Ron was brought to his cell for the night, he recovered his calm he started to think, 'they have not mentioned any names of the other arrested. Probably they are just bluffing about the other arrests. I must stay calm can't afford more mistakes. I'm exhausted, I need to sleep.'

The next day Tuesday morning detective Eddy came back to Ron with the same question: 'were you in Amsterdam on May 4?'

Ron answers: 'I already told you I've never being in Amsterdam.' Detective Josh asked him: 'ok if not in Amsterdam, where were you on that day?

Ron paused for a short moment then he said: 'I don't remember. I probably was working.'

Detective Eddy raised his left hand pointing upward with his index finger and exclaims 'Aha! You said probably working where? Doing what?'

Ron dismisses the whole expression of the detective with a contemptuous glare says 'where? Here in the city, doing what? My job, you know, what else?'

Then the detective tells him: 'you need to prove what you allegedly said is true.' Ron changed his assertion for: 'maybe I was not at work, maybe I happened to be at home by myself, watching tv or just resting.' The detective agreed and added: 'ok, tell me with solid evidence what about the two days before that date and the two days after.

I'll tell you what we'll do for you I'll give you a calendar and let's look at your cell phone, we'll check what numbers did you call and calls that you receive, including messages SMSs, that will help you to remember more details, don't worry we're here to help you, pal. You need to review your computer to trace all expenses that you did on those days, you'll get to answer what we asked you and more.'

At this point Ron knew he could not prove any of his affirmations. He tried to detain the inescapable. He asked if he could go home to check his computer.

Detective Josh said: 'let's start with your cell phone.'

The only delay in favor of Ron which provided him an ephemeral hope was his cell phone was at home.

Jack Wayne tells Miller: 'did they find the phone? It was hard for Ron, wasn't it?'

Miller: 'I'll tell you what happened, wait.'

He Asks the Question

It was Friday Doctor Chan had rested in better health, she called detective Liam and told him that they could meet later after work they could catch up. Detective Liam was delighted. He wanted to give her belated birthday present also deduce if she was interested in marriage before saying goodbye before returning to Monaco. There were only two more days left on his vacation.

Detective Liam was ridiculous nervous he almost forgot the birthday present when he left for dinner with Doctor Chan. He realized this could be the last chance he would have to talk to her about marriage. This thought somehow calmed his nerves and helped him to be more objective to face his feelings.

Doctor Chan was caught up on her work right after she called detective Liam it was time to go home to change clothes before going to dinner that will bring a lifetime change, but at the last minute a call from a patient delayed her for few minutes. She tried to rush but time said it was better call him to reschedule dinner for later. There were only ten minutes left before their meeting time. She called him but no answer. She had no choice but go to the restaurant The Boulevard on Embarcadero. It was detective Liam's choice for the reservations at six fifteen. She thought on how fast the week had gone and until now she had no idea how long detective Liam was staying on his vacation. She winced at the idea that he may be departing soon, perhaps right after dinner. She felt guilty wanted to tell him how much she enjoys his company. The question is: 'how does he feel about my company?' She wonders if 'he would want a wife. It is the man who is supposed to proposed not the woman, unless she is desperate willing to make a fool of herself.'

Detective Liam walked into the lobby of the restaurant few minutes before the reservation, then he requested a special service, he disclosed that he intended to propose to the lady after dinner, but before desert and would appreciate no disturbance for few min-utes. The restaurant applauded the occasion informed him that the desert was on the house for such a wonderful event. Doctor Chan walked in after she left work in a rush, she was not prepared for a date she felt more as a work-related dinner. She had no time to go home to change into a more appropriate dress, fix a bit her hair and have some make up. The restaurant host pointed at her table saying this way please, detective Liam was sitting looking down to a publication or some sort of file, work related perhaps. She walked up to the table detective Liam stood at her presence he was wearing the most elegant shirt and necktie that she had seen on him before. He looked radiant with a huge smile greeted her and gave her a soft hug with a timid kiss on her left cheek. Doctor Chan received it she felt underdress not being ready for the occasion.

Detective Liam looked at her eyes for a long moment then asked her how her day was. Doctor Chan looked at him, she was impressing and intrigue of his behavior. She answered right away with a short fine, immediately corrected: 'I've been so busy with hardly any time to even go home and be more presentable.' That was her excuse for looking shabby. Detective Liam waited until she finished then replied: 'you don't need to add anything, you are beautiful just as you are.' Doctor Chan felt blushing whispered: 'thanks.' Detective Liam proceeded to offer a glass of wine and asked her if she was very hungry to order right away eat or have some appetizer and order later. Doctor Chan confessed that she was starving, she had skipped lunch. Detective Liam called to place their order.

Detective Liam did not want to rush over anything, but time was at the essence. He then asked in a very candid way: 'Judy, would you marry me?' Before she had enough time to answer the waitress came back with the salad plates and interrupts Doctor Chan. The waitress completely oblivious to what was taking place set the salad plates to mention quickly that dinner was coming in a few minutes. Doctor Chan thanked then looked at detective Liam who was staring at her all the time with an expression of anticipation but very tender. Doctor Chan answered: 'Nolan Are you sure do you want me for a wife?' But before detective Liam said anything she added: 'sure, I mean yes I want to marry you Nolan, I know I want to be with you.' Detective Liam open his eyes wide and was about to reply when the waitress came back to check on them, Doctor Chan told the waitress 'Please go away he is proposing'. The waitress replies 'yes madam, but we, I mean you were supposed to be on the dessert after dinner to pop the question.' Doctor Chan very surprised asked: 'What did you say?' Detective Liam asked the waitress 'please come back later, thank you.' The waitress feels a bit embarrass, apologize and left.

Doctor Chan asked 'he knew? What is going on? Nolan?'

Detective Liam just waved with his hand and said, 'I'll explain later, would you marry me?' Doctor Chan leaned back on her chair took a deep breath and said: 'Yes, I love you Nolan' Detective Liam pulled the ring box opened and presented the ring to his bride and said: 'I love you too Judy. Here is a ring as a token of my sincere love' Then he got up went to her side kneeled to put the ring, she extended her hand waited for him to put the ring. Then she looked the ring and showed it to him with a sensuous grin, she pulled him off his knees, hugged him and kissed. The other two tables close to them applauded detective Liam, wave to them and bow as a gesture of gratitude. Doctor Chan blushes for long time and fan her face, as she felt very bashful. Detective Liam returned to his seat and told her. 'This is the best moment of my life.' Doctor Chan told him that she had dream attending a very beautiful wedding she could not see the bride, but she saw everything from the bride's eyes. Then she told her fiancée, 'You are my dream.' Dinner was excellent they conversed about few things but no details about the wedding. After dinner, detective Liam presented her birthday gifts that he had brought and explained the sequence of his shopping gifts first the birthday present in Monaco, then the engagement ring with the collaboration of his ever-faithful assistance Lorraine, 'by the way' he said to Judy 'she would be on the guest list'. Judy nodded in agreement with a smile. Then she thought 'I'm already doing what an obedient, loving wife does. I love this.'

Detective Liam looked at his watch realized that he needed to go and check on the investigation since he only has two more days left. Doctor Chan knew, she stood up asked for the bill. Then she tells him 'My dear husband to be we need to make some plans when you are returning home?' Detective Liam just nodded in agreement, 'I have two more days, and proceed to pay.'

He thought 'how in the world does she know that I have not pack?' I am following instructions like an obedient husband, this is preposterous!' Then he utters to himself, 'but I like it'.

On their way to his apartment there was only a small exchange of ideas for the wedding plans. Doctor Chan proposed to have a modest wedding. Nolan affirmed adding: 'with a group of family and friends. To celebrate all we need is a small-scale reception in San Francisco.' Judy adjusted by saying to him: 'unpretentious' we'll gather together to boogie like there is no tomorrow.' Detective Liam turned his head with his eyes wide open, Judy busted laughing soon Nolan laugh loudly with her for a long moment. Then with a loving smile they look at each other to kiss and hug tenderly. Doctor Chan was driving; she approached the house were Nolan stayed. Suddenly, she says, 'I must tell my sister, you must meet her, oh my! I need to tell my parents, although they live in Boston, they must come for the weeding.' She went around the block looking for a spot to park. Nolan asked what she was trying to do. 'There is no need for you to park, I can get off quickly and you continue to go home.' Doctor Chan smiled pull over closer to the sidewalk cross street from the house. She came close to Nolan and closed her eyes expecting a kiss. Nolan unclipped his seat belt grabbed his bride and kissed her embracing all of her. Then he whispered 'love you...doc Chan.' He got off and walked to the house.

He waved to Doctor Chan as she drove away.

Doctor Chan went home after dropping him off. She called her sister Naomi to tell her the great news about her coming nuptials. Naomi, her sister screamed hysterical! She was so happy for Judy. Next, Doctor Chan recounted the part that she told Nolan about unpretentious and dancing all night. Her sister laughed so hard that she starting to cough. They said good night and best wishes for the next few hours, Naomi added, 'love you, this is beyond crazy.' Doctor Chan could not go to sleep thinking in everything that it was her future. She needed to make numerous preparations, to leave her current employment, her home, find a new job in the city where they were going to live. Judy felt a bit overwhelmed. She looked at her ring with a smile a thought emerged 'you are in for the adventure of a lifetime' she took a deep breath felt encouraged and energized. She knew 'I don't have to do everything right now, just go to bed dream about my future! 'Nolan, you make me so happy, thank you."

THE BEGINNING OF ARRAIGNMENTS

The next morning detective Liam had couple of messages from police chief Craig Nelson 'please come to the station we have a suspect in custody.' Detective Joshua also had left a message indicating 'we had an anonymous call identifying a suspect from the heist in Amsterdam.'

Detective Liam called police chief Nelson to tell him: 'I am on my way to the police station. Thank you.'

Detective Liam called his bride Judy on his way to the police station and told her quickly the encouraging news about the suspect under custody.

When detective Liam arrived at the police station Ron's laptop and cell phone had been revised, they found many details of the critical dates providing hard evidence that Ron had physically spent time in the cities that had been robbed. The missing parts where the jewels. Detective Liam was introduced to Ron. He asked Ron a question: 'where are your allies Rudy Miller and Brat Walker? One more thing we know about your fourth member.' Detective Josh added: 'his name is Pete, we learned that from Mr. Ron's cell phone contact list.' Ron had no answer for such question, even if he knew theirs whereabouts, he would not tell. After hearing the same question again Ron responded: 'I have no idea.' Detective Liam asked Ron: 'tell me about the costumes, in fact let me see the file.' The large file that he had put together was brought to him. Nolan said: 'let's start from the beginning how many members are in the band?' Ron could not deny and uttered: 'four.'

His next question was: 'when did you started to hit the stores?'

Ron covers his face with his hands to answer: 'I don't remember exactly maybe a couple years ago.'

The interrogation continued for the entire morning. The three detectives took turns from an hour each at the time. Ron was exhausted he could not hide any answers from the police. The search for Rudy and Brat had become vigorous because through the information pulled out from Ron's devises and some of the answers from Ron the detectives had send few units to places where the suspects could be hiding out. The hunt for Pete was much simpler, he was a technician that should be located at his apartment or at his office besides, he has a list of possible jobs that the police could go to check.

Two undercover police officers were posted at Pete's apartment to wait for his coming and apprehend him. Two police officers went to his small shop, but he was not there. Detective Liam asked detective Josh to text Pete using Ron's cell phone, a simple and short message. 'Let's meet at my place in one hour.' Detective Liam went with two undercover police officer to wait outside Ron's apartment. One car park at the end of the block and the other car across the street in front of the front door. Detective Josh waited for Pete to answer, ten minutes passed there was a replied from Pete.

"I'm in the middle of a trouble shooting in a customer's warehouse security system, can't promise I'll be there in an hour, what's up?'

Detective Josh replied to the text: 'I need to check something with you. How soon can you come?' Pete answered: "How long do we need to check what you have?'

Detective Josh called detective Liam and explained what Pete is asking. 'What would you like to do?' Detective Liam indicated: 'continue with the exchange of text tell Pete that they just need some 15 minutes or less to get together.'

Pete read the text from detective Josh coming from Ron's cell phone, then he answered: 'I'll see you in about 25 minutes, I have to go and get some cables and other parts for the customer, I'll stop by before I return to this job.'

Pete did not suspect anything from the text, when he arrived at Ron's place, he noticed the front door ajar open he became suspicious and turned around back to his vehicle. Detective Liam was walking crossing the street towards him, the other two police officers came from the apartment calling him by his name asking him to stop. Pete saw detective Liam at the same time heard the police behind him calling his name. He stopped looked down the street another police car approaching very fast with the lights flashing. He realized there is no point in running. Neighbors peaked at the windows and watched how he was ordered to raise both hands then hand cuffed and taken into a patrol car. Once he was in the police vehicle he was identify as one of the suspects of jewelry burglars, he was under arrest and there was evidence to prove it.

One hour later a police car returned with the keys of Pete's vehicle drove it away to the police station for inspection.

Detective Liam was invited by police chief Craig Nelson to have lunch together and discuss the next step on progress of the investigation. Police chief Nelson said: 'It looks like only one suspect is still at large.' Detective Liam kept looking at his watch but very much engage in the conversation due to the unexpected events taken place since the day before. Chief Nelson asked detective Liam: 'how you would like to proceed with the case, we are going to charge these individuals for the robberies based on the evidence that you presented and the information we have collected. We still need to find the jewels or figure out what happened to them.' Detective Liam expressed his appreciation for all the help and work that chief Nelson had done, he also mentioned: 'I only have one more day before I return home. I have also a bit of personal business to share with you. First, I must say Lorraine is a fantastic assistant in every aspect thanks to her genuine and committed labor I gather much valuable data to figure some of this complicated investigation, but also, she was in part responsible for finding the right engagement ring for my bride.' He was all smiles. Chief Nelson wasn't sure what to answer first, he started by congratulate detective Liam for his engagement. Then he added: 'may I ask who the lucky girl is?'

He says: 'the lady is Doctor Judy Chan' with a cheerful smile. Chief Nelson clears his throat to say: 'well, detective Liam you have your hands full and not a whole lot of time.'

Detective Liam nodded in agreement: 'I'll call my boss to update him the lattes development I need to request three more days to establish the next steps with the suspects, the charges and who will take command of their custody, designate a criminal court for their prosecution. That also will provide me a little bit of extra time to organize the wedding.'

Pete was brought into a separate room from Ron's for interrogations. Detective Eddy came first, he gave to Pete a sheet of paper to read, he asked him to corroborate his name, address, occupation sign it if everything was correct, if not they will rectify. What Pete read was correct and he signed the sheet. Detective Eddy asked: 'where were you on the week of August 20, 21, 22, 23, 24, 25, and 26?' Pete was in dismay to hear the question. He stammered answering: 'I... I, don't remember.' Detective Eddy continued: 'how about on May 4?' Pete repeated: 'I can't remember.' Detective Eddy said: 'let me help you, probably you were in Amsterdam, weren't you?' Pete in a low voice answered: 'why would you say that?' Detective Eddy responded: 'there is plenty of evidence that incriminates you and your colleagues, the surveillance video at the jewelry store in Casiss, France, the testimony from your ally who is also in custody.' When Pete heard about his ally giving testimony incriminating him, he wondered: 'who is he talking about?' Detective Eddy observes Pete's demeanor, it was a clear expression of defeat on his face. The eyes glazed to the harsh reality of the end. Detective Eddy continued with the same question: 'now tell me were you in Amsterdam on May 4 or not? Pete looked down withdrawn. After a short moment Pete heard the same question again but this time with emphasis on naming the city of Amsterdam. Pete just nodded in a silent capitulation.

Rudy feeling perturbed after calling the police station fixed himself a cup of tea to calm his nerves and have a chance to meditate on what step he should take. After some 40 minutes he left his apartment for a walk, some fresh air he wanted to continue with his reflective thoughts. He did not have any place to go to, or how long did he intend to walk. After an hour or so he decides to go back home to rest, his brain felt heavy from the burdensome.

The night was a mixture of fictitious scenarios that went from bad to worst tormenting the exhausted Rudy's mind. He did not have a soothing sleep, instead he had a long continuous nightmare. The next morning, he felt awful with a bad taste on his mouth.

The thought of surrender started to emerge, he wanted to sort things out find a vindication for himself for betraying Ron and the Brits, even though, he did not give any other name of the band, but he realized it was inevitable the downfall of the rest of the Brits. Rudy reasoned, the police will arrest Ron, search his home ask few questions, soon they will have enough information to find the rest of the guys.

Some time had passed as Rudy was absorb in his deeply thinking. He looked at the refrigerator door magnets the ornament of the Sea cliff Aptos log cabin brought the loving memories of the romantic trip to Aptos. Rudy saw in his mind the most relevant events of the evening. He could see the armoire, the window, the fireplace and how they both enjoyed the warmth, he could hear the rain outside how they cuddled, sharing the snacks and loving each other. The memories reinforced his unconditional love for Angie. He remembered what he told Angie about surrendering to the police confessing his involvement with the band, this helped him to make up his mind.

He walked out the apartment with the hope to resolve some of the mess he was deeply involved. He thought calling Angie but realized at this hour she is busy at work, it was 8:30 on Tuesday morning the sky was partly cloudy. 'I must end this apprehension, I will do it for Angie, after all I had told her I will do it. I will do it for myself.'

Rudy went to his vehicle with the intention to drive up to the police station, but he asked himself in loud voice: 'then what might happen to my car, Angie could come and drive it away for me.' He got out the vehicle started to walk. He told himself: 'I will not impose my mess on her.' He was contemplating a chain of events when he noticed he was in front of the building. It was the police station.

Rudy crossed the street and went inside to give himself up. He explained in a calm voice who he was what he had done along with the other three members of what they call themselves the Brits. He explained where some of the jewels, that were part of his loot were kept at his apartment. The police could go and retrieve the loot, he gave them his apartment front door key, no need to break in and damage the landlord's property. He did not know where the other three guys were at the time of his surrender. Detective Josh was notified of Rudy's detention. Rudy was granted a phone call.

Angela received a call from an unknown number, she did not answer. There was a voice message from Rudy. The short voice message indicated that he was arrested, for few days he didn't know exactly how many days he would be silent, unable to see her or even talk to her. After 6 days Rudy left another voice message to Angela, he named the place where he was in detention. Angela came to visit. Rudy told Angela that he was having mixed feelings about the act of betraying his friends. There was no redemption, he did not feel any better by confessing. Angela explained to him that there were consequences to the wrong deeds. Rudy, she said: 'I know and hope that you will gain wisdom learn to discern right from wrong after the police clears everything and the court determines the penalty. If you accept and take responsibility for what you had done.' Rudy just stared the floor replied: 'what good is it? I mean what good is to have a virtue.

of wisdom? I can't buy anything not a car or a house, not even a cup of coffee for you! Can I take it to the bank and invest it? Could I exchange it for freedom? It won't even warm me at night or keep me company in a lonely cell. This wisdom stuff can't take you on a date for me, ha! I don't feel very wise.' Angela thought for a moment and responded with a tender heart: 'Rudy I admire your courage; I see your heart is in the right place. You are thinking on buying me a cup of coffee, while you are facing many legal issues. You are on the right track. You put me first and take your eyes from you. I don't have all the right answers. I can only tell you this I am with you. Besides there are few things that you can do with wisdom. Knowledge comes easily to the discerning mind.' Angela tells him that is Proverbs 14:6 The wisdom of the prudent is to give thought to their ways. Then she adds Proverbs 14:8 How much better to get wisdom than gold, to choose understanding rather than silver. Rudy has a puzzle face, but Angela mentioned one more. Proverbs 16:6 You can't take it to the bank because what you take two the bank you could lose, but with wisdom you can enrich others without losing your own wisdom. You meant wealth is require buying material goods like a car, a house, but the wealth has a potential to be stolen. It may bring satisfaction but also may have a preoccupation and worrisome, it needs to be guarded, and even so it can be lost like the jewels stolen from the stores. It can be destroyed wisdom and understanding do not decrease when they are shared. It will not be depleted by is use. No one can steal your wisdom and discerning. Providing guidance to those who want to listen your depth of understanding. Wisdom provides insight and reduces stress.' At this point Rudy was silent and somehow, he felt comforted by Angie's words about wisdom.

Jack Wayne asked the question that had chased his mind for some time: 'did Rudy and Angela get marry or ever lived together?'

Miller dropped his head and said: 'No, she got married to another guy who she met 2 years prior to the Brits went to prison. They moved to Chicago soon after they married. I only heard from her once, about 10 years ago.'

Doctor Chan got up few minutes earlier with multiple ideas of things chasing each other in her brain. She set the teapot as usual, got her note pad to write out the list of items to do in order of priorities.

1. write names of wedding guests this should not take too long. My dad and mom said they are coming!
2. select the place for the reception we don't need fancy or grandeur.

3. the date is having to be really soon yay!
4. wedding dress, oh my god I'm in a big trouble. Who could help? She was about to write couple of names when the teapot whistle startle her, giving her a slight jolt on her chair. She got up to fix her cup of tea. She only wrote two more items before rushing to get dress ready to go to work.
5. Cancel all appointments after today and present my resignation.
6. I could rent my apartment instead of selling it hastily.

Doctor Chan calls her fiancé, no answer, she left a message. Dear Nolan, I must find a wedding dress I need help any suggestions? Love you, bye.

Doctor Chan once at her office engaged on all the work that was waiting for her, before she remembered any of her personal big plans it was past 11:00, the whole morning was almost gone. She stopped for a moment and wrote quickly a resignation letter, stating 'as a result of living life one comes to enjoy the day, the very special day when one meets the person that in part is responsible for altering the best plans or better said, one realizes I have lived for this day to make the loving plans for the rest of our days.'

She read it reflected for 3 seconds and told herself, 'GREAT! Future here I come!'

She added a big thank you to her staff, to her boss, then she signed, and dated.

The afternoon was busy for the first 2 hours, then she collected her personal items, gave away everything else including books with a couple of desk ornaments. There was no time to pack.

'I better call Nolan he must be very busy at work with the investigation.' She texted Nolan asking him: 'call me as soon as you can, please. Love you.'

It was 3:45 in the afternoon when detective Liam saw the text, he excused himself from the room where they had Rudy to call Doctor Chan. It was a brief exchange of updates from Doctor Chan the request for help finding the bride gown, actually a fine dress will do. Detective Liam had the right person for help Lorraine. He told Doctor Chan: 'let me call her now, I'll ask her to call you. Please Judy do not worry you will be just fine. Love you.'

He needed to get back with the case to close his part before leaving for Monaco.

Lorraine was so excited to help Doctor Chan in finding a bride dress for her wedding.

The first place that Lorraine looked was wedding gowns online.

The plunge neck, appliqués tube dress, beaded backless split thigh, shirred back dress.

The dress is simple, but on her is elegant.

Detective Liam knew the fourth suspect full name and address, he had been at his apartment before once by himself then a second time with detectives Josh, and detective Eddy, both times he was not home, neighbors provide some information about the times they had seen him come and go. The police department had posted an officer around the hours the neighbors had pointed when Brat was usually home. Up to this point no results. They had a warrant to search his home.

Detective Liam had texted Brat, several times using Ron's cell phone, but no response from Brat. Detective Josh presumed Brat had learned about Ron's arrest and somehow figure that Pete was apprehended by answering Ron's text.

Brat received a text from Ron the next day after he was arrested. The text was nothing customary from Ron. It read: 'hey, I need to talk to you. Come meet me at home in about 20 minutes. Let me know what time you are coming. It is very important.'

Brat knew it was not from Ron, he supposed Ron's phone was hacked, someone is trying to set a trap on him. Brat called Pete to find out what was going on, but Pete did not answer. Brat texted Pete using his nick name: 'hey Techie this is Tin man what's up with Gru?' Detective Liam saw Pete's phone buzz and he read the text from Brat. He asked Pete: 'what is this? Who is Tin man and who is Gru?' Pete saw the text from Brat shrug off pretending he did not understand the text and answered: 'I don't know.' Detective

Josh asserted is from Brat's number. Pete maintained his initial dismiss, he said: 'It means nothing, someone is fulling around with his contact list.' Detective Liam review Ron's phone he investigated the texting history there were no such names on his messages. Ron and the Brits had made an agreement to keep those names from exchanging any type of messages.

When detective Liam asked Ron: 'who is Techie? Who is Tin man? And who is Gru?' Ron responded with a strong disdain, 'you are playing around with my phone and now you got some fool pulling your leg, so you come to me for answers? Aren't you the detective?' Detective Eddy came face to face to Ron and yelled: 'watch it buddy! Don't get smart with us.' Ron kept staring at detective Eddy's eyes without a word for a long silent moment, that grew into a completely quiet iron curtain.

Detective Liam called detective Josh and detective Eddy outside the room where they had Ron for questioning. He had them both sit around the table where they had all the information regarding the jewel's robberies case. Then he started by pointing what they had gathered the last few hours, and the latest data from Rudy after he surrendered himself, which included the names of the band members and nick names. Detective Liam suggested: 'we could go back to Ron reveal to him what we know, he will have to confirm as part of his confession, he will not have any more excuses and surrender the jewels.'

The three detectives walked one after the other back into the room where Ron was sitting in front of a small table with a police officer standing behind him. Detective Eddy asked the police officer to bring some water and a cup of fresh coffee.

Detective Josh proceeded to read the statement from Rudy.

I Rudy Miller, 28 years old with a current address 482 Liberty Street, San Francisco

Occupation sound technician self-employed independent contractor

Under myself decision hereby state my involvement as part of a group of thieves to steal jewels in France, Italy and Netherlands. The band was named the Brits. The members are

Ron Johnson nick name Gru, he is the leader and responsible for the sale of the loot.

Brat Walker second in command nick name Tin Man

Pete McNeill nick name techie.

Myself Rudy nick name, mate.

Rudy did not include the trips to Miami, Mexico, and the small jobs in San Francisco Bay area and in Monterey Peninsula, Carmel-by-the-Sea.

Then he asked Ron: 'do you confirm Rudy's statements?'

Ron remained unemotional seating with both hands resting on the table looking down to his fingers. Detective Liam proceeded: 'Mr. Ron you do not have any alibis, on the contrary we do have evidence that incriminates you and your band of so call Brits. Spare yourself the extended agony. Return the jewels, any profits from the sale of the loot, and disclose which stores have you and your band robbed.' Ron was not listening to any of the questions, he was not interested in providing any information or helping the police. He did not have much more to lose. Detective Liam ask detective Josh, 'we need to work on the documents for extradition. I am going back to Monaco with the criminal profiles and the indictments of the suspects. I going to the desk that you had provided here to report to my superiors with the updates.'

Detective Liam called his boss back in Monaco even though it was around two in the morning in Monaco, he left a brief message stating the progress in the investigation including the apprehension of three suspects and retrieval of some of the jewels. Then detective Liam wrote the lengthy report including the names and police photographs of the suspects. He left the office at 7:30 pm after talking to Judy informing her about all the progress. Doctor Chan complimented him for the progress in solving the case, in contrast she has unpleasant reports because she could not find a dress that will be of her satisfaction, despite the fact, Lorraine has done an excellent job searching and showing her an abundance of beautiful wedding dresses. Lorraine very supportive told Doctor Chan 'Please don't be dishearten, you'll find the perfect dress.'

Detective Liam was back at his room in the Sunset district Thursday evening, for the last night of his visit in town he has not pack a single item, there was too much to do concerning the documents for the case, besides he needed to talk to his superior with respect to the extradition of at least three suspects, one was still at large, that was Brat. It was 9:00 pm when detective Liam received an international call from Monaco, monsieur Blanchett, his boss.

The conversation started by asking the latest updated of the jewelry heist suspects. Detective Liam explained to his boss the apprehension of two suspects, a third one having surrender himself to the local police. There was still one more individual at large, the investigation for the jewels has had good progress. Monsieur Blanchett longtime colleague of detective Liam, and lately in charge of the police division where both had work for several years, treated detective Liam as a good friend. He was proud of the outstanding job his friend Nolan has done.

Monsieur Blanchett: 'congratulations! Nolan, you transcend the police work in every aspect. I'm proud of you.'

Detective Liam: 'merci Remy, I am writing a complete report of this case with the updates and other details. I need to request a couple more days to complete all the documentation for the extradition and the arrangement to transport the suspects to Monaco.'

Monsieur Blanchett: 'I have to confirm about the extradition, that will require few more days, don't worry about it.'

Detective Liam: 'I also have some personal news. I am..I er'

Monsieur Blanchett: 'Nolan Are you ok? What's the matter?'

Detective Liam: 'I don't know how to explain it, I'm getting marry!'

Monsieur Blanchett: 'You what? Well, congratulations! Are you coming back at all?'

Detective Liam: 'Thank you Remy. Yes, I need a job since I'm going to have a wife to feed,'

Monsieur Blanchett: 'Listen Nolan you have done excellent work as usual, although, you were supposed to catch only the suspects, but you have also caught a bride, or perhaps is the other way around a fine lady has capture you. She must be wonderful, congratulations to both of you. Take another week to complete the documents for the case, let me know if you two are spending honeymoon on the states and you could have more time outside work. I'll see you when you come back and ready for work.'

Detective Liam was elated with the extra week for the wedding preparations, then he immediately called Doctor Chan for the good news. He, in addition, felt appeased with the progress in the investigation, he can gather more information to coordinate prosecution of the suspects under custody with the local authorities.

That Red Skirt

Judy resolved to find a dress of her liking, and suitable for the occasion. According to Nolan now they have until next Friday to do zillion things including the wedding. That is four more days to plan the weeding and two days to pack before they both head for Monaco, as a married couple. Doctor Chan somehow is at peace, possibly because she has the faithful, willing help of Lorraine to continue the search. Lorraine goes online under traditional white wedding dresses some of the styles are too much revealing for Judy's preference. There was the long v-backline, Judy commented: 'maybe for a twenty-some years old girl.' Lorraine smiled pointing to a Polina style sleeveless gown with a v-back and embroidery lace in white satin. Judy shook her head indicating 'no.' Then Judy happens to catch a glance of a Chinese blouse, which made her think, what about the traditional Chinese wedding dress? Lorraine was quick to search online stores with traditional Chinese wedding gowns, she found one store with a dress in fabric brocade with a floral pattern embroidery. By coincidence, there was a store two blocks near, they decided to walk there. The enthusiastic clerk shows the dress, when Judy sees the bright red dress, raises her eyebrows. Lorraine pleads with the clerk to convince Judy, she hesitant tries one full length with Mandarin collar 3/4 sleeve pleated skirt.

The answer is 'No,' the color is too brilliant for her own style. Then she sees the floral embroidery cheongsam top ruffle strait, a close-fitting silk dress with high neck, short sleeves and a slit skirt. Lorraine convinced Judy that Nolan will be crazy for her in that dress the slit on the skirt is just couple inches above the knee, very romantic not too much revealing. Judy after few encouragement comments from Lorraine and the clerk accepted in a delightful giggling with her left hand (wearing her engagement ring) covering her mouth, with one joyful tear in her eyes. She was a beautiful radiant bride.

Jack Wayne animated with curiosity to learn the origin of the wedding band on the left-hand asked Miller: 'Please tell me why the wedding ring is worn on the left hand?'

The answer was simple, 'I'm not sure if this is true it is based on what the ancient Romans believe the 4th finger on the left hand had a vein that run directly to the heart. The vena amores, meaning "vein of love."

Jack Wayne responded: 'Wow! Sounds credible.'

The Official Charming Knot

Detective Nolan Liam and Doctor Judy Chan got marry in the presence of some family members among them Judy's parents Mr. Matthew and his wife Sarah (Judy's mom), her sister Naomi with her husband David, Judy staff three members from the office/clinic, some coworkers, and Judy's next-door long-time neighbors. Nolan's side had detectives Joshua with his wife Liz Ferrigno and Eduard with his wife Vicky Ness, interim Lorraine and her boyfriend. A gathering of some 28 people which resulted in an intimate reception. Everyone had a time to chat with the bride, detective Josh was fascinated by the work of the 3-D figures that Doctor Chan had created from the DNA samples, but he was equally mesmerizing by how the couple had met. He told detective Eddy: what are the chances that detective Liam working in Monaco finds his bride who works in San Francisco in a totally different field? Detective Eddy answered that's beyond me, man!

DNA BUST

On a partly cloudy Friday with the temperatures in the mid 60s and a light Eastern breeze the location was decorated, beautify with flowers, some white satin ribbons forming small bowties hang on the back of the chairs for the ladies and some black ribbon on the back of the chairs for the gentlemen, linens and lace hang on the walls on both sides of the main entrance.

Everyone helped to find a modest but beautiful venue for the wedding with a small reception the log cabin turned out to be the ideal place. A rustic romantic building in one secluded area in the Presidio Park, in the middle of conifer trees.

Judy was on a small back room getting the last touches on her dress, hair and make-up. She was supposed to walk a small brick pathway to the front doors. She was ready and excited to walk the isle at her father's arm, her sister came to point everyone is waiting for her at the altar. She started to walk on the small brick pathway and noticed the Brazilian Pepper tree, the place was serene, from some distance children were playing she can hear them laughing. Next to the brick pathway there is a park bench, her sister had decorated the back with two letters an N for Nolan and a J for Judy pasted within a heart. Judy sees the bench. The sun was on her back because she observed her shadow was in front of her, she turns her head to see the white rose bushes, then the two small stone steeps just before the double oak doors. She can hear the music inside. At that moment the sound of sirens afar causes Judy to a sudden stop.

That was her dream! Now in a surreal way she is having a dejavu. Her father looks at her then asked what's wrong? Judy shakes her head and continues to walk through the front doors. The minister standing waiting for the bride asks 'if everyone please rise' for the bride's procession to take her position and joint her groom to face the minister. The exchange of vowels takes place.

Nolan: in the name of God, I Nolan Liam take you Judy Chan,
To be my wife to have and to hold from this day forward,
For better, for worse, for richer, for poorer, in sickness and
In health, to love and cherish, until parted by death.
This is my solemn vow.

Judy: in the name of God, I Judy Chan, take you Nolan Liam
To be my husband to have and to hold from this day forward,
For better, for worse, for richer, for poorer, in sickness and
In health, to love and cherish, until parted by death.
This is my solemn vow.

The exchange of rings followed, the minister concluded by 'I pronounced you husband and wife. You may kiss the bride.'

Everyone cheered joyfully. The minister announced, 'may I present Mr. and missis Nolan and Judy Liam.'

On that Friday afternoon (4:50 pm) The newly wed had barely enough time to go to the airport for the flight to Monaco. No time yet for the honeymoon.

Judy for some strange reason remembered the lithograph of Yosemite Park in the room that she rented for Nolan at the house of Mr. Lu, the thought where we are going to stay for our honeymoon came to her mind briefly.

Judy with the help of her sister changed her wedding dress to wear a light pullover blouse, a pair of new jeans that her sister bought as part of wedding gift, the final added item for comfort for the long flight a pair of converse All Stars Chuck, red to contrast her blue jeans. Nolan did not change any clothes. He teased Judy telling her she can say he is her hired guide for the trip. Then he corrected himself: 'you can say I'm the proper hired guide.' Judy smiling replied: 'you are my proper husband and guide, but not for hire.' Nolan said: 'yes doctor.'

Doctor Chan promised Lorraine to come back in few months to visit, she wants to express her gratitude for all the help she had provided in her personal affairs as well as assisting her newly husband detective Liam with the jewelry heist case.

Three days had passed since Ron was in custody, Brat had received few text messages from Ron's cell phone and from Rudy's cell phone. The messages from Ron were odd, it did not seem texting from Ron, the message was an order, highly unlikely, Brat knew better. The text from Rudy was just the opposite, it was absurd, Rudy beseechs for the meeting, both messages were the same asking Brat to meet Ron at his apartment in a very short time. Brat had ignored all the text messages not responding to any, he suspected they were from either a hacker or the police. Brat had gone out of town to Russian River after he received the first text from Ron. He had the shrewdness to grab from his apartment the few jewels he kept from the last two jobs as part of his loot. He also took the money he had before he fled out of town. He could sense police were very close and catching on him.

A NEW BEGINNING

Brat did not waste any time to utilize his trickery to live another chapter as a dreadful fugitive.

He bought a large shoulder pad to wear under his double extra-large shirt and a double extra-large coat to appear bigger, much bulkier that what he actually is. He grew his hair long enough to cover his ears, he wears a hat, and dyes his hair and eyebrows in gray color making himself look much older. He added one half insole on the left shoe to help him walk with a limp. He wears slightly tinted gray nonprescription glasses, and a fake small mustache that matches the gray color of his eyebrows. When he talks to anyone, he pauses a lot pretending to concentrate, he simulates, that is difficult for him to remember or maintain focus. All these schemes helped him evade the police for few months.

Brat used his cell phone to find a smoke shop tobacco store in Windsor town, then he calls the store from Healdsburg. The police tracked his cell phone then sent a search team in both towns following the GPS with the expectation to locate and arrest him.

That afternoon Brat is walking from the smoke shop to his vehicle, sees the undercover patrol car but the police officer can't recognize him because the cosmetics, the costume he wears, also he walks simulating a tensile limp. Brat realizes his cell phone is the culprit. He decides to send a false beacon to the police by turning his cell phone off then driving to Reno and leaving his cell turned on under a park bench. He returns to Sebastopol to buy a new cell phone.

In an effort to hide from the police, have a place to live without much worry, he tries to rent an apartment in a senior only resident, it is for fix and low income, for this reason is a restricted community but he needs to prove he is old enough to qualify, he is not 55 years old. He has enough cash to sustain himself using the profits from the sale of the stolen jewels. He rents a studio detached from the other units for $1,100.00 a month in Santa Rosa. The property is in the Southwest neighborhood of the city, with a small market, a convenience store, a gas station nearby, and easy access to freeways. Brat looks in the downtown area for a job in a jewelry store, because of his knowledge of the gems. He is confronted with the requirements of his background. He needs a letter of recommendation indicating he can be trusted, a criminal background check, and fingerprints. Brat is not desperate to be hire; hence he walks away of that line of work. He tells himself: 'what were you thinking?'

There are other types of jobs that he could get, he likes coffee, a job in a coffee shop as a barista will be just fine. He finds a barista employment as a part time with no benefits, for weekends only from 5:00 am to 1:00pm Saturday and Sunday. He starts two days after the interview for the position, even though he has no previous experience, he can learn on the job.

A NEW BAND?

Brat gets acquainted with few individuals that are regulars on the late morning weekends. He contemplates the idea of forming his own band, he approaches one who is a bit younger than him, however, their conversations are for the most part humorless, and about how hard it is to make ends meet. On one occasion, Brat's customer mentioned about doing a "job" that could bring fast profits, but he needs a dependable guy. Brat did not answer to his remark, just kept listening. In a different day Brat asked how the 'job' was and if he got the fast profits. The other person blew some air in exasperation. Then went on to tell Brat that he is still looking for the right person to help with the project. At the same moment he realizes Brat might be the right guy. Brat did not wait to be ask if he was interested, and said: 'I have a job, my question is are you ready for a good profit?'

Jack Wayne could not wait for whatever Miller was about to tell him next and interrupted by asking: 'excuse me if I understood correct, Brat did not wait for his customer to say you are hire! Or something alike?'

Miller answered: 'that is correct young man! Now let me tell you where they go before talking about the profitable job.'

That afternoon after Brat finished his work, they met in a different coffee shop, the place was in a corner of a small alleyway with an outdoor seating area two small tables around a cherry tree, and a park bench on the sidewalk along the curb.

Miller added: 'it probable was an old bus stop but when the alleyway was closed due to the development of the main building at the end of the small street. The short alleyway was converted for deliveries only.'

Brat asked A.J. do you mind if we sit outdoors, I smoke and I would like to have a smoke while we talk about business,' they were in a different neighborhood, A.J. didn't mind. Brat had check couple of the small jewelry stores in St Helena. He had his target store selected after he himself had gone three different times to surveil two jewelry shops. The one on Main Street call Affinity Jewelers, has alleyways on two directions the Spring St on the Eastern side, and the Cypress Way, one long block, traffic flows one way only, which is the backstreet behind the gems building.

Brat and his acquaintance spend some time talking over the reasons why they should join their efforts and work together rather than one under the other like a boss-employee relationship. Brat asked what his plan was, what kind of project would yield fast profits and how long would the actual job take. The answer did not sound too good for Brat.

'Look man, we just go to the seven-11 store pull a gun on the clerk taking all the cash that he has on hand, then we just run out of the place.' Brat kept looking at him waiting for some more details, but after an awkward moment Brat said: 'that's it?'

The replied was: 'Yeah! That's it man. Quick cash, easy.'

Brat was having second thoughts about his candidate for the project. Then he pulls out a cigarette, lights it before he comments to A.J.: 'listen you don't need a helper to get busted for petty cash.' Then he asked: 'how much money do you think you could get from one time if all goes well for you?' A.J. thought for a moment and said: 'Oh, I don't know, maybe $1,200.00 or maybe more.' Brat says: 'let's say it goes really good for you and you hit a good pot of about $3,500.00. Are you wearing any mask, glasses, a coat I mean do you hide or disguise your identity?' A.J. says: 'not really, I just put on a hoodie and go to work. But I yell loud and let them know who the boss is, so they don't resist and hand over the cash.'

Brat takes a deep breath, and tells him: 'ok, now let me tell you about my project. I have a detail plan; we get a vehicle for the job with switched license plates. I had surveillance the place checked for security guards, number of employees, the easy access to inventory on breakable glass cases, we will deactivate security cameras, if possible, we park the car two short blocks on one of the less traffic alleys, there is a public bathroom where we can go and remove our costumes before we go back to the car. Before we go to the store, we will create a commotion by calling 911 anonymous call to report a fire and a suspicion backpack left outside the coffee shop cross street from our target shop. It should take no more than 7 minutes from the moment we tell the store manager we are there for the merchandise, as soon as we hear the sirens from the fire engine trucks approaching, that is our cue to pick our items.

After A. J. Hears Brat's plan, he does not know what to say, he has a big grin, and rubs his hands frankly with enthusiasm. Brat adds: 'aren't you asking how much do we expect from this job? I'll tell you, from my estimates the small rings, earrings and bracelets perhaps couple pendants we could get something around $20,000.00 or more.' Brat knew it was probably double, but he was not about to tell that to his recruit. Brat looks at his watch, and says: 'one more important thing, with a stern warning, this a very serious proposition if you think the possible profit is high, the risk is even higher, I'm talking about the danger if you go around talking about this operation. The worst mistake could be telling someone, and you could get kill and have me murder before we do anything. Let me repeat it again don't mention this to anyone whatsoever. Do you understand? A. J. Seemed to have his brain working overtime, after a short moment he looked at Brat and said: 'I got it! No words to anyone.' Brat added: 'do I have your promise?' A.J. nodded, touching his chest with his right hand.

We need to work the details and then set out, a tentative date. Brat ends the conversation telling A.J. 'come by the coffee shop Saturday, I'll have something for you to do for our plan.'

Jack Wayne asked Miller: 'what is the name of Brat's recruit?'

Miller raised his eyebrows and answered: 'his name Al Johnson, but he was called A. J.'

All seem to be working out for Brat and his recruit A.J. The coffee shop is the place where they meet for the third time to finalize details of Brat's plan including all the items needed for the costumes. A long wig natural looking for A.J., a walking cane for Brat, they dress up with long sleeve white shirts and bright red neckties, in dark blue trousers. They got a brown small backpack, a disposable cell phone to call 911 to report the false fire. One week after they completed the arrangements the day was pick, the last Sunday of the month. A.J. came out with a vehicle possible stolen a day before the heist. They drove in separate vehicles to Calistoga parked Brat's car in a public parking lot. Then they both rode to St Helena in A.J. car for the job. They dressed up with their costumes in an empty lot outside St Helena, then went to the alleyway to park the car, then walked to the coffee shop order a coffee cup and sat on one table outside to set the backpack. Brat called 911 speaking in a fake high pitch voice to report anonymously the fire and the suspicious brown backpack.

Brat was right the operation took less than 10 minutes from the moment they can hear at a distance the sirens from the fire engine trucks responding to the reported fire and suspicious backpack. The police and the fire department created a distraction that helped Brat and A.J. to pick a lot of merchandise after breaking few glass cases. They took over $50,000.00 worth in jewels. Brat was calm, concentrated. A.J. pulled a handgun from his canvas shopping bag and ordered the employees of ER Kuznetsov jewelers to lay down with both hands on their necks. Brat did not know that A.J. had a gun, but he followed what his recruit did. No shots, no one was hurt.

From Calistoga back to Santa Rosa they drove via Mark West Springs Road, Brat went home with the gems. The agreement between Brat with A.J. was after they get the jewels Brat will sell the jewels later provide his partner his share.

A.J. counted the total items in front of Brat

       10 rings, 3 with diamonds
       9 sets of earrings 2 with diamonds
       7 small gold pendants
       14 necklaces

3 gold pins
a result of 43 very expensive articles

After he saw the loot A.J. was thrilled, fist bump Brat with excitement. He commented how well the plan had worked. Brat gave A.J. $2,800.00 as an advance, Brat reaffirmed the rest of the money is coming after the loot is sold. A.J. had total confidence in Brat, and he could wait the cooling period that Brat mentioned before selling the jewels.

A.J. did not tell Brat the truth about the vehicle they used to go to St Helena. He rented it from his friend Paco. The price for the rent was based in how much profit Brat will get from the heist. A.J. recruited Paco in order to have the vehicle, A.J. told Paco: 'your job is very simple don't need to do anything other than give me the keys and the car, I'll pay when we get our profits.' Paco was a troublemaker, he was always arguing and never listen, hard-headed, but A.J. needed the car. Paco demanded from A.J. to meet Brat in person. Paco did not meet Brat, he only saw Brat from a distance, because A.J. showed Paco where he works as barista. Paco insisted to take the jewels from Brat all for themselves and get rid of Brat, 'we don't need to split the profit,' said Paco. A.J. asked Paco 'where are you going to sell those gems? You don't have any idea how to go about that kind of business, let's be smart and wait until he gets the money!'

One early evening Paco followed Brat from a distance to the smoke shop with the intentions to rob him. Paco was prudent he did not cause Brat to raise any suspicion.

WICKED INFLUENCES

Brat had work for a large company which managed several jewelry retail stores.

The company through few stores had a fraudulent method to mix low quality stones particularly diamonds with high quality diamonds. The system was used to sell at a high price set of jewelry to customers who had come to the store to select a set pay a deposit or part of the set then come back on a later day to pick their gems. The customer had examined and selected genuine items that were shown at the time of the purchase, however, when the gems were pick up at a later day, the store had mix some of the stones of high quality with some diamonds of low quality. Brat became aware of the corruption and because he was giving bonus from time to time with the condition that he would keep all knowledge confidential. Brat's responsibility was sales associate, in a short time he was promoted to assistant manager.

He stops working for them when the general manager was arrested for an investigation of some stolen gems purchased by the company.

Brat and Ron worked together in a diamond import corporation with several branches. Ron had an opportunity to select a small group of confident assistants to help him with the distribution of imported medium quality sets to the branches located on the Western region. Brat was one of the aids for updating inventory and organize sales events, such as graduations, engagement and weddings, Mother's Day, Father's Day and the like. Brat had learned many details about the fine cuts for diamonds. The corporation named Zahav distributes wholesale through small stores only quality items among them rings, chains, pendants set with earrings. Brat was in charge to identify the high-quality precious metals and the genuine stones.

After the Brits' last trip Brat had gone back to work for the Zahav company, his schedule was very flexible depending on the inventory, the availability of the wholesale from the suppliers. He was used to go to the stores in a sequence timetable. He was hopeful of being selected to be part of the company Zahav official buyer. He also met few outside dealers who buy questionable merchandise. Brat was planning to contact one or two of those dealers to present his latest loot.

Brat stop working for Zahav the day he learned the police had come looking for him at his apartment.

Santa Rosa's Dark Night

Brat frequents a smoke shop tobacco store for his cigarettes because the low price per packs. Although is in a dangerous drug traffic zone. The illegal dealing of crystal methamphetamine attracts rival bands and arm confrontations take place from time to time. One early evening Brat exits the smoke shop, he stops for a moment to pull out a cigarette at the moment he lights it two individuals start shooting towards the store front door, inside the store standing by the front door there are three guys with some narcotics, one is hit by the bullets, the other two inside the store shot back defending themselves but they escape running away through the back door of the shop. The two individuals outside at the front door kept shooting as they fled the scene. Leaving two dead bodies behind one inside the store and another out on the sidewalk.

Paco was sitting in his car parked across the street from the smoke shop, he watched the whole incident, when the bullets started to flight, he ducked behind the steering wheel and stayed there until the shooting stop. He heard the two men who starting the shooting ran to a vehicle that pulled over, he saw them get on the car and fled the scene. Paco got off his car and ran to check on the victim laying on the sidewalk, he knew it was Brat. Paco had followed him with the intentions to assault Brat, as it was mentioned before. Paco hoped to obtain money from the gems but also make the incident be seen as part of the narcotics altercation. Paco was cautious, he looked both directions and observed Brat was still holding the cigarettes pack in his hand, one cigarette was laying on the ground still lit, close to Brat's head. He was barely breathing but did not move his chess was covered with blood. Paco had the intension to check Brat's pockets, but he hears people getting close and sirens of emergency vehicles approaching. He started to walk away slowly as more bystanders got close to the front door to see the mess inside. Paco turned around and left the scene. Paco knew one of the individuals from the shooting. Paco was also involved in dealing meth.

The police department in Santa Rosa had received a notification from SF police department for the suspect Brat. The SFPD had follow his GPS on the cell phone usage on the city of Santa Rosa and neighboring towns. The photograph and relevant information were included, which was used to identify the dead body on a narcotics related shooting incident. The information only provided a short list of close friends incarcerated who cannot claim the body, cannot go to the morgue to identify or sign any documents at the coroner's office. Police went to Brat's apartment with the front door keys, after the search two satin sacks are found containing jewels, along with a substantial amount of cash. The report of a robbery jewel Store in St Helena is also in the bulletin of Santa Rosa law enforcement. The detective assigned to Brat's case calls the manager of ER Kuznetsov Jewelers to inform him about a few jewels found in a suspect apartment, he asked the manager to stop by the department to identify the items and prove they belong to the store. The manager gives the exact account, the kind of stolen jewels. The store recovers all the gems in perfect condition.

The SFPD updated the death status on Brat's file along with a photograph of the dead body from Santa Rosa forensics police.

Detective Josh read the report of Santa Rosa police department, then he gave a copy of the sheet mentioning the identification of one of the victims shooting to Ron. The one page included details of the event mixed with the crystals of meth. The report did not mention Brat as part of the confrontation between the two rival groups, rather indicated a casualty caught up at the wrong spot. Detective Josh did not want to explain any of the report to Ron, he prefers to let the written report tell what happened.

Ron was greatly saddened by the death of his longtime friend. Ron felt he had deserted everyone, more importantly his close friend. He was dismayed, he blamed himself. Many agonizing thoughts went through Ron's head. It was the beginning of a lonely, and lengthy mourning. Detective Josh gave a copy of the report sheet in the early afternoon, around 1:45, Ron could not stop thinking on the details how many bullets impacts the forensic indicated, the pack of cigarettes were still on his hand.

The fact that his body was never reclaimed for any family member or friend.

That night Ron did not eat dinner, he refused any food, he could not sleep more than 20-25 minutes despite being exhausted. For the following 5 days and nights Ron suffered nightmares, and bad headaches. After a week of a terrible anguish, Ron spent two days experiencing numbness, but gradually as he recovers his determination to not admit his participation of any crime grew stronger. He made up his mind to keep from disclosing to anyone the location of the stolen jewels. He made a promise to Brat, actually to honor his memory to die before giving up what the police had requested. He grew bitter. Once he was found guilty and condemned, detective Eddy, and detective Josh thought they could consider the case closed, although.

They had received some gems from Santa Rosa police that were recovered from Brat's apartment, they send notification to detective Liam's office. Detective Eddy needed identification from the store in Amsterdam in order to process the return of stolen goods. Rudy had contributed by identifying some of the jewels that they stole, Pete also had helped confirming the jewels from

Amsterdam. The money found in Brat's apartment was near impossible to determine where it came from. A judge had to rule the distribution. Rudy and Pete could not figure how much was precisely from any specific loot. Ron was no longer taking in consideration for inquires, he was not answering any questions. It took over a year for detectives Josh, and Eddy to resolve the returning of the stolen gems with the assistance of detective Liam's office, after all that time detective Josh close the case.

The police department had joint efforts with FBI to have the indictment for the three defendants, since one is deceased, identified as Brat Walker, a victim in a shooting incident. Detective Eddy was successful in finding the hidden jewels at Ron's apartment, on the garage roof, near the back corner up on the gutter. The DA prosecutes the suspects, a jury finds them guilty, the court condemns Ron to 35 years, Pete to 30 years, and Rudy to 20 years. The court was lenient to him because he surrendered himself, he provided information to the arrest of Ron also, he returned jewels with all the money as part of his loot. The suspects to serve the full term on federal prison. Detective Liam was formally congratulated and relieved from any more responsibilities in the jewels case.

LIFE UNFOLDS

L ife was as it should be in Monaco-Ville, less than two years later, 18 months to be precise, Jack Wayne was the name for the baby boy born to Detective Nolan and his wife Doctor Judy. They settle in Avenue Henry Dunant In a modest apartment but with excellent access to Liam's office. Judy applied for a position as medical doctor to a private clinic within walking distance from their home. She needed to study local regulations and pass a certification on her degree to have the valid medical license with working permit as a foreign doctor. Detective Liam asked his wife to stay home with the new son and take care of him, Nolan's nice in her teen's years wanted to help babysitting the adorable nephew. Judy trusted the niece; she could work three days a week and the rest of the time be with her son.

Rudy New Quest

Rudy was released under supervision of a parole officer after serving 17 years in prison. Nolan and Judy came to the states for Jack Wayne their son to study two years in high school, detective Nolan learned from detective Josh that Rudy was out on parole, Judy is talking with Nolan about Rudy writing his story about the robberies, he would like to interview Nolan. Jack hears this he is intrigued. He asked his dad if he can meet Rudy. Nolan is baffle by the question, then asked his son: 'why do you want to meet this person?' Jack Wayne: 'I have some questions for him, why is he writing about his wrong doings?' Nolan answered: 'let's find out, I'll see if he is ok meeting you.'

Detective Liam called police chief Craig Nelson to inquire about Rudy's behavior.

Lorraine's husband now works as part of the (investigation) special agents' unit for the FBI. He keeps contact with detective Joshua and is through him Lorraine learns about Rudy writing the story of the jewels heist, also the desire from Rudy to interview detective Liam. Lorraine received an email from Judy about theirs coming to California for their son's schooling, Lorraine tells Judy Rudy's writing plans.

Police chief Craig planned for detective Liam to meet Rudy for an interview, 'how ironic life can be, now you are the interviewed' said Rudy to detective Liam, 'you mean unexpected encounter' replied Nolan. 'If you think that is odd, here is something surprising even for me, let me introduce you, my son Jack Wayne. He has some questions for you, therefore, you will be interviewed by him, if you don't mind.' Rudy was not ready for an expected surprise like that, he thought the young son was curious to meet the jewelry robber and maybe say hello, but when he saw Jack Wayne with an inquisitive and penetrating look, he decided to let detective Liam's son ask the questions that he wanted. Rudy appreciated the favorable occasion to find unsuspected information that he could welcome for his writings. Therefore, he agreed.

Jack Wayne greeted Rudy by telling him how sorry he was to learn that his parents created a 3-D image that help to catch the band. Rudy observed Jack for a short moment then in a collected manner replied: 'no need to be sorry. I had learned so much about discerning between right and wrong, believe or not my case is the one that needed to get worse before it could turn to a better place.

Jack Wayne: 'really what do you mean?'

Rudy: 'for long time Angie pointed trying to help me to correct my wrong doings all those robberies, but I was comfortable, I was not under any physical or economical trouble, I must say I was going through emotional affliction.'

Jack Wayne: 'why?'

Rudy: 'well, you see Angie read and recited so many moral rules for respect, own protection I tried to dismiss all of them by being confused for my own interpretation of loyalty. The result of my neglect of these principles a hefty consequence. Loss of everything starting with my own liberty, go to jail, all my loot, legally confiscated, lost contact with friends, financially broke in other words in total bankruptcy.'

Jack Wayne: 'wow! But how that help you get better, you have nothing, and you were in prison, no one could help you.'

Rudy: 'Yes, I basically proved what Angie told me. You will harvest what you sow.

Now answering your question, let me say it this way. I was at the bottom the only way to go was up! Now let me ask you why you asked your dad to meet me?'

Jack Wayne: 'Yes and thank you for agreeing. My question is why you want to write a tragic story, you said, you lost everything.'

Rudy had to start by pointing the meaning of what you harvest is what you sow.

He underlines the Brits committed a series of robberies motivated by the desire of obtaining wealth in dishonest ways. This is the first step on the wrong path. After they planned and prepared by rehearsing and acquiring the different make-up kits and costumes, then they moved to act on the plan, committing offense or sin. They had sown the wrong seed. The result is ruin, and death, they gather their harvest. Three went to prison, lost everything, and one was shot and die. That is the miserable end of their deeds. Then Rudy explained the end is not the lost but the gain of something better than the jewels, money or any other possession, the attaining of wisdom. Rudy finally realized the value of wisdom, is a treasure that can't be lost, robbed, or diminished by using and giving it away, on the contrary it expands the benefits to the one who possess it. Now I would like to talk to your dad for a while, we can continue our conversation after I find some facts from him, if is ok with you.'

Jack Wayne replied: 'yes, will you tell me as much of the story as you can?'

Rudy said: 'I will tell you the whole story from the beginning.'
Jack Wayne smiled and gave thumbs up in agreement.

This is the end of the story; Rudy was granted a series of sessions with detective Liam with the object to complete the data for his writings. The sessions took few days for both of them to verify aspects that Rudy did not know with regard to the investigation done by detective Liam, Doctor Chan, and the different police departments. Rudy realized conducting interviews was a competent way to clarify and supplement some points of view from everyone, here are the interviews as addendum.

The Interviews

Rudy Miller

Rudy conducted interviews to the main characters of his story.

Rudy asked himself his impressions of the role he carried out. He answered his own questions made a statement reflecting on his part.

His answer: Well, the strong moral dilemma is very hard and complicated. The issue to choose between loyalty to friends or betrayal in order to do right and understand wrong, has no immediate results or favorable gains. The guilt feeling is bigger and at times harder to fight, you see in every human heart there is a need to be loved and to love. I was depressed when Angela showed up in my life. There was my need to belong to a group, to a club, belong to a community, to a family. Pete showed up with the offer to do some projects in a group. Planning the robberies, all the rehearsals, the traveling and executing the robberies were social events, that gave us adventure and bonding.

Brat Walker

I tried Rudy's method to reduce the number of smokes (cigarettes) on a day, I really did and it work for some time, I remember on those long trips on the airplane force me to hold off, but when I was on certain tension, you know stress out the smoke calmed my nerves. Greed force me to look for more robberies and commit mistakes. At the end the smokes did cause my fatal detriment. No one came to see after the body, no one was present for burial or cremation, no friends, no family all alone perhaps a reflection of my own behavior when I alone decided to perpetrate the crimes. What is the meaning of this tragic end? Is it a result of my own deeds or is a fortuitous event. Brat character leaves it to the reader to decide. Brat says I take what I think with me to my grave.

Ron Johnson

Ron The role he performs as a leader of the band from recruiting, to planning every operation with details snares himself in a spiral decay encouraged by greed that causes his own demise and the rest of the members of his band. He resisted to concede his defeat until the end, he never confessed the crimes or having possession of any money despite all the evidence and confession of his own accomplishers, Rudy and Pete. He learned his longtime friend and ally die as a result of his own criminal activity while the police were tracking him down. He never talks to Rudy after police told him who revealed his identity and what he had done in Amsterdam, at the end he was betrayed. Ironically, he started the band with the hope to enrich themselves, perhaps not conscious that the nature of the business was a betrayal to moral principles and to society.

Pete McNeil

Pete reformed while in prison and was released on parole after serving 26 years. He studied advance security and computer systems for ten years in prison, he graduated and work on designing his own systems while incarcerated. He sold few systems that provided him an excellent income that enable him to help other inmates. He was in a different prison that Rudy. They did not communicate each other during the time that Pete was in jail.

Angela Kendall

Angela based on truth provides moral counseling for Rudy. She knew he had the capacity to discern right from wrong. She modeled to Rudy many of the moral principles that she talked to him. Angela did not control Rudy's will, and she knew it, but her heart was captivated by Rudy's unpretentiousness.

What Angela's love did for Rudy, it helped him to have courage to make a radical change.

Angela takes many situations that Rudy face to explain the lesson or message and glean wisdom from those events, interesting to note some are appalling, or so are perceived by Rudy. It is Angela's walk with Rudy's struggle that brings her to a safe place where her heart in a sober moment decides to stay at the right distance to avoid a deeper emotional involvement. There is a different person for her to marry.

Doctor Judy Chan

Judy the long hours I spent on the DNA search to produce an image led me to the idea of creating a three-dimensional sculpture. Little that I knew all that work will help to resolve the mystery of the suspects, to be exact it provided a close resemble to identify two of the criminals, but that was not the end, I was rewarded with a wonderful husband and family in a very exclusive city. I had a dream that resulted in a vision revealing my future wedding, even details as the park bench with our initials!

The willingness to leave everything and move in an adventure in a total trust displayed the courage transmitted, by Nolan's sincere love.

Detective Nolan Liam

Nolan police work is always risky, a challenge for the unpredicted. The series of robberies and the call from monsieur Laurent the insurance adjuster for the gems was the initial of a long investigation that took years with a successful identification of the suspects, the indictment and imprisonment of the thieves, well at least three of them. One of them suffering fatal wounds in suspicious activity. Unfortunately, not all the jewels were recovered, only a small portion and some money confiscated from the criminals. I was extremely rewarded with a beautiful-intelligent, and talented wife with a great son. Doctor Chan did not hesitate to leave everything and run with me to a new life. She was confident in our love and trust me. Doctor Chan my wife assisted with an incredible three D image of two of the suspects, which made possible to find out details leading to names and home addresses of the suspects.

The total unexpected turn of events I had to answer few questions in an interview conducted by one of the convicted suspects. Thanks to such interview I had a chance to learn few facts that took place out of my involvement in the investigation. I'm referring specifically to the moral values shared with love from Angela to Rudy who I never met.

Hm, I wonder if such values are not just for Rudy.

Story written by Rene Mauricio Menjivar
Il nonno

Thank you to Melody Cheung for the software assistance.